RUNNER

Books by Tracy Clark

BROKEN PLACES

BORROWED TIME

WHAT YOU DON'T SEE

RUNNER

Published by Kensington Publishing Corp.

RUNNER

TRACY CLARK

KENSINGTON
PUBLISHING CORP.

www.kensingtonbooks.com

KENSINGTON BOOKS are published by

Kensington Publishing Corp.
119 West 40th Street
New York, NY 10018

All Kensington titles, imprints and distributed lines are available at special quantity discounts for bulk purchases for sales promotion, premiums, fund-raising, educational or institutional use.

Special book excerpts or customized printings can also be created to fit specific needs. For details, write or phone the office of the Kensington Special Sales Manager: Kensington Publishing Corp., 119 West 40th Street, New York, NY, 10018. Attn. Special Sales Department. Phone: 1-800-221-2647.

Library of Congress Card Catalogue Number: 2021931068

The K logo is a trademark of Kensington Publishing Corp.

ISBN-13: 978-1-4967-3201-9
ISBN-10: 1-4967-3201-4
First Kensington Hardcover Edition: July 2021

ISBN-13: 978-1-4967-3203-3 (ebook)
ISBN-10: 1-4967-3203-0 (ebook)

10 9 8 7 6 5 4 3 2 1

Printed in the United States of America

ACKNOWLEDGMENTS

As always, thank you to my agent, Evan Marshall, for his great care and advocacy, and warm thanks as well to my editor, John Scognamiglio, at Kensington Publishing, my fantastic publicist, Crystal McCoy, and the entire Kensington family, for banging the drum loudly on my behalf. Thanks to family and friends for their continued support, encouragement, and understanding, especially when I appear to be listening and in the room when I am actually on the page working my way out of a story jam. Thank you to Detective Gregory Auguste, Chicago Police Department, for helping me get it right. To Cassie Jones, whose hilarious childhood story told around a table gave me the idea for Pouch's TV remote swipe, thanks. I'm still laughing. And a warm hand to heart to my pals in the writing community and my writing families at Crime Writers of Color, Mystery Writers of America, and Sisters in Crime, who have been so generous, gracious, and kind with their huzzahs, advice, and fraternity. To all the talented podcasters, bloggers, and reviewers who have been, and continue to be, so enthusiastic and supportive, thank you. My undying gratitude also to all those wonderful readers who have embraced Cass and followed me along on this amazing journey. You are all so fantastic. Until we meet again.

Chapter 1

I yanked the door open and all but flung my half-frozen self into the snug White Castle, the hawk clawing up the back of my neck, my lungs shocked rigid by the subzero wind chill. Chicago. *Brutal.* Winter's threat—keep it moving, sucka, or die where you stand.

Winter, apparently, didn't own a calendar. It was just a couple days past Thanksgiving. I still had leftover turkey in my fridge. Winter had a sick sense of humor and was as welcome as an IRS audit . . . on your birthday.

I stomped my feet to clear the slush off my ankle boots, and then stood there a second inhaling warmth, the smell of fried onions and thin, square meat sizzling on the wide griddle already starting the thawing process. It'd just been a short dash from my car, but the tips of my fingers were already beginning to tingle, and my toes felt like ten frigid fish sticks right out the freezer, despite my having cranked up the car's heater to its highest setting. My fault, totally. I'd miscalculated and dressed for cute when I left the house this morning—jeans, short puffer jacket, a beanie puckishly placed atop my head, thin gloves, and the boots, good-looking in an everyday, schlepping-around kind of way, but several critical inches shy of adequate. Seriously, I didn't know what I was thinking. I mean, I didn't just meet Chicago. I was born here, raised here, live here; I know full well winter does not play. I slipped the beanie off and scanned the tables, finding what I would have expected to find in a White Castle at two o'clock on a Saturday morning—club rats easing down from a stupid night out, street folk looking for a sheltered stop before they ventured out again, and those coming from or going to shift work for painfully low but honest pay. The Castle was cheap, open 24/7, heated, and unless you came in and started tossing the place or harassing people, you were left alone.

I was looking for Leesa Evans, a prospective client. She'd called my office the day before looking for help to find her missing fifteen-year-old daughter, Ramona, but she hadn't given me a lot of details over the phone. Truthfully, though, she had me at *missing fifteen-year-old,* so I was here to get the rest of it, and to see if I could do anything for her.

My eyes landed on a lone woman sitting at a far table, burrowed deep in a light jacket, no hat, no boots, her eyes fixed in a faraway stare. She was dark, middle-aged, forties, maybe. There was no one else waiting alone, so I assumed she was who I was here to see. I watched her for a moment, trying to get a feel for her. She looked sad, beaten down to the ground, and she wasn't eating. There was only a paper coffee cup on her table. She tugged at her jacket sleeves. One foot tapped busily under the table.

The smell of the onions made my stomach growl. I'd spent most of the day tying up paperwork on closed cases, sending out invoices so I could get paid for the work, so it'd been hours since I'd stopped to eat, and my body was just now complaining about it. But I bypassed the counter, ignoring the pull of greasy sustenance, and went over to the table with the sad woman sitting at it.

"Ms. Evans?"

She startled, looked up, took me in warily; then her eyes left mine and she appeared to focus on something over my left shoulder. I flicked a look to see what had caught her attention, but there was nothing but an empty table behind me. I looked back. Evans's eyes dropped from mine. She'd seen nothing; apparently, she just had a difficult time looking at me.

"You're the detective. Cassandra Raines." She said it in a clear voice, loud enough for the half-buzzed night owls nearest to us to clearly hear. I cocked an ear, then waited for what I knew was coming. I'd planned on counting to five, but it didn't take that long for the half-in-the-bag party revelers and seasoned working girls on a break to get up from the tables and slip out into the cold. Detectives, even private ones like me, got no love at all, and it said a lot when a person would rather risk frostbite and hypothermia than share space with one of us. If I were the type of gal who gave a twist, I'd have taken offense.

I began to unzip my jacket, thought better of it halfway through the zip, and zipped it up again. I'd give it another minute . . . or twenty . . . to warm up some. I watched Evans sitting there, her leg bouncing nervously under the table, her not looking at me. She was thin, now that I saw her up close, and her eyes had dark circles under them.

"You're not hungry?" I said.

Evans shook her head, the denial unconvincing. She took a sip from her cup. There was no steam coming off the top. She'd obviously been sitting with it a while.

"Well, I'm starving. I haven't eaten anything since breakfast. You mind me getting a little something? We can talk while I eat."

She nodded an okay and I walked up to the counter, ordered double, and waited for my sliders, fries, and onion rings, sneaking the occasional peek back at the table, but finding Leesa Evans unchanged each time.

My order was up fast. Not much of a line at 2:00 AM. I carried the bag back to the table, sat, and then dug in for the first slider. I offered Evans some, but she shook her head no.

"Oh, come on. I can't eat all these by myself. I mean, I *could*, but I'd regret it almost instantly." I offered up the bag. "Help me out?"

Tentatively, like a shy kitten coaxed toward a bowl of buttermilk, Evans took a slider from the bag, bit into it. I spread the rest of the tiny boxes onto the table, positioning them between us, easy access for whoever wanted more.

"Two a.m.," I said, smiling. "Unconventional."

She finished the slider, eyed the line of boxes in front of her, but didn't go for one. It looked like I was going to have to coax her along, one slider at a time. I pushed a few boxes closer to her. She smiled slightly, then took another.

"I got a job. Cleaning places at night." She cocked her head. "The bus lets me out at the corner there."

I glanced out at the corner of Seventy-ninth and Stony, the stop on the west side of a cage-match intense tangle of intersections, which at the height of the day had cars flying from all directions on mistimed traffic lights. The hub of confusion was loathed by locals, ignored by the city, and had earned a decades-old reputation for being a flat-out death trap. If you were bent enough to try and cross the streets walking, you had better be quick about it. If you were driving and stuck at a light, you'd be wise to cross yourself and get right with Jesus before you pushed off on the green.

I ate another slider, watching Evans as she avoided looking at me, wondering how old she was. I'd pegged her as being in her early forties, but closer to her now, she looked younger than that. Something had hit her hard somewhere, that was evident, and her shoulders drooped from the weight it left behind.

I snuck furtive glances at her hands and wrists, wondering what was hidden under the jacket. She didn't look high or drunk; she was lucid, though slightly morose. She tugged at her sleeves again, as though she was trying desperately to hide something. I thought *addict*—recovering, at least. I thought *alcohol*, too, maybe. It would account for her skittishness, the tugs.

"How can I help you, Ms. Evans?"

She flicked a look at me. "Leesa."

I grabbed another mushy slider, but mostly so it would encourage her to do the same. "Leesa."

"Like I said on the phone, it's my daughter. She ran away. I need somebody to get her back for me." I plucked an onion ring out of a box, then offered the rest to Evans. "Her name's Ramona. Ramona Titus. Me and her father . . . Well, we wasn't married, or anything. She's fifteen. They say she's been gone since last Thursday. That's nine days she's been out there by herself."

I sat up straighter. "Who's *they*?"

Leesa looked embarrassed. "She don't live with me. The state took her five years ago. She's been in the system since." She eyed me sheepishly. "I got caught up in the drug life. That's why they took her. They moved her all over, but this last time, she was staying in a good place, I thought, with a woman named Deloris Poole. Ramona seemed to be doing okay there, but it must not have been so good, if she ran away."

"How long had she been with Poole?"

"About a year. I call her all the time, though. Poole gave her a phone and I called my baby to make sure she was all right, I sure did. Only the last time, I couldn't get through to her. I got worried, so I went over there." Her eyes fell to her lap. "I wasn't supposed to. No contact's what the judge ordered."

"Ramona told you where she was living."

Evans bristled. "I have a right to know where she's at, don't I?"

I fiddled absently with the empty slider box in front of me, giving Evans a moment to pull it back in. "Poole couldn't have been happy to see you on her doorstep."

Evans sneered. "She acted like I was something she stepped in. Told me straight off, Ramona had run away, like that's all I needed to know about it. That I'd go away and leave it like that. I thought at first she was making it up because she didn't want me seeing her, but it was true. She never even tried to call me to tell me she was gone. She should have. Ramona's *my* child, not hers."

I let a moment pass. "I agree. You should have been notified. Did Poole call the police?"

"She said they were looking for her, but I know how they look when it's us they're looking for." Evans looked as though she wanted to spit in disgust. "Detective Hogan's the one in charge," she said. "She gave me his number." Evans wrapped her arms around her body, glanced out the steamed-up window. "I don't trust the police. I got good reason." She turned back to me. "That's why I need somebody working for *me*. Maybe I'm not much of a mother, but Ramona's mine. I want to know what they're doing to find her. I want her back so I can do better." Evans swallowed hard, and her eyes began to fill. She brushed the tears away with the back of her hand. "I need her back with me."

I sat watching her, ignoring the food on the table and the new activity behind us at the tables in the wee hours on a Saturday. It wasn't my place to judge her. Whatever she'd been through, whatever failures led to Ramona being put in the system—it was inconsequential to the problem at hand.

"Before you tried calling and couldn't reach Ramona, when was the last time you actually talked to her?"

Evans thought for a moment. "Maybe a week before that. We didn't talk long. I asked about her schoolwork, she said she was doing fine. I told her how good I was doing, that I was making plans to bring her home with me." Evans's eyes held mine. They were weary eyes, frightened eyes, but I saw hope in them too. "I made a lot of promises. I let her down bad, but I'm going to do it this time. I know it."

"How long have you been clean?"

Evans stared out the sweaty window again. "Ninety-seven days. If that means you won't look for her, just . . ."

I stopped her. "That doesn't mean that at all. Where are you staying?"

Evans exhaled. "Redemption House. It's a—"

"Halfway house, sober living. I know it."

"I'm on probation," Evans said. "I did my time. Possession. I'm clean. I want my baby."

I reached into my jacket pocket and pulled out a pen and small notepad, set the pad on the table. "Detective Hogan. You talk to him directly?"

"He and another detective came to see me. They said it was to tell me what all they'd been doing, but they just wanted to see if I had her. Like I took her. That's how they do people." She reached into her pocket and slipped a business card out and handed it to me. "Here's his card. The other one with him was named something Italian. I can't remember it. He didn't say one word the whole time, just stared, like I wasn't even a person."

The cops had been reading her. It's what they had been trained to do, to size people up, read their body language, listen for inflections in the voice, physical cues that someone was lying—excessive sweating, body tics, nervous leg movements, averted eyes, whether a person wet their lips too much or laughed too hard and at inappropriate times. It wasn't personal; I'd done it just a few minutes ago at the door. It was just part of the training, but Leesa Evans didn't want to hear that. She'd already formed her own opinion on it.

I read the card: DETECTIVE DAN HOGAN. I didn't know him, but maybe I'd start with my ex-partner, Ben, and see if he did. I held the card between two fingers. "Mind if I take this?"

"Go ahead. When I tried calling to see if they'd found her, I got his machine. I left a message. He never bothered calling me back. I guess he didn't feel he had to."

I slid the card in between the pages of my pad, smiled at Evans. "I'll follow up."

She dipped a hand in one of her pockets, drew out a small wallet. "I don't know how this is supposed to work, or how much you charge. . . . My job's not much, but it's steady." Evans opened the wallet, drew out a small stack of bills, maybe a couple hundred dollars' worth, and set it on the table between us. "I been saving up for an apartment for me and Ramona, and I'm real close. My time at Redemption is up soon, but right now, this is more important."

I kept my eyes on her. A couple hundred was less than a day's pay for the kind of work she needed done. I sat there for a moment and tried to figure out in my head whether I could absorb the financial hit, calculating quickly how many days I could afford to work for Evans for free. "Thanks. But first, has Ramona run away before?"

Evans paused a moment. "I don't know. I wasn't exactly in a place where . . ."

"That's okay. Any idea where she might go?"

Evans shook her head solemnly, flicked a look at the money. "I can't think straight right now. Is this enough?"

I gathered up the bills, folded them, and handed them back. "Hold on to this for the time being, how's that?"

Evans's eyes fired. She put the money back on the table. "I don't imagine you work for free, do you? I sure as hell don't. If this isn't enough, then you tell me how much more, and I'll figure it out. I'm no charity case. My money's the same as anyone else's."

We stared at each other for a time, coming to a silent understanding. I picked up her money and slid it into my pocket. "I'll prepare a standard contract before I start and have you sign it. I'll give you a receipt for the money and send you an invoice for the rest when I'm done. If I need more, I'll let you know how much, and then have you give me the go-ahead. That's how it's done."

Evans sat back, her shoulders relaxed. "That sounds all right."

I picked up my pen, prepared to take notes. "But right now, let's go over everything again. Tell me as much as you can about Ramona."

Chapter 2

I followed up with Evans later that morning after I'd gone home for a few hours of sleep, showing up at Redemption House with a contract and a receipt for the two hundred she'd given me. That made things official. A half hour later, I was walking into Area Two headquarters to hopefully talk with Detectives Hogan and something Italian.

The place was hopping for a Saturday, even though it was just shy of 10:00 AM. Crime and stupidity never took a holiday. Someone on staff had made an effort to Christmas-up the place, maybe to take the sting out of being arrested? There were cheap felt stockings hung from the front desk, red and green tinsel everywhere, and red-and-white paper candy canes tacked to the walls, lopsided, as if thrown instead of carefully placed. *Ho, ho, ho, you're going to jail, but Merry Christmas, you low-life bastard.* I stopped at the desk and explained to the sergeant what I was there for, offering ID and an honest face; then I stepped back and waited while she called back for Hogan.

While I waited to see if he would see me, I stood off to the side, watching what went on at the desk. There was some cop clowning, something about doughnuts for someone's birthday. A PO named Green, apparently, had taken the last chocolate glaze and his coworkers had taken mock umbrage. I smiled, remembering my time in a squad, the ribbing, the camaraderie. There was a Green in every cop house, every office, every family. Greens always hit the doughnut box first and last, and they always took the last chocolate glaze.

A couple of civilians stood at the desk, too, opposing forces in a fender bender between a yellow cab and a Sebring, both vehicles parked at the curb out front. I glanced out the window at the scraped cars. Not much damage. The cabbie, an East Indian gentleman, had plenty of official-looking papers in his hands, but none of it appeared to be proof of insurance or a valid driver's license. The driver of the Sebring glowered at him. The desk sergeant waited patiently for the man to pick through the papers, knowing already, or at least having a sense, that he wasn't going to be able to produce what she needed. The cabbie was going to get dinged good.

A detective showed up at the desk, conferred with the sergeant, and then they both looked over at me. He was maybe in his late forties, white, dressed in blazer, white shirt, tie, his thinning sandy hair, receding at the hairline. He walked over to me, bringing a plume of sweet-smelling aftershave with him, his hard-soled shoes shined to a professional turn.

"Dan Hogan," he said. "Cassandra Raines?" His eyes swept over me. He was sizing me up, figuring out what box to stick me in—ally, foe, crackpot, pain in the ass. I'd explained to the desk sergeant that I was here about the Ramona Titus case, so Hogan knew what I was here for already. The question was would he be willing to share information with me.

I held out a hand for him to shake, which he did, though he looked at it first, as though the shake was some kind of trick.

"Thanks for coming down," I said. "I wonder if I could talk to you about Ramona Titus?"

"Sarge says you're a PI?"

"That's right." I pulled a card and my PI license from my bag, handed them to him. He didn't look impressed. "Anything you could share with me would be appreciated."

He tucked my card into his shirt pocket, handed the license back. "We're still working it. Who put you on the scent?"

This was a question I didn't normally answer, but Hogan had information I needed, and I wasn't going to get it playing tight-lipped. I smiled sweetly, the very picture of cooperation. "Her mother's worried." Hogan stared at me blankly. "If you could give me an update that I can pass along to her? Ease her mind."

"The *mother*? She didn't look to me like she had money to hire private."

I took a moment, taking my turn to size Hogan up. Hadn't *looked* like? "Oh? What *did* she look like?"

He ignored the question, wisely, and jabbed a thumb toward the front desk. "You told Sarge you used to be on the job?"

"Yep. The last bit working murder cases." Hogan's brows lifted. "Doesn't look like you have the years. What'd you do, find Hoffa?"

"No, I worked my ass off."

"One of those, hotshots, huh?" Hogan gave me a slight smile, then waved for me to follow him. "I'll give you a few."

His desk was littered with files, papers, cop debris. The room smelled of old sweat, scorched coffee, dust, and oiled holster leather, not wholly unpleasant, even a little nostalgic, given my history.

He sat behind his desk, gestured for me to take the seat facing him. "Ramona Titus."

I pulled my chair in. "Any leads?"

Hogan leaned back, laced his hands across his middle. "Not yet. I'm going back out in a few minutes to cover more ground, but so far we've come up with zilch."

"You and your partner?"

"I'm with Spinelli on this one, and everybody else around here's pitching in. You know how it is. All hands on deck when a kid's missing." He looked at me for a long time. "Her mother doesn't trust us, doesn't think we're working it, but we are. The kid's run away before, she tell you that? By all accounts, Ramona's real savvy, tough, and's got no problem taking care of herself. That's something."

"She's still fifteen," I said.

Hogan stared at me, getting it, not getting it. "Yeah, I know. No one can figure out why she keeps taking off. The last time she came back on her own after a couple days."

"Not so this time," I said.

Again, the long look. "Right."

"How'd you find out she was a chronic runaway?"

"The foster mother. Poole. She had the kid's whole history. And, of course, I was able to pull up two past reports, but those only recorded the times they called it in."

"Was there something that prompted her to run this time? Something happen at Poole's?"

"Not that she knows. One day the kid was there, she says, the next day she didn't come home from school. She had a little part-timer at a burger place in the neighborhood, too, but nobody there has seen her, either."

"And you're not looking at this as a possible abduction?"

"Nope. Kid planned it. Never even went to school the day she went missing. Poole checked. All her stuff was gone, right down to her toothbrush and socks. A real head-scratcher. Poole's place was a good spot, too—nice neighborhood, safe home. It can be real hit or miss with a lot of foster places, some good, some horrible. I know, I used to be a foster kid. Some of the places they stuck me in . . ." Hogan whistled, rolled his eyes. "It's a miracle I'm sitting here talking to you."

"Did you choose missing persons?"

"I got assigned. Wasn't till I was doing it for a while that I found I was good at it. Been doing it almost six years now. The kid cases are the worst, though, especially the system kids." He sat up and opened his top drawer and drew a notepad out, flipped it open. "I got shoved out of the system at eighteen and went right into the army. It made a man out of me. Taught me to fend for myself. After I got out, I joined up here, met a nice girl, got married, had kids. American Dream.

"Ramona Titus has bounced around for years, one home after the other. From what we could find out, she's a ghost everywhere she's placed. Quiet. Barely leaves a mark." He glanced up at me. "I knew kids like that, so broken by their circumstances, that they just shut down, stopped fighting it. Most of them don't make it. Poole said she was working with Ramona, trying to draw her out."

"Guess that didn't work?"

Hogan frowned. "Like I said, most don't make it."

"Are there other kids in the house, anyone Ramona might have confided in?"

"When we got brought in, Ramona was the only kid there. Poole says another girl, Tonya Pierce, had just gone back to her family, maybe a week or so before Ramona took off. Not unusual. These kids come and go through some of these homes like shoppers through a turnstile. That's the life, Raines—it either makes you or breaks you."

"You talk to Tonya?"

Hogan shook his head. "Poole said they barely spoke two words to each other the whole time they roomed together. I've seen it. Don't think we'd get much from her."

I made a mental note to talk to Ramona's former housemate. "Maybe the problem was at school, then?"

"Checked. Nothing. Not even a bully taking an interest. Ramona flew under the radar everywhere, like I said. Teachers liked her. She caught on quick to most things, they said. Had a real talent for numbers."

"How about Poole? Anything off with her?"

"Like?"

"I don't know. Anything?"

"She seems on the level. Likes kids, obviously. She's been fostering for a while. No abuse reports on record. She called it right in when Ramona didn't come home and seems real broken up now, with her out there somewhere. Nine days the kid's been gone, but I'll find her."

"Do you have a photo of her?"

Hogan opened a folder, pulled out a school photo of a sweet-faced fifteen-year-old with big brown eyes and deep dimples. Ramona stared squarely at the camera, almost as if daring the photographer to take a single look, a single expression she didn't want to give.

"Her mother said she had a cell phone."

"We tried it. No pings. She likely ditched it."

I thought about that for a moment. Most kids would rather cut off an arm before voluntarily separating from a mobile device. I looked over at Hogan, skepticism in the look.

"I told you she's smart. It wouldn't be hard for her to pick up another phone somewhere. And just in case you're thinking we're moving too slow, I've got six files on my desk right now, just like Ramona's. We're moving as fast as we can."

"Tough job," I said. "Runaways."

Hogan closed his notepad. "Tell me about it. I ran away from a few places. You get so you'd rather be on your own than confined to a place filled with strangers paid to keep you. You know when I finally got a real home? When I got married and bought one."

I thought of my childhood after my mother died and my father took off. How my grandparents' home, though familiar, welcoming, took some time to feel like home to me. But the world kept turning. It always does.

"How many homes were you in?" I asked.

"Eight, and, believe it or not, my number was low compared

to some of these kids. I always had to be ready to move at a moment's notice. Just pack up, move out. It was like you were a couch somebody bought, then decided they didn't want, so they just sent you back to the store." His eyes met mine. "I want to find Ramona. I will find her."

"Mind if I help?"

His eyes widened. "You have something special I don't?"

"Nope."

Hogan appeared to consider things; then he stood, straightened his tie. "I'm not about to turn away another pair of legs or another set of eyes. I want the kid, and I don't care who finds her first. Matter of fact, I got an ex-cop helping on this, too. He retired a couple years ago. Guy by the name of Frank Martini. You know him?" I shook my head. "He put in close to thirty years, can you believe it? Real old-school. I figured I'd toss him a bone."

I stood. "Retired? And he's still chasing runaways?"

Hogan chuckled. "He's a warhorse who can't turn it off. He does some light legwork, hits up his old contacts. If it were me, I'd spend my time lounging on a beach with a drink in my hand. He hasn't shaken anything loose on this yet, but he's out there." Hogan picked up a pen, pulled his notepad close, and scribbled on it. "Here's his number. Call him." He ripped a sheet clear, handed it to me. "Maybe you two can work together."

"A cop with no ego. That's a first."

Hogan grinned. "I got plenty ego, just not about this. Kids first, right?"

I slipped the paper into my bag. "I'll talk to Martini, but I'd also like to talk to Poole and Ramona's case manager, and anybody else I need to."

His arms akimbo, he stared at me. "I appreciate the courtesy call. Shows class. Most cops don't like PIs buzzing around, you know that. Tell you the truth, I think half of 'em are hacks, the

other half kooks. You seem okay, though." He went back to the
pen and notepad, scribbled some more, then ripped off another
sheet. He'd written down Poole's address and phone number,
and a number for a Ronald Shaw, placement counselor for Bettle House. The case manager.

I looked up at Hogan. "Bettle? I assumed we were dealing
with DCFS."

"Nah. Bettle's private. They work with older kids about to
age out. There's some cross-pollination, I think, but Bettle's its
own thing. Again, we checked them and Shaw, who used to
work with DCFS, and Bettle's a legit operation and Shaw's
your typical paper-pusher—overworked, underpaid. It doesn't
look like Ramona's running away has anything to do with
them. Shaw told me he's got files for at least thirty kids, just like
Ramona, sitting on his desk at any given moment. Personally, I
don't know how he does it. I'd have cracked up a long time ago.
Just keep me in the loop, will you? You latch onto something,
I'd appreciate a call." I shook his hand. I held the paper up.
"Thanks for this. I will."

I turned to leave. He stopped me. "Hey, who'd you partner
with on the job?"

"Ben Mickerson. Know him?"

I could tell by the blank look on his face that he didn't. He
shook his head to confirm. "You two still in touch?"

I grinned. "I see more of him now than I did when we
worked together."

Hogan smiled. "I like it when partners stick."

"What about you and Spinelli?"

Hogan smirked playfully. "Being honest? I'm tired of carrying the guy, and he's tired of carrying me."

"Funny," I said, "I thought that's what partners were for?"

Chapter 3

There was at least a half inch of snow on my car by the time I made it back outside. Right out the door, a mean, strapping wind socked me in the face like a brass-knuckled fist. I burrowed into my jacket, pushed into it, and ran for the car, skirting patches of slick ice, rock salt crunching underfoot. I dove for the car, slid inside, and started it up, flicking a stunned look at the weather readout on the dash. Seven below zero. Oh, my God, I was going to die out here in these streets.

Blowing on the tips of my fingers to get some of the feeling back, I watched ice on my windows loosen and melt, hoping I didn't have to get out of the car and help the defroster along with the ice scraper from the backseat. "Frosty the Snowman" jingle-belled out of the speakers like sickly-sweet sugar canes rolled in silver glitter, reminding me that Christmas was just weeks away, and I hadn't bought a single gift yet. I punched the radio off, hoping out of sight out of mind worked, wishing that not hearing Frosty could somehow push Christmas back until spring when I'd be ready for it.

I wondered about Deloris Poole. Fostering troubled kids

couldn't be an easy deal, though a lot of people did it well, and for all the right reasons. Some kids did make it out the other side—look at Hogan. I wondered, too, about Ramona moving through life never engaging, barely leaving a mark, forced to fend for herself when her mother couldn't hold up her end. It was gray and cold and lonely out here. Where could Ramona have gone? How was she surviving?

As ice melted on my windshield and back window, I got out the slip of paper Hogan had given me and tried calling Poole, but the phone rang several times and never kicked into voice mail. I hung up, checked my watch. Almost eleven. The only number I had for Shaw was his office number, and there was no point trying that on a Saturday.

There was also no point in driving around aimlessly looking for Ramona. She'd been away from home for a little over a week now, she'd likely found a place to hole up, or even managed to get out of the city altogether. I wasn't likely to happen upon her walking the streets, or at least I hoped I didn't. Street life was hard, unforgiving, it wouldn't take much for some scum to latch onto a runaway fifteen-year-old and turn her out. I dialed Frank Martini's number. Maybe he'd be willing to have a conversation.

"Martini," the man answered.

"Detective Frank Martini?"

"Who's this?" His voice was suspicious.

I knew I didn't have long to explain myself, so I rattled through the info: my name, my purpose, my meet with Hogan, my past with the department. My bona fides, my entry card. When I finished, I waited for Martini to say something. He didn't for a few moments, and I wondered what he was thinking about.

"You know where Clancy's is?"

Clancy's was a cop bar not too far from where I was sitting. "Sure."

"Meet me there at noon. You're buying."

He ended the call. I tossed the phone back in my bag. The windshield was clear, the car warmed up sufficiently. I took off for Clancy's.

I wouldn't call Clancy's a restaurant, though they served food-ish things to sop up the alcohol consumed at the messy bar. It was a place, a spot, with drinks and who cares what else, and it was as underwhelming as it had been the last time I'd seen it years ago. It sat just off Western Avenue in Evergreen Park, a couple doors down from a hot dog joint, a Baskin-Robbins/Dunkin' Donuts, and a sad-looking Pizza Hut that had the nerve to offer a drive-thru window. One story, frosted glass fronting it, beer signs and green shamrocks in the windows. There was no sign over the door or anywhere. The bar had been here forever. Everybody in the neighborhood knew Clancy's. Every cop in the city knew Clancy's. Irish cops knew it better.

There were three people in the place when I walked in, a white guy at a back table nursing a beer, a white guy at a front table nursing a beer, and a white guy behind the bar, who, when I asked for Martini, pointed me toward the back table white guy.

"Frank Martini?"

He looked me over. "Cassandra Raines, PI." He gestured for me to sit. I did. "Hope you're hungry. Clancy's makes a mean shepherd's pie."

Shepherd's pie. At Clancy's. Nope. "I'll pass. Thanks."

"Oh, c'mon, you gonna make me eat lunch alone?"

Hell yeah. It's *Clancy's.* I scanned the dingy dining area, which consisted of about eight tables, most of them leaning. Nothing in the place looked as though it had been updated since the Reagan administration, including the sleepy-looking white guys sitting around me. "They make anything else?"

Martini's eyes widened. "You don't like shepherd's pie?"

"It's okay."

"What's wrong with it?"

"Nothing. I'm just not a fan."

He put the menu down, stared at me. "What are you a fan of, then?"

"Clancy's make cheeseburgers?"

For a moment, there was complete silence at the table; then Martini leaned back and began to laugh, hard, his face turning red and everything. I didn't see what was so funny about a cheeseburger, frankly. I was the one who should have been laughing at him going for shepherd's pie in this place. You really had to work at it to mess up a cheeseburger.

"Cheeseburger in an Irish place," Martini said, shaking his head. "Like ordering fish at a steak house."

"You Irish, *Martini*?"

"On my mother's side. O'Shaughnessys. From Dublin."

I took him in. Hogan told me he was retired, and he looked it. His thin, once-dark hair was almost completely gray, and he was a little paunchy. His eyes were blue, with a touch of gray, and deceptively keen behind all the friendly talk of burgers and shepherd's pie. I noticed the nice watch on his wrist, much nicer than the everyday dad jeans and old-man sweater he had on. Maybe the watch was a retirement gift? A memento from his brothers in blue to commemorate his thirty years on the job? Maybe I would have gotten such a watch if I hadn't turned in my badge twenty years too early.

Martini wagged a stubby finger at me. "And anybody else woulda eaten the pie to get in good with me. You ask for a cheeseburger."

I grinned. "And fries."

We ate lunch and talked cop. Martini had a lot of old stories; I did, too. He seemed like an okay guy. When we were done eating, Martini ordered another beer, and we both pushed our plates away and got down to business.

"So tell me about the Ramona Titus case."

Martini wiped his mouth on his napkin, then tossed it down beside his empty plate. "Hogan likely told you as much as I know. Things are early yet, so I think we'll have a good outcome. Still, I haven't been able to get a bead on her. The thing holding me up is her being so solitary. No friends. No boyfriend. No contact with family. She's like a leaf that blows away from a branch and just keeps going."

"Hogan mentioned you had contacts from your time running missing persons cases like this."

"Sure. I've hit every street kid, pimp, dealer, and hooker out there, practically. I got eyes working night and day, but nothing's popped yet. Something will, though. Hogan tell you I worked kid cases for more than half my career? I seen it all. I've bumped against all the bureaucracy at DCFS and the private agencies, too."

"Bettle House?" I asked.

"Sure."

"Why'd you retire? You're not that old, and you obviously still like the work."

Martini paused. "It was time, and you're wrong, I am that old. I'll hit double nickels next March. The job's different than it was, the department, too." He looked around. "Too much waste, too many kids floating around aimless, not enough happy endings. Some of them have been out there so long it's like they're not even kids anymore. It wears on you, you know? But what I'm doing now is great, I can do just enough to keep a hand in." He tapped the side of his head with a finger. "And all that know-how is still right up here. There ain't a street in this city I haven't walked at least twice."

I said, "The department's loss, then."

Martini shifted in his chair. "Damn straight."

"You got kids?" I asked.

Martini beamed. "Three boys. One about to finish NYU, the

other two heading that way. Thank God for our pensions, right? You?"

"Not yet."

"Don't like 'em?"

"They're all right," I said.

Martini chuckled. "Like you and shepherd's pie?"

I smiled. "You talked to Deloris Poole. Did you get anything hinky off her?"

His brows rose. "Did you?"

"I'm just starting. I haven't talked to her yet."

Martini readjusted in the creaky chair. "She seems okay. Only talked to her once, but I didn't get any sense she was up to something. The kid just took off. It happens."

"Any indication that Ramona might have left town? She had a job after school. She could have saved up, bought a train ticket."

Martini shook his head. "Way ahead of you. No tickets. She could have hitched, though, if kids still do that, which they damn well shouldn't. I don't even want to think about all that could happen there."

I shivered. I didn't, either. Martini stared at me. "You got a lot of experience with runaways?"

"Some."

His eyes held mine. "Good to know. You asked about Poole. She's single. Never married. No record. Passed all the background checks. I think in the last twenty or so years, she said, she's fostered at least that many kids. Ramona, however, just didn't settle in. She couldn't break through to the kid at all."

"Fits with what Hogan told me."

Martini leaned forward, lowered his voice. "Poole didn't tell Hogan, so it isn't in the report, but apparently there are valuables missing from the house, including a ring Poole's mother left her."

"That's important. Why'd she hold that back?"

"Because she can't prove Ramona did it, though it's curious everything went missing the same time the kid did, and because she's still trying to get the kid on track and didn't want to brand her a thief. I've got eyes on likely pawnshops, in case she tries to hock it. Till then, I keep digging."

"That explains Poole," I said, "it doesn't explain why you haven't shared any of that with Hogan."

Martini smiled. "Like I said, I've got my feelers out. When I get something, he'll know about it." I sighed. Hogan professed not to have any ego when a child's safety was at stake. It didn't look like that held much for Frank Martini. "Well, I guess I'll start running the bases." I motioned for the check. "Next stop Deloris Poole. Thanks for the meet."

"Anytime." His jacket was hanging on the back of his chair. He reached in and pulled out a card case. "Take my card. It's got my cell, my house. You get something, call me. I get something, I'll think about calling you." He winked. "Just kidding."

I set three 20s on the check to cover the food and Martini's beers, then stood. "I will. Thanks."

He doffed an imaginary cap. "Tell Poole I said hello."

I tried Poole's number again from the car, and again got nothing. I was dead in the water until I talked to her. I started the car and the radio came to life. "Frosty the Snowman" was playing. *Again.* I turned the dial and got more Christmas carols with bells. I switched again and got Tammy Wynette singing "White Christmas." I flicked the radio off. Bah, humbug.

I ducked into Deek's and walked back to the last booth, my booth, relieved nobody was sitting at it. Luckily, there were only a few hungry weekenders sitting at tables this morning, a little light for a Saturday. Deek's never hit capacity, though, mainly because the man had zero social skills and a tendency to chew diners out if they got too precious with their food orders. I eyed them as I passed, getting snippets of excited conversation. Christmas shoppers, I deduced. Fueling up to hit the stores to get their grandma that battery-operated backscratcher they saw on a late-night infomercial. *She was gonna love it.*

There wasn't a festive decoration in the place, however. Not one single strand of tinsel, not a tree, no angels or wooden soldiers, nary a hint of red or green. Deek was a curmudgeon, a grouch, and apparently a Scrooge.

I looked around for Muna, but didn't see her waiting on any of the tables or standing behind the counter. I wasn't here to eat, but for warmth and to kill a little time until I could get in touch with Poole. I dialed her number again from the booth. Nothing. Maybe she was hitting the stores early?

Teen runaways were a tricky business, not like regular missing person cases. Usually, you couldn't track them by bank activity or ATM withdrawals, rental cars or airline tickets. Ramona's phone would have been the best bet, but Hogan and his partner, Spinelli, hadn't had any luck with that, which told me Ramona had thought about what she was doing and had made a conscious decision to make it more difficult for anyone to track her down.

Poole's stolen ring was an added layer. The alleged theft might explain Ramona's disappearance. Was Ramona into drugs, like her mother had been? If so, she would likely have hocked the stuff by now and blown the proceeds. Maybe she'd met someone on social media or in some dumb chat room who'd worked her and then convinced her to come to them. The world was full of sleazebags, cons, and grifters. Ramona might think she was capable of maneuvering around the filth, but to those who took advantage of the defenseless, the naïve, she was just prey.

Evans had given me two hundred dollars. How long had it taken her to save up that much? How much harder would she have to work to make it up? If I were lucky, maybe I could get a line on Ramona quick? Even as I thought it, I wasn't confident that would happen. Hogan, Spinelli, and even Martini had come up with nothing after nine days. Cases like these were either fast or slow. Fast, the kid was taking a little breather after a dustup at home. You maybe found them at a friend's house hanging out, ignoring frantic calls from their parents, or at a local hangout spot way past curfew. Or slow, like in Ramona's case, where the cops had looked everywhere she could be, used every weapon in their arsenal, and still hadn't found her. That's when things got dour and everyone got antsy and began thinking about tragic outcomes.

I didn't feel right about taking Evans's money. She needed it, and more, to find a place for herself and her daughter, to start over, to make things up. She'd been right, I don't work for free, and in my business, most times I couldn't count on working steady or banking a lot. I had a building to maintain, tenants, a car note, gas, utilities, *life,* just like everybody else. But I was currently in the black, not the red. Call it a pre-Christmas miracle. Maybe I could find a sneaky way of slipping the two hundred back to Evans without her taking offense?

My phone rang in my pocket. It was Ben.

"Yo." He sounded winded, like he was running, but that couldn't be it. Ben never ran. "Guess what I'm doin'."

It was an impossible task. His windedness was really throwing me. There was a rhythmic mechanical sound in the background, a steady whir I couldn't identify. "Ah." I took a second more. "Nu-uh. I got nothing."

I had nothing because I knew that, though my ex-partner sounded like he was running, he couldn't possibly *be* running. I knew for a fact he was opposed to the entire concept on principle. Ben was big, solid, like a defensive lineman, not built for wind sprints or even short trots to the mailbox. When we'd worked together, I was the one Flo-Jo-ing it through alleys and gangways, while he screeched up behind me in the car.

"I'm running the hills of Tuscany," he said. "Bought one of

those fancy treadmills that lets you cue up video of exotic lo-
cales. Beaches in Bimini. South American rain forests . . . Think
I'll go Great Wall of China next. Really, this baby does everything but burp and diaper you. Heart rate. Calories burned.
Stride measurement."

I scanned the restaurant, still looking for Muna. What the
hell? The other diners were eating, so I assumed she'd served
them. I wasn't hungry, but maybe a cup of hot tea or cocoa
would be nice? Maybe she was in the kitchen arguing with
Deek. The man really was a cantankerous old sod. "What
prompted all that?"

"Well . . . I'm done with rehab, so I figured I'd keep the momentum going . . . get in . . . some kind of shape, overall." His
words were choppy, punctuated by heavy breathing and a
slight wheeze that didn't sound good.

The mention of rehab reminded me of the knife attack
months earlier that almost killed him. There'd been so much
blood. I shook the memory off. "That's great. Can you run in a
rain forest? I'm thinking there'd be too many trees, poisonous
snakes, and such."

"I don't know . . . but wouldn't snakes make you run faster?
Anyway, I'll let you know. Tuscany's sweet, though."

I slid a fruitless look toward the kitchen. "Hey, glad you
called. You know anything about a couple of detectives—Dan
Hogan and a retired cop, Frank Martini. Hogan's at Area 2,
Martini used to be, before he retired."

The machine slowed a little on Ben's end. "Don't think I've
come across either of them. What's up?"

"Missing persons. Ramona Titus, a runaway foster kid. Fifteen. Her mother doesn't think CPD's doing all it can to track
her down, so she hired me to look at it. Hogan and Martini
seemed okay when I talked to them, though. Surprisingly ac-
commodating, actually, which is freaking me out.

"Hogan was a foster kid himself, so he has a soft spot. Best part was he didn't threaten to lock me up if he saw me nosing around his case. He said he welcomed an extra set of eyes. That's refreshing."

"A foster kid running away is common."

"I know. Martini says the foster mother's missing some valuables, and thinks Ramona took them."

"Unfortunately, also common." The machine sped up. Ben growled. "I'll ask around. See if . . . anyone I know . . . knows either of them."

"Thanks. I'd appreciate that. I'll do the same on my end."

"Whoa. I'm coming up . . . on a vineyard. Gotta go."

"Hey, wait. You called me. What'd you want?"

"Told you. I'm running the hills of Tuscany. On a bitch-ass robot treadmill. And *killing* it."

Curious, I asked, "How long have you been on it?"

"Ten . . . minutes."

"How long's it been out of the box at your place?"

"Halloween."

"Ben?"

"What?"

I thought about it, then decided to leave it. "Talk to you later." I ended the call, smiling.

"Help you?"

It was a slow, lazy, drawly voice, not Muna's. My head snapped up, and I stared into the face of a bony white woman with flame-red hair pulled into a neat top bun, heavy black eye makeup. She looked bored out of her skull, tired of the bullshit, a woman not to be messed with, now or ever.

"Who are you?" It shot out of my mouth before I had time to filter it. This was Deek's. My spot. I'd expected Muna. My waitress. I looked around the place again, as if Muna might be hiding under a table waiting to pop out and yell *surprise*. I turned back to the stranger with the bun.

The woman frowned, tapped a stubby yellow pencil against

the red nameplate on her chest, which I hadn't bothered to even pay attention to at first glance. Her name was AGGIE.

She blinked. Slowly. Like a sloth might. "I'm new. Started yesterday. You ordering?"

Yesterday? Had I been in yesterday? I gave my memory bank a quick scan. No. I hadn't. Yesterday I was hip-deep in paperwork and invoices, then there'd been Evans. I'd skipped Deek's.

"Where's Muna?" I hadn't expected the question to come out with quite so much panic in it. I mean, it wasn't like Muna and I were related or dating; we didn't go out shopping or clubbing. But this was my spot, and she was the person I'd come to expect to be in it when I got here. We were *friends-y,* in a close-acquaintance kind of way. Muna got in my business a lot, but, truthfully, her advice made a lot of sense, which was why I was here—in a diner—in six-below-zero weather when I'd just eaten a cheeseburger and fries with a retired cop in a grungy cop bar-restaurant. Panic? Who, me?

Aggie's sleepy eyes stared back at me. "Taking the day off, but if you're worried I can't cover a diner station, put your mind to rest. This isn't my first rodeo. Been slinging hash for now on twenty years." Her dull eyes held mine. "You're that detective Muna told me about. Extra whipped cream on your chocolate shakes. No butter on your pancakes. You always sit in this booth, with your back to the wall."

I said nothing, just stared at her, not liking any of it.

"Gangsters do that, too," Aggie said.

I squinted at her.

Aggie said, "They face the door, so they can see who comes gunning for them. You don't like change, Muna said." The pencil twirled in Aggie's bony fingers. "Says it throws you off. I know people like that. It's not healthy. You eating or just sitting? Muna also said sometimes you just come and sit. If this is one of those sit times, I'll leave you to it. If it isn't . . ." She poised the pencil over her order pad.

I said, "I handle change just fine."

One Aggie brow lifted. "Doesn't look like you're dealing too good with this one. We could test it, you know. You could sit up front at a table instead of holing yourself up back here like a hermit crab under a rock. Like an experiment."

I studied her, getting only a deadpan expression and a dull look back. Aggie waited. Life went on around us, same as usual. I changed my mind right then about the tea or the cocoa and got up from the booth to leave. "I've got to go."

Aggie took a step back. "Muna said you'd get up and leave. It takes you a while to warm to people, she said that too. Doesn't twist my knickers in a knot. Like I said, I worked all kinds of places, dealt with all kinds of folks. Nothing fazes Aggie."

I picked up my newspaper. "Jung still work here?"

Aggie gave me a head nod, just one. Who gives just one? "Yep."

"And Deek? He's in the kitchen? He still owns the place?"

"Yep."

I slid my hat on, getting ready to step out into the cold. Only a little change, then. Nothing new, except for Aggie. I guess I could handle that.

"Nicetomeetyou." I said it quick, not completely sure it was the truth.

Aggie nodded slowly. Again, just the one. What the hell *was* that? "I'll look after your booth for you."

"Uh-huh."

I grumbled. Walked out into the cold.

Chapter 4

My office was a couple doors down from Deek's, but I bypassed it, deciding instead to ride past Deloris Poole's house to see if she was at home. I was halfway there when my phone rang. It was Whip.

"Hey," I said.

"Hey, what's up?" he asked.

"Working. Missing kid. How's it going?"

Whip paused. "Same old, same old. You know how it is." He paused again. "Just checking in to make sure you weren't getting trapped in any fires."

I chuckled. "Not for months."

"How's the flying nun?"

I laughed out loud. "I'm telling her you called her that."

Whip laughed. "Hey, I ain't scared of no nun."

The three of us had grown up together, under the direction of Father Ray, our mentor, father figure: Whip, his real name Charles Mingo, Barb, and me. Our lives had gone off in different directions—Whip to prison, Barb to religious service, me to the police department and eventually to what I was doing now. Funny how things turned out.

"Maybe you can stop by and see me when you got a minute," Whip said.

"Sure," I said. He hesitated, and that wasn't like him. Whip
usually talked a mile a minute about everything and nothing.
"Everything okay?"

"Sure." His voice brightened. "Living the dream. I'll see you
soon. I'll cook you something nice."

Out of prison, he'd found a job at a West Side diner where he
was not just the cook, but the heartbeat of the place. It was a
nice diner, homey, and Whip knew his stuff.

"Crab cakes?" I offered hopefully.

"You got it. Hit me up when you're on your way."

We ended the call, but it stayed with me. I'd heard something
in his voice, something off. I'd have to call back at the earliest,
check on that. But for now, Poole.

She lived in Chatham in a small yellow-brick bungalow on a
slopey street that hadn't likely seen a revitalizing project in
over a decade. The street was cracked and littered with pot-
holes, the streetlight poles were rusted, their green paint peeling, looking as though they hadn't seen a fresh coat since they
went up, and I'd bet good money that once the sun went down
and the lights flicked on, at least one of them wouldn't be
working. I espied a weathered and leaning block club sign staked
into several inches of dirty snow, a dog, or several, having
marked territory, spraying yellow swirly lines around it. I
hoped the block club was heartier than the sign.

I rang Poole's bell, then turned to watch the quiet street,
turning back when I heard the door unlock and open. A thin
black woman dressed in a heavy cardigan and baggy slacks
stood there, the storm door between us.

"Good morning, Ms. Poole. I'm—"

"Cassandra Raines. The detective."

I blinked. I usually had to do a lot of stuff to introduce myself, show ID, state my business, occasionally BS my way if all of that didn't work. Deloris Poole had just made all that unnecessary, and it was taking a minute.

She held the door open for me. "Detective Martini said I'd be hearing from you. Come in. Get out of that cold."

I stepped into the house and stood planted on the doormat, aware my boots were wet. "He must have given you a good description."

She smiled. "He described you to a T. Tall, pretty, a *real looker* is what he said, but you know men. Can I offer you something warm? Coffee?"

I kicked my boots off, left them on the entry mat to dry. "No. Thank you. I tried calling earlier."

"I'm slow getting to the phone, and don't do voice mail." I followed her back to the living room, noticing that Poole walked slowly and unevenly, not with a limp, but as though she were walking on legs that might give out at any moment. I noticed again how thin she was and wondered about her health.

The front room was small, quiet, decorated in muted greens and soft tans. There were throw pillows on the couch, delicate knickknacks on the coffee table. The house smelled of frilly potpourri and lemony furniture polish. I sat in an end chair, Poole across from me on the couch. Not only was she thin, but there were dark circles under her eyes and her skin was sallow.

This appeared to be a nice place for a foster kid to land, if they were lucky, which, I suppose, was the point. To give at-risk kids a home, or some semblance of it, security, normalcy. What hadn't Ramona liked about it? I spotted a cane leaning against the end of the couch, and though the house felt warm, Poole gathered the sweater around her, as though she were freezing. She sat watching me as I sat watching her.

"It's mine." The small smile she gave me almost felt apologetic. "I have trouble getting around these days."

"I'm sorry to hear that," I said.

"Cancer. In my bones." She waved it off. "But that's not important now, Ramona is."

Cancer. I was afraid that's what it was. The thinness, the circles. I'd seen them in my mother as she slowly morphed into a shadow of herself. Her eyes, which had always held such intelligence, such a spark, dulled as the light slowly left them. Twelve. That's how old I'd been. I hated cancer, even the word itself set me off. I hated it then, I hate it now, I'd always hate it. I pulled myself back when Poole spoke again.

"I thought I was getting through to her, getting her to trust me. She came to me completely shut down. I tried everything. When she ran away . . . I'm just sick about it."

"You told Detective Hogan that as far as you knew, things were fine with her, here and at school, nothing that she might have wanted to run away from?"

"That's true. Ramona had problems adjusting. I try to give all my kids the things they didn't get in their own families—structure, boundaries, discipline, fun, too. A firm foundation, you know? Ramona's not used to any of that. She struggles. She doesn't know how to hold herself accountable or to be a contributing part of a household."

"Was she disruptive?"

"I wouldn't say that. If you've never been taught how to behave, or told what's expected, you don't know, do you? Ramona was never taught, but she was beginning to catch on, really get it. Then . . . I guess, she gave up." Poole glanced over at the cane. "I told her it was arthritis. Bad hips. She doesn't know it's cancer."

I'd known about my mother's cancer. I'd felt it in the air, in the hushed conversations whenever I entered a room, the loud rattle of dread from all the unsaid things that cast a pall over our home and all the frightened, solemn people in it. I didn't know much about Ramona yet, or her life here with Poole, but I would bet good money that Ramona had all the information when she walked out Poole's door. People were always leaving her. She was always being moved from place to place. Maybe this time she decided to be the first to leave?

"You told Mr. Martini she stole from you," I said. "You kept that from the police."

"I didn't want to get her in trouble. Detective Martini can't arrest her, Detective Hogan can. I don't want to ruin Ramona's life any more than it already has been ruined. When they find her, she'll return the ring, and that will be that."

"What else did she take?"

Poole's eyes held mine. "Nothing important, a little cash from the cookie jar."

"She's not on drugs, as far as you know?"

Poole bristled. "Absolutely not. None of my girls have ever been." She angled her head. "You're working for Ramona's mother." The way she said it let me know she didn't approve of my client. "I don't come between families, just so you know, I'm only here to help. Leesa Evans isn't good for Ramona. How does she expect to help her, if she can't help herself?"

"She's still her mother," I said.

Poole went on, as though I hadn't spoken. "If you could see Ramona's disappointment every time she lets her down, you'd know how devastating it is. Every broken promise chips a little more away from these kids. Sometimes it begins to feel they'd be a lot better off if they didn't have any family at all. If they could only learn the things they need to learn, well, then the world opens up for them, doesn't it?"

"But isn't the ultimate goal here to reunite kids with their families?"

Poole's smile was condescending, yet patient. "I've been doing this a long time. Would you like to know how rare that is?"

I glanced at the mantel over the fireplace. There were a few shiny awards sitting there; one looked familiar. "Is that a real Emmy?"

Poole followed where I was looking. "My other life. Spent my thirties in LA. I got lucky after ten years of struggling and landed a part on a sitcom called *Two by Two*. I played the sassy neighbor. I won that, oh, more than twenty years ago now."

The show didn't ring a bell, but I hadn't spent much of my teens watching sitcoms. I was too busy running the streets and getting into all kinds of trouble with Whip and Barb and other kids, half of whom were probably in prison now. I pointed to the Emmy. "Mind if I take a closer look?" It wasn't every day you got to hold an actual Emmy Award.

Poole beamed. "Go ahead."

The statuette was surprisingly heavy. "Wow. You could work out your biceps with this thing."

"It makes a good nutcracker, too."

"You got tired of the Hollywood life?"

"More like it got tired of me. The show got canceled, no other jobs came along. I needed to make a living, so I moved back here. I taught acting for a while, then saw where I could make a difference, a real difference in the lives of at-risk children, so I decided to foster. Best decision I ever made."

I placed it back on the shelf, along with the other honors. No other acting awards, but there were certificates of appreciation and commendations from various service organizations for volunteer work and for her tireless efforts in fostering children.

"You do good work," I said. "Tell me more about Ramona. What kind of kid is she?"

Poole sighed. "Quiet. Resigned. Sad. Like her entire world is painted black and gray and she can't even imagine that it could be anything else. It's like she's waiting for the next bad thing to happen, and whatever good thing she may be experiencing won't last."

"You have no idea where she might be?"

Poole shook her head. "I've looked everywhere I can think of. I've driven the whole neighborhood. The police are doing all they can, at least that's what they're telling me. To think what she could be going through, whom she might be with. She's a baby."

I could hear the anguish in her voice. "No friends."

Poole shook her head, then stood with some difficulty. I reached out to help her up, but she waved my hand away. "Come with me. I want to show you something."

Poole led me into the next room, flicking on the light as we entered it. She'd turned her dining room into a makeshift command center of sorts. The table in the center, large enough to seat six, was covered by maps and flyers. The flyers had the same school photo of Ramona on it, and underneath the photo, in bold black letters, the word *MISSING*. I took a good long look at the photograph again. Ramona definitely had her mother's eyes.

"It's the only picture I have of her," Poole said.

I picked up a flyer. "Can I take one?"

"I wish you would."

I folded the flyer and slipped it into my pocket. A larger map with colored pushpins sticking to it had been taped to a wall, the pins aligned in a grid pattern.

"I've checked everywhere," Poole said. "Her school. I've talked to her teachers, the kids in her classes. I searched as much as I could. I went street by street at all hours, looking. Ramona has a part-time job. I thought it'd be good for her. Get her out there with people, to learn the value of a dollar. No one there has seen or heard from her. Between me and the police, you'd think there'd be something. I can't sleep, knowing she's out there alone."

I walked over to the map, noting the streets Poole had already checked, knowing I'd check them again, though my chances of success would be low. "You concentrated on a tight area. Just a few blocks up and back."

"I don't know how it's supposed to be done, but I thought

maybe searching around the places she's familiar with—the school, the house, her job, would be the best places? That's probably not right."

I turned to face her. "No. Good thinking."

"She's on foot," Poole reasoned, "or at least I think so . . . unless, God forbid, someone picked her up. If they did . . ."

I didn't tell her that there was a chance Ramona might have made it farther than a few blocks. "How much was in the cookie jar?"

Poole paused to think. "Not much. Maybe thirty dollars? She couldn't have gone far on that."

I slid her a look. "You said she had a job." I pulled my phone out and snapped a picture of the map. "Detective Hogan mentioned there being another girl in the house with Ramona, Tonya? She went back to family right before all this? Have you checked with her?"

"Tonya Pierce. I wouldn't know how to. Once they leave me, I rarely see them again. All I was told was that Tonya's grandmother was able to take her back. But Tonya couldn't have had any idea what Ramona was planning to do. The two didn't share confidences. Ramona barely spoke to either of us. You have to understand, these kids are damaged, they're nomads. When Ramona came to me, everything she owned fit in a small bag. She had one pair of shoes, one sweater. She wouldn't accept anything from me at first. I had to add little things a little at a time—a bracelet, a watch, a bookbag, a cell phone, the kind you load up with minutes. For emergencies. She left all of it behind, except the phone." Poole moved past me. "Come. I'll show you."

The small pink-and-white room upstairs looked as though there ought to have been a fairy princess in it, too. The two twin beds were covered in frilly white spreads with matching pillowcases. The dressers were white, the vanity tables. Two of everything, everything the same. A Disney fantasy come to life.

"Maybe I went overboard," Poole said, moving clumsily around the room. "I always wanted a room like this when I was a child. I never got it, and I never had children of my own to do this for. When I started fostering, I wanted my girls to have it. Something nice, something all their own, a perfect place." She turned around to face me. "A room that said somebody cared about them."

"But that didn't work for Ramona?"

"I've fostered a lot of girls over the years with varying degrees of success. Most loved this room. Ramona barely ruffled the sheets. She always sat on the edge of the bed. Slept in one spot. It was as if she wouldn't allow herself to enjoy it because she knew it would only be temporary."

I moved over to the table, opened a couple drawers. There were a few shirts, socks, neatly folded and balled. There was a watch inside and a tiny gold bracelet, the things Poole had given her? I checked the closet. There were two pairs of jeans hanging from plastic hangers, one pair with the tags still on. There was no use checking anything else. "Tonya went back to her family?"

"That's what he said."

I looked at her. "*He?*"

"Ronald Shaw."

"Ramona's case manager?"

"Tonya's, too. I don't make decisions about where the girls go. I'm glad Tonya was able to go home. I'd hoped Ramona's mother would get to a point where she could go back, too, but that's a long way off, if it ever happens."

I parted the pink frilly curtains to look out the window onto the snowy street. "*Girls,* you said. Only girls?"

"I wanted daughters. This way, I figure I could at least make a difference for someone else's. I prepare them to become productive young women, to take pride in themselves, to contribute to the world, to stand on their own two feet, and to make their own money. They go to school, study, do chores. I'm raising women."

I was listening, following along, but also thinking at least two steps ahead, my mind on Poole's grid map, trying to come up with a course of action the police hadn't taken. It didn't help that Ramona was a loner who guarded her secrets, and that she was distrustful and savvy, or so it seemed. She had certainly evaded the police for this long.

"The police tried Ramona's phone. Have you?"

"A thousand times. It's turned off."

I stepped away from the window, turned back to Poole. "Could you give me the number?"

Chapter 5

I paced around the front room of Leesa Evans's halfway house, waiting for her to come down. She'd called me right as I left Poole's, saying she had something she wanted to show me. I hoped whatever it was led me closer to Ramona. Driving the streets with a missing person flyer, like I was searching for a pet bulldog that had breached the backyard fence, was not a good plan. Without the exhaustive resources of the CPD, I was going to have to work smarter, not harder.

When Evans came down the stairs, she looked as worried and as on edge as she had at 2:00 AM. I wondered what effect Ramona's disappearance was having on her newly minted sobriety, and whether she would be strong enough to weather it, even here at Redemption House.

She carried a small Crown Royal drawstring bag and we sat side by side on a lumpy couch in the front room as residents passed us by, offering only quick glances. *Not my problem, got my own*, their looks seemed to say.

"I know you just started," she said. "But I thought maybe this could do something." Evans opened the bag and emptied its contents into her hand, setting the empty bag on the scarred coffee table in front of us. "These are Ramona's."

I stared at the jumble of small things: a ceramic kitten with blue glass eyes, the kind you'd win at a carnival or county fair; a gold key on a silver neck chain; a small rusted harmonica; a faded photo of a house; a small rubber ball in kaleidoscope colors. I looked up at Evans, not sure what I was supposed to be seeing.

"Her *treasures,*" she said, "that's what she calls them." Evans set the items on the table next to the bag, as if the very act solved the mystery surrounding Ramona Titus's whereabouts.

"A harmonica and a ceramic kitten," I said gently. "A ball."

Evans looked abashed. "Not those." She picked up the photo, the key. "These. This is a picture of my mama's house. We used to live with her before I messed everything up. Ramona was happy there. I was, too. I just couldn't hold it together." She handed the photo to me. The house was unspectacular, a small wood frame with a sagging chain-link fence around a scraggly yard, drooping curtains at the windows. "You asked if there was anyplace Ramona would go. I didn't forget Mama's, but I never thought she'd go there. Then, after a while, I started to think maybe she would."

I studied the photo. Looked over at Evans. "And the key?"

"Ramona let herself in after school when Mama wasn't home. A latchkey kid? She knew how to take care of herself, even then."

"I'm sure Detective Hogan has already checked the house, Leesa. It'd—"

"I didn't tell him nothing about it. I didn't tell him anything after he came in and talked to me like he did, like *I* hurt Ramona, like I was no better than dirt." Her eyes fired. "It's how they always do. I knew then I was going to have to find Ramona myself. I just needed somebody working for me. That's when I found you. I got no problem giving you Ramona's things, telling you about the house. I trust you."

"What I'm saying is, you wouldn't have had to tell him about your last known address, he would already—"

She shook her head violently. "No. Believe me. He didn't care enough to do all that." She shoved the key in my hand. "*You* go. See if she's there." Evans dulled. "Mama's gone, passed not long after Ramona went into foster care. Maybe that and me doing what I was doing had something to do with it. Something else that's my fault. I don't know who's there now."

"Other family?"

"I got a sister and a brother, but we don't speak, haven't in a long time. Lester is always in and out of trouble. Marla gave up on both of us altogether. She tried to get them to give her Ramona when things got bad, but they wouldn't, so she gave up after a while. She's in Shreveport now. Maybe she stayed in touch with Ramona. I don't know. She sure didn't stay in touch with me."

"When's the last time you heard from either of them?"

"Lester, not since the funeral. Marla sent me a letter while I was inside. That's how I know she's in Louisiana. She blames me for Mama dying like she did, worried sick about Ramona and me. She's right."

"Do you still have that letter?"

Evans offered a quizzical look.

"It'd have her address on the envelope."

"You're thinking Ramona got all the way down there? How could she by herself? She's a child and she's never been anywhere before."

"She's fifteen and resourceful," I said. "And she has a job. We have no idea how long she's been planning this."

Evans started to rise. "I'll go get it."

"Wait," I said. "Would Ramona run to Lester?"

Evans eased back down, a stricken look on her face. "I hope not. Lester has always been just bad to the bone. I never did trust him around my baby. He ran with all kinds back then, probably still does. I don't talk to him. I don't even know where he is, and I like it like that." Her eyes met mine, pleading. "But he could have changed, maybe? If she did go back, and he was still there, maybe he wouldn't do nothing to her?"

"You didn't tell Detective Hogan about Lester or Marla, did you?"

Evans shook her head. "I wasn't going to get any help from him, and even if he went by Mama's, in that neighborhood, nobody was going to tell him anything."

Evans was right, the neighborhood closed ranks when white cops came around asking questions. Hogan wouldn't have gotten much, even if Ramona had come home. Hell, I might not get anything, either. Strangers were strangers, no matter what color they were.

I took out my phone, pulled up the photo of Poole's map, and showed it to Evans. "Do you know of anyplace in this area where Ramona might want to go? Maybe someone she knows? A family friend, a special place, someone she might trust?"

Evans took the phone, studied the photograph, then shook her head. "No. I don't think so." She handed the phone back. "Some mother I am."

I slipped the photo of the house and Ramona's key into my bag. "That's okay. The letter, please, and your mother's address."

It was after three and getting dark, winter dark, gray and desolate, as though the sun had backed away and left the world to freeze to death. The old Evans house didn't look like much from the curb. It was small and sunken in, rotting. There were rusted bars on the dirty windows. It looked empty. The block was unimpressive, dotted with small bungalows, a few of them displaying flashing Christmas lights strung along spindly bushes. In front of the house across the street, a half-inflated snowman and three angels were bent over at the waist, foreheads in the snow, as though they'd been shot and left for dead.

I walked up the front steps, an official-looking clipboard in my hand, a fake ID pinned to the front of my jacket. No one paid much attention to folks with clipboards and official-looking ID. No one wanted to engage for fear the bad news was there for them and not their neighbor. The trick was to act like you belonged, that you had important business to do—and not a lot of time to do it in. Often this was enough.

There was a yellow sticker pasted across the front door that informed me the Evans home had been lost to foreclosure. The lock on the door was new, courtesy of the bank. Ramona's key would do me no good here. Around the back of the house, I found the same situation—yellow sticker, new lock, but by way of an early Christmas gift, there was a busted window opening access to the covered porch. It was likely the work of neighborhood kids, knowing the house was empty, looking for a place to do things they weren't allowed to do at home, or maybe Ramona had busted it.

I put the clipboard down on a step, unclipped the fake ID from my jacket and put it on top, then took a quick look around to make sure no one was watching. Nobody I could see, so I crawled gingerly through the opening. Up, over, in, landing on all fours with zero footing, my boots slipping, scraping, sliding, on icy planked flooring covered in patchy snow blown in through the hole.

I stood, dusted off my gloves, blinking into the dark, smelling must and cold. The tiny flashlight from my pocket did little to light my way, but I wasn't supposed to be here in the first place, so I didn't really need a big, booming burst of light bouncing off the windows to announce the fact that I was trespassing on bank property. The house had been emptied out of furniture, from what I could see. It was just a shell now, murky, lifeless, and a little creepy, like the bare walls were watching me as I made my way along.

The floors were bare, hardwood, but there was no give in the frozen slats, so every step I took sounded ten times louder than I needed them to. I felt like Frankenstein's monster stomping through a village. I scanned for shoe prints, but saw only the ones my boots were making. It was clear nobody had been in here in a while. My flash lit something standing in a corner, and I jumped, thinking it was a man lying in wait, but it was only a grungy, raggedy settee covered in plastic that someone had stood up on its end and propped against the wall. Still, my heart beat a mile a minute. If Ramona had come back here and had chosen to stay, she was made of sterner stuff than I was.

The second floor was just as desolate—empty bedrooms, a gutted bathroom, layers of dust, again not a single shoe print. I went back the way I'd come, flicking the flash off at the back window, crawling back out, legs first, glad to be free of the creepy house, even if free meant being back outside where it was as cold as a witch's tit. When I came back around to the front, there was an old man shoveling his walk across the street.

He looked up and saw me. "Hope y'all are about to do something with that house. Leaving it sitting empty like that is asking for trouble."

I walked over to him, the clipboard in my hand. "You see people hanging around over there?"

"Just you folks with your stickers and such. Heard somebody bought it for the taxes, once Corlene died of that stroke. Couldn't expect her kids to take care of it. No account. Real shame." He leaned on the shovel, a blue skullcap with a Bears logo on it pulled low on his head.

"You lived here a long time?"

"Fifty-two years. I was one of the first ones on this block after the white folks ran for the hills."

"So you knew Marla, Leesa, and Lester?"

The old man made a face. "Oh yeah. The whole neighborhood knew them. The last two stayed up on the corner doing all kinds of stuff. Marla was the only one had something about herself, but she got up and away from here a little after Corlene died. Last I heard, Leesa was in jail for drugs and carrying on."

"And Lester?"

"Where he always is. All but lives out of Lippy's pool hall, up the street, but if you're looking to get money out of him for that house, you can hang that up. Lester steals money, he don't do nothing legal to make it."

I pulled the flyer with Ramona's photo out of my bag. "Have you seen this girl hanging around over there?"

The old man squinted at the flyer, then back at me. "What's a runaway child got to do with you selling Corlene's place?"

"We can't get the ball rolling," I said, "until we find all Mrs. Evans's relatives who might have a stake in the proceeds. This girl is her granddaughter."

His eyes widened in surprise. "That's little Ramona?" He stared again at the flyer with renewed interest. "Well, I'll be. She lived over there since she was a baby. We used to see her running up and down the block, riding a little tricycle and all." He shook his head solemnly. "They took her from Corlene right before she had that stroke. Leesa had got picked up again with drugs on her. Them taking that baby's what killed that poor woman. Now she's run off? Lord, have mercy. I haven't seen her hanging around, but I'll surely keep an eye out for her now. Least I can do for Corlene." He trained a steady gaze on me. "As for you folk, we don't need a crack house popping up over there, so if you got plans for the place, get on with them."

"Yes, sir." I took a pen from my bag, wrote my number on the back of the flyer. "If you do see Ramona, would you mind giving me a call? The sooner we get all parties assembled, the faster we can get that house settled." I handed the sheet to him. "And the better off the neighborhood will be, right?"

The old man stuffed the paper into his pocket and moved off the shovel. "If I see her, I'll call you."

"And Lippy's, you said?"

The man's eyes widened. "Look, I know you ain't planning on going down to Lippy's looking for Lester Evans."

"Why not?"

"*Why not?* Because Lippy's place is about as next to nothing as they come. Because it's full of thieves and gangbangers and women who like to hang out with 'em. And Lester Evans ain't a bit of good, and never will be." He shook his head adamantly. "No, you'd do well to stay away from over there. Whatever stake Lester's got in that house, you best mail it to him or give to him in court."

"Thanks for the advice, Mr. . . . ?"

"Morley. Zeke Morley. And that *advice* is the same I'd give my own granddaughters. Yes, indeed, you best stay away from Lester Evans."

"I'll let the police handle it, then," I said to put his mind at ease. "Do you know if Lester has a car?"

Morley frowned. "*Wish* he had a car. That fool rolls around here on that motorcycle all hours of the day and night like he still lives here. I think he's trying to check to see if anybody's moved in, so he can do something about it. Lester's like that. Trifling."

"Do you remember what his bike looks like?"

"Of course, I remember. I'm not that old. It's big and black, with red flames licking on it. And loud. Revs it up, too. Just to show us, I guess. I don't know how he bought it, in and out of jail like he always is, but however he did, you can bet it wasn't legal. Riding a bike in the middle of a winter like this. That shows you right there, he ain't right in the head."

"Thanks for your help, Mr. Morley. You be careful with that snow, now."

"I'm not worried about this snow, young lady. Been taking care of business since I burst into the world in 1945."

I gave him a thumbs-up, then headed back across the street, but stopped for one last question.

"You didn't happen to see the police over at the Evans place, did you? Two white cops?"

"All I've seen over there is you bank people. If the police are looking for Lester, they best do it down at Lippy's."

The shovel started back up as I pulled away from the curb. I gave Mr. Morley one final look as he slung a shovelful of snow off his walk. *He wasn't worried about this snow.*

Chapter 6

I dialed Ramona's phone, but got nothing, no dial tone, no voice mail, just dead air. I slid my phone into my bag and stared out my car window at the pool hall Morley had warned me away from. It was a pool hall, all right, and it looked rough. The front windows were grimy and had neon beer signs covering them, like Clancy's, like any bar, only no shamrocks here. Nobody had bothered to shovel the sidewalk in front, there wasn't even any rock salt thrown down. Lippy, apparently, didn't give a blip if you slipped, fell, or sued for damages. If it was the latter, I had a feeling you'd probably live to regret it.

From the sidewalk, I could see tables lined along the window with roughneck-looking patrons sitting at them hoisting bottles of beer. I spotted the motorcycle Mr. Morley described right outside the front door, black with red flames. I snapped a photo of the back plate, then stood on the sidewalk between the bike and the front door, watching dodgy folks walk past me, staring curiously like I'd lost my way and all good sense. Still, I felt safer out here in the open than I would have inside the place.

I backed up, stepped off the curb, and took up a spot close to Lester's bike, my hands in my pockets, my collar up, cars slipping up and down the street behind me. Then I waited for someone inside to glance out, see me, and tell Lester about it.

The bike was surprisingly clean, given the elements, and it looked like he babied the hell out of it. The streets were messy as heck, with all the snow and slush and salt, but Lester's bike appeared to have repelled most of it. It almost looked like he'd airlifted it here right from a custom car wash. I was sure I wouldn't have to wait by the bike too long, and I was right. In less than two minutes, a big, dark man, well over six feet and around two-fifty, came charging out of the pool hall straight toward me.

"Hey, what the hell you doing with my bike? Back up!" His dark eyes were wild and mean, and there was a deep, jagged scar running down the right side of his face. He wore a short-sleeved T-shirt under a black leather biker's vest, gang and prison tats running down both arms—arms the size of paint cans. His jeans rode low on a thick waist, and his biker boots had to be at least a size 13. No coat, but Lester didn't look cold.

I watched as the windows to the pool hall filled with half-drunken spectators and the foot traffic on the street slowed, then stopped with the promise of a Saturday night ass-kicking they could talk about in church tomorrow. I took a step back from the bike. It had served its purpose.

Lester checked the bike for damage, a scowl on his face, black ratlike eyes daring me to make a move while he did it. When he was satisfied his bike was as he'd left it, he turned to me for an explanation. He looked a little like Leesa Evans, similar features, but Lester was prison hard, likely broken beyond repair and unreachable to right reason. I'd encountered a lot of Lesters in my time. You didn't turn your back on a Lester. You didn't give a Lester a single opening. You kept your wits about you, your head in the game, or you walked away crooked from a Lester, or maybe not at all. I kept my right hand in my pocket. Let Lester worry about what I had in there.

"Lester Evans?"

He blinked, then sneered at me. "Who the hell are you?"

"I work for your sister Leesa."

He looked confused, then turned back toward the windows, scanned the street. Looking for witnesses? A cheering section? Maybe a little bit of both? "What you talking about *work for*?"

"Your niece, Ramona, has run away," I said. "I'm looking for her. Maybe you've seen or heard from her?"

"What's that got to do with you all up on my bike?"

"I don't want your bike." I held the flyer up so he could see Ramona's picture. "Have you seen your niece? Maybe around the old neighborhood? Your mother's house?"

"Wouldn't know. I got no reason to go around there no more."

"That so?" That wasn't what I'd gotten from Morley. According to him, Lester rode routinely down the block, revving up bike noise. "I heard different."

"From who?"

I didn't answer.

He gave me an oily grin. He was working something through his lizard brain, working up an angle. I could see it in his feral eyes. "There a reward out on her?"

Those on the street, disappointed there wouldn't be anything good to see, slowly moved along. I glanced over at the pool hall to see that most of the people in the windows, too, had gone back to what they were doing, which likely wasn't much.

I put the flyer away. "No reward."

His face fell, his interest flagged. Suddenly whether I found Ramona or not appeared to lose all relevance to him, since either way it wasn't putting a single penny in his pocket. "I ain't seen Leesa or her kid in years, so their business ain't none of my business." His greedy eyes took another slow survey. "But if you need help looking, well, that's another story. We can talk about that inside, in the back. I'll tell you how much it'll cost you. Hell, I'll even buy you a drink first."

I stared at him. He stared back. This was Ramona Titus's uncle. Family. This is who she had out here waiting for her? Leesa Evans had been right to keep her brother away from her kid. Score one for her.

"So you haven't seen her?"

"That's what I said."

"Not even interested in how Leesa's doing?"

His scowl deepened. He'd given me his answer.

I turned for the car without another word. He was useless. I wasn't going to find Ramona through him.

"Hey, I'll still buy you that drink," he yelled after me. " 'Cuz you got it like that."

I tuned him out and eased into the driver's seat, hurrying to start it up and get the heat going. I called Hogan, but got his voice mail. I ran down my encounter with Lester, such as it was, and passed along his bike's plate number. Maybe something would come out of it; until then, Lester was a dead end. I also passed along Marla Evans's address in Shreveport. Ramona could have made it that far.

I peered at Lester through the quickly de-icing windshield as he gave his precious bike one last look. He shot me a rakish grin, and then walked back into Lippy's, me fighting a very strong impulse to roll over his bike on my way out of the spot. I tossed the phone on the seat and pulled away from the curb, giving the bike a wide berth. *Merry Christmas, Lester Evans.*

It was well after four now, and getting colder, but there was one stop I wanted to make before I stopped for the night, so I made a U-turn midblock and drove east to the Burger Joint, Ramona's part-time job.

The place was small, just a divey food spot with a few tables out front, a counter with a register, and a couple of kids flitting about in short aprons and paper hats. There were two men behind the counter, a tall one at a long grill, and a shorter one at the counter waiting on a man in a UPS uniform. The menu board on the wall didn't veer from standard fare. There were burgers, fries, shakes, chicken nuggets, pizza puffs, mozzarella sticks, shrimp in a basket, cans of pop for $1.25 each. When the UPS man put in his order and moved back, I moved toward the counter guy.

"Hi," I said. "Can I speak with the manager or owner, please?"

He sensed trouble and tensed. I put him at about fifty, average by all standards . . . "There a problem?"

"No. I just need a little information about one of your employees." He just stared at me. "Ramona Titus."

Everything in the shop stopped, the guy at the grill, the teenagers behind me wiping off tables, even the UPS man standing behind me looked up from his phone.

"You police didn't find her dead, did you? Please tell me y'all didn't find her dead?"

"No," I said hurriedly. "No, she hasn't been found yet, and I'm not with the police. I'm a PI hired by Ramona's mother. I'm Cassandra Raines. Do you have a minute to talk?"

"PI?" He looked me over as though he didn't believe me, as though what I'd just said couldn't be possible. "You?"

"Yes."

He stood there for a moment considering things, I guess. "I got a minute. Meet you out front. Can I get you something?"

I eyed the menu board. "Hot chocolate?"

"Sure. I'll bring it out."

I found an empty table and sat watching as the kids slid me curious looks. The boy was lanky, thin; the girl the same; off to the side, replenishing paper napkins in a silver dispenser, was a girl with Down syndrome. They all looked to be about Ramona's age.

"Here you go." He set my cocoa on the table and then slid in across from me. "On the house. I'm Dangelo, by the way, manager and part owner. My brother back there's the other owner. He's Clint."

I took a sip of hot chocolatey goodness, my insides warming instantly as it slid down my throat to my stomach. "Thanks for taking time out."

"Ramona's one of our kids. If I can do anything, I'll do it."

"Had you noticed any change in her behavior? Did anyone here get the feeling there was something going on with her?"

"She seemed fine. No different. She's not a big talker, so it's hard to really say. The police asked us all the same thing, but if you want to talk to the kids again." He raised his arm to gesture for them.

"In a minute?" I said, holding off the kids. "First, did you see anyone hanging around the place for Ramona specifically?"

Dangelo shook his head. "I wouldn't have allowed that, even if I did. We're about the business around here. I tell them when I hire them, I'm not running a social club. They get breaks. Till then, the phones stay in their lockers and they keep working. We give them work, but we also teach them how to work."

"So Ramona came in, did her job, and that was it?"

"Light conversation, some fooling around, same as anyplace, but, like I said, they're here to work."

Dangelo called over the kids and they crowded in around the small table. I took another sip of chocolate, watching them in all their teenager tenderness. I couldn't remember ever being that young. I don't think I ever was. By the time I'd gotten to their ages, too much life had happened that it washed the child right out of me. Watching them now, I wondered, not for the first time, what I might have missed.

"She's asking about Ramona," Dangelo said. "This is Jamal and Kenya." Hanging back behind the two was the girl from the dispensers, who eyed me suspiciously. "And that's Rose."

"We told the police before," Kenya said. "Ramona never said

anything to us about anything. To tell the truth, she was a little stuck-up."

Jamal shot her a look. "She wasn't stuck-up. She was shy."

Kenya rolled her eyes, made a face. "Same thing."

I asked, "Did she ever mention a friend, maybe a boy she liked, or a place she wanted to go?"

They both shook their heads no. Rose stood quietly, mouth clamped shut, eyes wandering. I watched Rose.

"I'd sometimes see her taking her break with Rose," Dangelo said, peeking over at her. "Anything you can say about that, Rose?" The girl shook her head, then dropped her eyes to her shoe tops. Dangelo slid me an apologetic look. "She gets nervous around strangers."

Rose looked at me, then quickly looked away.

"The police talked to all of you?" I asked.

Dangelo scanned the group. "Everybody here, except Rose. She was off the day they came."

"It's sad about Ramona," Jamal said. "But we really didn't know all that much about her."

I pushed my cocoa aside. "How about you, Rose? Anything you'd like to tell me about Ramona?" I kept my voice light, friendly, hopefully nonthreatening.

Rose startled, eased back, her eyes searching the front windows, but she said nothing. Suddenly she broke away from the table and retreated to the dispensers, keeping her back to me.

"Don't mind Rose," Dangelo said. "Like I said, she doesn't take to people right off. You think you all have a chance at finding Ramona?"

"I hope so." My eyes were on Rose's back. She wasn't doing anything, her hands were idle, but she was listening to every word we said. She was shy around strangers. That could be it, or was it something else? I watched as Rose turned to stare out the front windows. She wrung her hands, bit her lower lip. Our eyes held for a half second, then Rose looked away again. She was afraid of me.

I stood, but kept my distance. Suddenly Rose bolted for the front door and ran out of the shop. I turned to see a blue Subaru Forester at the curb with a woman behind the wheel. Rose jumped into the passenger seat, slammed the door, and the car pulled off.

I turned back to the others. "Rose gets picked up every day?"

"And dropped off," Dangelo said. "By her mother. She only works a couple of hours, a few days a week. Why're you asking about Rose?"

I walked back to the table, pulling a card out of my bag. I handed it to Dangelo. "Do you think you could call her mother and ask if I could talk to Rose? And I'd like her to be there when I do."

Dangelo glanced at the card; the kids stared at me, eyes wide. "I can do that. You thinking Rose might know something about Ramona?"

I glanced out the window again at the spot where the car had been. "Rose work tomorrow?"

"None of us do," Jamal said. "We're closed Sundays."

"She's back Monday, though," Dangelo said.

"I'd appreciate your making that call as soon as you can, Dangelo. Thanks."

Chapter 7

Sunday warmed up nicely, the temperature soaring to a balmy sixteen degrees. The sun was bright, the air biting. I had my half brother, Whitford, in the car. I'd promised him pizza, but before we got to that, I wanted to drive around Ramona's neighborhood to get a feel for it. I drove slow, checking both sides of the street, ducking down alleys, side streets, and main drags. I doubled back around to the Burger Joint and around Poole's place, too.

I slid a look at the twelve-year-old in my passenger seat and found him watching me. "You said we were going to have pizza. We've passed this street a million times already."

"I know. We are. I just needed to check something first."

He scanned the street, turned back to me. "Who're you looking for? Bank robbers?"

I pulled a face. "What is it you think I do for a living?"

"You're a private investigator. You investigate."

"Not bank robberies."

"What, then?"

"It depends." He stared over at me, waiting for me to elaborate. "On a lot of things."

I turned the corner heading for a stretch of neighborhood where a lot of teens hung out around a game arcade, my eyes tracking the cars around me, the people walking down the sidewalks, the doorways. It was warmer, so more folks were out. I didn't expect to get anything for my efforts. I mean, it wasn't like I expected to see Ramona hanging out on the corner waiting to be spotted, but I wanted to see where people congregated and what types of people congregated there. Patterns.

I flicked a look over at Whit. It didn't look like he was about to give up on his line of questioning. I didn't know kids well; I didn't have any, and didn't spend a whole lot of time thinking about them. Was this par for the course, or just Whit being Whit? We'd only just recently met months ago—when my prodigal father returned after more than twenty years. Ted Raines came back searching for a do-over, a reunion, and he'd brought with him a new wife and Whit, who'd latched onto me and was not letting go. Family, most people would call it. I wasn't sure yet what I considered it. Right now, things were still slow going, except, apparently, for Whit, who had gone all in.

"People usually come to me with a problem," I said. "I figure out if I can help them. That's it." He sat there, his eyes on me, silent. "Nonbank related, usually."

His eyes narrowed; then he peeled off, glancing out the window again. I exhaled, glad to have the pressure off. There was nothing promising out on the street, and I'd heard nothing from Rose's mother yet, either. I didn't want to approach Rose without her okay, so I was kind of stuck until I heard from her. There was something there, though—I was sure of it, and I hated having to wait to find out what it might be. What if Rose knew something and wasn't telling it, because no one bothered to ask her?

"You're treating me like a kid again," he grumbled.

"You *are* a kid."

Whit and I caught the occasional pizza, or he hung out at my place with Mrs. Vincent, Barb, and Whip, which had instantly presented a problem. Charles Mingo was my pal. We'd nick-named him Whip way back when we were kids. Now Whitford was in the picture. Whit. Whip and Whit.

You couldn't confuse them physically. Whit was wiry, short for twelve. Whip, on the other hand, once a slip of a thing at thirteen, hence the nickname, was now a burly ex-con who wore a size-fourteen shoe and could body slam a full-grown man without breaking a sweat. We were going to have to come up with some new names around here. We just hadn't gotten around to it yet.

He shrugged, turned to glance out the window. "For now."

One more street, I told myself, turning another corner. "Any idea what you want to do with *your* life?"

"Not yet. Maybe a detective, like you."

I didn't say anything. Didn't know what to say. It wasn't an easy life, that was for sure. There was never enough sleep or pay, the hours sucked, and the odds of your getting brass knuckles upside the head were great. "Lots of other things. Doctor. Law-yer. President."

He thought it over. "Nah. So, *who* are we looking for?"

"*We?*"

"I have eyes, don't I? I'm in the car. I figure we can be Raines and Raines Investigations."

"Uh-huh." I gave the street we were on one final sweep. "There's a flyer in the console. I'm looking for a runaway, not much older than you. If you see her, call out."

Whit picked the flyer up, stared at it, then peered out the window. We were quiet for a time, both of us watching for Ra-mona, only one of us certain the effort was futile.

"We're getting along great, right? You, me, Dad, Mom." It came out of nowhere, and he wasn't looking at me when he said it. "You like us, right?"

I held my breath. Whit wanted desperately for the family thing to happen, but how did you bond again with a man who abandoned you on a doorstep a day after your mother's funeral? There was a lot to adjust to, a lot to forgive, a lot of anger and resentment to choke down. I didn't trust the man. I didn't know if I ever would. But his wife, Sylvia, was nice, so was Whit. It was going to be a process.

"The first rule of surveillance," I said, avoiding the question, "is hypervigilance. That means more watching, less talking." I gripped the wheel tighter. "And yes. I like you very much."

He turned to face me, smiled, then went back to watching. "If I was going to run away, I'd wait until it got warmer."

I took in the snow, the slushy streets. "Maybe she couldn't wait."

"Why?"

I sighed, grasping the magnitude of my task at hand. "That's where the investigation part of all this comes in." I turned the corner, deciding to call it. "Okay. Let's go eat."

Whit pumped his fists excitedly. "Yes! Thin crust. Pineapple and pepperoni."

I slid him a horrified look. "Deep dish. Sausage. Period."

"It's that serious?" he asked.

"Oh, it's that serious."

"Is it some kind of Chicago thing?"

"All day, every day."

"Okay. I guess I can deal."

I snorted. "Right answer."

I was sitting in the lot in front of Bettle House before nine on Monday, waiting for the office to open. I was there to talk to Ronald Shaw, Ramona's case manager. I didn't have an appointment, and no guarantee that he would talk to me, but I was here, anyway, waiting.

I'd looked them up, of course. Bettle was a for-profit agency that worked exclusively with older kids who were about to age out of the system. Bettle fostered them, and in some cases facilitated adoptions, finally giving kids who'd bounced around their entire lives a home and parents of their own. I wondered how Ramona got hooked in with Bettle and how she'd ended up at Deloris Poole's place in that frilly pink bedroom. I assumed Shaw had something to do with it, and wanted to talk to him about it.

Cars filed into the lot steadily as it got closer to nine. Employees making their way to the job. A few noticed me sitting in my car with the engine running, but no one approached me or made a federal case out of it. At exactly nine, I got out, leaned into a cold wind, and ran for the front door like the hounds of hell were chasing me. I snatched the door open and barreled inside.

"Whooo." I bent over, hands on knees. "Son of a . . ."

The blond woman behind the front desk smiled knowingly. "You're not used to it yet, either, are you?" I looked up, then straightened. "It went right from a nice fall to this," the woman added, shaking her head. "There was no time to prepare ourselves."

There was a tiny Christmas tree on her desk, lit up with tiny colored lights, and Christmas tree earrings in her ears. Festive. "You're right, but we'll get there. We always do. I'd like to speak with Ronald Shaw, if I could? I don't have an appointment. It's about Ramona Titus. I understand he's her case manager."

Smiling, she asked for ID, which I supplied; then she picked up the phone and called back. While I waited, I walked around reception, which was fronted by glass that winter had nearly frosted over. I saw my car sitting in the lot frozen stiff, a light snow falling. There was little feeling in my toes and fingers.

There were collages of happy, smiling kids all over the walls. Black kids, white, Asian kids, all smiling, all happy, all paired with what appeared to be loving parents. Families, at long last. I could have been one of these kids trapped in an endless series of placements, were it not for my grandparents. Would my father still have left me behind if I hadn't had them to go to? I hated to think so, but, truthfully, I didn't know the man well enough to say for sure. Where would I be now if I'd ended up at Bettle? Would I have spent the better part of my twenties in and out of prison, like Whip, or would I have ended up right where I was now, doing what I was doing?

I turned when a woman called my name. She was Hispanic, petite, and dressed in a thick ski sweater I envied more than I should have. She led me back and deposited me at an office door where inside a black man in his late forties sat behind a cluttered desk. The woman introduced me, then walked away.

Shaw stood, came around the desk, and waved me in. "Ms. Raines."

I held my hand out for a shake. "Mr. Shaw. Thanks for seeing me."

He looked like he hadn't gotten a lot of sleep, his cheeks sagged, there were deep lines around his eyes, and his dark face looked a little washed-out, but it was Monday morning, early, maybe he hadn't yet had his coffee. He tugged at the ugliest tie I'd seen in a while. It was purple with pink dots and neon blue swirls all over it. His clothes, too, were a bit of a mess—his pants too long, too ill fitting, his shirt too loose.

His ID badge hung from a lanyard around his neck. I looked at the photo, taken, presumably, years ago when he started this gig. That Robert Shaw, heavier, less gray, bore little resemblance to the Robert Shaw standing in front of me now.

"You said it's about Ramona Titus?"

I sat in his client chair. "Yes. I've been asked to help find her. I was hoping you could give me some information on her, some insight."

Shaw sat in his chair, closing the file he'd been reading and pushing it aside. "A private investigator and the police on one runaway girl. That's a new one. Don't get me wrong, I think it's great—the more eyes, the better—just saying it's not usually how it goes."

I knew what the usual was, but asked, anyway, curious about Shaw's take. "What's usual?"

"Usual is a kid runs away, some cops half look, and either the kid, by some miracle, is found, they come back on their own, or . . . I'm counting on it not being *or.*"

"When's the last time you checked in with Ramona, spoke to her?"

Shaw looked at me for a moment. "You know, I'm not supposed to share anything with you. Privacy issues. But when a kid's missing . . ." He sighed. "I went by to check on her maybe a week before she took off. I do monthly check-ins, just to make sure my kids are okay. She seemed fine. Ramona didn't talk much, but she was going to school, getting good grades, doing okay."

"So no signs that she was unhappy or in any kind of distress?"

"The police asked me the same thing. No, there was no sign of any of that. Like I said, she was okay. Whatever was going on with her wasn't related to her living at Poole's."

I leaned forward. "How do you know?"

"How could it? Poole keeps a nice home. First real one a lot of these kids have ever had. Why are you and the police so quick to think something happened there?"

"Because she ran away in the dead of winter," I said. "That sort of suggests that everything wasn't fine."

Shaw rearranged his tie so that it lay perfectly aligned down the front of his shirt. "Ramona's run away before, not from Poole's, but other places. These are damaged kids. Not their fault, of course, but sometimes you can do everything right, and it's still not enough to fix them. You can't imagine some of the things these kids have been through."

"I don't have to imagine," I said. "I used to be a cop. I've seen it. I got to deal with the result of all that brokenness—too late in a lot of cases, when all I could do was pick up jagged little pieces off the street."

Shaw offered a small, tired smile. "Same problem, different ends of it, then. I wish I knew what made Ramona run, but I don't. I wish I knew where she ran to, but I don't know that, either. I do know, I did everything in my power to help her, to get her situated. I do that for all of them. Ramona had real potential. She was smart, sharp, you know? But her mother . . ."

"What about her mother?"

Shaw shook his head. "Into drugs, in no way prepared to be a parent. If Ramona had had a stable home to begin with, we wouldn't be here now."

"People make mistakes. She's trying."

His expression soured. "They're *all* trying. Every day, all day long, that's what I hear. *'I'm trying. I'm trying.'* A lot of times that's as far as it goes. Kids need more than promises. Here, our job is twice as hard. Everyone wants cute babies, not so much older kids. They come with too much baggage, too many issues. They need a lot more patience, understanding, they need time to come around. Most of them have spent their entire childhoods in care, mainly because no one wants to take on the mess."

"How'd Ramona end up at Bettle in the first place, instead of DCFS?"

"Sorry. Privacy."

"Was she in counseling?"

He shook his head. "Can't tell you that, either. What I will say is, I made sure she had access to every resource we have available. Her running away is a good sign that wasn't enough. I've accepted, reluctantly, that I can't save them all."

I glanced at the many files on Shaw's desk, likely cases much like Ramona Titus's, children thrown away, lost, ill served by parental instability or neglect. There were thousands of Shaws out there, thousands of Ramonas. I was tired just thinking about it.

"No red flags with Deloris Poole?"

His brows rose. "Poole? You're looking to blame Poole for this?"

"I'm not blaming—"

He cut me off. "Because if it weren't for people like her, we really would be in a state." He put his hand on the stack of files. "She's a godsend. If I could, I'd put all these kids with Poole. At least I'd know then they'd get some direction, some purpose, some way forward in life. She makes sure they get what their parents didn't give them—discipline, self-reliance, a work ethic. Ramona didn't appreciate how good she had it. It was completely disrespectful what Ramona did."

"*Disrespectful?* To run away?"

Shaw scowled. "Is that ever the answer to anything?"

"To a fifteen-year-old? It might seem like it." I paused. "You're pretty high on Deloris Poole."

"What's that supposed to mean?"

I shrugged. "Nothing."

We sat silently for a moment as I watched Shaw looking a bit nervous. Nothing wrong with Bettle, according to him, or Poole, who, by his account, was the best thing since sliced bread. Ramona's the fly in the ointment, the disrespectful child who couldn't get with the program. I wondered about Shaw. I sat there mentally ticking through my contacts to find someone I could ask about him.

I stood. "Thanks for your time."

Shaw rose, too. Was that relief I saw on his face? "Ramona was a good kid. But if I were you, I'd leave it to the police."

I loved it when men felt compelled to tell women what to do in that patronizing tone they might give a meddling child, and by *loved*, I meant the opposite. In fact, it guaranteed I'd do more of the thing they didn't want me to do, but they didn't know that until much later.

"You're Tonya Pierce's manager, too. She was at Poole's with Ramona. You moved her a few days before Ramona ran away. To her grandmother's, wasn't it? Was that when you last checked on Ramona?"

He appeared to flinch at the mention of the name, but then brushed past me to open the door. Our talk was over, and none too soon, it appeared for him. "I'm not going to discuss my entire caseload with you. Tonya was transitioned to another home, and that's all I'll say. She did fine in the new place." He worried his ugly tie, tried a smile, but missed. "Nothing to do with Poole."

"The new place? So *not* her grandmother's?"

Shaw stiffened. "I can't say more."

"I'd like to talk to Tonya. She may know where Ramona . . ."

Shaw's head had begun shaking before I was even done talking. "Not possible. She didn't know anything about Ramona planning to run. Sorry." The last word was thrown in, almost as an afterthought, which meant Shaw wasn't sorry at all, just very committed to getting me out of his office.

I grinned, watching as he stood there with the door open, sweating the seconds until I got the hell out.

"If you think of anything else—"

"I've said all I can."

I was curious about his sudden curtness, but I finished my interrupted sentence. "I'm in the book. One more question, though, as long as I'm here, and since you won't be calling. Why do you speak of Ramona and Tonya in the past tense?"

Shaw's face paled. "I didn't."

"You did, actually. This whole time."

He opened the door wider. "Please leave." I stepped out into the hall, turned to face him. "And just so you know," he added sternly. "I'll be mentioning this visit to Detective Martini."

I didn't have a chance to respond before the door slammed in my face. It wasn't a new experience, and I didn't take it personally. I'd had tons of doors slammed in my face, and would have a ton more before I packed it in and retired to the sticks with a dog and a tomato garden. That's if somebody didn't knife me in an alley first.

Wait. Did he say Detective *Martini*?

Chapter 8

There was an unmarked cop car idling a couple slots from my car when I got to it and I stopped to watch as Detective Dan Hogan got out and walked over to me. "I know I said I didn't mind the extra eyes, but things are getting a little crowded, aren't they?"

"I'm playing catch-up," I said. "Shaw seemed like an important person to talk to."

"And? Get anything?"

"I think I would have gotten more if I'd been official."

Hogan chuckled. "Missing that star, Raines?"

I shrugged. "Not really. I got nothing from Shaw other than a lot of covering. He did his job—according to him, Ramona's the problem."

"I got that, too, last time out. I thought I'd come back and try again, see if he could tell me a little more."

"Speaking of crowded fields," I said, "Shaw's spoken to Martini. Did Martini mention that to you?"

"Martini? What the hell was he doing here?"

"Maybe you should ask him?"

Hogan considered for a moment. "It's starting to feel like I've got too many cooks in the kitchen here."

"Well, this cook has a client and a license. Nobody's paying Martini to stick his nose in, as far as I know."

"He's ex-police," Hogan said.

"So?"

He paused. "You always this—"

"Yes." I'd heard it before. I was always too something. "Did you have a chance to check Lester Evans?"

He slid his hands into his coat pockets to warm them. "Ramona's uncle. I'm wondering how you got on to him, and the mother didn't give me jack."

"She doesn't trust you. You burst in on her and all but accused her of snatching Ramona and hiding her. Next time? A gentler, more respectful approach might be more effective. Lester? Who, by the way, offered to help me look for Ramona . . . for a price."

"You might want to take a pass on that," Hogan said. "He's fresh out of Stateville. Hasn't been out a month after spending four and a half in. He squats out of Lippy's pool hall, working odd jobs in and around, and by *odd*, I mean illegal. I asked a couple guys who work that area, and they knew all about the guy. He's a real lowlife, a thief, mostly. I can't see him taking a kid in—selling one, maybe, sad to say. The aunt in Shreveport checks out. She's been down there for five years. An aide in a retirement place. She says she hasn't seen or heard from Ramona or her sister in all that time. I've asked Shreveport PD to double-check her place to make sure."

"Ramona wouldn't have known where to find either of them, then. She would maybe have gone back to her grandmother's, but I didn't see any signs that she'd been there." I was running it through, talking to myself more than to Hogan.

When Hogan's face blanked out, I realized I'd said too much, aloud, and in front of the wrong person.

"How'd you get in the house? It turned up owned by the bank. It's empty, off limits."

I pretended I hadn't heard. "What's that?"

He shook his head. "Careful, Raines."

I took a step back, dug for the keys in my pocket. "Always careful, Hogan." He turned for the building. "One more thing about Shaw," I said. "He talks about Ramona like she's never coming back. Could have been a slip, but I'd be interested in your take on it."

He nodded, but didn't say anything. I had a feeling my unauthorized house creep was still on his mind.

"I'll check in with Martini," I said, keeping it light. "See what he has to say."

"Maybe Spinelli and me will talk to Evans again, since she's got so much to say to everybody else but us."

I looked around at all the frozen cars, then back at Hogan. "Maybe this time be a little nicer?"

He flicked his chin in my direction. "Were you always nice?"

"To mothers grieving a lost kid or one shot dead in the street? Absolutely."

He watched me closely, his lips set in a stern, tight line. "We could have crossed off the brother and sister sooner."

"Shaw likely had that information, too, right? Why didn't he give it to you? The badge, the gun, you being you, it's intimidating, you know that. Most people wouldn't give up their brother, even an estranged one, if he were Jack the Ripper. You know that, too."

"But they want us to solve the problem, catch the guy, find the kid, whatever." He shook his head, eyed the quiet lot. "It ain't easy being blue these days."

My toes grew numb, and I craved warmth. "You want easy, you're in the wrong job."

"I want to find that kid," he said.

"Me too, and we will, because we're just that good, or at least I am. I don't know yet what you're made of."

A sly smile spread across his face. "You're a pain in the ass, you know that?"

"*I* know it. Now *you* know it."

"Maybe two steps back, though. I'll tell Martini the same."

"Two steps. Got it. Hey, one last thing. Do you know why Martini retired?"

"No. It was abrupt, though. He just announced he was packing it in, and that was that. Why?"

"Just asking," I said. "Thanks."

A gust of bitter wind whipped past us, and Hogan drew his coat collar closer around his neck and walked toward Shaw's office. "Stay warm," I called after him.

"Stay in your lane," he yelled back. "I mean it."

"Message received," I answered. I slid into the car, started her up. "And totally disregarded."

Chapter 9

I scrolled through the contacts in my phone while my car heated up in Bettle's lot. Shaw wasn't the only game in town. I had contacts at DCFS who might be familiar with him and with his entire setup. Maybe if I knew a little more about Ramona, her past, her history, it would give me a clue as to where she might have gone. That was my hope, anyway. I dialed a familiar cell phone number and got a familiar voice.

"Gwen Timmons."

"Hey, Gwen."

"Can't do it."

"What kind of attitude is that?"

"The kind that doesn't get me fired."

"You know I wouldn't ask if it weren't important."

Gwen said nothing, but I could hear her breathing.

"Gwen, are you sitting near a window?"

"Yeah, so?"

"Look outside. What do you see?"

"I see a whole lot of snow. God, I hate winter."

"I'm looking for a runaway girl. She's out in all that cold,

Gwen. Lord knows what could be happening to her right now as I'm talking to you. The police have nothing. I have nothing." I stopped, listened, but there was nothing going on, on Gwen's end of the line. "And it's almost Christmas."

"That's low. Hauling out Christmas."

I smiled, knowing I had her. "Just a couple names. And you know I won't abuse it."

"You going to feed my kids? Put shoes on their feet?"

I thought about it. "How many do you have again?"

"Three."

I grimaced. "I'll take the first one. The other two are on you."

She groaned, groused, but I knew she'd help me. Gwen had a soft spot for every single lost or abused thing, which I'd found out when I met her five cases back when she helped me track down a kid whose noncustodial father snatched him out of his school's yard at recess, only to get back at his ex-wife, whom he'd cheated on repeatedly.

"What is it?"

I gave her Tonya Pierce's name, then asked where Ramona had been before landing at Bettle. She'd been taken into care when Leesa went to jail. Gwen put me on hold, and I waited out the silence, holding my frozen hands in front of the heater vents, which blew out semiwarm air that smelled like hot plastic. No worries. I'd take it. Warm plastic air beat frigid outside air, hands down. Gwen clicked back.

"You know, you're the only one I'd do this for, right?"

I smiled. "I appreciate you, Gwen, you know that. Thanks."

She grumbled. "I sent you a text. Merry Christmas." Then she was gone.

I checked my phone. Lena and Ernie Knowles, Ramona's previous foster parents. For Tonya Pierce, inconsistency. Her parents were dead, both dying from drug overdoses. No other close family. She'd been in DCFS care for twelve of her sixteen years before landing at Bettle. No close family meant no grandmother. Hadn't Poole believed that was where Shaw was moving Tonya? Shaw hadn't mentioned a grandmother. He'd just said that Tonya had been doing fine in the new place. Had Shaw lied to Poole, or had Poole and Shaw both lied to me? I pulled out of the lot with the unsettling feeling that someone was leading me around, and I didn't much like it.

The Knowleses didn't live far, but before I could point the car in that direction, I got another text, this one from Dangelo at the Burger Joint. He'd talked to Rose's mother and she agreed to let me talk to Rose. At his place. In twenty minutes. I checked my watch. I was at least that far away. I texted back that I was on my way. Burger Joint first, then the Knowleses'.

For some reason, Rose had seemed afraid of me when I saw her last. She hovered in the background, eyed me warily. I didn't want to spook her again. Hopefully, her mother being present would help with that. I made good time on the slushy streets and parked right in front of Dangelo's place, my front bumper kissing a dirty wall of snow a city plow had banked on the side of the street. I sat for a time with the motor running, going over the best way to approach Rose, deciding finally that slow and easy would work best. I unclipped my tuck holster, slid my gun into my bag, zipping it up tight. There. Just another gal off the street, here to have a harmless little chat. At least that's how I hoped this whole thing would go down.

The place was all but empty when I pushed through the door, except for Clint at the grill and two men, leaning against the wall, eating heart attack Polishes out of grease-stained brown bags.

"Detective?" I turned to see Dangelo waving for me from the back. "Here."

The two leaners were now dialed into my business, staring, chewing, waiting for something interesting to happen. They were going to be disappointed. I brushed past them, ignoring their interest, lowering my voice when I got to Dangelo. "Yeah, I'd really like it if we could low-key this, all right?"

Dangelo looked over at the watchful men. "Got it. Sorry. We're back here in the breakroom. I figured we'd need some privacy."

We'd? I stopped. "Hold on a sec."

"Yeah?"

"Rose is back there with her mother?"

"Yeah, in the breakroom. It's private back there. I figured that'd be the best place."

I let a couple seconds pass. "Anything else you forgot to tell me about Ramona?" He shook his head. I looked down the short hall to a doorway, which I assumed led to the break room. "You mind if I take it from here, then?"

"You want me to stay out here?"

"Would you? I think the smaller we keep this, the more comfortable Rose will be, right?"

He looked disappointed, bummed he was being left out of the loop.

"If there's something more you need to add, though, I'd be happy to swing back and talk to you some more."

He flicked a look at the breakroom door, frowned. "I'll be out front, then. If you need anything." He turned and walked off down the hall.

"Dangelo?"

He turned.

"Thanks for putting this together."

He smiled. "For Ramona, right?"

I gave him a thumbs-up and watched him go, then turned for the breakroom. At the door, I took a deep breath, then went in. The room wasn't much, just a repurposed kitchen table and four cheap plastic chairs. Along the wall were shelves of provisions—buns, large tubs of ketchup, mustard, lard. A counter with a mini-microwave, coffeemaker, assorted tea selections, and next to it two beat-up school lockers with combination locks on them. The room smelled of burned coffee, overripe fruit, and mold. I kept my breathing light.

At the table sat Rose and her mother. They looked a lot alike. Same build, same coloring, same nose. Rose glanced up at me, then looked away, like she had the last time we met. Her mother stood and studied me carefully, getting a bead.

"Ms." I stopped, realizing at that moment I didn't know Rose's last name. "Ah, I'm sorry . . ."

"Leighton," she said. "Millie Leighton."

"Ms. Leighton. Thanks for seeing me." I glanced over at Rose. "And you, too, Rose." I got nothing back.

"Dangelo said it was about Ramona," Leighton said. "That poor child."

I gestured toward the table. "Please. Sit." She sat down again next to Rose, and I scooted one of the empty chairs a little away from the table, farthest away from the girl, placing my bag on the floor by my feet, trying to look as nonthreatening as I could.

"Dangelo told you, I guess, that I've been hired by Ramona's mother to help find her?" I spoke to Leighton, but tracked Rose out of the corner of my eye. She was the one I wanted to talk to, the one I felt knew something, but slow and steady. "The police are doing the same, but she's fifteen. Vulnerable. It doesn't hurt to double up."

Leighton shook her head, a sorrowful look on her face. "I know. If it was Rosie out there, I don't know what I'd do. I can't imagine what Ramona's mother is going through. But what do you think Rosie can tell you?"

At the mention of her name, Rose looked over at me and our eyes locked for a second. She sat there, her back straight, her eyes set, her lips pressed tightly together as though only that would be enough to keep to herself what I needed to hear. I realized then that I'd pegged it wrong. She wasn't afraid of me.

Rose had a secret she didn't want to tell. What I was seeing was defiance and resolve.

"Rose? Will you talk to me?"

She looked to her mother. "Go on," Leighton said. "Help your friend, if you can." Rose turned back to me.

"You and Ramona are good friends," I said. "Spent time together talking, a lot more than she did with the others."

Rose nodded. "Best friends. She said so. And best friends look out for each other."

Now I was in business. Rose was talking. I scooted my chair a little closer to the table. Not too far, just a little closer. "Yes, they do. Do you know where Ramona is, Rose?"

She looked again to her mother for affirmation, then shook her head. "She didn't say where."

"Did she say *why*? Did she tell you she was planning on going somewhere?"

Rose grinned. "When she comes back, we're going to the movies. We'll have popcorn and candy. Mama said I could go with Ramona. Remember, Mama? You said."

Leighton placed a gentle hand on Rose's knee, smiled. "That's right. I did. I like Ramona. You and Ramona are good friends."

"See?" Rose shot me an accusatory look, as though I hadn't believed her before, that she and Ramona were the best of friends.

"That's nice," I said. "Did Ramona say when she'd be coming back, Rose?"

"When she finished."

Leighton and I exchanged a worried look. I said, "Finished what?"

Rose shrugged. "I don't know. That's what she said. But when she comes back, we're going to see something cool at the movies. That's what friends do sometimes. Friends also don't tell things. Sometimes you keep things for friends."

Leighton said, "What do you mean, Rosie?"

"Ramona's my friend, so she asked me to keep things very, very safe."

I think I stopped breathing then. Not literally, but it felt like I did. "What things, Rose?"

She shook her head, her lips clamped shut. She wasn't going to say. I started to move even closer, but stopped myself. "You want to help Ramona, don't you, Rose?"

"I *am*."

"I'd like to help her, too. Do you think you could help me, so I can help her?"

"If you have something of Ramona's," Leighton said gently, "something she left you, can you show it to us?"

Rose looked at her mother, shook her head. "No one can see it. It's her insurance. In case . . ." Rose stopped suddenly, her lips compressed into a thin, hard line.

My palms were sweating. I rubbed them against my thighs. "In case, what?"

Leighton glanced over at me, a bewildered look on her face. "What'd Ramona tell you, Rosie?"

"Can't say. I promised."

"Rosie, look at me," Leighton said, a frightened edge to her voice.

I sat still, watching, as Rose's mother took the lead, an anxious feeling growing in my gut. Finished what? Insurance for what?

"We're going to help Ramona," Leighton said, "by telling this nice lady what she needs to know to find her." Rose darted her eyes at me, blinked. "*Now*, Rosie."

Rose glared at me. "Sometimes bad people look nice."

Leighton brushed her hand gently against Rose's cheek. "That's true. I taught you that. But this is different."

She considered for a moment before speaking. It was a long, painful silence, mostly for me.

"Rose?" Leighton's voice took on that mom tone, the one

that instantly broadcast that things were about to go a different direction, and not in a good way.

"A little box," Rose blurted out. "It's in my locker, where it's safe. Because it has a lock on it, and only I know the numbers." I glanced over at the dented gray lockers against the wall. Hardly impenetrable, even with a combination lock. I could devise five ways of getting into one of them in two seconds' time.

Leighton stood. "Then let's get it."

Rose shook her head, crossed her arms against her chest. "No. It's *my* locker, and Ramona's *my* friend."

"Rose Ann Leighton," Leighton commanded. "Open that locker. *Now.*"

Rose's arms went down, her defiance disappeared in an instant; then, without another word, she got up from the chair and went over to her locker, opened it up, and pulled a small tin cigar box off the top shelf and brought it back to the table and sat down.

Leighton looked worried. I didn't blame her. If someone had asked my daughter to hold on to a box of unknown origin or content, I would have worried, too. I stared at the box as if it might bite, then looked over at Rose. "Can I look inside?"

"What if Ramona wouldn't like it?" Rose said.

Her mother placed a hand on the girl's knee. "We're helping Ramona, remember?"

Rose stared down at the box, then at her mother and me. Finally, after an interminable amount of time, or so it seemed, she nodded her go-ahead. I slid the box toward me and removed the lid.

"What's inside?" Leighton asked, peering over, trying to get a better look. "Please don't tell me it's drugs or a gun, or Lord knows what else. I do not want to believe Ramona would leave drugs for Rosie to watch over."

I peered inside. "It's not drugs."

She sat back, relieved. "Thank you, Jesus."

There was a small key in the box, the kind that fits bus station or mall lockers. I pulled it out and set it on the table. At this point, it was meaningless. I had no idea what it fit, why it was important for Ramona to hide away, anything. It might as well have been a wad of gum or a grain of rice. I drew out a small brown envelope, with a thin metal clasp in back. Nothing written on the front of the envelope. It hadn't been mailed or assigned to anyone. I was aware that Leighton and Rose were watching me with rapt interest, each of us rabidly invested in what was inside the envelope.

I undid the clasp and slid out the contents. A state ID, the name on it, Tonya Pearson. Pearson, not Pierce. Was this the same girl who shared the pink bedroom in Deloris Poole's house with Ramona? I studied the ID photo. Nice face. Sweet kid, it appeared. She was dressed in a simple blue sweater, a gold butterfly necklace around her slender neck. Sad, hard eyes, though. Height. Weight. Average. Age. "Eighteen," I said it aloud, a bit incredulously.

I turned the card over in my hands. It looked legit. But Tonya Pierce, if this ID was hers, was, according to Timmons and Poole, sixteen, not eighteen. A fake ID? It wasn't as if I'd never seen one before. As a cop, I couldn't count the number of kids I'd rousted out of bars and clubs in the wee hours with crudely manufactured ID in their pockets. Kids did all kinds of stupid things. But what was Ramona doing with this ID? Why had she hidden it, here, with Rose?

I set the ID down next to the key, still worrying over it, then reached back in and took out a couple sheets of paper folded in quarters. I unfolded them. Two color copies of photographs. I stared at them a moment, a sinking feeling growing, a dread, anger, too. In the first, Deloris Poole was talking to two men, confidentially it appeared, somewhere outdoors, a stand of lush trees in the background. The second was much the same, only the photo appeared to have captured the three talking on a city street, snow on the ground. In each, it looked like they were familiar with each other, like they were discussing something vital, their expressions grave.

"What is it?" Leighton wanted to know.

I looked up to see her and Rose staring at me. I must have paled. I felt like I had, because Leighton looked concerned, Rose too. I didn't know what to say.

Leighton said, "It's something bad, isn't it?"

I breathed evenly, trying to resettle. Yes. Or maybe. Maybe it was bad? According to the date stamps, the first photo had been taken July eighteenth, four months before Poole had reported Ramona as a runaway on the eighteenth of November; the second, just a week before Ramona went. So, who took the photos, and what did they mean? And what had Deloris Poole, Frank Martini, and Ronald Shaw been talking about?

Chapter 10

The photos made no sense. Martini, Shaw, and Poole? Martini, who would have had no reason to come in contact with Poole or Shaw, as far as I knew, certainly not way back in July or days before there was even a Ramona Titus case to work on. Hadn't Martini told me he had only met Poole once, when he came to ask her about Ramona's disappearance? It had been at Clancy's over shepherd's pie and a cheeseburger. It wasn't the lie that bothered me, it was its implication. If Martini lied about knowing Poole, he did it for a reason, and I wanted to know what that was.

I put everything back in the box, hurriedly, then stood. "I'll need to take this, Rose."

Rose started to object. Her friend had trusted her to guard her secrets and now here I was coming in and snatching everything from her. I got it. I still needed the box, though.

"Ramona told *me* to keep it. To . . ."

"To what?" I asked. Rose drew her lips tight as though the words would fly involuntarily out of her mouth unless she did. "Rose?"

"Tell her, Rosie."

"I'm not supposed to tell the police about the box. It's not safe." She glared at me. "Ramona said so."

My heart sank. I turned to Leighton. "It's important."

She put an arm around Rose, soothing her. "It'll be okay, Rosie. You're a very good friend."

I squatted down in front of her. "Rose, did Ramona tell you she was afraid of the police?" The girl wouldn't answer me. She even turned her head so she wouldn't have to look at me. I kept pushing, anyway. "Did she tell you what was inside this box?"

Nothing.

"Rosie, speak up," Leighton prodded.

But Rose wouldn't budge. She'd gone as far as she was going to go, having been forced to give up Ramona's things.

Leighton looked at me, hopeful. "I'm sorry. But you'll find Ramona?"

I stood, nodded. It was all I had in the way of assurance. I went out to my car, slid into the driver's seat, and called Ben. "I need to see you," I said when he picked up. "Do you think you could swing by tonight?"

"Sure. What's up?"

I peered out the windshield at the dirty snow and gunmetal sky that looked like it was threatening to open up and dump more snow on us, and then at the bundled-up people racing past the car. "I'll tell you when I see you, okay?"

"What happened? What's going on?"

"When I see you, all right?"

I ended the call, then started up and pulled off for the Knowleses'. I was beginning to question everything I'd learned about Ramona Titus up to this point, and everyone I'd heard it from. Had Ramona run away, or had something else happened to her? What did the ID mean? Were Tonya Pierce and Tonya Pearson the same kid?

Before, I'd thought Shaw's use of the past tense when speak-

ing of Ramona was strange, curious; now it scared me. Maybe
he had spoken of her like she was dead because he knew she
was? Was Tonya Pierce/Pearson dead, too? What was Martini
doing in the middle of all this? It was obvious from the photo
that he knew Shaw and Poole before there even was a runaway
case. And who had taken the photos? Ramona? Someone else?

Talk to Martini? Show him the photo? Or Shaw? Or Poole?
No. Not until I had more information. I didn't want to bungle
into something half aware. First the Knowleses, then the rest.
Slow and steady, lead by lead.

The Knowleses lived in a two-story apartment building on
the far South Side, in Gresham, on a block lined with buildings
that look almost identical. The sidewalks had been shoveled by
conscientious residents, even if the city hadn't yet plowed the
street, but that was how it went south of the invisible dividing
line between South and West, and the more affluent parts of the
city those in power cared the most about.

According to the nameplate on one of the mailboxes in the
entry vestibule, the Knowleses lived on the second floor. I rang
the bell twice, but got no answer. I rang the other bells, too, but
got the same response. The tenants were at work or behind
their doors not answering the bell—either way I was out of
luck. I dug in my bag and pulled out a notepad and pen to
scribble a short message letting them know who I was and what
I needed; then I tore off the page, wrapped it around one of my
business cards, and slipped both into their mail slot. The best I
could do for now.

I paced around my living room later that evening, working it
through, Ben watching me do it.

"It's six-thirty," he said. "You've been wearing a hole in the
carpet for an hour . . . over a couple photos?"

I stopped, faced him. "The three of them together. Back in

July, and then a week before Ramona took off, before Martini says he met Poole?"

Ben pulled a face. "Anybody else and I'd say maybe you misheard, but it's you, and I know you didn't."

Ben was sitting on my couch. Just off shift, his tie was loosened, the top button of his shirt undone. He nodded. "Okay, let's see. He's freelance. Ramona's a repeat runaway. Maybe he's dealt with the kid from a runaway or two before this one? Maybe he and Shaw met the same way. Or the guy's an old-timer. Maybe he misspoke. It happens."

I considered it for a moment. It made sense, I decided begrudgingly. Martini had said he'd dealt with DCFS and Bettle before. He could have run into Shaw at some point.

"Maybe," I said. "But that doesn't explain *this* case. Hogan, not Shaw, tapped Martini to assist. So, he goes straight to Shaw for details. Okay. Fine. Maybe Shaw's one of Martini's contacts. That doesn't explain him in the photo with Shaw and Poole in July. Where were they? Why were they together? Poole said she'd never had one of her girls run away before, so what was Martini doing?"

"Digital photography these days? C'mon. You can make anything look like anything. Hell, I could put me in a photo with Minnie Minoso and make it look legit."

He sipped from a bottle of sparkling cranberry-flavored water, the only beverage available from my kitchen besides the water out of the tap. He winced, then glared at the bottle as if it had slapped him across the face. "Gawd, how do you drink this shit? Where's my beer? You usually stock up. Do I mean nothing to you anymore?"

I waved him off. "I've been busy. Missing kid, remember?"

The photographs in Ramona's box worried me, I didn't care how much Ben downplayed it. They felt significant, and if they turned out to be, that meant someone I'd encountered was lying to me, running me around, and I could literally feel myself knot up and harden with resolve.

"She runs the perfect home," I said. "Poole. And her place is Shaw's go-to spot. He couldn't say enough about her, or it. Even Martini signed off on it."

Ben grimaced through another sip. "So?"

I stopped pacing and plopped down into a chair across from Ben, folding my legs under me, crossing my arms petulantly across my chest. I was in a sour mood, in the dark, and I wasn't happy about it. "So nobody's that selfless, right? There was only one Mother Teresa, and even she had an edge, allegedly."

Ben, giving up on the water, set the half-empty bottle on a coaster on the coffee table in front of him. He smiled over at me. "Is there no one sacred? Mother Teresa?"

I squinted at him. "Since when are you and Mother Teresa tight?"

Ben sighed wistfully. "One, she's dead, God rest her soul. And two, Poole's been in this game a long time, you said. No red flags? What makes you think she's not on the up-and-up?" He pointed a finger at me in a scolding manner. "You pick at nits. You always do. I, on the other hand, see the big picture. That's why we worked so well together."

I glowered over at him. "I think they did something to that kid."

Ben cocked a brow. "*They?*"

"Shaw, Poole, Martini. Maybe even Hogan. I don't know any of them. I can't vouch for their character. Why the weird ID? Why did Ramona go to the trouble of hiding it? Why did Ramona tell Rose to not trust the police? You don't think any of that means something?"

Ben leaned back, draping his long arms across the back of the couch. "Try this on. What if Ramona stole the ID, intending to use it herself? Switch out the photo and, *bam*, she's in business. Or, maybe she was running some kind of fake ID business out of her locker at school. She hid that ID because she didn't want the foster mom finding it in the house. Or . . ."

I held up a hand to stop him. "All right."

Ben smiled, triumphant. "See? Big picture. You? Nits."

We were silent for a moment. "Why'd Shaw threaten to report me to Detective Martini, then, not Hogan? It's Hogan's case. Martini's retired, about as official as I am. That hints at a certain connectedness, doesn't it?"

Ben fingered his tie, thought about it. His eyes met mine and I could tell he didn't have any big-picture pronouncements. I grinned, triumphant. "Ha. Nit *that.*"

"Are you actively trying to take down the entire CPD, one cop at a time?" Ben grumbled.

"This is my fault now?"

"I checked around. Martini was a solid cop is what I'm hearing. A bit of a peacock. I got that from Dombrowski, who worked with him a few years back. Likes to talk big, Martini does, and maybe he's a crap golfer who throws the ball more than he hits it. Got that from Seles, who played a charity tourney with him. Seles swears Martini hit it into the rough, tucked into a blind spot, and then tossed the ball at the green.

"Not sure I believe that. Seles is kinda dodgy himself. He might have made that up to needle Martini for something. Bottom line, good cop, though a little pretentious. Not one to get hooked into whatever it is you think he's into. What is that, by the way? You think the kid was into drugs, what with her mom's history? The ID angle doesn't seem enough to make her run, unless it was hooked in some way with a larger operation."

"She's fifteen," I said. "We're not dealing with Al Capone, here."

"You don't know that," Ben said. "Al Capone had to start somewhere. Right out of the womb, he was likely stealing kids' lunch money."

I looked over at him, listening, but not really. "Hogan was

quick to sign off on me jumping into this. That's strange, right? Usually CPD is showing me the door. Maybe he did it so he could keep close tabs on me. I did run into him at Bettle House."

Ben frowned. "And here comes the paranoia." He leaned forward. "If you're so sure they're not shooting straight, that something's going on besides a runaway kid, show them the pics. Bring it right to them. See what they have to say. The direct approach, that's your usual."

I thought it through for a moment. "Not yet. Not until I have a better feel. I don't want to scare them off."

We were quiet for a time. I lifted my head to see that Ben had been watching me think. "What?"

He cleared his throat, leaned back on the couch. "I'm counting on it not being a cop who's the goat in all this, and I'm going to need you not to burst that bubble for me, okay?"

"Why are you looking at me like I've got it in for the CPD? Like I'm trying to pin Martini or Hogan, just because they're cops."

"Nah, that's not you, but you wouldn't shed a tear if it was either one of them into something shady."

"Why should I?"

"See? So, what're you going to do?" Ben asked.

"Go where the leads go."

Ben closed his eyes, leaned his head back. "Just measure twice and cut once, will you?"

I answered defensively. "I know what the hell I'm doing."

His eyes popped open, met mine. "I know that. Did I say I didn't know that? All I'm saying is, go slow. You're worried about the kid. I get it. It's written all over you, and there's not one rock you won't turn over. But Frank Martini doesn't appear to be one of them, okay? Benefit of the doubt."

I didn't say anything.

"*Cass?*"

"*Ben?*"

He sighed. "I'm wasting my breath here, is that it?"

"I heard you. If Martini's clean, he's clean. And Hogan."

Ben appeared to relax, his shoulders lowered.

"But if they're not, I'll measure it any way I need to."

He chuckled softly. "Just like old times."

I smiled. "Shove off."

My doorbell rang and I answered, finding Whip standing there, bundled up, breathing heavy after the three flights up. I took him in, his dark eyes peeking out from beneath a Kangol cap, earmuffs on his ears, a heavy scarf wrapped around the lower part of his full dark face.

"Hey," I said.

"Hey."

I stepped back to let him in, but he just stood there. "Hope you don't mind. Mrs. Vincent saw me at the door and let me in."

I held the door wider. "Of course not. Come in, warm up."

Whip started to enter; then his eyes left my face and slid over my shoulder to see Ben on the couch. He stopped. "I didn't know you had company. I'll come back." He backed up toward the stairs.

"What? Don't be crazy. Ben's not company."

Whip pulled up his coat collar, prepared to get back out in the cold. "Seriously, it's okay. It can wait."

He started down the steps; I followed him out into the hall. "What can wait? Whip?"

"Bean, it's good, all right? I just wanted your advice on a couple things." His voice was light this time, but I could tell he was forcing it. "Career advice. Figured you'd have a take on it. We can touch base in a couple days. No big deal."

He'd used my childhood nickname—Bean, short for *string bean*—but he didn't sound like his old self. Career advice? He always seemed happy at the diner, well suited to it. Had he changed his mind? Or, God forbid, was he feeling the pull of the streets again? Why wouldn't he come inside? All of this was cycling around in my brain as I stood there on the landing, looking down on him, as he tried desperately to get away from my door. Away from . . .

"Is it Ben? You won't come inside because he's here?" We exchanged a look, and I knew that was it, but Whip chuckled and forced a little more lightness into his voice, and onto his face. He sounded like the same old Whip, then—the one I'd known more than half my life. Then it was gone, underneath the chuckle, there was something else there, something that was beginning to worry me.

He said, "Hanging around with cops does take a little getting used to."

I gripped the landing railing, looked down at him hard. "You okay?"

"Sure, don't I look it?"

I hesitated a moment. No, he didn't. "If you weren't okay, you'd tell me, right?"

Our eyes held. "You'd be the first one I'd come to."

We stood silently, watching each other.

"Let me grab my coat," I said finally. "We'll find someplace to talk."

Whip waved me off. "Are you nuts? Stop being so dramatic. It's minus a million degrees out here. You're home, warm and safe, stay there. I'm telling you, this can wait. Tomorrow or the next day, we'll talk."

"About that career advice," I said.

"Right. And if you stop by the diner, I'll cook you something good while you're giving it. Those crab cakes you asked for. That'll put some meat on those bones of yours. Go on back in there now. You don't want to leave a cop alone in your house too long. He'll start searching the place like a drug-sniffing dog."

I stepped away from the railing, shaking my head. "You are not right."

He gave me one last look, a wink, then trotted down the stairs, hollered back up, "See ya, Bean!"

I called Whip later that night, after Ben had gone, after I'd settled in bed, but got no answer. I left a voice mail asking him to call me as soon as he could; then I rolled over and tried to sleep. Tried, and failed.

Chapter 11

Tuesday morning, Ronald Shaw wouldn't see me. The woman at the front desk had called back to his office, and whatever Shaw had told her, her attitude toward me changed in an instant, and she ordered me out of the building. There was little I could do at that point. Barging past her wasn't an option, unless I wanted to spend Christmas in jail eating bologna sandwiches, so I walked back to my car, drove away, and then doubled back and parked at the outer edge of the lot and waited for Shaw to come out. I'd spent many a night on stakeouts waiting for drug dealers or killers to make their move, I could certainly cool my heels for a few hours waiting for jittery Ronald Shaw.

He could play it two ways, I guess, either he'd hunker down inside, where he knew I couldn't get to him, or he'd try to make a break for it, hoping I couldn't catch up. Shaw struck me as being the streaker type, and I didn't think I'd have to wait long for confirmation, so I settled in, turned up my radio, and kept my eyes on the door. I wasn't worried that Shaw would sneak out a back door, either. This was the only lot. His car had to be in it. This place was nowhere near an "L" station, and the bus stop was a good four blocks away. No chance at all he'd try to walk home, either—it was too damned cold. He'd die of hypothermia before he got a quarter mile out. Maybe he'd chance it, I thought, and leave his car in the lot overnight. Nah, not in this neighborhood. Shaw would likely not find his car here in the morning, or if he did, only parts of it would be in the spot— a rim, half the chassis, maybe a bumper.

It was a little after noon when Shaw finally poked his head out the front door, looked both ways, and then rushed to the lot, his battered briefcase clutched in his arms, his eyes wild, his feet moving fast, slipping along the icy sidewalk. I watched which car he made for, then put my car in gear, sped over, and blocked him in. When he realized it was me, he looked like somebody had just tased him.

I jumped out, walked up to him. "Going to lunch?"

He backed up against his car door. "You can't block me in like that."

I smiled, looked his car over. It was an old beater, white. The briefcase, which had looked distressed a distance away, looked expensively made up close. "I won't be long. I wanted to talk to you, but you were obviously busy this morning and couldn't fit me in."

Shaw looked up and down the lot, clutched his case tighter, his car keys in his hand. "I told you. I can't discuss . . ."

I held Ramona's photos up, inches from his face. Shaw looked at them. Despite the frosty temps, he began to sweat, a difficult feat, given the fact it was minus three degrees. "I wanted to ask you about these."

"I don't know anything about that. Where'd you get those?"

"Unimportant." I tapped a finger against the most recent one taken. "Tell me about this one. What did you three have to talk about . . . before there should have been anything for you to talk about?"

Shaw paled. "What? That's wrong. She—"

I held a finger up, just one. He clamped his mouth shut. "You're lying to me. What are you, Martini, and Poole up to? Where's Ramona?"

Shaw gave me the dirtiest look. He wanted me gone, but he didn't know how to make it happen. He decided on the hard approach. "Move your car now, or I'll call the police."

"The police, or Frank Martini?"

Shaw slammed his case on the roof of his car hard. I think he meant it to frighten me. The photos were still up where he could clearly see them. He turned, yanked open the driver's door. "Move it, or I'll wreck it. It's up to you." He grabbed his case, tossed it onto the passenger seat, and then slid in behind the wheel, his window partly open.

"Tonya Pierce," I said. "Or is it Pearson? Where is she? Are there others?"

Shaw started his car, stared straight ahead, his hands gripping the wheel. "Last chance."

"About the case," I said. "What is it? Designer?"

He revved his engine, not bothering to look at me. I folded the copies of the photos and shoved them through the crack in his window. "Keep those. I made copies. Share them with your friends. I'll be back. I'll haunt your dreams, dog your steps. I'm going to stick to you like white on rice."

His jaw clenched, but his eyes never left his windshield. "Is that a threat?"

I leaned down, kept my voice low. "I don't stop. Ask anyone. I'll be seeing you, Shaw."

I got back in my car and reversed to allow him out of his spot, which he did with great speed, anxious, it seemed, to put distance between us. I watched him go.

"Definitely designer."

I spent the afternoon running Tonya Pierce, not Pearson, and the girl was, in fact, sixteen, not eighteen. The ID in Ramona's box was a good fake, but a fake. Was Ramona somehow involved in some scheme to produce and sell fake IDs, as Ben suggested? I hated to admit it, but he'd been right about us approaching things from different directions: big picture, nits. That's part of what had made our partnership work so well. Maybe he was right about this.

At least, then, Ramona leaving the box with Rose made sense. Deloris Poole ran a tight ship. Ramona would have wanted to hide what she was doing. But the ID thing didn't explain the photos or Shaw's jumpiness, and it didn't tell me where to find Ramona.

I slid the box into my top drawer, then closed and locked it; I next checked my watch. After five o'clock. My neck was stiff from hunching over the computer all afternoon, my back and legs, too. I'd sat too long in the chair without moving. I stood, stretched, glancing out at the street below, ready to pack it in for the night. No closer to finding Ramona, an inkling about Shaw and Martini, but no proof. I liked my job, but sometimes I hated it, too.

My office door opened and I turned to see Martini walk in, dressed like a cop—shirt, tie, overcoat, slip-on rubber galoshes over his hard-soled cop shoes. He smiled, but his eyes somehow hadn't gotten the message. Cop eyes. Assessing, unreadable most times, like mine, like Ben's, like every cop's. Martini took a slow sweep, as though committing everything to memory. I stared at him, keeping my mouth shut, having a good idea what was coming.

"So this is where the magic happens, huh?" he asked.

I pulled my swivel chair out and sat behind my desk. I'd trusted Martini three days ago at Clancy's, and thought him an okay cop; I had no reason not to. But I hadn't seen the photo of him and the others then. Knowing now that he might be hiding something about Ramona, it burned me that I'd paid for his shepherd's pie.

"Martini."

There was no warmth in the way I said it, and Martini noted it with a slight raise of his brows. He didn't look impressed with the office, but in my defense, I hadn't done much to it in the years I'd been here. It was an office. Except for a couple Annie Lee prints on the walls, it held only what I needed: a battered desk and file cabinets salvaged from a police auction, a small table with my computer and printer on it, a barely used coffeemaker, off to the side, and the caned coatrack with Pop's umbrella hanging from it. And a closet, but a closet was just a closet.

"Thought I'd stop by," he said, "see how things were going."

I said, "Going well. You?"

He eased over, ran his hand along the handles on my file cabinets, then slid me a look out of the corner of his eye before turning to face me. "Still working my contacts. Nothing promising, then? No leads?"

I pulled my chair in closer to the desk, guarding the drawer I'd put Ramona's box in without appearing to guard it. "Nothing."

Martini walked over to one of the chairs facing my desk, sat down, taking off his gloves, sitting them on his thigh. Again, the smile. He shook his head, his eyes held mine, and we matched cop stare to cop stare.

"You re-up, or something?" I asked. He looked confused. I nodded at his attire. "You're dressed for the job."

He smoothed his tie. "Old habits, right? No word on the girl?"

"Ramona Titus," I answered pointedly. "No. What have your contacts given you?"

Martini shrugged. "No one's seen her. Yet. Look, I had an idea on how we might work this. Coordinate, so to speak."

"Oh?"

"We team up. Work it together. Maximize our efforts."

"I thought that's what we were doing. I'm working it, you're working it."

He adjusted in the chair. "That's just it, we're working it separate. I mean we work it like partners. You remember those, don't you, Raines?" He chuckled. "What do you say? An old-timer with bad knees, but years of street experience, and a hotshot private dick? We'd crack this thing in no time. You might even be able to teach this old dog a few tricks."

I folded my hands on the desk, listening, of course, but thinking, too, and I had a good idea why Martini was here. Shaw had gone crying to him about our encounter in the Bettle lot, hoping probably for a little protection, thinking Martini, the ex-cop with the lethal stare, could warn, scare, or divert my attention. It had zero chance of working, but neither of them had any way of knowing that, because neither of them knew me.

Martini's offer of a partnership was what, then? His way of leading me off course? Maybe he thought he could steer me well away from whatever he had going with Poole and Shaw? The human equivalent to hurling a stick past a bear, hoping it went for that and not your jugular? I grinned, nodded. Yep, that's what this was, I was sure of it.

I squared my shoulders, ready to play. "I doubt that. I appreciate the offer, but let's keep things as they are. I work better, and faster, alone."

"No deadweight, huh?"

"Only, on occasion, my own," I said.

He shrugged, casually, like my turning him down was no big deal, like he hadn't cared one way or the other what I'd say. The lie to that was in the intense way he looked at me. "Just a thought." He slid a hand into his pocket and pulled out his cell phone, checked it. "Here's something just came in. I've got a kid who thinks Ramona met a guy on some meet-up site." He looked up at me. "Maybe he and she planned her escape together, some kind of Romeo-and-Juliet thing."

I angled my head. "Which site?"

Martini consulted his phone again. "Didn't say, but I'll fol-

low up, get more details. It might not be a bad idea if we explored that angle. See if there is some moony kid in the mix."
He stood, buttoned his coat. "What do you think?"

I stood, too, happily anticipating his exit. "Sounds promising. Get the details. You can take it, or I can. We can talk about it."

Martini hesitated for a moment. I could tell he was deciding something. Maybe he had expected to have an easier time baiting me? "Lone wolf."

"Excuse me?"

"I said you're a lone wolf. I get it." He opened the door, his hand stayed on the knob. "We should look into there being a boy linked up in all this. We find him, we find her. I'll be in touch."

Martini left, closing the door behind him. I listened to his squeaky footsteps as he walked away down the hall. I was sure of two things in that moment: one, something about Frank Martini was off, and two, everything he'd just told me about Ramona and some unnamed boy had been a lie.

When I heard Martini's rubber overshoes hit the stairs, I unlocked my desk drawer, took the box, grabbed my bag, locked up, and raced for the back stairs that led to the basement four flights down. It was a spidery journey, one I didn't relish taking. The narrow, dusty stairwell was lit only by dim bare bulbs covered in cobwebs, greasy grit, and decades-old soot. It was stuffy in the stairwell, airless, and smelled of dirt and furnace heat. As far as I knew, no one in the building came this way, except me and Turk, the tatted-up, full-bearded biker dude who served as the building's custodian.

Turk, a fix-it-all man, could look at anything once and figure out how it worked and how to fix it. He kept the furnace running, the water flowing, the garbage cleared, the windows washed, all of it. And he guarded his basement lair as ferociously as a lion guarding its den.

When I got to the fire door at the bottom of the narrow stairs, I rapped loudly and waited. I knew Turk was inside. He seemed always to be here, watching out for his building. I had no idea what kind of life he led off the premises, but whatever it was, I was sure it was unconventional.

I stepped back when the door opened. Turk stood there in broken-in jeans, a long-sleeved Henley with the sleeves rolled up to his elbows, and scuffed biker boots that looked like he'd walked from here to California in them . . . and back again. Without a word, he stood back and let me in, latching the door behind me. We had a deal. This was it.

"In deep shit again, huh?"

I noted the no-joke pipe wrench in his hand, then brushed past him. "Not yet deep, but it has that potential."

His blue eyes locked on mine. "Anything I can do?"

"Thanks, but I got it."

I glanced in Turk's "office" on my way back. It was little more than a utility closet into which he'd crammed a narrow cot and a fifty-two-inch television (with cable access), but he'd done it up nice. There was a hot plate, a coffeemaker, a small fridge, and AC/DC and Harley-Davidson posters taped to the walls, even a cute faux Tiffany accent lamp. I didn't know for sure, and I'd never asked outright, but there was a very good possibility that Turk lived down here full-time.

Turk stopped at his spot, flicking a look at the TV screen, which was turned to a football game. "Yell if you need a big guy with a wrench."

It sounded kind of dirty, but I waved him off. "I'll only be a couple minutes. I'll let myself out."

"Cool."

I ducked into a small room, flicked on the overhead light, and headed for the small wall safe I'd had installed down here, which would come as a surprise to the company that owned the building. I turned the combination lock, opened the door, set Ramona's box inside, and then locked the safe up tight again.

Since my office had a tendency to get turned over on the regular, with bad guys thinking they could slow me down by kicking my door in and trashing the place, I'd decided to build in an extra level of security for myself. There was a safe under my desk in my office, of course, but then there was this one down here, too. If somebody wanted to get at it, they were going to have to get past Turk, which wasn't going to be easy, and then they'd have to blow this baby sky-high.

I waved to Turk on my way out. " 'Night."

"You out?"

"Yep. Locked up. Going home."

The volume on the TV rose. "Stay frosty."

"Always do."

Chapter 12

I woke at six Wednesday morning to more snow. It was the first of December and snowing like crazy. Pretty from my front windows, not so pretty on my windshield or my front walk. I padded into the kitchen and made myself a cup of tea, then stood at the sink and looked out the window at the kitchen window next door. The Volkners' place. Mrs. Volkner had pretty kitchen curtains of lace, with little yellow bumblebees woven into it. They were nice curtains. I looked at mine critically. Just plain white. No bees. I could have gone in for a fancier setup, I guess. But thinking about it now, I still couldn't work up much enthusiasm. Still, the Volkners' bees were a nice touch.

Martini was a solid cop, according to Ben and the solid cops he'd talked to, which left me confused, because my radar was telling me Martini was two people in one body. I didn't know how to describe it better than that, but I had the distinct feeling that I hadn't yet met the real Frank Martini, the one Ronald Shaw apparently had on speed dial, the one who knew Deloris Poole before he should have known her, the one Ramona Titus felt it necessary to capture in a photograph.

I switched on the small TV mounted under my kitchen cabinet to catch the 6 AM news. They were still on the weather, the meteorologist and anchors lamenting the temperature and the snow, as though it were a new phenomenon. Meanwhile, the news crawl recapped the highlights: five shot, two killed overnight; the list of schools closed because of the snow; which politician got caught with his pants down—again. I settled on a bowl of oatmeal and was sitting eating it with a sesame seed bagel when there was a knock at my door.

I padded down the hall, peeked through the peephole. At this hour, I expected Mrs. Vincent or my second-floor tenant, Hank Gray, but it was Eli, the detective I've been seeing. I looked myself over. I was in sweats and an old U of I T-shirt, my feet bare on the paisley hall runner. Whatever. I opened the door.

"Hey," I said.

He smiled, walked in, and we kissed. "Mrs. Vincent let me in. She really monitors that door all hours, doesn't she? I didn't even have time to ring the bell. And I think she's warming up to me." He held up a bakery box. "Doughnuts."

We walked back to the kitchen. He set the box down on the counter. I opened it, peeked in. Glazed and chocolate. I plucked out a chocolate. Who wouldn't? I hadn't exercised in weeks, my treasured racing bike hanging from its stand in the corner waiting for dry weather, but one doughnut couldn't hurt anything.

"Thanks," I said, taking a bite. "What'd I do to rate fresh doughnuts on a Wednesday?"

"I'm trying to butter you up."

I grinned. "For what? Something fun, I hope."

"Dinner. With me."

My grin got bigger. "You didn't need doughnuts for that. Yes."

He let a beat pass. "And Dana."

I stopped chewing. The grin died. Dana was Eli's sixteen-year-old daughter. We'd never met, but I'd heard all about her, including the bit about her holding me personally responsible for her parents' separation and divorce, which was bogus. The papers had been signed for months before I even gave Eli Weber the time of day. But when was the last time anyone could get a wounded teenager to think straight?

I finished the doughnut, though the subsequent bites paled in taste to that first blissful nibble. I hadn't known then that the doughnuts came with strings attached. "Um."

"I think it's time you met. It's the holiday season. What better time, right?"

I needed milk to wash the doughnut down, so I grabbed the carton out of the fridge, got a glass, and poured some. The milk thing also gave me time.

"Cass?"

I took a sip, watching him over the rim. I swallowed slowly. "Yeah?"

He leaned back against the counter. "What's wrong?"

I put the glass down, thinking seriously about a second doughnut, not for pleasure but for stress. "It's too soon."

"What do you mean?"

"You said she was having a hard time dealing with everything. That she's angry?"

"It's been almost a year since the divorce."

"And we've been seeing each other only about half that." He stared at me blankly, not getting it. "That's like two weeks in teenager time."

"I think I know my kid."

He was getting defensive. "Okay." I poured more milk.

"Sounds like you don't want to meet her."

He was a great detective, dedicated, smart, tough, insightful most times. Today? Right now with the doughnuts? Completely clueless. I walked my bowl and cup to the dishwasher. "I'll think about it, okay?" I tried keeping a lightness in my voice that I did not feel. "But I'm in the middle of something right now. A runaway."

Eli pressed. "I was thinking somewhere nice. Downtown. Two hours tops." He looked at me hopefully, a lot apparently hanging on my response. "We can always reschedule if you get tied up."

I looked over at him. "What's the rush?"

"It's just dinner. A breaking of the ice. You don't have to make it more than it is."

"What does Dana say about all this?"

He played with his tie. "I haven't told her yet, but it'll be fine."

"Eli—"

He stopped me. "Look, it's no big deal. You'll meet, we'll eat, that's it. Unless you don't want to meet her. Is that it?"

"You know that's not it."

"Then, yes? Dinner on Friday with me and my daughter?"

For a moment, I said nothing, just watched him waiting for my answer. I could see this was important to him, but I knew this was a train wreck waiting to happen.

"All right. Dinner. Friday. *If* I'm not tied up."

He came over, pulled me into a hug. "Fantastic. It'll be fine. Trust me. She's going to love you."

I sighed. "What's not to love, right?"

There was a message waiting for me on my phone. The Knowleses agreed to see me if I could get there before nine, so I bundled up, shoveled my car out, and slipped and slid my way to their place, the Friday dinner on my mind. It was a bad idea. I knew it. I mean, Eli and I were okay, but we weren't locked into anything. Why was he pushing his daughter into the mix so soon? What could he be thinking? Hell, what was I thinking when I agreed to the whole thing, knowing it had the potential of blowing up in our faces? Family drama. I had zero tolerance for it. Family drama played out in a restaurant on a Friday night? With a sixteen-year-old who thought I broke up her parents' marriage? God help me.

Back in the lobby of the Knowleses' building, I rang the bell, identified myself when the intercom engaged, and was quickly buzzed up. By the time I got to the second floor, the door to the Knowleses' apartment was open and a couple stood in the doorway dressed for work.

"Mr. and Mrs. Knowles," I said at the door in my most polite voice. "Cassandra Raines. Thanks for seeing me."

They welcomed me in, led me to the front room. The apartment was nothing out of the ordinary, comfortably furnished, not ostentatious, homey. The Knowleses were comfortably in their fifties, and looked like they were happy together. Mrs. Knowles placed a gentle hand on her husband's knee when they sat down on the couch. They both had kind faces.

"Sorry it had to be so early," Mrs. Knowles said. "But we both work. You said it was about Ramona? Is she all right?"

I sat opposite the couch in a wing chair. "She's run away. I've been hired to help find her."

"Oh no," Mrs. Knowles said. "What happened?"

I set my bag down at my feet, then perched on the edge of the chair. "I was hoping you might be able to help me with that. Ramona lived with you for a time. What can you tell me about her? How did she get along here?"

Mr. Knowles stared at me. "Just fine with us. We have a couple other kids, too."

"Lexie and Max," Mrs. Knowles added. "They're at school now."

Mr. Knowles went on. "Ramona was with us for only about six months. She started off real quiet at first, but she was just beginning to come into herself—"

"Then last year they up and moved her," Mrs. Knowles said, cutting in. "We got a call on a Friday, and they came to get her the next morning. We wanted to keep her. She wanted to stay, but . . ."

"There was no explanation?"

They both shook their heads at the same time. "We both know these placements are temporary," Mrs. Knowles said. "That we have to be prepared to let them go, no matter how much we love them."

"Mind if I ask *who* called?"

Mr. Knowles slid his wife a look, then said, "Ronald Shaw. He said he had gotten Ramona into some specialized therapy that she needed, and the new place he was putting her in was going to help with that. How could we argue? If she needed the help—"

"But she really did love it here," Mrs. Knowles said. "Some kids act out because they're hurt so deep. Ramona's different. She never lets things bog her down for too long. She never cut school or hung out with the wrong crowd. She reads and she studies. I always say about Ramona, she knows exactly where she wants to go, who she wants to be, and she's not going to let anyone or anything keep her from it. That's rare in a child her age. How long has she been gone? Are the police looking for her?" She looked over at her husband, reached out for his hand. "What can we do to help?"

"Did somebody do something to her?" Mr. Knowles asked. "Is that why she ran?"

Mrs. Knowles gasped. "Sweet Jesus, tell me they didn't do anything to that child."

I couldn't give her that assurance. I didn't know what had happened to Ramona from the day she left the Knowleses' a year ago to the day she left Deloris Poole's.

"She never ran away while she was with you?" I asked.

"Never," she said. "Like we said, she was happy here."

"But you were told Ramona had run away before?"

The couple shared a look. "Shaw never said anything about that to us."

"But Ramona did." Mrs. Knowles gave her husband's knee a squeeze. She obviously had information he didn't have. "One place they put her, they were very strict. They used a belt. She said that's why she ran from there, to avoid the beatings." Her expression darkened, anger bubbled up in her throat. "I'd like to say that's unusual, but it's not. Some of these fosters are not in it for the kids. They don't know how to parent. I've never beaten a child in my life."

"Do you know Deloris Poole or Frank Martini?"

They shook their heads; Mr. Knowles answered. "Should we?"

"She's Ramona's current foster mother," I said, "he's a retired detective."

"We never had any contact with any detectives," Mr. Knowles said. "We've had some great kids."

"They aren't bad," Mrs. Knowles added, "they're just babies caught up in bad situations. Give them a little love, a little understanding, and they bloom like roses."

Shaw had painted quite a different picture of Ramona as a problem child steeped in psychological trauma, one for whom he'd recommended therapy. It was the reason he'd given for taking Ramona from the Knowleses. But they saw Ramona in a totally different light.

"Stealing," I said. "Has Ramona ever—"

"Never once," Mr. Knowles shot back. "Ramona's no thief! Is that what they're saying? That she's a thief?"

Mrs. Knowles bristled, opened her mouth to speak, but I held up a hand. "It's information I was given. I have no idea whether it's true or not, so I ask."

"Well, that's a lie," Mrs. Knowles said. "She never took a thing from this house, and we never heard of her taking anything from anywhere else, either. Whoever told you that's a bald-faced liar."

That would be Shaw and Poole. They had portrayed Ramona as a troubled kid in need of help, a serial runaway, a thief. If I had to choose which version of the girl to believe, I'd have wanted to go with the one from the Knowleses, the people who appeared to genuinely love her, but I wouldn't know for sure until I found Ramona and saw for myself.

"Did Ramona have any friends she was particularly close to?" I thought of the box left with Rose. "Or did she leave anything behind?"

I could see they were scared, worried. The child they loved was somewhere out there unprotected, alone, and I knew by looking at them that neither would have a moment's peace or a full night's sleep until Ramona was back safe. Mrs. Knowles's eyes filled with tears. "You find her. You bring her back."

I stood, feeling no closer to anything. This was still a big city. Ramona was still out there in it. I had photographs that made no sense and liars lying. It was a lot, and I wasn't sure where to go with it, or if I had enough to get it done.

Standing alone in the hall after the Knowleses' door closed behind me, I took a moment to breathe. I closed my eyes, inhaling, exhaling, slow and easy. When I opened them again, I was good to go. It was a lot, but I was a lot, too, depending on the day. I bounded down the stairs, buttoning up my coat, and headed out into the cold again.

Chapter 13

I was driving the streets, checking out spots on Poole's map, when I got a call from Hogan. A body had been found smoldering in a trash can under the Stevenson, and he was on his way there.

"It might not be her," he said, "but . . ."

He didn't have to finish. "On my way."

The can was at the edge of a makeshift homeless encampment, whose residents had wisely scattered when the body was discovered and the cops showed up, leaving behind their tents and blankets and carts and buckets crammed with everything they owned and held dear. There was a good chance the city would come in and dismantle the camp before the homeless had a chance to return. Nothing like the discovery of a body to get slow-moving government wheels to suddenly turn fast as lightning.

Police cars, ambulances, the medical examiner's van ringed the slushy gray plot of underpass strewn with bits of garbage tossed from the cars above and detritus dumped by haulers and ragmen who, instead of disposing of tires, old appliances, and assorted car parts in the city dumps where they belonged, sneakily dumped truckloads of it in the dead of night to save a trip, pocket a buck, and blight the neighborhood, as though garbage was all it deserved and it should be lucky to have it.

From a distance, held back by red crime-scene tape, I stared at the can, the smoke snaking out of it, the stench of burning rubber, trash, and flesh stinging my nose. I was sick to my stomach, sick to my head of evil and soullessness. I glanced around at the people watching, the reporters standing in several inches of snow facing cameras as they told the city what had been done here. I wondered how many watching would even care? How many would take only a passing interest, then turn away and get back to their lives?

No one had said it was Ramona Titus, not yet, but even if it wasn't her, somebody's someone was dead. If Ramona was there, my job was over, and I'd mucked it up; if it wasn't her, I was still no closer to finding her than I was yesterday or the day before. I kept my eyes on the can and on the backs of the first responders, Hogan among them. I looked for Martini, wondering if he was this dialed in that he'd made it here before I had, but I didn't see him anywhere. What would I tell Leesa Evans if Ramona was dead? She was desperate to do better, to start again. What would the loss of Ramona do to her? I watched as Hogan pulled himself away from the group and approached me, his face a slate of stone. This was his job, the expression on his face said, and he was damn well going to do it. Emotions would come later, I knew. Often over one too many at a cop bar, or at home, alone in the dark, downing a glass or bottle at a time from a liquor cart, or a pill or two from a medicine cabinet. Numbing, anesthetizing the human parts, the parts that thought too much, felt too deeply, the parts that ached at the waste. Or maybe Hogan handled it differently, better. But for now, it was all business.

"I got a call from homicide when it looked like their body

might be my missing person," Hogan said. "No ID. The body's badly charred. ME's going to have to take it from here." He scanned the scene, peering up at the overpass, cars whizzing past oblivious. "The hands and teeth are missing. Female is all we know."

"How?"

"Some hair left. Earrings in the ears, a bracelet half melted into what's left on her wrist. Hopefully, they'll get more."

I sighed. "Somebody didn't want to make this easy."

"Tell me about it. We won't have anything for a while. I'll let you know. You okay?"

I'd been staring at the can and wasn't aware that Hogan had been watching me. "Thanks for the call." I turned, walked back to my car. I wanted to go home. I wanted to go home and stay there and not think about the can or the smell of burning flesh. I wanted the world to be different, and for pain to stop. And I knew I wouldn't get any of that.

I sat on my couch, lights out. Hours ago, I'd opened the drapes so that I could see the snow coming down in big, fat clumps of magic. Perfect snow falling down on an imperfect world, a world where monsters dumped bodies into cans and set them on fire. I wished I could say the whole thing shocked me. It didn't. I'd seen it more than once and would likely see it again, but it always pulled me up short, at least for a moment. It never failed to distress me and plunge me into a pit, briefly, until the fire in my belly, doused for a second, roared back and I got angry that there were monsters with human faces who walked the streets, hunting for prey.

I glanced over at the digital readout on the TV's cable box. It was 8:00 PM. When had the snow stopped falling? When had it gotten dark out? I stood. I was going to bed. Maybe I could pretend for a time that the world wasn't what it sometimes is, and that innocents always had the privilege of remaining so.

* * *

The next morning, I held the receiver in my hand, not wanting to call Leesa Evans. What would I say, anyway? It was too soon to have heard anything from Hogan. Why distress her further unnecessarily? I'd wait until I knew for sure. Instead, I dialed Ramona's cell. Hogan had gotten nothing from it, no pings, no activity, and so considered the phone a dead end, but I couldn't believe that Ramona would toss her phone away. Still, no pick up. Dead end.

My doorbell rang and I padded over to the intercom. "Yes?"

"It's me," Barb said, a rush to her voice.

I buzzed her up and left the door open for her before heading back to the kitchen to start coffee.

The front door shut. "Kitchen," I said.

I heard her take off her boots, hang her coat up in the hall closet, then walk back, her stocking feet brushing along the wool runner that ran the length of the long hall.

"Brrr," she said, rubbing her hands to warm them. Her red hair was a mess of curls, her green eyes bright, her skin flushed from the cold. Sister Barbara Covey, frozen snownun.

I took a coffee mug from the cabinet and set it on the island as the coffeemaker began to gurgle.

"You look terrible," Barb said. "Something you're working on?"

I nodded. "A runaway girl. Haven't found her yet."

Barb flicked a look out the kitchen window at the frost inches deep on the glass. She made a face. "In that?" Worry creased her face. "Runaways. They break my heart. Can I help?" Barb taught English at our old school, but somehow she felt secure in her abilities to tackle investigative work on top of everything else she had going on. And, to tell the truth, she wasn't half bad at it. She had a logical mind, bulldog tenacity, and she was frighteningly fearless. Maybe having Jesus firmly on your side gave a person a certain feeling of invincibility. I certainly didn't have that confidence. I knew what lurked in the corners, hid in shadows, and most of it scared the crap out of me.

I gave her a weak smile. I was tired, my head filled with the stench of human flesh burning. "Don't think so. I may not even have a case anymore." I told her about yesterday's gruesome discovery and watched her face pale.

"Who would do something so . . . heinous?"

The coffeemaker beeped and I retrieved the carafe to fill Barb's mug. "A lot of people, unfortunately."

"And you don't know if it's the child you're looking for?"

"I don't."

She took a sip, a faraway look in her eyes. "Evil is real."

"No school?" I asked, hoping to change the subject.

"Not for me. Personal day. I had something I needed to take care of."

She sat there. I did, too. I stared at her. Barb stared at me. She was straightforward usually, almost to a fault. If she had something to say, she said it. No bush beating, no hemming and hawing. Direct, like iron balls shot out of a cannon. A quiet stare-off was not something she did as a rule. The fact that we were engaged in one now felt weird.

"And this is it?" I asked. "The thing you needed to do?"

She smiled. "It is."

A moment went by. Two.

"Fun," I said.

"Your runaway. How long has she been missing?"

"Two weeks."

Barb began rubbing the small gold cross hanging from a chain around her neck. "Children wandering the streets, lost, physically, spiritually, scared out of their minds, but trying not to show it, like they have it all handled. They don't. Who could? Throwaways, most of them. I don't understand how a parent can just throw a child away."

My jaw clenched. "They aren't parents. Your mistake is assuming they are."

Barb noticed a short stack of flyers with Ramona's photo on it. She picked one up. "She's beautiful. Two weeks gone. Mind if I take one?"

"No, but why?"

"You don't know the body's hers for sure. She could still be out there. I just started volunteering on a mobile outreach bus. We see a lot of runaways, street people. I can keep an eye out, ask around."

I perked up. "You never mentioned anything about that."

Barb slid the flyer into her pocket. "I didn't take out an ad, or anything. Besides, I've only been out twice so far. We hand out blankets, food, toiletries, books, anything anyone might need, but not have access to. No judgment. We don't preach or try to convert anyone. We're just there to fill a need and offer resources, if they ask for them. The Love Bus is out midnight to dawn most nights. That's where I've been." She sipped her coffee. "It does good work. I hope it's making a difference."

"It might not be Ramona," I said. "I need to get on that bus. You think you can set it up?"

"We can always use another set of hands." Barb put her mug down. "But right now, the thing I needed to do . . ." She reached into the pocket of her pink fleece jacket and pulled out a small travel chessboard, the kind you took on planes or on long car rides to keep kids busy so you wouldn't have to stop or turn the car around. Barb slowly set the board on the table in front of us and placed her hand on it. I looked at her, but said nothing for a time.

I'd played chess every Wednesday with Pop since I was about thirteen. It was our thing. The games had been part pastime, part therapy session, a weekly check-in, a reunion, a recharge. I didn't play chess anymore—not since he was killed . . . I got through Wednesdays now by keeping my head down, not thinking about it. Like yesterday when I'd kept busy, like the Wednesdays before that and all the other Wednesdays yet to come. I looked down at the set, resenting the memories it forced back.

I'd packed Pop's lucky board away so I wouldn't have to see it. I'd thought at one point it'd be a good idea to donate it to a community center or a children's hospital, but I couldn't bring myself to part with it, even if I couldn't bear to look at it. It was mine. He'd left it to me. Just like he'd left me his ratty old umbrella, which I kept in my office, hanging from the coatrack. I glanced over at it a million times in a day. The board and the umbrella were all I had left of him. Barb knew all that.

I pushed the board back at her. "No."

"I know, I'm not much of a player. I'm a checkers gal, you know that. But I don't think the playing is as important as what goes on while we play, right?" She opened the board and began to set up the pieces. "The talking and the working things through. For instance, we could talk about your case, or whatever you want." Barb lined up the pieces, tiny bishops, rooks, and knights, deliberately, taking great care that they were neat and straight. "I'm no priest," she went on, conversationally, as though this were a thing of little consequence, a simple chess game between friends, not a transition, not a moving forward, a getting past. Finally, with all the pieces in place, she picked up a black pawn and a white one and placed one in each fisted hand. After a brief shuffle from one hand to the other, she presented her fists to me. "But I am sort of in the same profession. Working from the same operating manual, you could say. And I've known you just as long as he did. *And* even though you always say everything's fine, and you have nothing to talk about, I know it's a crock." She grinned, held her fists higher. "Choose. Let's get this gabfest started."

I stared at Barb's hands, at her. "Barb . . ."

She kept talking, "And I realize it's Thursday, not Wednesday. I thought about it and decided we needed to pick a new day. New day, new start, new tradition."

"Barb—"

"He's gone."

The bluntness of her words drew me up short, blunt but not mean, not meant to be hurtful, but definitive, final. "He was here. He did what God called him to do, and now he's gone," she said. "The good part is that he gave us everything we're ever going to need, so we're going to get on with it. We start by doing this." She jutted her fists out farther. "Choose."

I bristled. I hated being pushed. It brought out the stubbornness in me. "And if I don't?"

"Then my arms are going to get really tired. One of us will eventually have to use the bathroom, and we'll get hungry at some point. It'd be a shame if they found us here starved to death, me with chess pieces in my emaciated fists, inches from your fridge, and a block away from a Starbucks." She shook her fists impatiently. "C'mon. Choose."

Moments passed before I slowly reached over and tapped her right hand and got the white pawn. I'd go first.

Barb shook her head, grinning. "You always come out smelling like a rose, don't you? Make your move."

I slid the pawn from b2 to b3. Barb's face lit up; so did her triumphant smile, as though I'd given her the greatest gift, instead of it maybe being the other way around.

She pumped her fist. "Thursday chess. Day one. Now, tell me more about your runaway."

Chapter 14

Barb left a couple hours later with a batch of Mrs. Vincent's homemade oatmeal cookies, our game of Thursday chess having done more good than I could have ever thought possible. Then I got a call from Leesa Evans. She'd seen the report on the burned body on the morning news and, like me, like Hogan, thought the body might be Ramona's. I said the usual things—told her not to worry, I'd keep on top of it and call her with any updates. She seemed satisfied with that, but I knew it wouldn't last, that she wouldn't rest or stop worrying until she knew for sure her daughter was alive or dead. The waiting was the difficult part.

I spent the day at the office checking in with Hogan, avoiding Martini, studying the photographs looking for something I might have missed. Martini wasn't the only one with contacts on the street. I checked in with mine, but no one had seen a kid matching Ramona's description. I'd already papered the neighborhood with flyers. Every other thought that went through my head was of the unidentified body left smoking like garbage. Female, Hogan said.

I dialed Ramona's number several times, but got more nothing. What did they say about insanity being defined as doing the same thing, over and over again, expecting a different result? With no leads to follow, no move to make, I finally went home around six PM to shower, eat, and brood. Waiting on the ID. Waiting to learn if Ramona Titus was still among the living.

My doorbell rang. The voice over the intercom was unexpected.

"Miss Cassandra?"

"Pouch?"

"Yeah, it's me. I need to talk to you?"

I buzzed him up, but not before taking a quick look at my place to memorize my stuff and where I had it. Pouch was a master pickpocket with kleptomaniac tendencies, a friend of Whip's whom he was trying to keep on the straight and narrow. He was nicknamed Pouch for obvious reasons.

When I let him in, I stepped back and took in his outfit. He was a short white guy, about fifty, maybe—it was hard to tell. Pointy head, hair always looked greasy, steady eyes, beady, and the most elegant hands you'd ever see on a man, long, slender fingers, neat nails. Like he was a surgeon or a concert pianist. Pouch had the hands of an artist, which, I guess, you could argue he was—he was an artistic thief, a guy who could part you from your wallet without your feeling a single tug.

Pouch only ever wore one color at a time. Today, he was all in black—jeans, turtleneck, jacket, boots, skullcap. He looked like a five-foot-tall cat burglar, or a nonblue member of the Blue Man Group.

"Pouch," I said. "What is it?"

He stepped inside, looked around nervously. "Have you seen Charlie?"

"No. Not for a couple days. Why?"

Pouch looked uneasy, which was beginning to make me uneasy. "Heard from him?"

I shut the door. "Pouch, what's going on?"

"Maybe nothing. I been trying to call him for a few days. He never answers and he don't call back. I even went by the place he cooks at, they said he up and quit." Pouch scanned my entry-way, the living room beyond it. I knew he was looking for something to pinch.

"Pouch! Focus."

His eyes slid back to me. "Right. Yeah, so I figured I'd come by and see if you knew where he was at?"

"I knew it!"

I banged a fist against my thigh, recalling that strange visit Whip had paid me when he refused to step inside the apartment to talk. I'd had a sense then that something was wrong. Pouch blinked. "Knew what?"

"Hold on," I said. I moved into the living room, grabbed my phone off the table, and dialed Whip's apartment, but got no answer. Voice mail kicked in, and I left a message asking him to call me right away. Then I punched END and dialed his cell, get-ting the same. "When was the last time you talked to him? Ex-actly?"

Pouch was wandering around my front room like he was browsing the shelves at Macy's. He hadn't heard me.

"Pouch!"

He startled, turned, a guilty look on his pinched little face. "What's that?"

"When was the last time you actually talked to him?"

"What's today?"

I had no idea what Pouch did when he wasn't in my pres-ence. He could be a vagabond or a CPA. He could sell shoes out of the back of a truck or train greyhounds for the track. He was Whip's friend, not mine.

"Thursday," I said testily. "All day."

He thought about it, his ratlike eyes pointed upward, an empty look on his face. "Then Tuesday? We were supposed to hit up the indoor swap meet, but I couldn't get hold of him. Had to go solo. It's never good when I go solo." That meant he stole something from the swap meet. "Maybe he's taking some downtime, but I thought I'd check with you to see if you'd heard from him."

I dialed Barb's number. She picked right up. "Yep?"

"Have you heard from Whip?" I watched Pouch browse. "Hold on." I covered the phone with my hand. "Pouch? Freeze. And keep your hands to yourself."

He looked hurt. "You don't trust me?"

I looked right at him. "No." I went back to Barb. "Pouch is here. He says he hasn't been able to get hold of him in a few days, and that he quit the diner."

"*Quit?* Why? He loved that job."

"I don't know. He stopped by on Monday and he was acting strange. Not himself. I just tried calling, he doesn't answer."

"I don't think we should worry. He's a grown man. He can take care of himself. He's been doing great, anyway, right? Maybe he's just taking some time for himself."

"Yeah, that's what Pouch just said."

Barb paused. "Pouch and me on the same wavelength. Should I worry?"

"Yes," I said. "I'm going to run by his diner and see what I can find out."

"I'll try his apartment, then," Barb said. "It's probably nothing."

I ended the call, turned to Pouch. "Thanks for letting me know." I showed him to the door. "I'll let Whip know you're worried about him."

Pouch bowed. "My pleasure, Miss Cassandra."

I watched as he descended the stairs until he was out of view, and then went back inside and locked the door. I dialed Whip's number again, nothing, and while I had it in hand, dialed Ramona's, too, also nothing. Looking around the coffee table where I kept the TV remote, I didn't see it. I turned over the couch cushions, looked between the chair cushions, under the couch, on the bookshelves. Pouch!

I ran for the door, grabbed up my keys, and tore out of my

apartment, bounding down the stairs, out onto the front stoop, looking up and down the block for a small black blob. Found it. Half a block up, on the other side of the street. I took off running, no coat, only a long-sleeved T-shirt and jeans, and a pair of running shoes, death in the snow. I'd have been cold if it weren't for the burning indignation in my belly.

"Pouch! Stop!"

He stopped, reeled, his eyes wide. He raised his hands in surrender. I caught up to him, grabbed him by his jacket collar, twisted, and slung him against a parked car, scattering snow. "Hands on the roof. Spread 'em." I kicked his legs apart, started the pat down.

"It's a sickness," he whined. "I really am working on it. Charlie's helping me. Old days, I woulda walked out with half your stuff."

I wasn't listening, I was patting pockets. I found my remote tucked into one of his socks. I grabbed it, tucked it into my back pocket, and then turned Pouch around. "Am I going to have to frisk you every time you come into my place?" He didn't answer. I yanked him by the collar. "*Am I?*"

"I swear, no. I'm keyed-up. Charlie calms me down, but I can't reach him. The remote was sitting there. Before I knew it, I'd palmed it. I regret it. I apologize. You're family. I *know* this." He buried his head in his hands. "I can do this. I know I can do this."

I stared at him, instantly regretting the frisk. I let go of him, smoothed his collar down. "Go home, Pouch."

I walked off, with him still explaining himself. I didn't need this; really, I didn't. Why did I do this to myself? A pickpocket klepto, a missing ex-con, a runaway teenager. I got back to my building, mounted the stairs, and locked myself into my apartment again, grumbling the whole way. I pulled the remote out of my pocket and put it back on the table, where it belonged. It was the only win I had on my side for the day. Pitiful.

Chapter 15

Whip worked at a place called Creole's on the West Side, which specialized in down-home Southern dishes, Cajun favorites, Creole basics, and whatever else he felt like cooking up fresh and well-seasoned in the tiny kitchen he ran like a tight ship. I walked in Friday morning, looking around for him, but didn't see him out front. I walked back to the kitchen and entered it, but there was a short, wide black man in a white apron. Not Whip.

"Hey, you can't come back here," the man said.

"Where's Charles Mingo?"

"Who's asking?"

"I am."

"Quit," the man said.

I scanned the small kitchen, taking in the pots and pans and whatnots, as though grill man was hiding Whip under a colander, or something. "Why?"

"How the hell should I know? You can't be his old lady, 'cuz his luck ain't that good. So, what's all this?"

The kitchen door opened and the manager of the place, a guy

I'd met before when I'd stopped by to visit and eat—Kenny something—walked in. "What's going on? You can't come back here." He stopped talking when I turned around and he saw it was me. "Oh, hey."

"Kenny, right?" I asked.

He nodded. "Yeah, still, you can't be in here."

I flicked a look at the cook, back at Kenny. "I need to see you out there, then."

I walked back out into the dining area, sat at an empty table with a red-and-white checked tablecloth. Kenny sat across from me, looking as though I might bite.

"Charles quit," I said. "When? Why? What happened?"

"You two are tight, aren't you? Seems to me you should know more about it than me."

I didn't, and felt guilty about it. Kenny was right. Whip was my friend. If something was going on with him, I should have picked up on it, instead of having to get the news from a remote-filching Pouch. "Tell me what happened."

"Nothing happened. One day he was here, next day he wasn't. He didn't show up, didn't call. Then he didn't show up the next day or the next. I called his place, got no answer. I got a business to run, so I had to bump Tennessee up to head cook. He's nowhere near as good as Charlie. Matter of fact, he's lousy, but I needed somebody in there. Make no mistake, I'd take Charlie back if he walked in here right now. That's how good he is, but he'd have to do a lot of explaining to get back in my good graces. I took a chance on him when nobody else would, remember that, seeing as he's a con."

"Ex," I said defensively.

"Maybe," Kenny said. "Maybe not. Either way, he ain't here, is he?"

"So he didn't say anything. He just didn't show?"

Kenny shook his head. "Yup. Not a word or nothing. It's been a full week since I laid eyes on him."

A week. I'd seen Whip on Monday. Four days ago. "The last

time you saw him, how did he seem? Was he stressed? Worried?"

Kenny thought about it. "Same old Charlie, I'd say. Cracking jokes, cooking up a storm. Then he ghosts me."

I got up, then placed one of my cards on the table. "If you hear from him, see him, would you call me, please?"

Kenny slid the card toward himself and read it. "I can do that. Hope everything's all right with good old Charlie. Tennessee . . ." He frowned, shook his head. "Well, he's Tennessee."

I slid into my driver's seat, called Barb. "Anything?"

"He's not home. I talked to his neighbors. Last time they remember seeing him for sure was Tuesday morning getting into his car."

"He came to see me the night before that," I said. "The manager at his diner says he hasn't shown up for work in a week. Did he have luggage or a bag or anything like that with him when his neighbors saw him?"

"I asked that. He was empty-handed. One neighbor said he seemed in a hurry. Whip usually stopped to talk with her, but not this time. Straight to his car and gone. You really think he's in trouble?"

"I hope not." I was thinking of ways I could track him down. He wouldn't like it, but I didn't care. I wasn't going to lose another person out of my life without doing something about it.

"Best thing we can do is stay calm," Barb said.

I said nothing.

"Cass?"

"Yes. Calm. I'll call you later."

Ben's car heater was on full blast to cut the bite of the air seeping in from outside. We were parked in front of my office, the car idling. It was a gloomy afternoon, the sky a depressing shade of gummy gray as I sat and watched tiny snowflakes melt into water on the windshield.

"Yeah, why are we not inside the diner up the block? It's warm there and I can get something for lunch."

"Muna's off," I said. "There's some new woman in there. Aggie. Strange."

Ben looked at me, bewildered. "A waitress?" I nodded. "Who serves food? In a diner where it's warm? What's strange about that?"

"Muna should be back soon."

"So you're avoiding the place till then?"

I looked over at him. "I'm not *avoiding* it."

"You're not eating in it, either," he said.

He didn't say anything more, neither did I. He knew who I was. He reached into his glove compartment and took out an old granola bar, which looked like it'd been in there for a long time. He unwrapped it, bit into it. It was a sorry substitute for Deek's hot plates, but sometimes you just had to roll with it.

"Now I gotta see this Aggie," Ben muttered. "To run you out of your spot into cold like this, I mean she's gotta—"

"Can we please drop it? We're talking about Whip. This isn't like him."

"How do you know? Up until a few months ago, you hadn't seen or heard from him since you were kids, right? He'd been right here, stealing all kinds of shit, ending up in prison. You knew the kid. You can't say you know the man. This picking up and moving off without saying anything could be his thing."

"I know him," I stated. Ben looked skeptical. "As well as I know you."

His brows lifted. "Oh, you think you know me?"

"About as well as you know me."

It got quiet in the car, the heater whirring. Ben took another bite of granola. "Yeah, well, he'll be fine. When he's ready to tell you whatever he has to tell you, he'll tell you." He balled up the empty granola wrapper and stuffed it in his cup holder. "What's new on your case?"

"Not much. I may take another run at Poole. See what she has to say about those photos. I was holding off to see what else developed, but . . . I mean, if Shaw tagged Martini after I talked to him, and I bet that's exactly what he did, he probably tagged her, too. It feels like they're in something together, keeping some kind of secret. I just don't know what it is."

"Maybe," Ben said. "Maybe not."

"A photo's worth a thousand words," I said.

He smirked. "And just a photo doesn't mean shit."

A car eased into the spot behind us, its headlights on. Ben and I both checked it out in the rearview mirror, watching as the lights cut off, and Detective Hogan and a tall dark guy— who, I assumed, was his partner, Spinelli—got out of the car and headed for my office. "Hogan," I said to Ben.

He checked him out in the rearview. "Not much to write home about. Who's the swimsuit model with him?"

I checked the rearview. The second cop was about six-two, athletically built, full lips, droopy eyes, Stallonish, but young Stallone, not old Stallone. "I'm guessing that's his partner, Spinelli."

"What do you suppose they want?" Ben asked.

"Go see," I said.

Ben snorted. "You go see. It's cold as balls out there."

I opened the passenger door and a fist of cold punched its way inside and I seized up, lungs and all. The man didn't lie. Cold as balls. "Hogan!"

He and Spinelli stopped, turned. Ben got out of the car and we waited for them at his back bumper.

Hogan took Ben in, gave a single head nod of acknowledgment. "I'd recognize one of us a mile away."

Ben held out his hand for Hogan to shake it. "Ben Mickerson."

"My ex-partner," I explained, watching Stallone stand there and sizzle in the subzero temps. "Detective Spinelli?"

He said, "Vince."

He looked younger than Hogan, maybe forty, and stood stock straight, military bearing, serious. I turned my attention back to Hogan.

"I stopped by to give you an update on that body we found. We were on our way up. Guess this saves us the trip." His eyes moved over Ben, assessing. "Homicide got the prelims in. Female, like we knew. Age estimate sixteen, maybe seventeen. She'd given birth at least once, which doesn't match with the Titus girl. That's all they've got so far. So, I'm still on my missing persons and they got their hands full. I called her mother, *respectfully,* to tell her it wasn't Ramona."

"Thank you," I said.

I thought of the ID. The good fake. The one in Ramona's box of mysteries. "Did you try Tonya Pierce?" I said. "For a name. Maybe it'll match. Or Pearson." Hogan and Spinelli clocked in. Their faces hardened, like I was suddenly a suspect who'd been holding out on them.

"Pierce. The other kid at Poole's?" Hogan asked. "How's she in this?"

I took a second to choose my words carefully. "It's possible she might not have gone back to family, like we were told. In fact, it doesn't appear she has any family at all."

"And you think the body's hers," he said.

"I'm only saying it might be possible."

"And you think Shaw had something to do with it?"

"He's very jumpy," I said. "He's afraid of something, someone. We have Tonya, unaccounted for, and an unidentified body, female, around the same age." I left it there, watching Hogan and Spinelli. "It's Shaw who moves the kids around, isn't it? Home to home?"

Hogan looked like he didn't believe me, and I got the same incredulous look from Spinelli. I really should tell them about the key and the photographs in Ramona's box, but the fact that

Hogan's go-to man on the street was Frank Martini hinted at a certain familiarity, so I kept my mouth shut.

"Where'd you get Pearson?" Spinelli asked, stone-faced.

"I stumbled on it as a possible, that's all."

Hogan asked, "Stumbled on it where?"

"I can't recall *exactly* where."

A moment passed.

"Anything else?" Hogan said.

"Nothing yet, but I'll keep in touch." Hogan's and Spinelli's cop faces were unreadable, but the smirk on Ben's face came through loud and clear. He knew I was tap dancing like crazy. Still, in my opinion, I was holding up well to the cop heat. Kudos to me.

"You know where to find us, then." Hogan looked over at Ben. "Mickerson. You look familiar. You ever work with a cop named Anton Bosko?"

"Never did," Ben said. "But I have one of those faces you see everywhere. Comes in handy on a drug buy."

Hogan smiled. He got it. Understood it.

He and Spinelli turned to leave, I stopped them. "Hogan? Why didn't you just call with the prelim news? Why drive all the way out here?"

"Just covering all the bases, Raines."

Ben and I stood there freezing while Hogan and Spinelli got in their car and left, leaving us there to watch them drive away.

"Covering all the bases my ass," Ben said. "He definitely could have called with that body info. He came here to feel you out, to make sure you weren't getting ahead of him. You got that, right? And that Spinelli? Cold as ice. They know they dropped the ball on Pierce. They're gonna be scrambling now to catch up, and watching you like a hawk."

"Maybe," I said. Poole, Shaw, Martini. Why not Hogan? I flicked him a look. "Solid cops, though, by all accounts. Like Martini."

Ben sighed. "You don't let a damn thing go, do you?"

Chapter 16

I called Leesa Evans just to make sure Hogan had been telling the truth. He had. I could practically hear the relief in her voice, like a huge boulder had been lifted from her chest. She was positive that if Ramona had had a child, she would have known about it. I wasn't so sure, given Evans's addiction, her incarceration, and her prolonged absence from Ramona's life, but I had nothing to counter it.

It took me the next couple hours of nonstop phone work to find out Whip hadn't been picked up anywhere and he wasn't in any of the area hospitals. Meanwhile, I kept calling his phone and Ramona's, too, with no results.

Armed with the missing flyer, I was back at it around three that afternoon, checking people walking down the street, peering into gangways, alleys, scanning deserted lots, underpasses, viaducts. It was slow, tedious work, and ultimately fruitless, but it was all I had. I wondered still about the key and ID, but they were safe where I'd locked them away. I wondered also about the young girl's body in the can. It wasn't Ramona, but it could be Tonya. If so, how had she ended up there? *Why* had she ended up there? How did a kid go from the most perfect foster home, with a pink princess bedroom, to a dirty garbage can, under a highway on-ramp? And, worst of all, burned nearly to ash? And, God forbid, had Ramona Titus suffered the same fate and just hadn't been found yet? Was that why I couldn't find her? Would there be another can with another body found inside it?

I walked blocks on frozen feet, the tips of my gloved fingers stinging from impending frostbite. I doubted Hogan or Spinelli had done an on-foot canvass. Maybe a couple of unis had been deployed at some point to knock on doors, or not. CPD was huge, their workload immense, and there were a lot of kids out here lost or thrown away. If they had done a door-to-door at the onset, they sure in hell wouldn't have had the time or man-power to double back and do it again, unless the case was a high-profile one, unless the world was watching. For a kid like Ramona, it was easy to slip through cracks that wide.

Back at my car, after hours of walking, and nobody telling me squat, I gave up and drove back to Whip's apartment to see if he'd turned up. I knocked on his door, the knocking loud enough to disturb the entire building, but got nothing. I turned when the door across the hall creaked open and an old woman peeked out, her chain still engaged.

"Sorry to bother you," I said, offering my friendliest smile. "I'm looking for a friend of mine? Charles Mingo?"

"That's how you call on people? By trying to break their door down?"

I stepped away from the door. "No, ma'am. Like I said, I'm a friend trying to reach him."

"Another friend? Never knew Charles had so many. You, that young woman yesterday. *White.*" She whispered the last word, her eyes holding mine. That would've been Barb. "I haven't seen him since Tuesday morning, like I told her. He dropped me off one of his tuna noodle casseroles, bless his heart."

I stepped a little closer to her door. "Was he okay when you saw him? Did he say he was taking a trip?"

"He seemed fine. His usual self, I'd say. Nothing about a trip. Nice young man Charlie." Her face compressed in the first signs of worry. "He's all right, isn't he?"

"Yes," I said. As far as I knew, that was true. "Besides the woman yesterday, has there been anyone else looking for him?"

"Not a soul. He doesn't get much company, except for that little man who comes by sometimes. Also white. Short, dresses funny. He's real peculiar. Strange eyes. The way he looks at me gives me a shiver. It's like he's planning on killing me and is trying to figure out how much I weigh and how big a bag he's going to need to cart me away in. I stay away from him."

I turned, stared at Whip's door. The creepy little man had to be Pouch; if so, it wasn't murder on his mind. He was likely trying to assess how easy a mark the old woman might be.

I dug into my bag and pulled out my card and slid it past the chain. "I really need to talk to him. Do you think you could give me a call the next time you see him? Or if he drops off another casserole, could you please tell him Cass is looking for him?"

She read the card aloud. "'Raines Investigations.'" She looked up at me. "You said he wasn't in any trouble."

"He isn't. That's just where I work."

She looked relieved. "Well, next time I see him, I'll tell him you stopped by."

"And maybe give me a call when you do see him?"

"I can do that."

I thanked her and watched as she closed her door and locked it. I heard at least three dead bolts engage. I walked back across the hall, knocked one final time on Whip's door, out of frustration more than anything else, and then I left. As I bounded down the stairs, I called his number again and left another voice mail, this one more insistent than the last.

He didn't have to check in with me. I didn't own him, but we were friends, old friends. I worried that he was doing something that would land him back in prison, forfeiting the rest of his life. If he were in trouble, why wouldn't he have come to me or Barb? But he had, hadn't he? He came to me needing to talk, then he wouldn't. I worried about that all the way home, crafting nightmare scenarios in my head to such a vivid extreme that my hands shook on the wheel. Ben was wrong. I did know Whip, and something wasn't right.

I'd lost so many people in my life—my mother, my grandparents, Pop, my father, though he'd seen fit to return. What if I was losing Whip? What if I'd already lost him, and didn't know it yet? His car hadn't been in front of his apartment; presumably, wherever he was, he was in it. Who could I tap to help track him down? What if I did, and Whip was fine? He'd hate that. He might even resent me for overstepping. Could I afford to wait a little longer before I did anything? What if I waited too long?

I pulled to the curb in front of my apartment. Dinner with Eli and Dana was in ninety minutes. I had just enough time to shower, get changed, and get to the restaurant for what I had a good feeling would be the most painful dinner of my entire life. I grabbed my bag, keys, and locked up, trudging through the deep snow to my front door, feeling like I had a date for my own execution.

The valet took my keys and drove my car off, and I walked into Stefano's on Erie, right on time. Friday night, downtown restaurant, River North. I'd need a bank loan to get my car out of the garage. I spotted Eli and a sullen, pint-sized, female version of him sitting at a corner table. I'd just paid what amounted to half a week's worth of groceries for parking, but I was trying really hard not to let that turn my mood to vinegar. Eli had offered to pick me up, but that would have meant time in the car with you know who; and I had a feeling the less time we spent together tonight, the better. He stood and waved when he saw me coming his way. I waved back and snaked through the tables.

"Hey, you made it," he said, giving me a peck on the cheek. "You look beautiful."

I'd worn a simple black dress, nice shoes, which explained the valet. "Thanks." Eli was in a gray slim-cut suit and tie. He'd gotten a haircut and was neatly shaved. I smiled. "You, too."

I glanced over at a glowering Dana. She was small for sixteen, I noted, but the aggrieved look on her face was full-on. She slumped a little in her chair, and watched me closely, even though she tried not to look like she was doing it. Sizing me up. Comparing me to her mother, trying to figure out what her father saw in me. At least that's what I thought might be going through her mind, but what did I know?

"Dana," Eli said, smiling, "this is Cassandra Raines."

"H'lo," she grumbled.

"It's nice to meet you, Dana," I said; to which I received a half smile, and averted eyes.

I sat across from her, settled in, resigned to a long, awkward evening, but more than willing to give a shot at turning it around. All through the appetizers, Eli tried, poor thing, to draw Dana out, but she wasn't having it. Trying to help him out, I came up with a few questions about school, her interests, her friends. For a good forty-five minutes, I tried. For my efforts, I got either one-word answers, no answer at all, or quick shrugs and pouts. Eli had wanted things to go well, but I could tell he was getting frustrated and embarrassed.

Having exhausted my best material, and being overly solicitous to the point of fawning, I finally gave up and checked out. When the waiter came by with the dessert menu, Eli and I ordered tiramisu; Dana rolled her eyes at the waiter, crossed her arms across her chest, and ordered nothing. We sat in silence until the plates arrived, and then I dug in, hoping to speed things along. Eli noticed.

He tossed down his napkin and leaned in toward Dana. "That's it. You're behaving like a brat, Dana. What's wrong with you?"

I ignored them, spooning tiramisu into my mouth, watching the other diners enjoy their meals and each other's company. I left Dana to Eli.

"You took my phone. What did you expect?" she snapped, then cocked her head in my direction. "You didn't take *hers.*"

Another bite of tiramisu. It wasn't half bad. Not the best I'd ever tasted, but decent. I smiled at Eli. Moral support. All you, dude. All you.

"No one brings their phone to the dinner table," Eli shot back.

Dana reared up, scanned the dining room. "Oh yeah? I see one, two, three . . . six phones all around us."

"That's it. Apologize for your behavior right now." He said it in that Dad voice, his teeth clenched.

"*Apologize?* I told you I didn't want to come to this dumb dinner." Dana cut her eyes at me. "With a *homewrecker.*"

"Enough!" Eli signaled for the waiter as he and his petulant, and misinformed, daughter were caught in a stare-off of monumental proportions. *Homewrecker.* Didn't sound like a term a sixteen-year-old would come up with on her own. I felt the hand of Eli's ex-wife at play here. Again, not my deal.

The title did, however, sour my appetite for the tiramisu. I put my fork down and glanced around the dining area to see who'd picked up on it. Yep, everybody. The room got quiet as gawkers craned to hear the conversation at our table; the wait staff lingered in the vicinity without trying to look like they were lingering. I'd gone my entire adult life without being the third party in someone else's relationship. On principle. Hell, I didn't even take on domestic cases in my job, preferring to stay well out of other people's love messes. Now, here I was, being called a *homewrecker* by a kid who didn't know the first thing about me. I was shelling out at least forty dollars for parking and taking time away from a case. Yet, here I sat. For Eli. Because it was important to him.

"We're done." Eli signaled for the waiter, who hurried over with the check. "And *you* are grounded." He dug into his back pocket for his wallet and slid the credit card inside the little folder, holding it up for our waiter. "Cass, I'm so sorry about this. I thought we'd raised her better. I guess I was wrong."

I said nothing, but I watched Dana carefully. What I saw was a kid in pain. She wanted her parents together, but nobody apparently had bothered to ask her how she felt about things. She was likely holding on to her mother's anger, taking her side, which I couldn't fault her for. She wasn't old enough to know how complicated adult relationships could be. She believed what her mother told her: I was the interloper, the *homewrecker,* the reason Dana had to toggle between two homes and negotiate for each parent's time and attention. I could try to relay the truth, but she was sixteen. It was a conceited age predicated on the belief that life was black and white, knowable, rational, fair.

I eyed the half-eaten tiramisu. Smiled again at Eli. I felt for him, too. Working out Dana's issues was going to be a rough one. The waiter came back, Eli left a hefty tip, and we got up from the table.

"Well, it was a pleasure meeting you, Dana," I said.

She said nothing.

"Dana!" Eli barked.

"Fine!" she shouted as she trudged to the door ahead of us. "Whatever."

"I'll talk to her," Eli said.

I smiled. "Great."

"She didn't mean it. She'll come around."

I turned to catch Dana's wake as the kid pushed through the front doors. "Uh-huh."

Later that night, I lay in bed fully dressed for the streets and watched the numbers on my alarm clock change. My bedroom was dark, it was dark outside, dreary, and all of it matched my mood. Barb had called on my way home from Stefano's to tell me she had gotten me on the Love Bus tonight. I was to meet her and it in an hour.

It would be a long, shivery night, and my plan had been to get a couple hours' sleep to, hopefully, dull my memory of my dinner with Dana. That didn't happen. I couldn't drift off. Too much rolling around in my head, not the least among them being called a *homewrecker* by a kid not old enough to take a legal drink.

Had I been that obnoxious at sixteen? Probably. I was a handful for my grandparents almost from the first day I came to live with them—here, in the building I was lying in now. I'd come with only a suitcase filled with small clothes, a hidden Raggedy Ann I refused to part with, my favorite books . . . and grief, not realizing soon enough that my grandparents were grieving, too. They had lost their only child, and here I was on their doorstep looking just like her.

I blinked up at the ceiling, arms behind my head, my cell phone lying on my chest in case Whip called, or Barb, or anyone. For want of anything else to do, I dialed his number again and got bupkes. Insult to injury, his mailbox was now full.

I scrubbed my hands across my tired face. Maybe Whip had run away, too. Tired of slinging dirty rice, he had just taken off for Santa Fe or Timbuktu or Boise. Or? Or a lot of things. He lived light. It was easy to pick up and leave a life like that. Like Ramona, maybe.

The little tin box, left behind with Rose? Ramona hadn't much else in the way of treasures. Everything else she owned, according to Poole, could fit in a small bag. So, why leave the box? Why leave it with Rose? Was she hiding its contents from Poole or Shaw? Martini? Hogan? If so, not a bad strategy, but what was the connection?

"Smart girl, Ramona, smart girl," I muttered. "So, where the hell are you?"

I glanced over at the clock again; only five minutes had passed. I sent Hogan a text asking if he'd heard anything else about that body, or been able to get hold of Tonya, so I'd know it wasn't her. I knew it was early stages, but that didn't stop me being desperate for answers. If the dead girl turned out to be Tonya, this thing would take off in a totally different direction, and Ronald Shaw would be my suspect number one.

Once more, since the phone was already in my hands, I dialed Ramona's cell. It was becoming habit, a thing I did as reflexively as coughing or blinking. It reminded me of calling in to a radio station, dialing incessantly, getting a busy signal, hanging up, and dialing back in hopes of getting through for concert tickets. I called Ramona's phone, hoping to get through, only to get nothing, and yet I dialed again, and again, and again . . .

Someone picked up. I startled, only half believing it. I eased up in bed, listening to the open line, afraid to even breathe. "Hello? Ramona?" Someone was definitely breathing on the other end. The sound was low, hardly audible, but it was there. My palms began to sweat. "I'm Cassandra. Are you safe? Do you need help?" There was just the breathing. I swung my legs over the side of the bed, sweating like a faucet. "I'd like to help you, Ramona, if this is you. No judgment, no hassle, just help." The breathing gave way to a slight rustle, like someone was moving the phone from one ear to the other. "Don't hang up, okay? Talk to me?" Nothing. "I have something of yours." I needed to keep the line open. "Ramona? The things you left behind in a safe place? The box." I wiped sweat from my forehead, my heart beating like mad. "You're going to have to tell me what they mean, though. I don't have a clue. I'm not the police, if that's what you're worried about. A lot of people are worried about you, Ramona. Your mother, the Knowleses, Ms. Poole . . . Maybe if you . . ."

The line went dead.

"Crap!" I shot up from the bed, dialed right back, but the phone had gone dead again. She was likely only using it in short bursts, turning it on for just seconds, then disabling it again. I'd gotten lucky last time. I kept saying her, but was it her? Her phone could have been stolen, sold, lost. I could have been talking to someone who hadn't a clue what I was talking about.

I tossed the phone into a chair, kicked shoes aside, knocked the pillows and blankets off the bed, then stood there, chest heaving, glaring at the mess I'd made. It was stupid. All I'd done was make work for myself. I paced the floor while I calmed down; then I went about putting everything back where it belonged.

It was now forty-five minutes until time to meet the bus. I squeezed my eyes shut, inhaled, exhaled. I wasn't going to make it. I was going to implode long before then.

Chapter 17

I heard the Love Bus long before I saw it, and I stepped out of my building and watched as the converted school bus lumbered down my street. Its engine burped, wheezed, choked to death, black exhaust puffing out of the tailpipe. It was the middle of the night, and I worried about the noise waking my neighbors. It had been Barb who insisted on the door-to-door service. Had I known the Love Bus was just this side of scrap, I'd have just tailed along after it, instead of riding it.

I stood at the curb and watched as the bus groaned to a stop in front of me, wheezing like an old man who had just mounted a flight of stairs. It was colorful, though. It was painted rainbow colors, with big red hearts, yellow suns and balloons all over it. Cheerful, no doubt, in July, out of place in December amongst all the Santas, angels and reindeer.

The door opened and Barb bounded out, bundled up like an Iditarod racer. She smiled, her red hair peeking underneath her cap, and swept her arms toward the bus with a welcoming flourish. "All aboard the Love Bus, baby." She looked excited, like we were embarking on a girls' trip to Vegas, or something. "Free as the breeze. No line. No waiting."

I took the bus in. "That's it?"

An older black woman climbed out of the driver's seat and stood next to Barb, grinning, her dark cheeks kissed by cold, her brown eyes alive, dancing. She looked happy, far too happy.

"Sister Marian, our driver for the evening," Barb said. "Marian, this is my friend Cass, the one I've been telling you about ad nauseam."

I slid Barb a look. "*Ad nauseam,* really?"

Barb grinned. "There was a lot to cover. Marian doesn't let just anyone on her bus."

Sister Marian chuckled, then held out a hand for a shake, pudgy fingers sticking out of fingerless gloves. "She's right about that. The Love Bus doesn't take just anybody."

Sister Marian was sixtyish, stout, round, dressed in a wooly sweater under purple ski overalls, heavy boots on her feet. I chalked her wardrobe up to the season, but also to the dodginess of the bus. The way it looked and sounded, there was a good possibility we would either have to walk or hitch home.

Barb and I were dressed almost alike—jeans, hiking boots, fleece jackets under warmer Thinsulate jackets, and beanie caps pulled low on our heads.

"We look like twins, or something," Barb joked. "Who'll be able to tell us apart?" She jabbed a playful elbow into my side.

I smiled, but I was still distracted by the one-sided call I'd just been on. Ramona, or not Ramona. If Ramona, why now? If not Ramona, who? Barb noticed, but kindly said nothing.

"Well, let's get going," Sister Marian said. "We're doing no good standing around here."

"Wait. It's just the two of you?"

"Sure," Barb chirped. "Why?"

"You drive into some rough areas. Where's your security?"

They were two nuns driving around in the middle of the night in a bus filled with goodies. Nothing about that sounded good. Whose idea was this?

Barb pointed a finger heavenward. "We have the best security ever."

I stared at Barb, worried now about her sanity. She was no babe in the woods. She'd grown up in the same place I did, seen the same things I'd seen. True, she was no cream puff. She could probably take me in a cage match, but she was driving around the streets of Chicago in a hippie bus full of sandwiches and blankets with only an old black nun in ski overalls as her wingman? "Are you serious right now?"

Marian jumped in. "We're perfectly safe. I give the police our route every time we go out, there's a two-way on the bus, and we've got our cells. The officers don't follow us the whole time, but they make frequent loops to make sure we're getting along okay. Besides, nobody bothers us. They love us. We're the Love Bus."

I stared at them both, blankly, not knowing what to say.

"You used to be a police officer, Barbara tells me," Marian said, grinning. "So tonight we'll have triple security." She clapped her hands together once. "So come on. Hop up, let's do this."

Marian started it up, which restarted the clatter. Barb hooked her arm in mine. "This is going to be fun."

I slid her a look. "Does your mother know you're doing this? Or your brothers, one of whom happens to *be* a cop?"

Barb stopped. "You wouldn't dare."

"Oh yes, I would."

She pulled her arm away. " 'Snitches get stitches.' "

"Better than *nuns get dead*."

She gave me a death stare. "Get on the bus."

"Oh, I'm getting on the bus."

She shoved me as I passed her. "For the record, no one likes a narc."

There it was, that tough-as-nails South Side Irish underneath all her *Sound of Music* nun sugar. I turned, stuck my tongue out at her. Inside, the bus had been completely reconditioned, most of the bench seating removed in favor of shelves holding almost everything someone sleeping rough might need, but couldn't get. There were warm blankets stacked high, the pile almost as tall as I was, bottles of over-the-counter meds (aspirin, cough syrup, stomachache remedies), toiletries (bars of soap, tooth-paste, toothbrushes, mouthwash, lotion, combs, nail clippers), snacks (potato chips, chewing gum, Ho Hos, hard candies), and even books, magazines, puzzles, and little toys for kids. All free. All courtesy of the Love Bus.

"Wow," I said. "You guys aren't playing around, are you?"

"The need is so great," Barb said rather solemnly. "We could give out a hundred times more if we had the space, and even that wouldn't be enough."

The bus took off, pointed toward the need. Barb and I shared a bench. "So, how's the case going?" she asked. I told her about the phone call. How it posed more questions than gave answers.

"It has to be her, right? Who else could it be?"

I shook my head. "I want it to be Ramona, but I can't swear it was her."

"We see a lot of runaways out here," Marian said from be-hind the wheel, over the noise of the grumbling engine. "Some as young as twelve. It breaks your heart. Tell me a little about the one you're looking for."

"Her name's Ramona Titus," I answered. "She's fifteen. A foster kid who took off from her foster home. No one knows why she took off, but she's out here somewhere." Neither Barb nor Marian made any comment. We all knew what that meant.

"There's a pied piper of sorts out here," Marian said. "They call him Scoot. He leads a close group of runaways. They never get too close, and none of them will offer any information about themselves, but we might see him tonight and get the tide to turn. With any luck, he's seen your girl." She glanced back at me through the rearview. "You're going to need a soft touch, though. We want them to feel comfortable coming up to the bus without being afraid we're going to turn them in to Social Services. No strong-arming, no pressure. Got it?"

I looked over at Barb, wondering exactly what she'd told Marian about me. "No problem."

The bus sped up, rattling to beat the band. "All righty, then. Here we go."

Barb grinned. "Buckle up, buttercup."

"You nuns are weird, you know that, right?"

After a time, the rattling bus came to a hissy stop in an empty lot off Garfield Boulevard in the Washington Park neighborhood. Not too far from my neck of the woods. Sister Marian routed the bus to circle the wide swath of gritty blocks where homeless and runaways were known to hang. It wasn't that far from Poole's home, either; Ramona could have made it here, though the area hadn't been marked off with a pushpin on her search map.

Marian parked the bus next to a dark, paint-peeled viaduct with a blinking streetlight nearby, the only source of half-light. The spot was just off 55th Street, a few blocks east of the Dan Ryan, a few west of the CTA's Green Line. I peered out the side windows to see makeshift tents strung up along the graffiti-filled walls, with humans wrapped in blankets and scraps of clothing huddled inside. The mounds of blankets, the scraps of clothing, began to move when the bus came to a stop. Homeless. People. Living out in the cold in America.

They came toward the Love Bus in pairs and in small groups from everywhere, it seemed, dragging their bags and carts, or lugging everything they owned on their backs. Everyone was looking for food or medicine or warmth—for human touch, a smile, compassion.

It didn't take long at all for a line to form. At one point, I counted twenty or so waiting at the door. Young and old, black and white, able and disabled, those who perhaps should have been hospitalized with mental issues, but didn't have the access. Lost people. People who had walked away from those who knew them, or, worse yet, had been rejected and asked to go.

"Finished that book I got last time, Sister M," said a gap-toothed Hispanic man of indiscriminate age, who was layered head to toe in dirty cast-off clothing two sizes too big for him. "That was some deep shit." He cackled.

Marian beamed, her hands on her hips. "Told you you'd like Faulkner, Ernesto. Ready to try something new?" She flicked her brows playfully. "Something downright subterranean?"

"Bring it on, woman," he said.

She handed over a paperback of Langston Hughes poems, not from the shelves or the boxes, but from one of her pockets; she'd apparently been saving this one special just for him. "Poems this time, but still deep as the ocean."

Ernesto took the book and shoved it inside his filthy parka. "Don't worry about me, Sister M. I learned to swim long time ago." The two shared a laugh and then he shuffled off.

I turned to Sister Marian. "That's all he came for? Something to read?"

"There are all kinds of need, Cass. Today, he needed just the book. Next time, maybe a pair of warm boots. We're here for all of it."

The plight of the homeless, of course, was not new to me, but seeing it again, at eye level, knowing there would be no end to it, made it somehow a new thing in a new way. I went back to handing things out, smiling, keeping an eye out for run-aways. Sticking to Sister Marian's request that I not badger anyone who showed up, I'd taped the flyer with Ramona's photo on it up at the back of the bus and at the front door, hoping that if anyone recognized her, they'd say so.

When the crowd thinned, a tall, skinny white kid, maybe

seventeen or eighteen, walked up, his eyes glued to the flyer. Did he recognize Ramona, or was he just curious? He didn't look as rumpled and scrappy as Ernesto had. His clothes were old, but neat enough, his army boots scuffed and broken in, but passable. The gray skullcap he wore was slightly threadbare, his black hair, long at the back, brushing his shoulders, and though his old leather car coat was peeling, he walked with a swagger, coolness personified.

He pointed at the flyer. "What's with that?"

I could feel Barb and Marian stop behind me, and knew they were listening. "She ran away. Her name's Ramona. I'm hoping to find her, bring her home safe." We said nothing for a moment or two. His gray eyes were piercing, shrewd.

"Your kid?"

"No. But her mother asked me to look for her. Have you seen her?"

He backed away. "Me? Nah. Don't know her."

"That's too bad," I said. "Maybe you could take another good look at the picture, then. If you do see her around, maybe mention her mother misses her, and would like to hear from her."

He pulled his cap down lower on his head. He gave me one final look, then looked beyond me to address Sister Marian. "Got anything good to eat back there?"

Marian rushed up with a handful of goodie bags with sandwiches, chips, juice, and cookies inside. She handed them to the kid.

"Here you go, *Scoot,*" she said cheerfully, sliding me a look. "You know, you would really be helping us out, if you could keep an eye out for Ramona, huh? We're here to help her. You, too, if you need it."

Scoot stuffed the bags into his pockets, backed away from the bus, from me. "If I see her, maybe." He watched me. "You a nun like them?"

"No. Just helping out. I like helping. It's good for the soul."

Scoot offered me a jaded grin, the kind of grin that said *sure, whatever.* How long had he been out here? I wondered. How had he come to be out here? He was a kid. He should be in his home doing his homework, sleeping in a warm bed surrounded by parents who loved him. There were far too many Scoots.

He turned to leave. I called out to him, unwilling to let him go, taking a final shot at getting through. "Scoot." He stopped, his back to me. "If you see Ramona, and she's in any kind of trouble, let her know I *can* help. She can trust me." He walked away without a word. "If you don't see me on the bus, Sister Barb or Sister Marian know how to get in touch."

I watched as he joined a small group of raggedy teens huddled up under a broken streetlight a few yards away. None of them looked like Ramona. He murmured something to them, and then they all turned to look at me, before walking off together.

Barb said, "You think he's seen her?"

"I don't know. What do you know about him?"

Marian said, "Just what you see. The best we can do is keep an eye out for them, feed them, and offer a safe haven."

Scoot and his crew disappeared around the corner, and a new wave of people crowded the bus. I went back to handing out goodie bags and books and such, my mind on the cautious kid in the leather coat.

Scoot.

Chapter 18

After the bus and a couple hours sleep, I was out in front of my building at seven shoveling the walk, too keyed-up about Scoot to sleep long or well. Besides, I didn't want Mrs. Vincent slipping or falling on the ice if she needed to go out for anything. I was halfway done with the walk when Hank Gray walked up, his backpack slung over his shoulder.

"Just getting off shift, huh?" I asked, leaning on the shovel, taking a break. Gray was a fireman with CFD, big enough to haul a grown man out of the flames, quiet enough to fit right in with Mrs. Vincent and me, in the three-flat we shared.

"Looks it?"

I grinned. "Maybe a little around the eyes."

"Two-alarm over on Cortez, no fatalities, thank God, so it was a good night." He eyed the shovel. "Need some help with that?"

"No. I got it."

He eyed the rest of the walk, the sidewalk running right and left, which I hadn't yet gotten to. "That the only shovel you got?"

"There's another inside the door. Why?"

"I'll be back out. Help you clear some of this off."

"Gray . . ."

"I know. You got it. Humor me. I'm CFD. We're special like that. Teamwork all the way."

I chuckled. "*Special*, huh?"

He pedaled backward, did a little football spike hustle. "You heard it right."

I went back to shoveling. "Yeah, we'll see about that, fireman."

"Save some for me now. 'Cuz I got all that." He pointed at the sidewalk along the curb, hardpacked with ice and snow. "Arms of steel, right here."

I shook my head and watched as he turned for the door. "Gray?" I called. He turned back. "Thanks."

He gave me a thumbs-up and disappeared inside, and I went back to the snow along my little patch.

Showered and dressed a bit later, I ate breakfast at home, skipping Deek's. I wasn't exactly change averse. I could deal if I had to, but in this, I didn't have to . . . yet. Aggie was going to take a lot of getting used to, a lot of energy, and I didn't have it at the moment. My bowl of oatmeal and slice of dry toast couldn't compete with Deek's half stack and bacon, but it'd have to do until Muna got back.

When I rang Deloris Poole's bell at 10:00 AM, in my opinion, a reasonable hour, I had a plan. I was going to ask her, point-blank, about the photo of her, Martini, and Shaw, and see what kind of reaction I got; then I'd see where that got me. I wished PI work was more exact, but it was just a lot of knocking on doors, getting doors slammed in my face, and whittling away at lies people told me. Drudge work, mostly, until you chased down the right lead, the one that tied it all up, if you ever did. Sometimes you got nothing but sore feet and an open file that stayed open for want of resolution. I hated when that happened.

Poole opened the door, and for a split second, it looked like she was not thrilled to see me standing there. It was just a fleeting flicker in the eyes—shock, then a guardedness I could almost wrap my fingers around. She smiled sweetly after that initial moment, and opened the door to let me in.

"I wanted to talk to you again," I said lightly, pretending I hadn't noticed how cautious she seemed. "I've come across something, and I'd like your take on it, if you have a few minutes?" She was fully dressed, smartly, in slacks and a wool sweater, like she was planning on going out. "I'm not keeping you, am I? I promise I'll be quick."

Her smile widened. "Of course not. I've got a doctor's appointment, that's all, but I've got a few minutes before I have to leave. Have you found something? Please tell me you have."

She led me to the living room. Same couch. Same chair. I sat, placed my bag next to me. "How well do you know Ronald Shaw?"

"The case manager?"

I nodded, watching her.

"I wouldn't say well. We've talked on the phone several times. He's been here to drop off girls or pick them up. He seems like a nice person, a bit frazzled, overworked. I'd imagine his workload is horrendous. I've offered him tea once or twice, and we've talked about the system, about the kids and how they're adjusting. Why?"

I reached into my bag. "I've come across something that doesn't seem like it fits. It's been worrying me, and instead of letting it keep worrying me, I thought I'd just come by and ask. See if there wasn't an obvious explanation."

Poole's eyes tracked my hand as it slid into my bag and then all the way back out again. I had her complete attention. I unfolded the copy of the photos and handed them to her without saying anything first; then I waited for her to look at them.

"This is us discussing Ramona. I was worried sick. Still am. I've hardly slept or eaten."

"That's what I figured," I said, my eyes steady on hers. "But notice the date stamp."

The stamp was in the top right corner, and Poole squinted at the small numbers, then at me, a quizzical look on her face. "I don't know what I should be seeing?"

"According to the date there, that photo was taken, I think by Ramona, a week before she ran away. Shaw, I get. You, I get. But there should be no reason why the two of you would be talking to a former cop doing legwork on Ramona's case . . . before there was a case. His name is Frank Martini."

She stared at the photograph a moment longer, then thrust it back at me. "The date has to be wrong then. Martini, yes. He came with Mr. Shaw. We discussed what we could do to help find her, but this is after she left, not before."

I took the photo back, not sure I believed her. "You're sure?"

She shook her head, adamant. "Absolutely sure. The date is wrong. It happens."

I refolded the copies, held them. "That's true. But just to be clear, you never met Martini before you reported Ramona missing? The first time you came in contact with him was after the police sent uniformed officers around to take the report, and after the case was bumped to Detective Hogan? That's when he showed up with Shaw."

I watched as Poole steepled her fingers, rubbed them, placed them in her lap, then clasped them there. Nervous movement, though she appeared unflustered and cool otherwise. She shrugged, confused, at a loss. "That's true."

I slid the copies back in my bag. "Then you're probably right. The date must be wrong." I rose, projected disappointment. "I'll press on."

Poole rose, too. "Thank you. I don't know what I'd do if I didn't know you were out there looking for Ramona night and day." She walked me to the door. "But those photos. Where did you get them? Not her room. You would have said."

I opened the door to leave. "Yes, I would have said. No, I got lucky and found a few things. Nothing significant to report yet, but one step at a time, right?"

"Right. I'm so glad you're making progress," she said.

I stepped out onto the porch. "Thanks again."

Poole was standing on her porch without a coat on when I pulled away from the curb. Half a block up, I glanced back at her through the rearview. She was still there.

Around the corner, I pulled over and texted Martini, keeping it short and sweet: **Found something. Just left Poole's. Busy now, but I'll be in touch.** I slipped the phone in my pocket, and then pulled back into traffic. If the photos meant nothing, then no harm done. If they were significant, as I had a feeling they were. I'd just tossed a match on a pile of dry leaves. So be it. I was tired of fooling around now. Let the leaves burn.

At a light, my phone rang. "Hello?"

"Is this Cassandra Raines?"

I didn't recognize the number, but the voice was vaguely familiar. "It is. Who am I speaking to?"

"Florence Kennison, Charlie's neighbor? You wanted me to call if I saw him?"

I tensed. "Yes, yes, of course, Miss Kennison. Thank you."

"Well, he just went into his place about five minutes ago. I tried speaking, but he just rushed right on by me. That's not like Charlie at all."

I marked the street I was on, calculating in my head the fastest route to Whip's place. I checked traffic, cleared at the intersection, and then made a sharp U-turn, heading back the other way to zip over to the Eisenhower heading south. "I'm on my way. Don't let him leave. Be there in fifteen minutes." I laid on the horn to get the car in front of me moving. "Or less."

Seventeen minutes later, I screeched to a stop in front of Whip's building. There was no answer to my knocks at his door. Across the hall, Kennison's door opened, this time no security chain.

"You missed him. He rushed in, rushed right back out. I stopped him on his way down and told him you'd been trying to catch him, that you were on your way."

"And he just left?"

"He ran down the stairs and out like the devil himself was chasing him."

I stood in the hall and eyed Whip's door, bewildered. What the hell was he up to? I turned to the woman. "He didn't say *anything*, or leave me a message?"

"Not a thing."

"Is there a landlord in the building, someone who'd have a key to his apartment?"

She shook her head. "Only comes around here to collect the rent, or raise it, more like. It did seem like Charlie knew you, though," Kennison said. "When I told him you were by here looking for him, it looked like he wanted to say something, but he just went on."

That was it. There was nothing more I could do. I was relieved he wasn't dead or lying in a ditch somewhere, but that didn't take much of my worry away. He was avoiding me, actively avoiding me, and I had no idea why.

"Thanks for calling. I appreciate it." I turned to leave.

"I have a key to his place."

I turned back. "What?"

"He has one to my apartment, too, for emergencies. But you being so worried has me worried. If something's going on with him, if you need the key . . ."

"I need it."

"I won't be letting you in to steal from him, would I? You're not some crazy ex-girlfriend?"

My jaw tightened. Valid question, though. "I'm a worried friend, that's all."

She gave me one last appraising look. "All right, then. Hold on."

She disappeared from the door, reappearing in less than a minute with a silver key on a string. She stepped out into the hall. "I'll be going with you, just to make sure nothing funny goes on. You look honest enough, but some of these young women nowadays are something else, flitting all over the place, half dressed, chasing after any piece of man. They need some home training, and if they were mine, they would have gotten it."

The woman moved slowly, but I couldn't rush her. I needed to take a look inside, and this was how I had to do it. "*Home training,* huh?" I was making conversation, barely, watching as Kennison slid the key in the lock and turned the knob. When the door was open, I slid past her with my apologies, and swept my eyes over the apartment as though I were searching for contraband.

Nothing stood out at first glance, nothing looked out of order. I'd been here a few times, but it wasn't like I was familiar enough with Whip's stuff or the layout of the place to know if something was missing or had been moved.

The kitchen was tidy, the bedroom neat. No drawers pulled out, no clothes strewn over the floor. I checked the closet. His luggage, a good-sized duffel and a rolling bag, were inside. The dresser drawers were full. I swept into the bathroom. The shower had been used, a damp towel on the floor, but his toiletries—shaving cream, razor, toothpaste—were still in the cabinet. Had he stopped home just to take a quick shower? I swept back into the bedroom.

"What are you looking for?" Kennison asked.

I spotted the hamper against the wall. "Found it."

I opened the lid to find a pair of dirty jeans, a smelly sweatshirt, and a pair of white athletic socks, which looked like they were encrusted with grease or sludge or something. I took a sniff, a chemical smell. Oil. Diesel? The legs on the jeans had the same stuff on them. The rust-colored splotches on the shirt looked like dried blood. I dropped everything back in the hamper.

"Oil and blood," I muttered low enough so Kennison couldn't hear. "What is he *doing*?"

Across the room, Kennison scanned the bedroom. "Looks like everything's all right in here. See? We worried for nothing." She smoothed down the edge of the comforter on the bed. "I expect he's taking care of some personal business, maybe even has a girlfriend he's spending time with." Kennison smiled. "That would be nice, wouldn't it? A woman would be lucky to have a man like Charlie."

I watched the old woman lock Whip's door and walk back across the hall to her apartment.

"Thanks for doing that," I said.

"Friends have to stick together, I always say. You want me to pass along another message when I see him?"

I didn't see the point. The last one hadn't done any good. "No, I think I'll leave it."

"I'm sure he'll call you when he's got a minute. You take care now."

She went back in her apartment and I stood there listening to the three locks engage again, baffled, worried, now more than ever. Oil and blood.

We were back on the Love Bus at 1:00 AM, doing the same thing we had done the night before, only it was even colder. Different spot this time, a few blocks east of last night's stopping point. I'd bundled up in extra layers, as had Barb and Sister Marian. Same overalls for Marian, though.

"Maybe we should just give him some space," Barb said. "Let him work out whatever he's working out?"

Marian chimed in from the front of the bus. "Couldn't help overhearing. You know what your problem is?"

Nothing that came after that question ever landed well, and I stood waiting for it. "No. What?"

She wagged a finger at me that took me all the way back to Catholic school. I slid Barb a look, a look that said, *You better come get your girl.*

"Finger wag," I whispered. "Finger. *Wag.*"

"Nun," Barb whispered back.

I said, "Who's about to tell me about *my* problem." I plastered a patient smile on my face. "Yes, Sister?"

"You're a control freak of the highest order. Unfortunately, life *can't* be controlled, except by God himself. Sometimes people fall away, sometimes you can help, sometimes you can't. But you have to be solid enough in your faith to trust that the Lord knows what's best and will see it done. In short, 'let go, and let God.' Pithy saying, but truer words were never spoken. Your friend, wherever he is, is in God's good hands. Your being there when you are needed is the best you can do. Patience. All in good time."

I let a few moments pass, watching as Sister Marian went back to passing goodies out the back of the bus. Barb looked over at me, grinned. "Truer words were never spoken," she said. "We'll talk about that control thing the next time we play chess."

Half the night went by without anything exceptional happening. The group was just as large as it had been the night before, with some of the same faces in it, which testified to the level of need in this community, and countless others like it. The entire time, I kept an eye out for Scoot, or any of the kids in his group. It wasn't until we were close to shutting down, around 4:00 AM, that I spotted him, alone, standing a little way from the bus, his arms crossed, leaning against a light pole, his eyes intently on me, his head cocked to one side, as though trying to figure me out before making an important decision.

I gently jabbed an elbow into Barb's side to get her attention.

"There he is." I kept my voice low, my lips barely moving. "Scoot."

Barb took a sly look, pretending she was looking elsewhere. "Maybe we should call him over?"

"That might not be the best move."

"Let's see." Barb stepped off the back of the bus, smiled at Scoot, and waved for him to come over. "Scoot! You wouldn't happen to like chocolate, would you?"

I kept my voice low, my lips barely moving. "Luring a kid with chocolate, Barb? How could you?"

"Shut up."

We watched as Scoot unstuck himself from the pole, but he just stood there, making no effort to come nearer. "Doughnuts," Barb said. "We're done for the night. It would be wasteful to throw them away. Would you and your friends like to take them off our hands?"

I held my breath, waiting to see what he'd do, breathing again only when he slowly approached the bus. I had about fifteen seconds to come up with something to say, more like ten.

"How many?" he asked when he got to us. He was talking to Barb, but looking at me, as though I might spring at him and pin him down.

"I'll check. Hold on." Barb climbed back on the bus. "How many do you need?" Subtle, I thought. Barb was trying to find out how many followers Scoot had. Smart woman.

"Whatever." Our eyes locked. "You still looking for that girl? What's her name?"

"Ramona. Ramona Titus. I'm still looking for her. Seen her?"

"You with Social Services?"

"No. Just helping out, like I said."

"What'd she do to make her run off in the first place?"

I could feel Barb behind me, hanging back, giving Scoot a chance to warm up. I didn't want to go into Ramona's specific situation. I knew nothing about Scoot, and my client's personal circumstances were hers to share or keep. "I'll need to ask Ramona that." I pointed to the flyer taped to the bus. "Sometimes, when you're fifteen, problems seem too big to solve. Sometimes it helps to have a little help. So, have you seen her?"

"Answer's still no." He looked around me, at Barb fiddling with the doughnuts. "Maybe she's better off out here."

"Nobody's better off on the street. She's a baby."

"No babies out here, lady . . . at least not for long."

My gut knotted. "Those kids with you last night." I thrust an extra flyer forward for him to take. "Would you mind showing this to them?"

He stared at it a long time, then took it and pocketed it. "Maybe."

"Thing is," I said, pushing. "From what I hear, you know everything that goes on out here. I could sure use your help." He said nothing, just stared at me.

"Silence," I said, "code of the street. That's how it's going to be?"

"First thing you got right tonight," he said.

Barb was back with the doughnuts in a box. "Here you go, young man. There are eighteen in there. Enough for all of you?"

Scoot took the box and backed away to leave.

"Wait," I called after him. There was no telling if I'd ever see him again. He'd been to the bus two nights in a row, he knew what I was here for. He'd likely avoid the bus now, at least for as long as I was riding it. I jumped off the bus, started toward him. "Give me another minute?"

"Cass, what are you doing? Get back here." There was a worried timbre to Barb's voice.

Scoot saw me following him, stopped. "Go home, *cop*. I got nothing for you."

I stopped too, giving him a lot of room. "Something happened to make her run."

He grinned, walked back toward me, close enough for me to

hear, but far enough away so no one else could. "Something always makes them run. Sometimes they have no choice. Sometimes they take too much, and people don't want to be bothered, so they lock the doors with you on the outside. Sometimes a lot of things. You don't know how it is." He ran his jaded eyes up and down my body, from head to toe, sneering. "Bet Mommy and Daddy were real good to you. Set you up real good." He leaned in slightly. "I'm taking good care of her, like I do all the rest, so go home. *Cop.*"

I tensed. "What's that mean, you're taking good care of her?" I moved forward. "Where is she?"

Scoot pedaled back, smiling. "Bye, cop. Go home, cop. See ya later, cop."

I rushed toward him. "What's that *mean!*"

He laughed, turned, and then ran off, the box of doughnuts under his arm. I took off after him. I didn't think about it, or decide to, I just went. Probably not the wisest thing I could have done, had I thought about it first, but I was in it now.

Barb shouted frantically from the bus. "Cass! Leave him! What are you doing?"

Scoot ran flat out, slipping some on the ice and snow, but not stopping or slowing. He was a kid, nimble, sure-footed. If he took a tumble, he'd likely spring back up and keep on going. I was of a certain age, four years from the big 4-0; if I hit the ice, I was going to break something and end up in the emergency room.

He checked for me, and found me there, my arms pumping, my legs, too, me praying the whole time I didn't catch a bad patch of ice and ruin the next six months of my life.

"Stop!" I yelled.

Scoot ignored the command. He gave up the sidewalk and darted out into the street between cars into oncoming traffic. I skidded to a stop before leaving the curb, waiting for cars to pass, then stepped off, having lost ground. Getting hit by a car was also not in my plan. That meant broken bones, maybe traction, months of PT, and that's if the darn thing didn't kill me right from the jump.

I ran across the street, brushing the back of a car's bumper as I passed it. "Scoot!" I plastered my eyes to his back, using it as my focal point. How long was he going to hold on to the box of doughnuts? You would think it would slow him down. Just then, I remembered I had left my bag on the bus. I had no cell phone, no ID, nothing. I should stop running. I should let the kid go, find him another way. I had no idea where he was leading me. A sane person would break off and go back. I dug in and sped up.

Up ahead, well ahead, Scoot suddenly stopped and turned, breathing hard, his eyes cutting, angry. "What is your problem, bitch?"

I pulled up to a much-needed stop, too. I was winded, heating up under my fleece and outer jacket, my vision blurred from the run. I hadn't been on my bike since the weather turned, and I was now feeling the effects of too little exercise. That, and the midthirties thing.

I leaned over, my hands on my knees, trying not to pass out. It took a few seconds. I straightened, pointed at him. "First, don't call me *bitch*. Second, what's *your* problem? Where *is* she? I swear, kid, if there's one hair out of place on her head"— I gulped in cold air, needing more of it, even though it hit my lungs like nail spikes shot out of a gun—"I'm going to beat the living crap out of you."

He smirked at me. "Doesn't look like you're so much." He hoisted the box of doughnuts higher under his arm. "Plus, I get nothing for helping you. I can't spend nothing. I can't eat nothing. Nothing gets me no place warm. So, bye." He turned, flicked me a look, then took off again. *"Bitch!"*

I wasn't ready, not by half, but I started up again, digging in the best I could, the word *bitch* still ringing in my ears. What was wrong with kids today? Homewrecker? Bitch? When I caught Scoot, we were going to have a conversation about respect, and by *conversation*, I meant something else entirely.

We ran for blocks, Scoot never once in danger of being caught. The only thing I could hope for was not to lose sight of him. Maybe he was leading me to Ramona, maybe he was luring me away from the bus. I knew I should stop, turn back, but couldn't do it.

We were heading back toward Garfield Boulevard, toward where Marian had parked the bus the night before. I saw Scoot zip into the alley behind the old Sunshine Bread Company. The block-long building, standing ghost-like in the dark, had been shuttered and boarded up for years, since Sunshine rolled the last loaf off the conveyor belt. The homey aroma of fresh-baked bread used to permeate the entire neighborhood, and jobs were plentiful before people started watching their carbs, wrapping their sandwiches in lettuce leaves, and Sunshine went bust. I stumbled up to the building, winded, in time to see Scoot peel a plywood sheet away from the back door and slip inside.

It was a big building, maybe a dozen floors, and all but the ground level had been wrapped in some heavy-duty covering, likely by developers hoping to revitalize the place. Bakers, packagers, line workers, delivery drivers, and office personnel often worked their entire careers right here, putting in the hours, manning the ovens, the kneading machines, keeping the files straight, some big pooh-bah at the top hiring and firing. I studied the layout. Dark out here, dark in there. Ramona missing, Scoot with the *bitch* and the box of doughnuts, and information I needed.

"I'm taking good care of her"—that's what he said. Maybe he's just messing with me? I eyed the boarded windows on the first floor, the door Scoot had gone through. What would I be walking into?

Leave it, Cass. Turn around. Come at it another way. Only a fool would go into that building.

I looked up to the roof at the battered blue-and-white SUN-SHINE BREAD COMPANY sign, then back at the door, the boarded windows. *He's taking care of her.* "No babies out here, lady . . . at least not for long."

I pulled the board away from the door and slipped inside into almost total darkness and an overpowering stench of rotting decay, like something living crawled in here to keep warm and then died. I blinked, and held my spot for a time, waiting for my eyes to adjust, as slowly a short flight of stairs leading up materialized. There was something else mixed in with the smell of the decay and emptiness. I could have sworn I smelled bread. It was impossible, of course, or had the bread smell gotten baked into the walls?

At the top of the stairs, through a glass door, I found myself in a long, wide room with crusted, paint-peeled pillars running down both sides. Everything else was gone. The Sunshine people had made a thorough job of clearing out.

Except for the sound my feet made on the concrete floor as I crept along, there was just the faint clicking sound of rat feet along the walls. I cringed and stayed well away. I got a whiff of charred wood, then. Squatters, maybe, or Scoot and his crew? Glass cracked under my feet as I made my way through what looked like a back lobby, the floor jade green tiles dusted over by years of grime, dirt, and rodent feces.

I moved fast, then, my eyes and ears open, figuring a fast target would be more difficult to get a bead on. Quickly, through the lobby, through the ground floor to the front of the building, where there was trash strewn everywhere: balled-up McDonald's bags, beer cans, whisky bottles, old clothes, broken chairs, and upturned buckets, which explained the rats. Squatters. I'd walked through hundreds of places like this while on the job. I knew it would take weeks before I stopped itching and got the smell of urine and rot, the sound of rat feet, out of my nose and head.

I found a staircase leading up to the second floor, wide, with ornate wooden railings with grand S's carved into the newel post caps. It must have been impressive back in the day. *"Welcome to Sunshine Bread Company. This way, please."*

I kept my back to the wall as I made my way up, on alert, hands up, ready to deflect anything that might come at me. Still, no sign of Scoot. The stairs ended at a long hallway with heavy wooden doors with numbers on them—201, 202, 203. Offices. Mr. So-and-So in packaging, Ms. So-and-So in human resources. All gone now. I passed a bank of elevators, only the doors had been removed, likely the cars, too, but I wasn't about to get close enough to the gaping holes to confirm that.

The smell of burning wood was stronger up here, and it seemed to be coming from somewhere way down the hall. Halfway there, hands still up, eyes scanning, focused, I heard a scraping sound and stopped. Metal on metal, or something like that? I followed it to a set of wide double doors; above them, MEETING ROOM A stenciled in flaked gold. I pressed my ear to the wood, hearing nothing at first, then the scraping again. It was coming from inside. I eased the doors open and went in, high windows to the left, the covering blocking out the light from the moon and the streetlights. It was as if someone had mummified the building, wrapping it tightly in strips of linen to preserve it for the afterlife. In the center of the room sat a fifty-gallon drum, a glow emanating from it. The source of the wood smell, someone's heat source. No clue to the scraping noise, though; I didn't hear it now, anyway.

Halfway to the drum, I felt a subtle shift in the air, an energy that wasn't mine. I wasn't alone. Startled, flat-footed, I reeled just in time to see a kid rush toward me, a baseball bat raised high, aiming for my head.

Chapter 19

I shifted, turned, which broke the kid's momentum, but also gave her a smaller target to aim for. She tried to adjust, to come at me again, but I kicked the back of her knee, buckling her left leg, then shoved her to the floor, grabbing the bat out of her hands as she went. Stunned, but unhurt, she scrambled to her feet and backed away from me, eyes wide.

I eyed the bat. It was an old Louisville Slugger, and it looked like some animal had chewed the crap out of it. If I hadn't turned around fast enough, the police would be bagging it as evidence to use at the kid's trial. I, of course, would be dead, or close to it.

I glanced over at the kid. She was a tiny slip of a thing, dressed in flimsy layers, her pink boots scuffed all over. She glared back at me as though I'd tried to bash her head in, instead of it being the other way around. That's when the shadows at the sides of the room began to move and I found myself quickly surrounded by Scoot and a ragtag band of half-pints. No one looked happy to see me.

"Hey, Scoot." I tossed the bat down, hoping to keep things

calm and cordial. The sound of the bat hitting the floor echoed off the walls. "Mind if we talk now?"

I counted six kids of varying heights, ages—a motley crew. Scoot made seven. Each kid had a weapon: one, a two-by-four; another, what looked like the leg to a dining-room table, spikes nailed to the tip. Scoot held a club that looked like it had been used more than once to stoke the fire. One gangly boy of sixteen or so had a shiv, dirty tape wound around the makeshift handle. *A shiv.* My tossing the bat now seemed premature.

"You crazy, or something?" Scoot asked.

"Probably." I looked around me, squinting into the dark. "Is she here?" My eyes held Scoot's. "Is she one of you?"

Nobody said anything. I walked over to the can, slowly, my hands up and out. The fire. It wouldn't last too much longer. I stuck my hands over the top to warm them, keeping my eyes on the kids, of course, and that shiv.

"You seem to think I'm the enemy here. I'm trying to help Ramona." I looked around the group. "Or any one of you, if you want it." I took in the room, what I could see of it. "Anything has to be better than this."

"Not stepfathers." A girl in back, wearing a bright red wool hat, glowered at me, her arms folded across her chest. My heart sank. What had she endured at home that she would prefer this to going back?

"What's your name?"

She huffed, turned away. The group chuckled, I didn't. I didn't see a single thing funny. I watched as she stepped back behind the others and shut down. The girl in the red wool hat. I wondered if after all this was done, would I be able to find her again?

"You're no cop, that's for sure," Scoot said. "No cop would be stupid enough to follow me in here."

He was right. No cop would have; *I* shouldn't have. "Good point."

"So we're supposed to believe you're here to help her." Scoot smirked; it was a tired, jaded, world-weary expression. Heartbreaking to see in a kid not yet twenty. "*Everybody* wants to help."

"Yeah, well, everybody's not here, *I'm* here. So, if you know where she is, please tell me."

"Or?" Scoot chuckled. "There's more of us than there is of you."

The group stirred, and it looked like the kids were deciding among themselves to make a move toward me.

"Nu-uh," I warned. "We're not doing that today." I stared each one of them down; everyone stepped back, except for Scoot. "At least tell me if you've seen her." For a moment, everything was still, quiet, except for the crackle of the dying fire.

"A body was found recently," I began slowly. "In a can much like this. A girl. Burned so badly they're having a hard time finding out who she is." My eyes held Scoot's. "It's not Ramona, but it could just have easily been one of you. This isn't a game we're playing here. Have you seen Ramona Titus, or not?"

She wasn't in the group in front of me; I'd checked every face, and none of them matched the photo I had of her, but she could be hiding in the shadows, watching me twist in the wind. "If she is here, it's safe to come out. All I want to do is talk."

I got nothing but blank stares. Scoot suddenly banged his club down on the floor, the echo of it whipping around my ears. He was calling our little meeting to a close. "We'll discuss your request. Be in touch."

"Discuss my request? Look, kid . . ."

The club came down again. "Kick bricks!"

"*What? Kick bricks?*"

They ignored me, and I watched helplessly as the band of baby marauders backed up into the dark, like specters melting into a witchy mist. Scoot gave me one final scowl, and then followed them. There was likely another door at that end of the room, had to be. That's how they had slipped in without my seeing them the first time.

I felt my front pocket, where I'd stashed a few business cards to hand out on the bus. I'd already written my cell phone number on the back, thinking ahead, though not perhaps for this exact situation. I'd also tucked a couple of twenties in my pocket, in case I needed to grease a few palms.

I bent down and placed the card and the money on the floor. "I'm leaving my card, and forty dollars. If you decide to trust me, and I really hope you will, call me? My office address is here, my numbers are on the front and back." I craned to hear, but got nothing back. "I hang out at a diner in Hyde Park. Deek's? If I'm not there, leave a message." I thought I heard breathing sounds from the dark; then, suddenly, it felt like I was totally alone.

"I'll have another fifty for whoever comes!" I yelled, hoping my voice carried to wherever they were. "No Social Services, no cops, just me!"

I eased out of the room slowly, back through the doors I'd entered from, and then hightailed it back down the hall, back down the stairs, and out the back door into the night, feeling lucky to be alive. Maybe closer to getting in touch with Ramona, maybe not. But I'd survived stupid. I felt light, reprieved, saved by Jesus himself, and I wasted no time putting significant distance between me and the Sunshine Bread Company.

As I walked back the way I came, I kept my eyes on the street, looking out for whatever. This was not the neighborhood for early-morning walks out in the open. Bad things happened to good people dumb enough to be out this early alone. You'd think me catching sight of the Love Bus turning the corner, and heading right for me, would be a good thing, a thing I would appreciate. However, even through the windshield at a good distance, I could see the heat of anger fizzing off both Barb and Marian. For a split second, I thought of taking off in the opposite direction, hitching a ride with a serial killer, but they were on me before I could get my feet to move.

The angry nuns bounded out of the bus and shot straight toward me, both harried and stricken with worry. I felt a little guilty at that point. They had no idea where I'd gone, which direction I'd run off in.

Barb shrieked, the high pitch drilling through my temples like kabob skewers. "What were you thinking?! What is wrong with you?! You just jump off the bus and run into the night like a crazy person?!"

Marian glared at me, her lips tight with disapproval. "On the bus. Now."

It literally sent a shiver down my spine, and I thought cops cornered the market on chilling deliveries. I sat next to Barb, beside the shelves of Ho Hos and donated paperbacks, filling her in, while Marian drove in silence. I'd hacked off a nun big-time. Was that a mortal or venial sin? I checked around for any of those old-timey rulers the old nuns in school liked to use. Didn't find one. Why was I suddenly ten years old again? I glared at the back of Sister Marian's head.

"I see you," she said. Her voice low, slow, and chilling. "We're not done." In that moment, she reminded me a lot of Pop. He'd have driven the bus through every street in the city until he found me, and when he did, I'd get an earful, then a lecture, then understanding, and finally a hug. Marian's eyes caught mine in the rearview. Just for a moment, before her attention went back to the street. It didn't look like I'd have any hugs coming. Barb shuddered. "A shiv."

I leaned back, closed my eyes, smiling. "I know, right?"

Chapter 20

It took me most of Monday morning to find Ronald Shaw's home address. I wanted to take another pass, rattle him some more to see what came of it. I couldn't wait on Scoot or the others. They didn't trust me and when you looked at it from their perspective, they had everything to lose and very little to gain from helping me out. Money was a temporary stopgap: It came, it went. The homeless stayed, the street stayed. Their hand-to-mouth existence didn't change. I'd made the contact and hoped it led to something, but I had to keep it moving. Ramona had now been on her own for almost three weeks, and in a couple of weeks the city would literally screech to a halt for Christmas. I needed a break, a lead, a miracle. Shaw lived up north, which meant sliding up Lake Shore Drive on a deceptively thin sheet of black ice, keeping well away from the taillights in front of me, monitoring the headlights behind. I could tell city plows had already been out, their tracks evident in the slush, but keeping up with the ice and the freezing temperatures, when more snow was predicted later, was a Sisyphean task.

I found Shaw's place easy enough, but had to drive past the address and park around the corner to avoid the residential parking signs and all the dib holders—old office chairs, busted baby strollers, orange traffic cones—sitting in shoveled-out spots, waiting for their shovelers' return. The practice of saving your spot on a city street was technically illegal, but so were a lot of things the city let slide until somebody made a big stink about it and ruined it for everybody else.

I'd stopped at Bettle House first, and was told that Shaw was out of the office, not feeling well, but there was no answer to the bell. I tried getting a peek inside through a small gap in the front drapes, but I couldn't see anything. There was no answer to a second or third ring. The street was quiet, but it was a workday, and most people were likely in an office downtown already dreading a miserable evening commute.

Nobody was around to tell me I couldn't, so I walked around the side of the house to the back gate. I rattled it, and waited to see if a dog ran up to bark at me or a neighbor next door stuck his head out to ask what the hell I thought I was doing. No barking dog, no neighbor. Nice garage, though, at the end of the walk. Looked like it was insulated. I checked the yard again, just for safety. No doghouse, no chain, no empty food bowl with *Fido* written on it, no gummed-up squeak toys left in the snow. Not a guarantee, but good enough. I eased into the yard.

Shaw didn't answer my knock at the back door, either, but there was a low hum coming from somewhere. It sounded like something mechanical, something running, and there was a faint hint of gas. I pressed an ear to the door, sniffed, thinking it was coming from inside, but it didn't appear to be. I turned, eyed the garage. The walk hadn't been shoveled. There were at least five or six inches on the narrow path from the back porch to the garage door. No footprints on the path, so Shaw hadn't walked that way since last night's snowfall. The hum, though. I suddenly got it. It was a car motor. Shaw had somehow gotten around me and was trying to get away. I ran for the garage, kicking up shin-deep snow. I was done being polite. A kid's life was at stake. Ronald Shaw was going to talk to me. Now. Today.

I yanked open the garage door and a wall of exhaust fumes flew out at me, knocking me back, stealing my breath, poison racing down my throat, up my nose, leaving a burning behind. I drew my jacket sleeve up to cover my mouth and nose, but my eyes watered and stung. I could feel the moisture freezing to my cheeks.

I stepped forward a bit, peering inside, and saw an old beater with a man slumped over the driver's seat. Shaw. I stepped back again, then bent over to cough my lungs out, grabbing up handfuls of new snow to rub across my face. What had Shaw done? Why this? Now?

I straightened, then covered up again with my sleeve. I needed to break the windows, turn off the car, stop the fumes. Simple tasks. Immediate priorities. I drew my gun out of the holster, turned it, and banged the grip against every pane of glass in the garage. The noise of it, at least in my head, was enough to rouse the entire neighborhood, but nobody came out of their homes. Not one person.

I rushed inside. All four doors on the car were locked. I peered inside. Shaw's lips were blue, his eyes half opened. He looked gone already. I ran back outside, grabbing needed air, more snow, then ran back in again, searching along the greasy floor for something to break a window on the car. I spotted an old crowbar sitting on a pile of junk. I grabbed it and ran around to the passenger side; after three hits, I managed to hammer a hole in the front side window. A quick glance over at Shaw. Nothing had changed.

Sticking an arm through the hole, I flicked the lock, swung the door open, and leaned in, turning off the ignition, a Porsche key chain hanging from the lone key. I checked Shaw. No pulse. He wasn't breathing. He was gone.

He looked a bit disheveled, unshaven, though he was dressed formally in a black suit and tie. Had he dressed for his own funeral? There was a half-empty bottle of Maker's Mark whisky at his feet, as though it had simply slipped from his hands when he lost consciousness. I noticed he wasn't wearing socks or shoes. In his left hand, he was clutching a brown medicine bottle. I looked around the floorboards for any loose pills, but there weren't any. Shaw had apparently taken every last one. No note. Nothing incriminating or out of the ordinary in the backseat. I eyed the glove compartment, but didn't dare touch it. I'd touched enough already.

I backed out of the car, out of the garage, leaving it all for the police. I stood in the alley, gulping air, feeling a little light-headed and sick to my stomach, then got out my phone and dialed 911. Had the stress of Shaw's job finally gotten to him? Was this tied to Ramona's disappearance? Maybe it was the photographs I'd confronted him with—the ones he didn't want to talk about?

Leaning against a garage on the other side of the alley, away from Shaw, away from what it appeared he'd done to himself, I waited for the police. The alley was quiet, almost peaceful, nobody out but me, and what was left of Ronald Shaw. At that moment, I knew only one thing for certain. Whatever Shaw knew, whatever secrets he had, he had taken them with him to glory.

Chapter 21

I walked into Giacomo's restaurant, and there was a big white guy at the door. He peered down at me, sneered. He was broad-chested; his arms as big as piano legs; his hair cut short, bristly. He looked like your typical strip joint bouncer, only this was an Italian restaurant on the northwest side at two in the after-noon. There was Christmas music playing—Dean Martin sing-ing *Frosty the Snowman*. I could not catch a break.

The big guy pointed toward a back table, where Martini sat drinking something dark from a short glass. I wove through the tables, catching snatches of friendly conversation on a day when I could have used some. Only I'd just discovered a dead man in a garage and then been subjected to repetitive question-ing from the police, and Ramona was still lost, and I was about to meet Martini, who wasn't firmly on the up-and-up, or so I suspected. Still, I'd called him and asked to meet.

"Since when does an Italian restaurant need a bouncer?" I asked when I got to the table.

Martini laughed. "He's no bouncer. He's the owner's kid. What else is he gonna do?"

I sat across from him, placed my bag beside me. "Shaw's dead."

Martini nodded, his eyes on mine. "Heard. Suicide. Also heard you're the one who found him. Tough day, huh?"

It was good to know the cop grapevine was fully operational. It was also good to be reminded that Martini was hooked into it and had his own eyes and ears. Was one of them Detective Hogan? Spinelli? The waitress appeared with menus. Martini took one. I didn't. "Nothing for me, thanks. I'm not staying."

Martini looked disappointed. The waitress didn't seem to care all that much. One less plate to bring out. "You don't eat?"

"Busy," I said.

He shook his head. "An army marches on its stomach, Raines. Remember that."

I reached into my bag and pulled out copies of Ramona's photos. I slid them across the table. "Shaw nearly swallowed his tongue when I showed these to him. Poole played it cool, swore the date was off, but I could tell they landed with her, too. The problem here is twofold, the date stamp and the three of you together." Martini opened his mouth to speak. I interrupted. "If you're about to lie to me again, don't. I don't have space in my head for another one. What do you three have going? Does it have anything to do with why Shaw's dead?" Of course, I knew Martini wasn't going to answer either question. I wasn't even sure I had the right end of the stick, but if I was going to push, and I was, I may as well push hard. Go big or go home, right? "What pushed Shaw over? Or maybe who?"

Martini put the menu down, stared at me; playtime was over. "I don't think I like where this conversation's going." I said nothing. He flicked a look at the photos. "You never said where you got those."

"You're right."

He played a bit with the menu, sliding it on the table, turning it. "Anybody ever tell you, you're a ball hog, Raines?"

"I never said I played well with others. Do you know what happened to Ramona?"

He didn't say anything.

"Does Poole know?"

Still nothing.

"Why'd Shaw end up in that garage?" I leaned back in my chair. "You can answer one or all, Martini, but your silence isn't going to put me off, if that's what you're hoping for."

His expression suddenly shifted from dark to light and he gave me a small smile. "I got no idea what you're talking about. I'm looking for the kid, same as you. Following leads, same as you. Maybe I met Poole before and didn't remember it. Shaw? Well, maybe I ran into him, too. If I'm looking for a kid and they got 'em in spades, paths cross, right?" He tapped the side of his head. "You get a certain age, things don't work as good as they did. Memory? Faces look the same." He looked down at the photos. "Maybe I could have met them, another kid, another time, but what I don't get is the heat you're giving off. It's almost like you're accusing me of something, and I don't like it."

I was and wasn't. I was nowhere near the accusatory stage, but something was sure beginning to smell funny. "No theories on Shaw, then."

"Shaw? I'm supposed to know the reason why on him? Maybe he was just messed up in the head. Maybe he couldn't hack that job anymore. There could be a million reasons why that went down the way it did. None of it's got anything to do with me. And as for the foster mother?" He stopped, bewildered. "I got no connection other than the one you see right in front of you. Period." He pushed his glass away. "But it seems to me you know more about this whole thing than you're saying. Like maybe you got a line on the kid. Funny *you're* the one who just happens to find Shaw? Why'd you keep going back to him? What did you think he could tell you?"

I wasn't about to answer. I stood. "Okay, then." I slid the photocopies closer to him. "See you around."

"Raines," he said. "We are on the same side, here, you know, cop to cop."

"Neither of us is a cop anymore, you know that, right?"

"Speak for yourself. I'll always bleed blue."

I wrapped my scarf around my neck, slipped on my gloves. "Suit yourself."

From the car, I e-mailed the photos to Hogan. Might as well stir that pot, too. He hadn't given me anything else on the burned body. Maybe he was holding out. But if the body was Tonya's that would hook her to Shaw, and Shaw to Poole, and Poole to Martini, who was just now sitting at a table not fifty feet from me, eating his lunch like he was a Mafia don with time and a half to kill.

I flicked on the heat and waited, knowing I wouldn't have to wait long. I didn't. The phone rang. It was Hogan.

"What's this?"

"Photos of your boy, Martini, with the now-dead Ronald Shaw and Deloris Poole."

"You took them?"

"In July and days before Ramona ran away? I think Ramona took them."

"Where'd you get these?"

I hesitated, not sure I wanted to tell him everything. "First, is there anything else on that unidentified body? Is it Tonya?"

"Raines!"

"I'll answer," I said. "I just need to know."

"Still, no positive ID, but I ran a check on Pierce. Bettle House had nothing on her. She wasn't even in their files. DCFS had her there, and guess who her case manager was?"

"Shaw?"

"Bingo. He quit DCFS under some kind of cloud. We're still trying to find out more on that."

"What about Ramona? Bettle knows about her, right?"

"Titus they have, so I've got no idea what's going on."

I ran a hand through my hair. "What did Shaw think he was doing?"

"No idea, and guess who we can't ask because he gassed himself? Now, where did you get these photographs?"

I thought about how much to tell him, deciding, finally, to keep it light. I mean, I didn't know Hogan any better than I knew Martini, and I had a gut feeling Martini was sketchy as hell.

"The where is not as important as the who and when," I said. "Ask yourself what would the three of them be involved in that might have led to Ramona's disappearance, and now, apparently, Tonya Pierce's?"

For a moment, Hogan didn't say anything. "You don't know for sure she took them, unless she told you herself, and if that's the case, we're going to have a problem."

"I haven't found her, all right? But check those photos, the most recent one. The vantage point? It was taken from the up-stairs bedroom at Poole's. The one Ramona shared with Tonya. You can see a bit of the pink drapes in the shot. If Ramona didn't take it, who did?"

And that's all I wanted Hogan to know for now. I'd shown him the photos, laid down the foundation for a possible the-ory—now I'd stand back and see what came of it. If one of them or all of them were dirty and up to something, they'd know I suspected them and maybe make a play.

"I've got to go," I said.

"Hell no. If you got anything else on this, I want to see it, all of it." He was angry. I could almost feel the heat coming through the phone. "I should have known this wouldn't work. You've been on your own too long, you forgot how this goes. I want whatever you've got on my desk now. And, God help you, Raines, if you're playing both sides of this—"

"Calm down. A deal's a deal. When I get something solid, you'll probably be my first call."

"*Probably?* Son of a—"

"Seriously, I have to go. My toes are getting cold."

"I ought to send a car and haul you in, you know it?"

I hung up, strangely comforted. Hogan's threat to lock me up felt more familiar than that partnership of cooperation we had been working under. This was how things were supposed to be, me working CPD's last nerve, them swatting me away like a fly buzzing around the potato salad at a backyard barbecue. I was grinning when I pulled away from Giacomo's, knowing that true balance had been restored to the universe. I had now played every card I had, and I was out of chips. It was time to see what the dealer had up his sleeve.

I watched the girls flit up the court toward the basket, the compact forward dribbling her little heart out, shoes squeaking on the hard court like an army of angry mice. A quick setup, the ball released, a sharp blow from Barb's whistle, and the ball ricocheted off the rim. Traveling. No basket.

"Watch that footwork, Shay! Fancy doesn't work if you get a call and can't hit the basket." She blew the whistle. "Okay. That's it for today. Practice again Wednesday. Don't be late, any of you, or I'll make you go to Confession."

A communal groan went up as the girls, all knobby knees and elbows, ran for the locker room. I sat watching the whole thing from the retractable stands at the side of the gym, my feet propped up on the bench in front of me, my elbows on the bench behind. I'd had a rough morning smashing out windows and looking into the eyes of a dead man, getting batted around by cops and used-to-be cops, so watching kids who hadn't had bad stuff happen to them yet was nice.

"Not bad, huh?" Barb climbed up on the bleachers and sat next to me, her silver whistle hanging around her neck, next to the small gold cross she never took off. "A little rusty still on the defense, but we'll be ready for Saint Aloysius."

"When do you play them?"

"Day after Christmas."

I grimaced, but kept my mouth shut. "I saw that," Barb said. "It's not all about winning, you know."

I looked over at her. "Since when?"

"Oh, hush. Anything new on Whip?"

"No."

Barb sighed. "Give it time. You still need to ride the bus?"

"I don't know. Scoot's not talking, but they know how to reach me. Besides, I think I'm on Marian's you-know-what list."

"Yeah, you are," Barb said. "You scared her bad. Me too, by the way. That was a dumb thing to do."

"I know. Sorry."

"You take wild chances," Barb said.

"Sometimes."

"Any idea why?" she asked.

I shook my head.

Barb stood, stretched. "Sounds like a topic for next Thursday's chess match. Meanwhile, you wait. For Scoot and for Whip."

"It's half of what I do for a living." My phone rang. I pulled it from my back pocket, read the number. It was Eli. "That's the part I suck at." My thumb hovered over the screen for a second; then I swiped IGNORE.

Barb saw the swipe. "Trouble?"

"What?"

She flicked a look at the phone. "Eli."

"I don't know. No. Maybe. I'll call him back later." Barb looked like she didn't believe me. "I will. Tonight."

"You want to talk about it?"

"Do you have a chessboard on you?"

She got up, dusted off the seat of her jeans. "Touché. Let me roust these kids out of here and then we can go get something to eat. I'm starving."

I stood, too, watching as Barb climbed down the bleachers and trotted toward the locker room to stop the giggling and the horseplay and herd the kids out the gym door. I blew out a breath, still smelling exhaust fumes on my clothes, in my hair.

Half my job? Huh, try most of it.

Chapter 22

The cops went through Shaw's house again Tuesday morning, but didn't find anything having to do with Ramona, Poole, or Martini. There were no office files; there was no suicide note, no old letters. Just one day, Shaw's there, living his life; the next, I find him slumped over in his car, good and dead. He wasn't married, so no marital strife to blame; he didn't even have a pet. I got all of that—not from Hogan, who still appeared to be in a bit of a snit, but from another cop I knew who owed me a solid. It didn't seem unfathomable at this point that Shaw might take his own life, but the question still kept popping up—why now? And by *now* that meant after two kids had gone missing from Poole's and I started asking about it. And why no shoes or socks? If you went through the trouble of dressing in a suit to meet your death, wouldn't you complete the look? Wouldn't you at least shave? The medicine bottle in his hand might explain it. He could have been impaired. That might explain his walking barefoot from the house to the garage, too, in the dead of night.

I was sitting in my office, thinking about that and other

things, trying to come up with a fresh angle, when Eli walked in. I smiled, stood to greet him, but the smile quickly faded when a sullen Dana walked in right behind him. Surprised? Yes. Happily? No comment. The dinner we had shared was still fresh in my mind. I had dressed up for the thing, paid a valet, made an effort, to be called *homewrecker* straight to my face in a crowded restaurant full of white folks by a petulant kid I'd never laid eyes on before. Although I felt for Dana, and sort of understood the spot she was in, that didn't mean I wanted a re-peat performance so soon.

"I hope we're not catching you at a bad time?" Eli asked.

The small smile he gave me told me he knew exactly what he was doing. He was forcing things again. If he'd really worried about catching me at a bad time, a phone call, even a text, would have done it. Just then, I remembered his call last night, the one I ignored. It appeared, then, that I'd brought this little encounter on myself. Shouldn't Dana be in school, anyway? I flicked a look at my watch. It was nearly 3:00 PM. Well past dis-missal time. Shoot.

Eli said, "This'll only take a minute."

That was a lie. It'd already been a minute, and that was one minute too many. I stood there and wondered what Eli had planned that he thought would only take sixty bogus seconds, but I kept my mouth shut.

He gently pushed the girl forward a step. "Dana?"

She glared at me, then saw her father looking and lightened up the look. "I'm sorry for my behavior at dinner. I was rude." Eli cleared his throat, a signal that more was required. "It was completely uncalled for. I apologize." She stepped back, hiking her backpack higher on her shoulders.

I gave it a second. That was it? I looked at Eli, then at Dana. Normally, this would be the point where I would peace out. This was far more drama than I usually went in for. I mean, my baggage was heavy. I had tons of stuff in there, but I owned it; I had it all sorted the way I liked it. I knew where it all was and how to maybe deal with it. Did I really want to add this on? A kid? Not mine, Eli's. Was I ready for the package deal?

I glanced over at Dana. The sour look was back. This little apology appearance hadn't been her idea, obviously. She was making nice to satisfy her father. She might not have been calling me a *homewrecker* to my face now, but I could see in her eyes that she wanted to.

"Give us a minute?" I asked Eli.

"Who? You two?"

I said, "Take a walk down the hall, maybe? Shut the door behind you."

Dana looked scared. She obviously didn't want to be left alone with me and turned to Eli for a little coverage. Instead, he gave her a reassuring nod, then stepped out into the hall and closed the door. I waited until I heard him slowly walk away from the door.

I sat down. "Don't worry. I won't bite. Sit."

"Look, I apologized, all right?"

I didn't say anything, just watched her standing there. After a few moments, she gave in and sat down across from me, her arms folded in front of her, defiant. She fidgeted some, avoided looking at me. I waited for all of that to settle down before I said anything.

"I did not break up your parents' marriage. Their divorce was final before I started seeing your father." She looked doubtful. "That's the truth."

"Like you always tell the truth," she snapped back.

"I make it a point, actually." That was true, unless I was working some low-life scum, or playing things loose with a cop. Those lies were tools of the trade and I didn't count them; real life was different.

"You ever meet my mother?"

"No, I haven't."

"You ever been to my house?"

Strange question, but I answered it. "I have not."

"But you *knew* him before the divorce."

"I met him last April on a case. Professionally. That's all."

"But you're sleeping with him now, right?"

She had meant to shock me, embarrass me, test me, maybe all of the above. "Yes."

She shifted in the chair, glowered. "I won't live with you if you two get married."

"We're not talking about getting married."

"Why not?"

"You want us to get married?"

"No!"

"Then what's it to you why not?"

She stared at me. "They'll never get back together with you hanging around."

"Who's hanging around?" I leaned forward, my arms on my desk. "Look, I get it. You want your parents together, but that's not up to you, or me. You obviously need some help working it all through, so talk to them, find a way to deal with it." I let a moment go. "As for me, my business is also none of your business. But I accept your apology, though it was coerced. Maybe a condition of getting your phone back?" I smiled when she looked up, shocked. I knew then I'd gotten it right. "I accept it because it's important to your father, who I happen to like quite a lot. Out of respect for him." I watched her closely. "But when, or if, we meet again, I'm going to expect some of that back. That's how civilized people behave, and that's how I'll expect you to act. Understand?" She ignored me. "Dana."

She looked over at me. "I heard you."

"Then tell me you understand what I just said."

She gritted her teeth. It evidently pained her to comply, but she really wanted that phone. "I understand."

I got up from my chair. "Then we'll wipe the slate clean and start again."

She stood, too, slung her backpack over her shoulder, shot me a look. "I don't like you."

"I'm not wild about you, either. You're a little snot."

She gasped. "I'll tell my father you said that."

"You won't have to. *I'll* tell him. Your plan to work one of us against the other's not going to work, either. Mainly because I'm not getting in the middle of this soap opera. You are your parents' problem, not mine. It's a big thing, maturity, but once you master it, you'll be well on your way to a happy, productive life."

"You don't scare me," she muttered, not looking all that sure about it.

"I'm not trying to scare you, Dana. But you might want to remember that feeling. The world moves fast, kid, it always has. Bad things happen. You have to learn how to absorb the hits and keep it moving. You'll learn. Thanks for stopping by, now beat it."

At the door, she stopped, turned with her hand still on the knob. "Who are you?"

"Good question."

After a moment of confusion, she eased out and closed the door behind her; only a moment later Eli opened it again.

"Sorry about this whole thing," he said. "You were right. Too soon. I didn't want to spring it on you, but I did want her to apologize for that performance the other night. It was important she do that."

"I get it," I said. "No problem."

He nodded, smiled, his eyes held mine. "We still good?"

"Yes," I said.

He smiled, opened the door to leave. "I'm glad. Call you later."

He closed the door behind him and I stood there for a bit listening as the two of them walked away.

* * *

A couple hours later, I was walking to my car when I heard someone behind me, their footfalls noisy in the hard snow. I turned slightly, just to get a peek, relieved to find it was a couple of kids, a boy and a girl, whom I recognized from Sunshine Bread. Scoot's kids. I slowed, and instead of going to my car, I walked toward Deek's, hoping they'd follow me there, praying they weren't hiding bats or shivs under their coats.

At the door, I turned to face them, shocked now that I had a full view of how underdressed they were for the cold. It was freezing, there was snow on the ground, ice in the air; yet neither kid was wearing a hat, gloves, or boots, and the jackets they had on were thin.

"Hello," I said.

The boy stepped forward to take the lead. He was light, with big brown eyes that looked like they had seen so much, not any of it good. "You said you got fifty if we told you about that girl."

The girl stepped forward. "For each of us."

"That's right. Come inside. We'll talk over dinner."

"The money first," he said.

I waited a beat. "Information and dinner at the same time."

They shared a look, began to back away. "What's to keep you from getting what you want and stiffing us?" he asked.

"What's to keep you from taking the money first and stiffing me?"

We stood there, the three of us, quietly.

"We're going to have to trust each other," I said finally. I looked through the diner windows. Muna was back. My mood brightened instantly. "I'm cold. You two cold? The food's good in there. We can warm up, eat, talk. Order anything you want."

They conferred with each other, then decided with an almost-imperceptible nod between them. I held the door and ushered them inside. We got some strange looks as we threaded past the tables to my booth in back. The kids looked like they had been living rough, which they had. Muna was standing at the counter when we came in and tracked us all the way to the booth. I saw her grab menus and head our way. I looked around the place. No Aggie. I could almost feel one tiny piece of the universe fall back into alignment.

"Got company, I see." Muna was talking to me, but her eyes never left the kids, who looked up at her with what looked like a mixture of awe and suspicion. Muna was a sturdy woman, stout, wide, commanding. She set three menus down on the table and then stood there with her hands on her wide hips, her jaw clenched tight. "Friends of yours?"

I looked across the table, smiled. "I hope so." I picked up a menu, though I didn't need to. This was my spot. I knew what came out of the kitchen. But I hoped if I picked up my menu, the kids would feel comfortable enough to pick up theirs. "The meat loaf's good." I peeked over the top of my menu. "The cheeseburgers are my personal favorite, but don't let me influence you."

Tentatively they both slid their menus closer and began to go over it, their eyes wide. I wondered when they'd last eaten a good hearty meal, and then I ran through my head resources I could tap to help them. Who could I reach out to?

I snapped the menu closed, handed it to Muna, who was still watching the kids. "That meat loaf will stick to your ribs, all right. It comes with mashed potatoes, a buttered roll, and green beans." She leaned over toward them, winked. "And old Muna'll even throw in a slice of chocolate cake for each of you, if that meat loaf don't fill you up."

Personally, I think she lost them with the green beans, but I sat quietly as they considered their choices, giving them plenty of time with it.

"Can I get a cheeseburger and fries?" the boy said, his voice tentative.

"I'll have the meat loaf," his companion said, gently handing the menu back to Muna. "Thank you."

"Meatloaf sounds good," I said. "I'll have that, too." I handed her my menu with a smile. I looked over at the kids. "And shakes? Chocolate okay?" They both nodded.

Muna took the menus. "Coming right up."

She shot me a look, one I understood. These kids were breaking her heart, as they were breaking mine.

"So," I said when Muna moved away. I put two 50s on the table between us so they could see it, keep tabs on it. "You can take it now, or take it later. Up to you." After a moment's pause, both reached for the money and slid the bills into their pockets. "First, thank you for coming to see me. I appreciate that. Maybe we could start with your names?"

"Why do you need our names?" the boy asked. He felt his pocket for the money, as though I might have plans to ask for it back.

"What should I call you, then?"

Another quick exchange between them. The girl spoke. "You can call me V, and him M."

I looked from one to the other, not wanting to push my luck. "All right. V and M. What can you tell me?"

"We know her. Ramona," said M. "She's one of us, sorta."

"Scoot found her," V said. "Like he found all of us."

"Where is she?" I asked. "Is she okay?"

"She's okay. We're all okay," M said. "We take care of each other. We're family."

"Yeah, Scoot holds us together. He keeps the pimps and pushers off us and finds places for us to hang out where nobody bothers us. He protects us."

M added, "And we watch out for him, too."

The girl said, "Ramona was there at Sunshine. Hiding. She heard everything you said. She thinks you might be okay. Scoot sent us to see if you were lying about the money."

Maybe that was the truth about Ramona being there, maybe it wasn't, maybe Scoot was trying to run a scam, string me along for the money. These were street kids, used to finding creative ways to stay alive.

"So, what happens now?" I asked.

M shrugged. "We tell him you were straight up."

The girl watched me for a moment, then reached into her pocket and handed me a note. "First we give you this. You gave us fifty, but if you want to see Ramona, Scoot wants his cut."

I read the note. Someone had written just the number 100. I looked at the kids. "I assume that's one hundred dollars?"

They both nodded.

"Ride the bus tonight," M said. "He'll tell you when and where from there. Bring the money with you."

Getting back on the Love Bus shouldn't be a problem, I thought, unless Sister Marian was still mad at me. "I'll be there. How'd you two get here?"

"What do you mean?" V asked.

"It's quite a walk from where we last met up."

M chuckled. "Lady, we get all over this city all kinds of ways."

V joined in. "By everything but a plane."

"There are easier, safer ways to live, you know that? People who can help? I could put you in touch with—"

"Save it," V said. "We're safer where we are."

"And we do okay just us," M added.

I sat back and let it go for now, but not forever. I was relieved to know that Ramona was safe—that's if the kids were telling me the truth and not just pumping me for cash. Time would tell on that, too.

The food came, Muna dropping off plate after plate, crowding the small table. The kids' eyes widened. Right on her heels came an angry Deek, who barreled up to the booth, frowned at the kids, at me, a vein throbbing at his forehead. Was he really going to make a big deal about feeding homeless kids? I braced, anticipating his nastiness, preparing to knock it back. "See you in the kitchen?" he asked.

I glanced over at Muna, then watched as Deek stormed back

through the kitchen doors. I slid out of the booth, headed that way. "I'll be right back. Dig in."

I shoved the kitchen door open and a wall of steam and sizzle from the old man's griddle smacked me in the face. The kitchen was just big enough for him, nothing fancy. The pots and pans and doodads were all worn down, as though Deek had been cooking with them since the dawn of time. Nothing shimmered or shined, there was no Spic or Span; it was as if he'd carved the place out of igneous rock. This was my first time past the doors. Deek was not the welcoming sort, so I'd never had a reason to venture past the dining area. Getting a good look now, I took everything in, as if the kitchen, *his* kitchen, would give me some insight into the grouchy old cur.

"What?"

He turned from his grill, his white apron smeared with whatever he'd been cooking, a white T-shirt and jeans underneath. His dark face glistened with cooking steam, his eyes hard, unreadable, his massive arms covered in Marine tats. Dealing with Deek on the odd occasion out in the dining room was horror enough; being here, in his spot, was like walking into hell and finding Satan sharpening Ginzu knives. "Homeless kids. In my place. What's your problem?"

I felt myself go cold, dangerously so. "*My* problem? Are you serious?"

"I'm running a business here, not some outreach center."

"They're kids. They're hungry and I'm feeding them. Are you really going to stand there and pitch a bitch about feeding hungry kids?"

He glowered at me, rough, gruff. "I been watching you. I see how you operate. Here's a lesson you haven't learned yet. You can't save everybody."

I took a step back, more for his sake than for mine. "What's that supposed to mean?"

"It means what you think it does. Every hangdog reject, and

you're off to the races. Who do you think you are, anyway? What're you trying to do? Save the world, one lost puppy at a time? Take it from me, it won't work. You'll burn yourself out, and the world will be the same messed-up place it always was and always will be."

I sputtered for a moment, not sure where to start. First, that was the most Deek had ever said to me in all the years I'd been coming to his place, and second, Deek didn't know me. We weren't friends; we weren't anything, really. Maybe once he and Muna had all but saved my life, but as far as I knew, Muna had driven *that* train.

"You're a horrible old man, anyone ever tell you that?"

He lifted his chin, slammed the spatula against the side of the griddle. "Not to my face, and not more than once."

"I'm feeding those kids. If they show up tomorrow or the next day, if they show up from now until I grow old and blow away to dust, I'm feeding them. I dare you to try and stop me."

"This is my place."

"So?"

We faced off for a time. I was breathing heavily, beside myself with fury. Deek just stood there, calmly watching me, no expression on his face. I couldn't tell if he was as angry as I was or amused at my declaration, given while standing in a room he owned, in a restaurant he owned, over food he cooked.

Finally he broke the stalemate. "You're as stubborn as a bulldog. Throwing you and them out would make me look like the biggest asshole around, wouldn't it?"

I was mad, itching for a fight, ready to start one, end one, I didn't care which. "You're already the biggest asshole around, and everybody around here knows it. Grousing about feeding *children*. What's wrong with you?"

He didn't answer. He just stood there glaring at me. After a moment, he turned back to his griddle. "Go on, then. Feed them. No charge."

I wasn't sure I'd heard him right. "What?"

"The kids. They eat free. Tonight. Whenever they need. Now get the hell out of my kitchen."

"Hey, you called me in here."

"Well, now I'm throwing you out. Go on!"

I stood there. Trying to figure the man out, getting nowhere. He was a grouch, a malcontent, since when did he have a soft spot? I wanted to know where he'd been hiding it, but didn't dare ask. Or what if this was some kind of fake? An offer he would deny making the next time.

He looked up. "You still here? Get out!"

I shoved the door open. We weren't done, Willis Deacon and me, not by a long shot. On my way out, I turned back, confused, to take one last look at the man, who, having dismissed me, went back to his orders and his griddle. I opened my mouth to say something, but he stopped me.

"No," he barked. "All you get."

I flounced out of the kitchen, cursing under my breath.

"What happened in there?" Muna asked when I slid back into the booth.

"I almost killed a man," I said. The kids were well into their meals, smiles on their faces. "Muna, while we finish talking, would you ask Deek to please work up a sack of burgers to go? He's paying."

Muna coughed. "*He's* paying?" She flicked a look toward the kitchen. "That old cheapskate?"

"In fact," I added, "let's just run a tab, okay?"

Chapter 23

I looked out for Scoot the entire night on the Love Bus, but hours went by, the entire tail end of the night, and he was a no-show. I'd just started to think I'd been had, when I saw him, alone, hanging off to the side of a group of homeless men, who'd just moved away from the bus with arms full of supplies.

Barb grabbed me by the arm, whispered into my ear, "You jump off this bus this time, and I'm jumping off with you, Marian too."

I turned to see the old nun giving me the stink eye. She did not look like a nun you wanted to test. I turned to Barb. "I don't tell you two how to pray, do I?"

Barb gave me a tiny shove. "I've said all I need to."

I watched as Scoot made up his mind and approached. "You got the message."

"I did," I said.

"Give me the hundred."

I smiled. Scoot smiled.

"You're the one wants to talk," he said.

"Doesn't mean I have to be an idiot about it."

I reached into my back pocket and pulled out a copy of the photos Ramona had taken, handed it to Scoot. "I came across these, along with a couple of other things. Ramona will know what, and she'll know where I got them. Tell her, if you know where she is, and aren't just jerking me around, that I need her to tell me why they were important enough to hide away."

Scoot watched me for a good while. He was a street kid, not prone to trust or confidences. He'd likely been burned a million times and would be slow to let that happen again. He slipped the copy into his pocket and backed away, pulling his collar up against the winter bite.

"Tomorrow. Midnight. Old junkyard close to the building you were dumb enough to chase me into." He grinned. "You're lucky it was me, and not some of these others out here. Half of them would skin you alive just because it's Tuesday."

I could feel Barb and Marian's eyes searing holes into my back. "This junkyard got an address?"

"I look like GPS? There's just the one. You're the PI. Find it. Just you, or we disappear. Show up at midnight, or don't even bother."

"I'll be there."

"With the hundred."

I nodded. "I'll have it."

He turned and hustled off into the shadows, gone.

"You cannot be serious," Barb said. "A junkyard at midnight? Why don't you just strangle yourself and fall dead into a casket?"

I frowned, not liking the picture she painted. "That's dark."

"You can't go alone."

"You heard him. It's me and only me. This is my best shot at finding out what the heck is going on. I know what I'm doing."

"What if he's luring you there for the money?"

"Then I'll find that out soon enough."

Marian slid in behind the wheel, prepared to close up shop

for the night. We'd nearly depleted our supplies; everyone had gone away with something they'd needed desperately.

"You're an obstinate woman," Marian pronounced. "Bull-headed, singularly unwavering in your tenacity . . . and fool-hardiness."

"Hey, you barely know me!"

"You're not that deep a pool, missy. I know enough." The bus started up and pulled away from the curb, headed for home.

Barb grinned. "She nailed it. You are stupidly tenacious."

"She didn't say *stupidly.*"

Marian jumped in. "I would have thought it implied."

I squinched my eyes, burning holes in the old nun's back as she whistled a peaceful hymn like she hadn't a care in the world. I plopped down into a seat, zipped my jacket up to the chin, and ignored them both.

I pulled up to the junkyard and peered out of the windshield at the weathered sign, hanging half off the chain fence: CHOLLY'S. I got out of the car to get a better look, though there didn't appear to be anything worth getting a better look at. It was a junkyard. It was cluttered, desolate, rusty, piled high with crap nobody with good sense wanted. It smelled like diesel and metal and there wasn't a light on anywhere inside the six-foot chain fence or outside it, as it was well away from the nearest building. It didn't look like a single soul had set foot on the lonesome lot in years.

"*I'm* stupidly tenacious?" I leaned inside the car, got my flashlight out of the glove compartment. My gun was there, too, but I left it. "*Stupidly.*" I'd been chewing on it for hours, rejecting it as hogwash. However, standing here alone in front of a beat-up junkyard at midnight, even I had to admit that maybe there was a little something to it.

There was an open padlock on the chain. I scanned the yard,

then unhooked the lock and swung the gate open. I hesitated before going in, taking a moment to look around and listen to the sounds around me. Inside the fence, there was a weathered construction site trailer that looked like it might have been used as an office at one time. Close to it stood a snow-capped pillar of truck tires stacked high and leaning precariously, a Tower of Pisa made of industrial rubber.

Sweeping the lot with my flash from the safe side of the fence, I saw no sign of Scoot or the kids. For a moment, I just stood there surrounded by detritus covered in snow, listening to the biting wind as it whipped around frozen car parts. Maybe this was a setup. Maybe Scoot got me out here for a laugh. I hoped not. I really needed to find Ramona.

I ran my flashlight along the fence to rattle it, make a noise. I was worried about dogs. That there might be feral ones inside that had taken up residence when the business of exhaust pipes and replacement windshields went bust. Nothing on four legs barked or rushed up to the fence. Good sign. I turned around to check my car. There it sat, all nice and warm and safe. I wished I were in it, headed home to a warm bed. Now was not the best time, but that scene from *Cujo* where the crazy dog had the woman and the little boy trapped in a car with no way out flashed in my head. Thank you, Stephen King. I rattled the fence once more, just for safety. All clear.

I eased inside the yard, the triangular cone of light from my flash guiding my steps. The windows on the trailer were busted out, I noticed, the door hanging drunkenly from twisted hinges. Some destructive kids or looters, no doubt. The growl was low at first, easy, and when I heard it, when my blood ran cold, I was well away from the fence. I froze in my tracks. The growl was coming from behind me, but I didn't dare turn to see. Halfway through the yard. That meant I was half a yard away from my car parked on the salvation side of the Cholly's sign. If I ran, even if I were an Olympic sprinter, I'd never make it.

Moving glacially, I brought the flashlight up, switched my grip, prepared to turn around. The growl grew louder as I moved, giving way to frightening baritone barks that were definitely not coming from a Chihuahua. This was a big dog, an angry dog, a dog I wished were not here. Hadn't I rattled the fence?

I made it around to find a mangy-looking black Rottweiler, his teeth bared, standing maybe twenty feet away from me, his muscled forelegs planted wide, his black marble eyes trained on me. There was a sturdy collar around his thick neck, with a small pouch attached to it. He belonged to somebody. Was he Scoot's? My second worry was that this dog had friends that also did not startle at fence rattling. My eyes swept slowly left and right and back. Just junk, as far as I could tell.

My gun was in the car. I'd left it there intentionally. I was meeting with children, and even though one of the tiny outsiders had tried to bash my head in with a bat, there was no scenario I could conjure where I'd ever consider shooting one of them. I didn't want to shoot the dog, either, though if he'd had the common decency to announce his presence while I was still on the safe side of the fence, I might have reconsidered leaving my weapon behind. I had my phone in my back pocket, though, and my feet were working just fine. I wasn't too proud to run. My stomach in my throat, I tightened my grip on the flashlight, one of those heavy-duty jobs. Best I could do.

The nearest junker was at least ten feet from me. I wouldn't make that—besides, all four doors had been stripped off. The dog was now barking his head off, inching forward with blood in his eyes, slobber dripping from his jowls. I tightened my grip on the flash, held it now as a club, then shifted to the balls of my feet, my mouth dry, hands shaking. Gnawed to death by a junkyard dog at Christmastime. I hoped to God I didn't die here surrounded by tires. The dog inched closer, slowly closed the gap between us. I braced myself and waited for its charge. I needed to keep him away from my neck and face. Lead with the forearms. Get the flashlight in there fast, give him something to think about. Okay. Eyes on Cujo. Ready.

"King! Come!"

Startled, I turned my head to see where the stern command had come from, thankful there was someone in this yard besides me, relieved that I wasn't going to have to knock a dog out in order to get out of here in one piece.

The dog stopped barking, twirled around in a tight circle, then moved back, just as Scoot and his family stepped out from behind a pile of car bumpers. The dog then fell in at Scoot's side, now as docile as a newborn kitten. My heart was in my throat, my legs shaking. I could have loosened my grip on the flashlight, as the immediate threat was gone, but I didn't trust either the dog or Scoot.

"You were going to fight my dog?" Scoot looked amused.

"This your idea of fun?"

He leaned over and scratched the dog behind the ears, grinning. "You didn't scream, or run, or anything. Points for you."

I could barely hear him over the sound of the blood rushing in my ears. I glared at the dog, who now couldn't have been more disinterested in me. I watched the kids in front of me, seeing the same faces I had seen before, the two from Deek's, three from Sunshine Bread Company, and one more.

In the back, a black hoodie pulled down over a thin, dark face, was a girl of about fifteen, with long braids hanging down past her ears. Her eyes left her boot tops only long enough to sneak a peek at me. She was trying so hard not to be noticed, yet she was all I saw.

Scoot interrupted my study. "Where's the money?"

I slid the flashlight into my pocket. "You're a little shit, you know that?"

Scoot laughed, pleased with himself. "The hundred?"

"I have it. Where's Ramona?"

"I'll take you to her. Don't worry," he said. "We're gonna take this slow."

I shook my head. "I'm done with *slow*. If Ramona *were* here, I would tell her that I found Rose and the box she left with her." My eyes stayed trained on the hoodie, the downcast eyes. "I'd tell her that I think she stumbled on something involving Detective Frank Martini, Deloris Poole, and Ronald Shaw. Something to do with the girls put into Poole's home?" The girl flicked a look up. Our eyes held for a fraction of a second; then hers were gone again.

Scoot chuckled. "Wasting your breath. She isn't here."

I ignored him. "The photos, the key, and a doctored ID for Tonya Pierce." I stopped speaking, but no one said anything, not even the dog. "Ronald Shaw is dead. Tonya is unaccounted for. There was a body found." The eyes flicked up, fear in them now. "If I had a chance to talk to Ramona, I'd tell her that I'm here to listen to what she has to say. I'd tell her that I'll believe her. I'd also tell her that I don't stop until she's safe."

The girl in the hoodie moved back farther from the group, but her eyes were locked on me. Scoot looked confused. Maybe Ramona hadn't told him anything about why she had run away. I looked around the yard. "This place can't offer much protection long-term. A baseball bat, a two-by-four, and even a shiv aren't going to get you too far." I turned to look at the boy who had brandished the shiv the other day. "I need Ramona to tell me why she ran, and what's going on at Poole's. I need her to trust me."

"We're done," Scoot declared. He snapped his fingers and the kids prepared to move out. "Give me the money, or I come and take it." He looked down at his dog. "With King."

I kept it up, my eyes on the dog, who perked up when he heard his name spoken. "There is way too much pink flounce in that princess bedroom," I said. "I thought so the first time I saw it. It's like she's working too hard to convince everyone she's doing the right thing for the right reasons. Maybe Ramona knows she isn't? Maybe Ramona has *proof* she isn't?"

The kids moved back a little; Scoot, the dog, and the girl in the hoodie stayed put. Then the girl with the braids reached up and dropped her hood, stepping forward. I recognized her now. Those big brown eyes, the dimples. She was thinner than the photo I had of her, and she looked like she hadn't been sleeping well, but I could see traces of her mother in her. It was Ramona Titus in the flesh.

"I'm here," Ramona said. "I'll talk to you."

I'd finally found her. Alive, well. Scoot and his gang likely had dozens of hidey-holes all over the city they could burrow into and I would never have found her, but here she was, not burned to nothing in a can, not stolen by predators, all innocence lost. Here in front of me, whole.

I exhaled. Took a step forward, damn the dog. "Nice to meet you, Ramona."

Chapter 24

Ramona and I sat in my car, the motor running, the heat on as high as I could crank it up. After the dog scare, I even locked the doors. I watched the others mill around the yard, lounging on cans, jumping on tires, goofing around like kids do, my crisp hundred-dollar bill in Scoot's pocket.

"How'd you hook up with him, anyway?" I asked, warming my hands pressed against the vents, glad to be out of that dirty yard away from King, who toward the end there looked downright disappointed he wasn't going to get a chance to gum my shinbones.

"He found me at the shelter. It was cold. I was hungry. I guess I looked like I needed help. He knows everything that goes on out here."

"And you just went with him?"

She shrugged. "He seemed okay. There were other kids."

I sat back, not sure where to begin. "Ramona, that wasn't smart or safe. What—"

She cut me off. "Is Mr. Shaw really dead?"

"I found him in his garage. It looked like he killed himself. You know any reason he might have done that?"

"Ask Miss Poole."

"She says you ran because you stole jewelry from her."

Ramona stared out the side window at the dark, at the snow. "You know, anybody could say my mother sent them."

"Oh, so now you're careful?"

She slid me a look. "I can take care of myself."

"Your mother told me about your grandmother and your grandmother's house, how you both were happy there. Looking for you, the police also contacted your aunt Marla down in Shreveport. I personally talked to your uncle Lester." Ramona frowned. "Yeah, I'd steer clear of him," I said. "Understand?" She nodded. "I can call your mother, put her on the phone. She'll verify everything."

She stared at me for a long time, then turned back to the window. "I don't want to talk to her yet."

"You've got good reason not to trust her, I know. But you're going to have to trust somebody. Hanging out in a junkyard and an old bread company is not a long-term life plan."

"If I didn't run, I had a feeling Mr. Shaw would come for me, like he did Tonya. I liked it at the Knowleses. They liked me too. I knew things probably weren't going to work out with my mother, so I hoped to stay there. Then I got moved to Miss Poole's. Something about therapy." She looked at me. "There wasn't any therapy. Then she said she got off drugs again and started calling. Then Tonya got moved out. There was something off about him. Miss Poole, too. So I started watching her, listening. She's doing something, I don't know what, but I think it has something to do with us."

"So you ran to get away from Shaw, and because you suspected Poole of . . . something. And she lied about your stealing."

"She has an office. She goes in there and locks the door. You can hear her a little through the door talking to someone on the phone. I could never make out what it was about really, but I know it was about us girls. When she finished in there, she locked the door, and she kept the key in her pocket all the time. I wanted to know what was in there. Why was she always so careful about locking the door? What was she saying about us and who was she saying it to?"

"Did you find out?"

"The day I ran away. She must have thought I left for school already, but it was late start that morning. I knew she was in the office, so I hung around. She was on the phone again. She stayed on it a long time. . . . When she finally came out and went to the kitchen, I could hear her making coffee. The office door was open. She didn't know I was there. I snuck in and took a thumb drive and a leather book off the desk, not jewelry. She saw me, ran after me, but I got away."

"You hadn't planned on running away, then."

"No, I was always planning to, but not until I found out what she and Mr. Shaw were doing. Girls would come in, stay for a while, and then he would come and get them. They'd always say they were going to another home or back to their families. I don't think that's true. That's why I had to see what was in that office. I had a bag with some clothes, food, and a little money in my locker at work. When I ran, I went and got it. Rose let me in the back, no one else saw."

"And you left her the box to hold."

"Not then. I went back later. I knew I needed to make copies of the drive and the book first, as insurance. I only left Tonya's ID and the photos I took with Rose. The other things I left somewhere else. It wouldn't have been smart to leave everything in one place. Do you think they did something to Tonya?"

"I don't know. The police are on it."

"But you think the body could be her?"

"It's possible." Ramona drifted away again to stare blankly out the window. "The body belonged to a girl about your age. She'd had at least one child."

Ramona turned back, stunned. "Tonya had a baby, a girl. She named her Sierra. They made her give her up. She said they told her she couldn't give her any of the things she needed. That's why she was so angry. She was always talking back to Miss Poole, not doing anything she was supposed to do, just to show them how mad she was. Then Shaw came." Her eyes began to fill.

"Poole and Shaw told me you and Tonya barely spoke. That you weren't friends."

"We were, though. We didn't have anybody else." She wiped a tear away. "They killed her, I know it. I hate them. I hate them all."

"How'd you get Tonya's ID? Why was there a different name on it, a different age?"

"I found it stuck in a crack by the window in our room, behind those ugly curtains. We hid stuff there all the time so Miss. Poole wouldn't find it. She hid the ID there for me, to tell me something. I don't know why she had it, but I'll bet it had something to do with what Miss Poole is doing." She raised her hood. "She wanted us to be little princesses, like little dolls. We did our homework. She taught us about table manners and how a lady's supposed to act. She bought us fancy dresses and showed us how to put on makeup. Tonya wouldn't do any of it. All she wanted was her baby back."

I didn't like where this was going and sat still, quiet, listening to Ramona, hoping I wasn't about to hear what I suspected I would.

"Family," she said, "that's what we were supposed to be, but it didn't feel like that. So I listened and I started to see things. Mr. Shaw and Miss Poole talked like they were friends, maybe more than friends, and they both knew that old detective."

"Where are the drive and the book now?"

Ramona shook her head, drew back. She only trusted me up to a point. "Safe."

I couldn't blame her, not really. The kid had been living off her wits almost her entire life, shuttled from one house to the other, unable to latch onto anything lasting. The only thing she had to count on was herself, she was the only one she trusted.

"Did you at least see what was on it?"

Ramona shook her head. "I only had time to copy it, not read it. The book had numbers and maybe initials in it? But I couldn't figure it out, and I had to get lost in a crowd somewhere. I knew Miss Poole would be looking for me, for her stuff. If I went into a library or one of those office places, there would be cameras all around. I couldn't take that chance. Whatever's on it, though, she wants it back bad."

I pulled out the photos from the box. "Explain these to me?"

"That's the three of them. They would meet, off and on, not for long, but it always looked like they were talking about something serious. I decided I needed proof."

"This one was taken last summer, July," I said. "This one, more recently."

She held the July photo. "That's at the farm. Miss Poole took us, and we spent the whole day. It was my first time, but Tonya said they went the year before, too." She pointed to Martini. "That's the first time I'd seen him." She stared at the second photo. "This is them again, Mr. Shaw had just come for Tonya like the day before, but he came back with that detective and they started arguing and shouting. Something was definitely wrong. I took that thinking it might be important."

"Poole told me that photo had to have been taken after you ran. That the date stamp had to be wrong," I said.

Ramona shook her head. "She's a liar. I took it after Tonya went. I didn't get into her office until like the next week."

"Did Martini, the cop, ever talk to you? Say anything?"

Ramona handed the photos back. "He only talked to Mr. Shaw and Miss Poole."

"A farm."

"Not *a* farm, *the* farm. That's what she called it. There were a lot of kids there, and hot dogs, pop, animals to pet and stuff. There were other people there, too."

"Men?" I braced for her answer.

"And women, too. Like they were married, maybe? It was a party. Everybody just walked around having a good time. They talked to Mr. Shaw and Miss Poole, and sometimes we'd have to talk to them, too. They'd ask questions about school and what we wanted to be when we grew up. Nobody ever said what it was about, but I think they were trying to get us adopted? But it was weird, like not the usual way you get adopted? Some of the people were nice, some were a little creepy."

I listened, my brain working overtime. *The farm.* Poole and Shaw and Martini at *the farm.* Adoption could certainly have been the intent of the outing, I mean that was what Bettle House was about, giving older kids a shot at a real family. A day at a farm felt odd, though, parading kids in front of prospective parents like they were rescue puppies in need of a forever home. And the entire thing didn't explain Tonya's disappearance or her fake ID. It didn't explain Martini in the photos when he shouldn't have been, and it didn't explain Shaw dead.

"Where is the farm?"

"I don't know. We'd take a van. Drive a long way on the expressway."

"Ramona, how many girls did Shaw pick up from Poole's?"

"I've only been there about a year. Before that I was with the Knowleses. They really were so nice. I liked them a lot, but I only got to stay with them a few months when Mr. Shaw moved me. Someplace better, he said. That turned out to be Miss Poole's." Ramona glowered. "It wasn't better. Tonya was already there. Miss Poole gave me the bed closest to the window. Tonya said a girl named Sarita used to sleep there, until she was moved out."

"By Shaw?"

Ramona shrugged. "Tonya didn't say. She never mentioned Sarita again."

"Do you know Sarita's last name?"

"No. I don't think Tonya knew it either. You try not to get too close to people."

"So it doesn't hurt so much when you have to leave them?"

Ramona looked back at Scoot and the others. "I guess that's it."

I thought for a time. Cycling girls in and out? Shaw. "How'd Poole run after you in her condition?"

Ramona turned to face me. "What do you mean?"

"She told me she had cancer, that it had spread to her bones and that she was very sick. She was on a cane when I spoke to her and had trouble walking."

Ramona smiled. "Nothing's wrong with her. She ran after me just fine. She almost caught me, too. You know she used to be on some TV show, right? In the basement, there's a big trunk with all kinds of costumes, hats, *and stuff,* even a couple of canes, too. Me and Tonya would mess around down there all the time, dressing up, pretending we were somebody else . . . someplace else." Ramona shot me a pity grin. "She played you. She plays everybody."

"Why would she do that?"

"Why do adults do half the stuff they do?"

I pulled my phone out of my pocket, dialed Leesa Evans's number, then handed the phone to Ramona. "Let your mother know you're okay."

I sat and listened to the short conversation, Ramona mostly answering in one-word answers, Evans's voice over the phone loud enough for me to feel her anguish, her relief. I closed my eyes, just for a moment, hoping that moment calmed me down enough to see straight. Poole *had* played me. I'd been so concerned for Ramona's safety that I'd taken her act at face value, didn't question it. I didn't think the outings were about adoptions. If they were, Tonya Pierce would have had a file at Bettle

House, the farm wouldn't seem so clandestine, and Martini's presence wouldn't be so alarming. Trafficking. That's what I was thinking. Shaw, Poole and Martini were peddling children. It was horrifying just to think about, and if it turned out to be true, God help them.

I had been applying heat to Shaw and to Poole. Is that why Shaw broke? And Poole, cool, playing the worried foster mother, when all the time it's not Ramona she wants back, but that drive and the book with the numbers in it. There were no words for what I felt for Martini.

"All right," Ramona said. "I will." She ended the call and handed the phone back. "She sounds like her old self."

"She's trying very hard," I said.

Ramona was quiet for a moment. "I left the drive in a safe place. The key you found unlocks where it is. If you bring the key to me, you can have everything I took from her. There's a closed-up dentist's office north of here a couple of blocks. It's got smiling teeth on the sign. Meet us there." She took me in, shook her head. "You look burned out, so maybe get some sleep first. Eleven. Bring lunch?" She got out of the car. I followed her out.

"Wait. Come with me. I'll find you a place to stay. I'll take all of you. Hold on." I reached inside the car to get my phone off the console to search it for Gwen Timmons's number. She handled emergency placements all the time; she'd know how to help. I punched the number, looked up, and Ramona was already inside the fence and heading off with Scoot and the kids.

I ran to the fence. "Hey! Hold up! Ramona!"

She and the others didn't bother to turn around, just kept walking away. Even the damned dog ignored me.

I tucked my phone into a pocket, then kicked a mound of snow. "Gaaaaaah!"

Chapter 25

It was late. I should have gone home, but I found myself at almost 3:00 AM in front of Poole's house. Her lights were off, as I would have expected them to be at that hour, but I came prepared to wake her up, only her car wasn't in the driveway. I got out and walked up to her door, rang the bell. No, 3:00 AM was not a polite time to visit, but I wasn't in a polite mood, and we weren't about to have a polite conversation. Nothing stirred inside, not a single light came on in answer to the bell. Had I spooked her enough for her to pack up and run? Was she inside hiding? I stared up at her darkened windows, no play to make. I'd have to come back for Poole.

Driving home, lost in thought, I was slow to notice the tail. It was the headlights that finally registered. The one on the right blinked like it was going out. Dark car. One male driver, no passengers. The driver stayed a couple car lengths behind me, with one car always in between; hard to do this late at night when traffic was sparse. He slowed when I slowed, sped up when I sped up, turned when I turned. As badly as I wanted to go home and fall into bed, I headed in the opposite direction of my apartment, the mouse leading the cat on a late-night car parade. I looped around side streets without appearing to do so, the car giving me all kinds of slack, but sticking with me, nonetheless.

Making another languid turn, I headed north on State Street, the Dan Ryan on my left, past a fish market and a store selling fresh fruit and vegetables, along with liters of pop, lottery tickets, and pork skins. The tail car well behind me, I stepped on the gas, made a turn, and raced a block up, fishtailing into an alley, driving halfway in and pulling to a stop.

A few seconds later, the tail barreled in after me, pulling to a stop at the mouth of the alley, idling there for a time. My hazard lights were on, my engine off. The alley lights were working, but the light was dull, murky, like it was shining through a cloudy drinking glass. A minute passed, two, five. Finally the driver turned his car off, left his lights on, and walked slowly toward the back of my car. I saw only the outline of the man. Average height. Average build. Dark clothing. Nothing in his hands. The sound of heavy feet on icy, hardpacked snow was the only disturbance to the cold, still night.

He stopped at my back bumper, angled to peer inside the slightly tinted windows. In the half-light, I made out the porkpie hat and stepped out of the shadows, my gun at my side. "Lenny Vine."

Lenny spun around, his eyes wide. He had likely expected to find me inside the car, not out of it, but tried playing it off with a cheerful smile. "Raines."

I checked him out, keeping my distance. "Get away from my car."

His flinty, calculating eyes swept down to the gun in my hand and his went up in mock surrender as he gingerly stepped back and away. "Whoa. Heard you loud and clear. Getting away."

Vine was a PI, sort of, but he did the profession no favors. He was a gap-toothed, feral-eyed, double-dealing scumbag who would sell his own mother for a nickel, a hooker, and a shot of cheap booze. Yet, he always approached me like we were pals; we were *not* pals. I wouldn't voluntarily come within two feet of Lenny Vine, even if my life depended on it. I didn't work for just anyone; Lenny Vine would work for the devil himself if the money was right. There were other differences, fundamental ones, but none of that mattered right at this moment. What was important now was that someone hired Lenny Vine to follow me. Who?

He feigned surprise, pointed at the car. "This is you? I didn't know. I was passing and saw the blinkers on. I'm thinking somebody's out here in some distress, you know? Middle of the night, like it is, and it's you? Huh. Small world." He started to put his arms down. I flicked the gun upward, he raised them back up. He kept the smile going, but his eyes hadn't signed on to the fake. I knew Lenny Vine didn't like me any more than I liked him. "What are you doing out so late, Raines? Didn't know you were the midnight-creeper type."

I stepped back, glanced down the alley at his car. The right headlight blinked, like it was about to go out. I turned back to Lenny. It was too late for razzle-dazzle. I was tired, I'd lost contact with my client's kid, and I was sick to my stomach about Poole and Martini. Restraint was a good thing to have. I was glad I had it now.

"Why are you following me? More important, who's paying you?"

"Following you?" He chuckled, slowly raised his hands to adjust that stupid porkpie. It was ten degrees out here. I doubted Lenny Vine had sense enough to come in out of the rain.

I waved him away from my car. "It's the headlight, Lenny. See it?" He glanced down the alley. "See how it blinks like that? Distinctive. Easy to pick up in the middle of the night. You've been on me for blocks. Who hired you?" He tried looking offended, like I didn't know he was scum. "I know for a fact you don't put on your shoes for free."

Lenny shrugged, seemingly amused at being caught out. "You know I can't tell you that." He began to back up, his hands still up. "But you win this one." He pedaled back until he was well away; then he stopped. "See you around, Raines." He turned and walked back to his car. He drove off, the way he'd come, peeling his bald tires away on black ice. I slipped my gun into my jacket pocket and jumped back in my car, headed in the opposite direction, keeping my eye on the rearview for a blinking headlight.

Lenny Vine was a problem. Had he been on me when I met Ramona at Cholly's? Had I led him right to her? It had to be this case he was interested in, I wasn't working any others, which meant he was likely working for either Martini or Poole or both. That meant I was getting close to something neither of them wanted me getting close to. But Vine was a worry. The man had no scruples. He'd go as low as he needed to, and wouldn't lose a single night's sleep over it.

I pulled into a well-lit gas station about a mile north of the alley and got out of the car to walk around it. Lenny Vine was a terrible investigator; he'd need a cheat. Everything looked okay, but I knew it couldn't be. I got down on my hands and knees in the slush and ran my hands along the bottom of the car, front to back, right side first, finding nothing. I repeated the search on the left side, again finding nothing. After checking under the back bumper and finding nothing, I did the same in front and found a tiny tracker underneath, on the driver's side. Lenny's cheat. I held the small black box in my hand. It weighed hardly anything, but it apparently worked just fine for Lenny, the small flashing green light told me that. "I hate you, Lenny Vine."

I stood up, the knees of my jeans soaked through. There was no one else in the station, just the lone cashier inside watching a small TV, his back to the pumps, safe behind bulletproof glass. I looked around for Vine, but didn't see his blinky light anywhere. I dropped the tracker to the ground and smashed it with the heel of my boot. The green light went out and stayed out. "Follow *that,* you porkpie jackass."

Chapter 26

I felt my pocket for the key as I ducked into the abandoned dentist office at eleven Friday morning with a bag of McDonald's breakfast sandwiches, paper cups, and a gallon of orange juice. But before stopping, I had looped the block a few times, making sure Vine or anyone else wasn't around watching. The tracker was gone, but that didn't mean I couldn't have picked up some low-tech attention. Thankfully, I saw no one.

It was a little warmer today, sunny, low twenties, and it wasn't snowing, which was a plus. I slid into the storefront through the open back door, picking my way through, broken glass crunching under my feet, light fixtures and wires dangling from the wrecked drop ceiling. There wasn't much left of the place. Like Sunshine, everything of any value had been stripped, stolen, or trashed outright, leaving only empty space, a shell, that had been boarded up haphazardly and left to waste away.

I turned at the sound of footsteps behind me. Ramona and Scoot stood there, the others behind them, even the dog showed up.

"On time," Scoot said.

"Can't we ever meet somewhere nice?" I asked.

Ramona stepped forward, took the food and juice. "Thanks." She handed it off to the kids, who crowded around the bag like ants around a picnic basket, then turned back to me. "Did you bring it?"

I drew the key out of my pocket, tossed it to her. "What's it fit?"

She clutched the key in her hand, smiled. "Follow me."

The group stayed put, enjoying breakfast, while Ramona led Scoot and me into a back exam room, the dental chair long ago removed, the room's cabinets left behind, forgotten posters, tattered and hanging from graffiti-marred walls, encouraging frequent flossing and warning against the scourge of gingivitis. The cabinets looked sturdy, despite the destruction of the place. They were where the dentist kept his medications, instruments and such. The small locks on the doors looked just the right size for the key I'd just handed over.

Ramona squatted down, poked the key in the lock, slid the door back, and drew out a small ledger, with a green rubber band around it. She tossed the book to me.

I looked past her. The cabinet was empty. "What about the drive?"

Ramona stood, exchanged a look with Scoot, who stood there with his hands in his pockets, rocking on his heels. "You remember what I said about spreading it around?"

Scoot whistled for the dog. "King. Come."

The dog trotted over, happy as a lark, like a puppy ready to play. Apparently, he held no grudges about our earlier encounter in the junkyard. I could not say the same. I stepped back, giving him all kinds of room. Scoot rubbed the dog's head and neck affectionately and kissed him on the top of the head. "Good boy, King, good boy."

Ramona bent down, kissed the dog on the snout, and then reached into the pouch around its neck, drawing out a thumb drive, which she tossed to me.

"Smart, huh? The pouch was Scoot's idea. No way anyone was going to get it there."

I gripped the drive in my hand, the ledger too. I turned to Scoot. We shared a knowing look. "You could have gotten big money for these, enough to pick up and go anywhere and live a real life."

He shrugged. "Maybe."

"What are you talking about," Ramona said, "he wouldn't have taken them."

He would have, he could have at any point, and Ramona would never have found him anywhere in these streets.

"Why didn't you?" I asked him, curious.

He glanced over at Ramona, then back at me. "That whole thing she said? About the woman and the house and the farm? I know what that sounds like, so do you. I don't help pushers or pimps. I got standards."

Ramona's eyes widened, the truth slowly dawning. It looked like she had not even considered that Scoot would have double-crossed her. She was smart—up to a point, yes—but also naïve, far too trusting, not at all accustomed to mean streets or those fighting to survive them.

Ramona faced Scoot, looking at him now in a new light, not as her savior, but as a stranger. She said nothing. What was there to say? It was what it was. She walked past me. "I'll wait for you outside."

"Ramona, wait," I said.

I hated to admit it, I hated even to think it, but she was probably safer with Scoot, moving from place to place under the radar, off the grid. If she went with me, where would I take her that she'd be safe? Her mother lived in a halfway house, teetering on the edge of sobriety. Did I turn her in to Hogan and Spinelli? What if Martini had friends at the district? What if one of them was Hogan? I certainly couldn't take her back to Poole's.

"I need you to stay with them for another day, or two, no longer."

She stormed back. "Are you serious? I can't stay with them now! He was thinking about stealing from me, or maybe even leading them right to me!"

"Thinking's not doing," Scoot said, smirking. "And you could do worse."

Ramona charged forward toward Scoot, angry, betrayed. I moved between them. Scoot appeared to find the entire thing amusing. "Let's sit in my car for a bit," I told her. "You," I said, turning to Scoot, "stay put. Do not leave. We won't be long."

"I can't believe it," Ramona kept saying, her head against the headrest, her eyes closed. "He's a thief. He thought about selling me out."

"He's had to be a lot of things," I said. "Or else he wouldn't have survived this long. It's not his fault, not all of it. It's a different world out here, Ramona, one no child—hell, no adult—should have to deal with."

For a moment, she said nothing. "I get it. It's just . . ."

"So you'll stick with them, you'll stay out of sight. I'll tell your mother you're okay, and I'll try and figure out what's going on. That's the plan." Minutes passed without us speaking. "You told me about the farm, that you got there by van on the expressway. About how long was the drive?"

"Two hours, maybe. Sometimes we stopped for snacks."

"Is there anything else you can tell me? Anything you remember about the place?"

"I don't know the address, if that's what you're asking. There was a big white house and a couple of barns. There's a gate, with all kinds of No Trespassing signs on it, and two statues of lions sitting there. You go up a long road through a lot of trees, and behind the house there are woods and a little lake."

"Lake?"

"A small one. We tossed rocks in it and jumped over it without getting our feet wet when Miss Poole wasn't watching."

"A stream, creek, maybe."

"I guess." She thought for a moment, then turned to face me. She'd remembered something. "We stopped for ice cream in a little town. They had all kinds of cones and flavors and old-fashioned candy, like something out of a Disney movie. Sally Sweet's Sweets."

"That's good. Do you remember the name of the town?"

She bit her lip, concentrating. "I was on my phone. I didn't pay attention."

"That's all right. You did good." I watched Scoot and the others hanging out in front of the dentist's office, waiting for Ramona. "A day or two, maybe less if I get lucky. Don't use your phone, throw it away." I took money out of my bag, handed it to her. "Buy a prepaid one. Check in with me once a day, no more. If something happens, you know where to find me. Okay?"

Ramona watched Scoot, too, only this time her eyes appeared to be completely open. "Sure. Why not?" She opened the door to leave.

"He could have picked you clean," I said. "He didn't. He came down on your side when he didn't have to. He's an operator, don't get me wrong, but this time, he did the right thing." I let a moment go. "Ramona, is there anything else you haven't told me that I should know? Anything you've hidden somewhere else?"

Ramona stuffed the money into her pocket, then zipped it closed. "That's all. I'll be in touch." She got out of the car and rejoined the others, and I watched as the kids crowded around her, welcoming her back into the fold. Even Scoot. Only when they all moved off and melted back into the city did I drive away . . .

And though I couldn't prove it, I'd swear to it that Ramona Titus had just lied to me.

Chapter 27

I found the nearest Office Depot and sat at one of the computers. The ledger was clear-cut enough. I fluttered the pages, leafed through. There were two columns on each page, neither labeled, one with initials, the other with numbers, no dates and no dollar signs, no indication what either column represented. It might have been written in Greek for all the sense it made to me, but it meant enough to Poole that she took great care to keep it locked in her office away from prying eyes, except for the one time she didn't.

There were several folders on the drive. I clicked the first one, which turned out to contain bio information on what I assumed were her foster kids. I randomly clicked through to see what was there. Each file contained a photo of the kid, info on height, weight, age, Social Security number, their family background, medical details, if they were relevant, allergies, food sensitivities, etc., and then special interests and talents were noted, too.

Debra Lynton's photo showed an unsmiling seventeen-year-old with a faraway look in her eye. There was nothing noted under special talents or interests or medical details, and for next of kin there was a zero with a line through it.

Nothing about any of that looked off to me. Poole would need information on the girls who came into her home, wouldn't she? She'd need to know where they came from and a little bit about their circumstances.

I opened several more files, including Ramona's, but they were all the same. No bombshell information, no smoking gun to something heinous. Poole had likely kept the drive private because it contained personal information for each girl. If she was doing something else with the information, it wasn't here, unless I was missing it.

The other folders had what looked like her household operating expenses detailed: her utilities, food costs, gas, clothing for the girls. There was a folder with a lot of photos in it of girls baking cookies, learning to sew, reading. A few of them had Poole in them, smiling, and except for the fact that there were no dark circles under her eyes, she looked much the same as I'd found her a few days ago. I clicked through the rest: girls talking in a park, playing volleyball.

"Nothing," I muttered, sitting back in the chair. I thought back through it all, Poole's search for Ramona, the pushpins, Shaw, the photos, Tonya's fake ID, the trips in the van, all that pink, and the cane for a disease Poole apparently did not have.

No, there was something, I just wasn't getting it. Maybe the evidence wasn't on Poole's end, but Shaw's? If that was the case, I was going to have a nearly impossible time getting hold of it. Or maybe there simply was no evidence. Maybe all I needed to do here was get Ramona back to where she belonged, where she'd be safe, and walk away from this with my job done. So why couldn't I just get Ramona, wrap it up, and move on?

"Because I'm stupidly tenacious." I hadn't realized I'd said it aloud until I saw the man sitting two computers over slide me a look. I mouthed an apology and he turned back to what he'd been doing, and I went through the ledger again, looking for special symbols or characters embedded somewhere that might connect to the files on the drive in some way. Maybe to understand it, I needed to look at them as companion pieces, not as separate entities? It was a good idea, I thought, but one that came to nothing. The files weren't color coded, either, or seemingly prioritized in any way. I checked my watch. It was nearly five; I'd been at it for over three hours, and I didn't have a single thing to show for it.

I spent another hour printing everything out, then copying every page of the ledger. The originals I put in my bag, the copies I slid into a large insulated envelope purchased near the front counter and addressed it to a PO box I maintained for just this purpose. Like Ramona had done, I was building in a little insurance, in case I needed it, but if the last three hours were any indication, I'd just wasted another one.

While I was there, I Googled Sally Sweet's Sweets. It was in tiny Pittston, Illinois, about two hours south of Chicago, downstate in Douglas County. I had never been there, never had call to venture that far out of the city into straight-up farm country. Pittston was well past Joliet Prison and Urbana, at the foot of the state, which might have been the moon for all I knew about it.

Why had Poole chosen Pittston for an outing, bypassing likelier choices, like Starved Rock or the Indiana Dunes? There were plenty of open spaces right here in the city, too, forest preserves, parks, beaches, in some you could even ride a horse or feed ducks. Or was the fact that Pittston was so out of the way the point? Had she been trying to get as far away from Chicago, Bettle House, and CPD as she could get? No prying eyes, no oversight?

I'd need to go to Pittston to see if I could find the farm Ramona remembered, but it was too late to get there tonight, the morning would have to do. From the car, I dialed Poole's number and got no answer. I left a message telling her I needed to speak with her about the things Ramona took from her; then I called Martini.

He answered right away. "Raines."

"Martini, good news," I said cheerfully. "I found Ramona. Well, I've got a lead on her, anyway. I arranged to meet her in about an hour. Ferber Park. At the old gazebo."

"You serious? How'd you track her down?"

"Would you believe her phone? I just kept calling it and calling it, and she finally answered the thing. She said she wants to tell me something important. I told her I'd listen to whatever she had to say. She sounded tired and worn-out, but thank God she's alive."

Martini hesitated. "Ferber? That's far south, right? I can be there in—"

"No. I told her it'd just be me. If you show up, it could spook her, right? I'll take the meet, and call you when it's done. With any luck, we can wrap this whole thing up tonight."

"Yeah, sure. Let's hope, huh? Good work there, Raines." He chuckled but it sounded forced. "You'd have made a good cop."

I punched end, then held the phone in my hand. It was a lie, all of it; now let's see what I got for my troubles.

Ferber Park in winter was a different experience than in summer months. In August, the wide, leafy plot of urban tranquility was full to the brim with baby strollers, canoodling couples, dogs on leashes, kids kicking balls around. In the dead of winter, it was like a snow-covered ghost town, its trees bare, not a soul in sight. The park used to be part of my beat. It was isolated and offered plenty of good places to hide. That's why I picked it.

The gazebo had fallen into disrepair years ago, and the changing neighborhood had made attempts to shore it up and bring it back to its original beauty. Somewhere, however, between the proposal stage and actual completion of the project, the half-shuttered gazebo had been left alone. It had been boarded up at one point, but over the years, the boards had either buckled and fallen away or been removed by those who wanted to use the structure to get out of the rain or snow or heat. It was a good spot to hide a drug deal, squat in, or in my case spring a trap. Maybe the cops who patrolled the area checked it on occasion to make sure no one was dead inside, maybe they didn't. Chances were good they didn't. I doubted little Pittston, Illinois, wherever it was, had a similar problem.

Another reason I picked Ferber is because it had four entrances: north, south, east, and west, each with an archway. Two of the streets bordering the park ran east and west, the other two north and south. I took up position at the west archway, the gazebo abutted the north. From here, I could easily see who approached from three sides. There was nothing behind me but a private parking lot for the apartment building across the street. I lifted my camera to get it in focus, training the telephoto lens on the gazebo's short steps. Perfect.

This was a test. I wanted to know if Martini would show up, and if he did, who might be with him. I told him about six, and it was that now. It was getting dark, and I'd planned on that, too. Darkness was excellent cover. Now all I had to do was wait to freeze to death. I tensed when an older man walked into the park with a dog, but they didn't stop or linger. Too cold for that. The pair moved quickly up the pedestrian path, past the gazebo, and out of the park at the other end. Leisurely park strolls were at least four months away.

At 6:10 PM, a car pulled up and stopped at the east edge of the park, but no one got out. I slid farther behind the arch, camera up, holding my breath, mindful that I was losing the sun and all I'd have to see by would be the park lights dotting the path in front of me. Two figures got out of the car and walked slowly toward the gazebo, where Ramona and I were supposed to be talking. Men, from their size and the way they walked. I aimed the camera, squinted through the viewfinder. It was Martini, all right . . . and Lenny Vine. That confirmed it. Martini was bad. No one with an ounce of integrity ran around with Lenny Vine. I started snapping photo after photo, an angry, pissed off thumb pressing the shutter button. I watched as Martini neared the gazebo, hesitated, and then pulled his gun. Vine, next to him, did the same. I gasped and pulled my eye away from the viewfinder, horrified. What were they up to? I pressed my eye back, began snapping again as the two inched closer to the gazebo. Separating as they went, Martini approached from the left, Vine from the right. They shared a confirmation nod, then took the gazebo in a rush, bursting inside, disappearing from view for a time. When they reemerged, they were running scared, scanning the park as they raced back to the car and sped away.

I lowered the camera, my heart racing, and leaned back against the archway in disbelief. Had Martini and Vine come here to kill Ramona and me? How would they have explained it, or covered it up? I knew Vine wouldn't have had a problem with it, but Martini? At least I knew now who had hired Vine. It was also clear they had wanted to get to Ramona before she told me anything, which drew Poole in. What they didn't know, and I did, was that both of them were too late. I stuffed the camera in my jacket pocket and slowly made my way out of the park, checking the street for cars, looking over my shoulder, aware that Martini and Vine were out there somewhere, and neither one of them seemed to have a single qualm about putting a bullet in my head.

Chapter 28

The photos I'd taken in Ferber Park weren't evidence of anything. Martini and Vine would be able to explain them away with some tall tale, but now I plainly knew who had it in for me, and that was a good thing. It was always better to know from which direction the arrows would be coming, and to be honest, I was relieved it hadn't been Hogan with Martini. Maybe that meant I could trust Hogan. Maybe he had no idea Martini was bad.

I waited for Hogan in the coffee shop around the corner from Area 2. It was after eight-thirty, but the night was still young, apparently. I was lucky to have found him still clocked in. I wanted to feel him out, see if I could trust him, then decide how much to tell him. After that, I'd go home, get a few hours' sleep, and then head out in the morning for Pittston to see if I could find the big white house with the long road and the stone lions at the gate. I had Googled the place, the town only had about four thousand people in it. How many big white farmhouses with stone lions could there be?

He walked in with the file I'd asked to see and sat across the table from me. I stared at him for longer than was comfortable for either of us.

"I shouldn't even be doing this," he said. "You're a live wire. I hate live wires."

I said nothing, just stared at him.

"You called me here to stare me to death?"

It wasn't Hogan in Ramona's photos. She hadn't mentioned seeing anyone who looked like Hogan, or Spinelli, anywhere around Poole's place or the farm. There didn't appear to be any deep connection between Hogan and Martini, at least none I'd found. So, I could trust him, right? I could trust Hogan and bring Ramona home.

"Your friend Martini came gunning for me tonight," I said. "He brought with him a bottom-feeding PI by the name of Lenny Vine." I took the drive and the ledger out of my bag, set them on the table. "I'm sure they were hoping to get their hands on these, but once they did, they were going to shut Ramona up, me along with her." I told him about my encounter in the park.

I'd shocked him. "Martini did what? And you found Titus? Where? When?"

I eyed the folder he'd brought with him, the one I'd requested a peek at. "That it?"

He clapped his big cop hand down on it. "Me first. What the hell's going on, and where the fuck is Ramona Titus?"

"I don't know what's going on yet." I tapped the drive. "I didn't find anything on this that made sense to me. Ramona thinks Poole, Martini, and the late Ronald Shaw were partners in some scheme involving the girls. Gut feeling? Either an under-the-table adoption business, off the books, or, God forbid, some kind of trafficking operation. Selling girls right out of Poole's hands. The girls she took in are listed there. The ledger, well, I don't know about that."

I set Tonya's ID next to the drive. "It's fake. It was found hidden at Poole's. They aged her a year to make her legal. That tells me it wasn't adoption they were about, at least not in her case. They had other plans." Hogan picked it up, studied it. "I really think that's who was found in that burning can. Tonya wouldn't get with Poole's program, according to Ramona. She had had a daughter and she was taken from her. The birth fits with the prelim findings. No hands, no teeth because if she was identified, that ID would lead you and the others right to Poole's front door."

Hogan tossed the ID down, glared at me, then opened the folder and slid out an evidence photo. He held it up for me to see. "Take a good look." It was a close-up shot of a mangled gold butterfly necklace. "We found it next to that can." He picked up the ID again. "The same one she's wearing in this ID photo. How long have you been holding on to this? How long have you been in contact with the kid I've been busting my back looking for for weeks?" He snatched up the drive and the ledger. "This is why I don't like working with PIs. You're all sociopaths, running around, doing whatever the hell you want." He pocketed the ID.

"I didn't know if I could trust you," I said. "You and Martini—"

His brows shot up. "Me and *Martini*? There is no me and Martini. He's an old blowhard who doesn't know how to turn it off because he's got nothing else going in his life. He hangs around boring the shit out of every cop in the place with his old street stories, half of them pure fantasy. He's more air than cop."

"Then why ask him to look for Ramona?"

"I would have asked Satan himself to keep an eye out. All hands, remember? Martini's got eyes and ears out there. I needed those eyes and ears, but that's the extent of it. We're not drinking buddies."

"He's been keeping tabs," I said. "Seeing how far you got in finding her."

"Where's Ramona?" Hogan was angry, not listening. Not connecting the dots.

"I can't tell you," I said. Hogan geared up, ready to let me have it, but I rushed in with the rest of it before he could. "Because I don't know exactly. I know who she's with; I know she's safe for now. I have a way of contacting her if I need to. That part of it is done, but there's more. You have a key to it in your hands."

Hogan stood, sneered at me, as though I were something that had just crawled out of a sewer. "We're done. Bring that kid to me by nine, tomorrow morning. If she's not there, I'm locking you up."

"For what?"

He leaned over, his eyes burning hot. "Kidnapping. Gun running. Arson. Pissing me off. Wasting my time. I don't give a shit, I'll find something that sticks." He straightened up. "You know, looks to me you and Martini are cut from the same cloth. A couple of crazy outliers trying to play cop. You bring me that kid, then you stay out of my district."

I watched him storm out of the shop, and then sat there, my eyes closed. The necklace match nudged us closer to identifying the body in the can. I knew it. Hogan knew it. Who killed Tonya? Who would be next?

Chapter 29

At nine Saturday morning I was supposed to be standing in front of Hogan with Ramona by my side; instead I'd been on the road since eight headed to Pittston, 150 miles south as the crow flies. It'd take me almost three hours to get there in this weather. It had begun to snow just before I started out, and it hadn't let up yet.

I didn't think Hogan would actually come to arrest me when I didn't show up with Ramona, but maybe he might. He could be standing at my front door right now with a couple of uniforms itching to put me in handcuffs. He'd been angry last night. Truth was, I couldn't blame him. I'd have behaved the same if our positions had been reversed. I didn't think he'd pay much attention to the drive or the ledger, given his state of mind, just on principle—just because I was the one who gave them to him. His main concern was finding Ramona. I'd found her, and now wouldn't give her up, only I had good reason. I had to keep going, staying ahead of Hogan and Martini and Vine.

I cranked up my radio and zoned out a bit, watching the

lines on the highway, checking behind me for Lenny Vine. Before I left home, I checked my car again for trackers; luckily, there weren't any. That didn't mean Lenny had moved on. I knew he was still in it, Martini too. It just meant they were laying low, coming up with another way to tackle the thing, tackle me. There were three more messages on my phone from Martini wanting to know how things went at the park. Bogus, of course. He knew how things went. He had been there. With a gun. I had no intention of calling him back. Let him stew.

It was just after ten-thirty when I turned off I-57 and eased onto Pittston's quiet main drag. There wasn't a car anywhere, except for mine. The snowy wide street, with sleepy shops on either side, looked like a quaint, friendly little Christmas town, with tinsel and wreaths and cardboard cutouts of smiling snowmen and happy angels in practically every shop window. It was a little freaky, everything too clean, too orderly, too cute, like I'd just landed in Stepford, but all the wives were inside baking bread or sewing Christmas stockings. Driving slow, I checked the street, searching for the ice-cream shop Ramona remembered, and I found it right in the middle, fronted by a red-and-white striped awning with ice-cream cones and bags of candy drawn on the front window in colorful paint. Sally Sweet's Sweets.

I didn't stop. First I wanted to see if I could find the farm on my own without stirring up too much attention. I didn't know this town, but I was confident there weren't a lot of people who looked like me living way down here, where corn, and whatever else they grew, had to outnumber the humans a million to one. I was a black woman driving around farm country in the dead of winter. I couldn't have been more conspicuous if I'd painted my car hot pink and affixed a megaphone to the top of it announcing my arrival.

I drove right through town and quickly out of it, taking a single lane road west past flat, fallow fields, and around doglegged bends, looking for the main house of the farm. It took more than an hour of driving, up jutted roads and looping back around, until I found it.

I pulled up and stopped at a metal gate covered in NO TRES-PASSING signs, with two stone lion statues on either side. I peered through the windshield at the long road beyond it that cut through a stand of trees with naked branches heavy with snow. Ramona said the road led to a white house. There were no tire tracks or footprints on the road that I could see, and the snow looked deep. Even if I could have gotten past the gate, I would likely not have been able to drive all the way through and up to the house without getting bogged down. No name on the battered mailbox out front, no numbers on the gate. Maybe they didn't do that out here in the sticks. Maybe it was like *Cheers.* Around here, everybody knew your name. Yet, visitors, trespassers, were not encouraged, as the gate signs made clear.

I got out of the car and walked up to the gate. It wasn't that high, maybe four feet. It was just a low metal closure, more like a barrier to entry than a sentry post. I wanted to get a look at the house to see if anyone lived there, but I couldn't do that from here, and I'd come too far to turn back unsatisfied. After one final look, up and down the road behind me, I hopped the gate and started trudging through the high snow.

It was slow going, my boots getting sucked into the wet, heavy snow as I went. The only sound was that of my heavy breathing and country birds chirping above my head. I stopped for a second to listen and to make sure I didn't hear footsteps behind or ahead of me, then started again.

It took about five minutes before a two-story white farm-house with black shutters came into view. It stood on a slight hill, unlit. The farm. Off to the side, yards away, was a red silo that looked a little worse for wear and a corral with weathered fencing surrounding it, also a decrepit gray barn that looked like it hadn't been painted or seen to in quite some time, its wide doors standing open.

The cameras at the front door threw me. Old farm, not much happening on it, from what I could see, but security cameras at the door. No front bell. No door knocker. How did you announce yourself? Maybe that's where the cameras came in? I waited for a good length of time, but nothing happened at the door, even after I knocked a few times.

There were no cars parked around, no evidence that anyone was here or had been here recently. Maybe this was someone's summer home? Abandoned in winter? If so, I couldn't blame them. It was brutally cold out here with nothing but winter trees shivering in the bitter wind to protect the house from gusts as strong as a freight train. I walked around the side to where the outbuildings stood. I didn't see any horses, no livestock of any kind. So, apparently, not a working farm. I stopped to stare at the woods along the back of the property. They looked deep and would likely provide good shade and coolness in the summer, but they felt a little creepy now—with no one around and just the trees watching. I couldn't imagine venturing in there when the trees were full and the heavy canopy shut the sun out, let alone now when it looked foreboding and haunted. Ramona said there was a lake beyond the trees somewhere. I'd take her word for it. I shuddered, some from the cold, but mostly recalling all the horror movies I'd seen that had dumb teenagers running through the woods chased by an ax murderer. It was a no-go on the woods.

The flashing blue police lights were an unwelcome sight as I rounded the final bend in the road to see a Pittston PD SUV parked behind me at the gate, right next to the NO TRESPASSING sign I'd blithely disregarded.

I plastered a friendly smile on my face and waited for the local law at my driver's door, my hands out in the open, my keys in my pocket. Two people emerged from the vehicle; on the driver's side, a white guy in a shearling jacket and a black skullcap with a Pittston PD emblem on it. On the passenger side, a white woman in her late twenties, maybe, in a dark blue police uniform and matching jacket, the town's crest on the front, blond hair stuffed under a similar cap.

Both walked over to me, working the flank. I kept real still, kept the smile going, kept my hands where they could see them. I was a stranger in a strange land, a trespasser on private property, a black woman miles from anyone who knew me.

"Your car?" the man asked.

He'd likely already checked. I had no idea how long they'd been blocking me in. Had they been alerted by someone inside the house? Or maybe this was what the cameras were for?

"It is."

He had gray eyes, sharp, steady. He was about the business, making no attempt to be folksy or polite. "Car trouble, is it?"

"No, actually." I cleared my throat, which gave me just enough time to work up a lie. "I wanted to take a closer look at the house. I'm in the market, and it looked like a nice spot, away from the road, plenty of open space, not too close to town. You wouldn't happen to know if it's for sale, would you?"

Neither of them said anything for a moment. "Can't really see the house from the road," he said.

"I got a quick glimpse through that stand of trees. Like I said, I'm in the market. You know the owner?"

He glanced behind his shoulder toward the empty road. "Kind of off the beaten path for you to see it in the first place." He turned back to me. "Must've been looking for this place, special. Were you?"

"Just got turned around. None of these roads are marked. I'm used to street signs, landmarks. I saw the lions first. Hard to miss them. The house was a happy surprise, you might say."

The woman spoke up. "You could've stopped in town and

asked about property for sale at the realty office. Guess you missed it when you drove through."

How'd they know I'd passed through town? "I kind of wanted to take a look myself," I said. "It's a nice Saturday drive. Small town. Not that many roads. But, like I said, I got turned around. Signs would be helpful."

"You some kind of reporter?" he asked.

"No."

"What do you do, then?" the woman asked.

"I'm a podiatrist." I said it with a straight face, too. Score one for me.

The two exchanged a look.

"We don't get many *podiatrists* down here," he said. "They mostly stay up north with all the other podiatrists."

By the way they both stared at me, I could tell we weren't talking about podiatrists, but I went with it. "I'm a different kind of podiatrist. I go wherever I feel like going."

Our eyes locked. He said, "Yeah, well, we're gonna have to ask you to move along. This is private property, as you see from the *signs*. No Trespassing means just that."

"Very well," I said.

The blond woman slid her partner a look. "We catch you out here again, we'll do something different, understand?"

It was the cutest little thing the way she tried to act all Dirty Harry when she was all of five feet tall with rosy cheeks. Maybe to impress her partner, maybe just trying badass out to see how it fit her; it didn't much. She'd have done better sticking with good cop.

I said, "Completely. Is that it?"

He let a beat pass. "Got ID on you?"

Slowly I reached into my jacket pocket and pulled out my wallet, which I'd tucked there in case I came up shot dead for trespassing by some unreasonable farmer with a hunting rifle. My fingers slipped past my PI license, my FOID card, nope,

nope, I handed over my driver's license. He looked it over, looked me over again, then handed it back. For a moment, he said nothing. "Long way from Chicago. Heckuva drive, especially in this weather. I guess you'll be headed back that way now."

I slid my license back in the slot, my wallet back in my jacket. "Actually, I thought I'd stop back in town, get some ice cream, then head out." I patted my pocket, faced them. "That okay with you two?"

"Kinda cold for ice cream," the woman said. "More of a summer thing, I'd think."

I shrugged. "I like it year-round. What's good there?"

Stern faces looked back at me, a couple of humorless gargoyles. I didn't know anything about Pittston, only the little I'd seen of it from the car, but if these two were representative of its residents, I couldn't imagine a more depressing place to live. Neither cop answered the question. Instead, they walked back to their SUV.

The woman stopped at her door, her hand on the handle. "Rocky road's always a good choice."

"Get it to go," her partner added. "Wouldn't want you to get lost around here after dark."

After dark? It was barely three PM, but the warning couldn't have been clearer. I was being told to git, hightail it out, vamoose, before nighttime found me here. It brought to mind those racist signs in Southern sundown towns years ago that warned blacks not to stop or tarry within their borders. "Don't Let the Sun Set on You in—" It didn't matter the name of the town. No place was safe.

Was that what this was? Or was I being warned away because I was paying attention to this house specifically? Had they been monitoring the security cameras? I watched the SUV pull back and go slow in the direction of town. Maybe they got so few visitors, they didn't know how to be hospitable. Or they had a thing about podiatrists from Chicago.

I glanced back at the gate. This was not a place that said,

Y'all come! Yet, Deloris Poole, black, had brought her girls here, also black, for summer outings and ice cream. Why? What was her connection to this place? I got back in the car and, curious, Googled the town's demographics. Not surprisingly, the town of four thousand or so was 97.75 percent white, 2 percent Asian, and a whopping 0.25 percent black.

I checked the rearview, got the car in gear. "Time to git."

Chapter 30

The Pittston PD SUV was parked across the road from Sally Sweet's Sweets when I pulled up in front, the same two cops inside the vehicle clocking my every step as I went inside. That's when Christmas smacked me full-on across the face. Everywhere I looked, there were Christmas trees and wreaths and stockings, tinsel and ornaments, holly and ivy. Even the air smelled like Santa slept in the back room, everything vanilla and cinnamon, pine trees and nutmeg. Beneath it all, there were white café tables with matching chairs, and walls painted baby pink and white, like an ice-cream cone, like summer on a boardwalk somewhere . . . in the early 1900s.

The sweets were displayed in glass jars sitting on doily-lined shelves along the walls; each large jar had a scooper in it and bags at the ready. The counter up front topped a long freezer case filled with tubs of all kinds of ice cream. Waffle and plain cones stacked on top. Behind it, a white woman stood, dressed as Mrs. Claus, silver spectacles and all. I stopped in my tracks. Watched her. She watched me back, smiling.

"Help you?" She looked about my age, and unlike tiny cop

sitting outside in the cold, the red at her apple cheeks was rouged on.

I walked over to her, carefully, trying not to pick up any yuletide glitter. "Ready for Christmas?"

She chuckled. "We've got a party coming, in a couple hours. A woman down at the senior home. Loves Christmas. Ninety-six she's turning—so, why not give her a thrill, right?"

I looked around the place, where even a look might lead to diabetes.

"I know what you're thinking," the woman said. "But she's ninety-six. Let her have her chocolate."

I glanced over the display, mindful of the cops outside. "How about a plain vanilla cone, one scoop."

Mrs. Claus's lips twisted. "Not very adventurous, are you?"

I shrugged, feeling cop eyes on my back. "Not with ice cream."

She picked up a scoop and opened the display. "We don't get a lot of strangers this time of year, or, well, anytime, really. What brings you to Pittston?"

"Just driving through." I turned around casually, to check on the cops. Yep. Still, there. Looked like they were going to stay until I went. Distrustful bastards. "Nice farms around here."

"I guess. Most of them owned by the same families that started them generations back. Can't say it's an easy life, and the town's shrinking every year, but Pittston's still kickin'." The way she said the last part sounded like she wished it wasn't. She read my curious look. "Don't get me wrong, it's okay, just a little . . . confining. Not for everybody."

"Speaking of farms, I passed one that looked like no one was living there. Out far, east from here. There were the cutest stone lions sitting out in front of it."

"That's the Whittier place. Another of our long-timers, but there haven't been any Whittiers since old Harold died almost ten years ago." She handed me the cone. I took it. "Harold never married, so there weren't any heirs. He left the farm to the town, God bless him."

I licked my cone. "And nobody's been up there in ten years?"

"Not to live." She ran a red towel along the case, keeping it clean. "I don't know how it all works, but there are all kinds of events and such there during the summer. The craft festival was there last July, and there's the Apple Harvest fair in September. Sometimes the church rents the grounds for their Sunday school picnics. All kinds of things." She folded the towel, slid it aside. "Where you from?"

"Up north. Chicago."

"Chicago," she said wistfully, like I'd just told her I hailed from the Emerald City. "I always wanted to see Chicago. Never got there."

"Not too late," I said, smiling. "It's a nice place."

"One of these days, maybe. We had some folks from up your way a few months ago, though." She scanned the walls where photos were hanging in between all the red and green stuff. "Hold on." She walked over to the wall. "We take pictures of all our summer guests, that's if they let us. Some folks are camera shy. I think the photographs are a nice thing to have from year to year. We have some customers who get theirs taken every year they come. You get to see the same kids grow up, then they come back with their own kids, and it starts all over again. It's the best thing ever."

"You don't look old enough to have been here long enough to see the generations change over."

She laughed. "My grandmother opened this shop in 1947. She left it to my mother, my mother left it to me. That's when I came back to town, I'd moved out on my own after community college. To Belleville, the *big* city." She glanced around the place. "But family is family. This place has been mine outright for the past nine years. Even as a kid, I worked the register, swept the floors, made the sundaes, waited on the customers—learning the family business." She winked. "Just like the farms."

I licked my cone, stared at the photos. "You know, you might have seen a friend of mine come through here from Chicago. Her name's Deloris. She's about five-six, black, average build. She would have come through with her girls."

She plucked a photo off the wall and turned to face me. "Sure, I remember her. Sadly, we don't get a lot of diversity down here, so when I get it, I remember it. She's been down here a few times. Nice. The kids too. You won't find her up there, though. She never wanted her photo taken and wouldn't let me take one of the girls. Said she needed to protect their privacy. I respected that. Funny, even their driver was camera shy."

Driver? "Was that Carlton?" I chuckled. "Her brother. Short, a little chubby, wild hair?"

"Oh no. This man was tall, average, short hair, black. The nervous type. He sweat the whole time. Kept asking for glasses of water. I thought maybe he was sick, or something, but he eventually calmed down. We don't see a lot of keyed-up people down this way. Things move a lot slower here."

That sounded like Ronald Shaw. The bell over the door chimed as the female cop from before strolled in. I watched as she walked over to the candy jars and scooped out a few licorice bites and tossed them into a bag, then dropped a dollar on the counter. My time was up.

The cop glanced around the place, then back at Mrs. Claus and me. "Hey, there, Doreen."

"Patsy. Help you with anything else? Maybe take a few salted caramels to your father out there in the car?"

I glanced out the window at the SUV. "He's your father?"

"Sure, he is," Doreen said. "Everything here in Pittston's a family business."

Officer Patsy rested a hand on her gun belt, where she, no

doubt, felt most comfortable putting it. "Thought our visitor here might need directions back to the interstate."

"Actually, no," I said. "I've got GPS that works just fine. Doreen and I were just standing here jawing about Pittston's summer visitors. Didn't realize Sally's had such an interesting tradition of documenting their visits. What a great idea." I slurped the last of my scoop and nibbled a bit on the cone before tossing the rest into a trash can, also pink, but with a paper candy cane taped to the front.

"Oh, I was going to show you this," Doreen said, holding up the photo she'd taken from the wall. "They're from Chicago. Nice family. They were down here to do some fishing last July."

I took the photo, looked at it, smiled. "No," I said. "I don't know these people, but you're right, they do look like a nice family." I handed it back, my heart racing. "Thanks so much for the cone. Love your shop."

Doreen beamed. "Come back anytime. I'll put your photo up on the wall."

Patsy walked me out. The SUV with her father behind the wheel followed me to the on-ramp of the interstate before it turned around and went back.

Two hours and change back to Chicago. That was plenty of time to think about Frank Martini's family photo on the wall at Sally Sweet's Sweets.

Chapter 31

I slid into the city at a little after six, but turned away from my house and office and instead drove to Shaw's. Peering through his garage window, I saw that his death car was still parked inside, its doors open, chemical powder used to check for fingerprints all over the hood, doors, and windows. My mind flashed back to the moment I'd found him, gray, still, dead. Had he killed himself because he felt the walls closing in around him? Had he killed Tonya? Had he stolen girls to profit from them, with the help of Poole and Martini? Or was I trying to shoehorn a man's unfortunate end into something bigger than it was? Why didn't Tonya have a file at Bettle House? Why move Ramona from the Knowleses when she'd finally found a home where she was wanted and loved? Why had both girls ended up at Poole's? Shaw was the link. Shaw, who had a connection to Martini. Money? Is that what they'd done it all for? If so, where was the evidence? If so, what had turned Poole, Shaw, and Martini so far from decency? Poole had been fostering for years. Where were the other girls?

The police wouldn't have done much if Shaw's death looked

like it looked, unless there was some other information that made them suspect foul play, and Hogan all but said that hadn't been the case. But I still wondered how Shaw got into the garage without leaving his footprints in the snow. Why had he gotten only half dressed for the last time? What had been in that medicine bottle? I burrowed into my jacket, pulled my cap down on my head. My eyes landed on a security camera attached to a garage across the alley, its lens covering the door. When I looked, I found several cameras up and down the alley, even one over Shaw's own garage. Had the police even bothered to check the footage?

I slipped through Shaw's back gate and up to his back door. It was locked, but the lock was laughable and the door flimsy. Hadn't Shaw worried about break-ins? This was the North Side, sure, but no neighborhood in the city was immune to crime these days, petty or otherwise. I put my back to the door, scanned the yard, the buildings next door, then back-kicked the door with the heel of my boot, and goosed it with a full-on body push. It took three quick tries, but the door finally popped open and I slid inside.

I was taking quite a few liberties on this case, busting into places without a scintilla of legal standing—Ramona's grandmother's house, Sunshine Bread, that farm, now Shaw's place. Maybe it should worry me that I was so unbothered by it. And did it even count if they didn't catch me at it?

The lights were off inside. I took out my flashlight. This had been a home, now it was just four walls and stuff left behind that somebody was going to have to pack up and clear away. Nothing appeared out of place; the kitchen, dining room, and living room were all neat and tidy, as though Shaw had just left for work for the day and was coming back at dinnertime—only he wasn't.

In his bedroom, I found the same, except for a carry-on suitcase pushed against a wall. When I lifted it, it felt empty; opening it confirmed that to be true. Had Shaw always kept the bag there, or had he been planning a trip, or an escape? His drawers were a mess, clothes stuffed in willy-nilly. I smiled. *Willy-nilly* had been one of my grandmother's favorite expressions.

Underwear, socks, shirts, all crammed in like Shaw had done a fast, down-and-dirty laundry day. I took a moment before opening the closet, bracing myself, flashing back to the time I opened one of these suckers and nearly got strangled to death by a man hiding inside. I eased the door open a bit at a time, ready to bolt if I needed, but there was no one lying in wait, and nothing inside of much interest. Clothes on the hangers, no big whoop, expected; ditto the shoes lined up on the floor. My eyes landed on another suitcase, this one bigger than the carry-on, this one heavy. I rolled it out, opened it. It was packed with clothes, shoes, toiletries, underwear. Shaw was going somewhere, and I doubted it was for the weekend. It looked like he'd packed for a move, not a jaunt. What did he do, change his mind? Instead of Vegas or an escape to the Dominican Republic, he'd decided instead on an eternity in a graveyard?

Nothing in the house pointed to Poole or Pittston or any van, and I didn't find any computers or a cell phone anywhere, which nixed my plans to access his security camera. The police would have taken those, of course, hoping to piece together Shaw's last days. There'd been only one toothbrush in the bathroom, one shaver, one can of shaving cream, one washcloth, and no women's things, so if he was seeing anyone, male or female, they had kept it tight. It would take a good-sized duffel to cart home all the stuff I had at Eli's place—makeup, bath salts, lingerie, T-shirts, my favorite ice cream in his fridge—and we were just fooling around.

When I eased out of Shaw's, I pulled the door closed behind me. The cleaning up, the clearing out, would be left for any family members left behind. My attention was focused now on the other cameras in the alley. They didn't stop the break-ins, of course—the best that homeowners could hope for was to capture the thieves in the act. The police didn't even bother looking for your stuff half the time, but it was some satisfaction taping the lowlife scumbag running away with your lawn mower or flat-screen.

The house directly across the alley from Shaw's was my target. I drove around the front and rang the bell. The door opened after a few seconds to a twentysomething white guy in sweats and a faded fleece jacket. His dark hair was rumpled, like he'd just gotten up from a late-Saturday nap, and his green eyes were bleary and bloodshot. He said nothing, just stared at me. Apparently, he was expecting me to start things off.

I held up my card. "Hi. Hate to bother you, but I'd like to ask you about your neighbor across the alley? There was an incident the other day . . ."

He cracked open the door, took the card, and read it. "Yeah. Crazy bastard gassed himself. All the cop cars tied up the alley for hours. Nobody could get in or out."

I stared at him, at the eyes, the whole rumpled package. Nope. There was nothing there that told me he realized how insensitive his remark had been. "I noticed you have a security camera on your garage. Did the police ask you about it?"

He frowned, confused. "No, why would they?"

"I wonder if I might take a look at any video you might have from that day? Specifically, from that day, but maybe a couple days prior, too? I'm looking for any unusual foot or car traffic around your neighbor's home, anything out of the ordinary, really."

He gave me the full-body sweep, then gave the card another look. "What for? You looking for the guy's ghost?" He grinned, satisfied with his own joke.

Maybe it was the age. Death didn't resonate with a lot of twentysomethings. It hadn't yet touched them personally in a lot of cases, or anyone they knew, so it was easy to make light of it, to see it as something far removed, like Mars or Machu Picchu. Or maybe he was just a nimrod. "Like I said, traffic, unusual activity around the time of . . . the incident. Mr. . . . ?"

He left me hanging on his name. He seemed adamant about not filling in one single blank. He was going to make me work for it.

"The cops didn't ask. What's it to you?"

"The deceased was related to a case I'm working. Sorry. I can't say more than that."

He held the card up, squinted at it. "Is this for real?"

I dug into my bag and pulled out my PI license, showed it to him. "Yes. I could really use your cooperation."

He grinned. "Why not, huh?" He stepped back and held the door open. "But don't do anything funny. I took three tae kwon do lessons last year."

I slid him a look. *Three whole lessons?* The place was a dude sty, a point hammered home by the two sloppy Millennials lounging on a saggy couch in the front room enthralled by video game action on a thousand-inch television screen.

"My roommates."

Neither guy looked away from the screen, their fingers assaulting controllers as characters in fatigues raced over hills with big guns in their hands shooting at Lord knew what. I didn't bother saying hello, neither knew I was there, anyway. The place smelled of guy feet, dirty dishes, and burritos. Guaranteed no woman lived here or would even consider it.

"Follow me," he said, pointing toward the back.

"Would you mind giving me your name first?" I asked.

"Why? What are you going to do with it?"

"Use it when addressing you. Or do you prefer The White Guy Who Opened the Door?"

He wagged a finger at me. "I like your vibe, Cassandra Raines, PI. Saucy." He leered at me. "You seeing anybody? If not, you want to?" He flicked his brows up and down suggestively.

I stood there, saying nothing, staring at him, letting the silence between us hang there just long enough for it to do its work. A duet of groans flew up from the couch as the pair of gamers suffered some kind of digital defeat, but, otherwise, nada.

He cleared his throat nervously. "Sorry." He smoothed down his hair, looked embarrassed. "Ben. Ben Lassner. This way."

He led me to a back room cluttered with textbooks stacked in unsteady piles on a rippled gray carpet. Economics and business appeared to be Lassner's field of study. There was a laptop on a small table, a folding chair behind it, like a work desk, but not a desk, like an office for a twentysomething who had no concept of what an office should be. The rest of the room was empty.

He sat down, booted up the computer. "Give me a minute to cue things up."

His fingers flew across the keyboard, the click of the keys the only sound in the room. He turned the laptop to face me. "There you go. Two days before, you said?"

"It's a good start. Do you have anything that goes back further?"

"I have a week out. You plan on going through all of it?"

I leaned in to see, my eyes on the screen, noting the time stamp. "It's good to have the option."

Lassner stood. "Take the chair. Get you something? A beer? Water? Doritos?" I looked up at him. "It's our go-to in the house."

I smiled. "No, thanks. Just this."

He backed away, perched a haunch on the lip of the bare windowsill, his arms crossed, legs too, as he peeked over my shoulder. A testosterone-fueled roar went up from the front room, where Heckle and Jeckle had apparently smoked an adversarial avatar in a virtual universe. Just a game, I knew, but joystick killing made the act of real killing look far too easy, far too clean.

"What's the case?"

I turned around to look at Lassner. "What?"

"You said the guy was involved in a case you were working." He shrugged. "What's the case?"

I turned back to the laptop. "Sorry. Appreciate your help, though." My eyes scanned the video. Lassner had been right. The alley appeared to get very little traffic compared to some others in the city. Quiet. Clean enough to eat a meal off the pavement, even the city's black trash carts looked new, not gnawed half to useless by rats and raccoons like they were on the South Side. But that was the North Side for you. Whole other world.

Lassner wouldn't let up. "Some kind of fraud, I'd guess. An insurance scam, or something like that?"

It was as good a guess as any, I thought, but I said nothing in response. The back of Shaw's garage came in clear. I could even see his back gate, and a sliver of his back walk. There was a good chance that Lassner's camera would have picked up anything unusual around Shaw's place, anyone coming or going out of the back; so, fingers figuratively crossed, I let the footage play through.

"A lot of that going on these days," he said, "insurance fraud, and why not? It's easy money, until you get caught."

"Guess so," I answered absently.

"I mean, I didn't know him personally, but he looked like an everyday guy with a nine-to-five job. He put his trash out on time. Kept his yard up. You'd never know he was a Tesla Roadster guy. He just didn't have that vibe. And if you've got that kind of money, what do you have to be depressed about? Try living on ramen in a house with two other guys. Now *that's* depressing."

I turned. "Excuse me? What's that about a Tesla?"

"The dead guy owned one. Matte black. Sleek as hell. Two hundred fifty thousand easy, but it's like he didn't match it, you know? It was like seeing Homer Simpson driving around in the Batmobile."

I found Shaw in a beat-up old clunker with a dodgy exhaust, a Porsche keychain dangling from the ignition. No sign of a Tesla. Anyway, how could Shaw afford one on his salary? You didn't own a $250,000 car and dress as messily as he had, and you didn't park it just anywhere with only a couple of low-end security cameras and a flimsy lock to keep joyriders at bay. "When did you last see it?"

Lassner shrugged. "I don't know. It didn't get out of the garage much. Shame too. It's sweet. I figured it was the reason he put the cameras up in the first place. You don't drive that kind of flash without putting eyes on it 24/7."

"It's December," I said. "That's not the kind of car you'd drive in this weather or leave in a garage until spring."

"Hell no," Lassner said. "I mean, I wouldn't. I'd board that baby somewhere dry, clean, and temperature controlled. But maybe he was getting around to it? He hadn't had it long. Less than a year?"

I eyed the laptop. I'd started with video taken a week prior to my finding Shaw, and hadn't yet seen a Tesla go in or out of his garage. Where was it? I looked over at Lassner. "Did you ever see a Porsche over there?"

"Porsche? Who was the guy, Elon Musk?" He laughed, but cut it off when he saw me staring at him. He cleared his throat. "Sorry. No, just the Tesla and that piece of crap he drove most of the time. I called it his decoy car. Drive the old car during the day to fool everybody, then sneak off at night and live the Tesla life when nobody's looking. Maybe he was going through a midlife crisis. Grabbing one last thrill before it all goes south."

I went at it again, lasering in on every grainy frame, concentrating on Shaw's garage door and back gate, day by day, hour by hour.

"What're you looking for, exactly?"

I ignored his question and asked one of my own. "You don't remember seeing anyone coming in or out across the alley?"

"You mean the cop?"

"No, not counting the 911 response."

"I wasn't. A cop showed up the night before they found him. He parked blocking the garage, went in through the gate. That's what made me think the guy was in trouble with the law."

I turned away from the laptop again. Lassner was proving to be quite the info dump. "The police didn't knock on your door to talk to you?" Lassner shook his head. "And you didn't call them to tell them any of what you're telling me now?"

"Was I supposed to?"

I let a moment go. "What'd this cop look like?"

"Beats me. It was dark. Didn't see much."

"In uniform?"

Lassner shook his head. "Regular clothes."

"Then how'd you know he was a cop?"

"The walk. All cops walk like they own everything their feet touch, you know what I mean? Cocky. He had on a dark coat, no hat, no gloves. Not too tall? He moved like he knew what he was doing. Cops do that, too. Move like they own it."

"You didn't see his face, even when he came out again?"

"I didn't stick with it that long. I figured whatever the guy was into had nothing to do with me."

Hours prior to me finding Shaw, at six minutes after one last Monday morning, there he was, the cop Lassner described. The hour was far too late for a routine call. He had gotten out of a dark car, blue or black, the camera catching just the front hood and bumper as he pulled up right at the gate. He kept his head down and turned away from the cameras.

"He knows the cameras are there," I muttered. "He's deliberately avoiding them."

Lassner leaned in to take a look. "What's he up to?"

"Good question."

I watched as the time ticked off from the moment the dark figure slipped inside Shaw's gate and disappeared, presumably, into the house. Twenty minutes passed before the figure appeared back at the gate, but this time he wasn't alone. I froze the footage, catching the two figures midstride. Neither man was Shaw, one was too short, the other too wide.

"Where'd the second guy come from?" Lassner asked. "Is it Tesla guy?"

I unfroze the video, advancing it frame by frame. I could feel my heart rate rise. Two men. Dark clothing. Moving quickly. There it was. I stopped the tape again. "That dumb porkpie hat."

Lassner squinted at the screen. "A what?"

Guy number two was Lenny Vine, which meant there was a good chance that his partner was Frank Martini. Martini got in his car quickly, while Vine disappeared out of frame. Then Martini's lights flicked on and he sped away, the camera catching just a quick shot of his taillights. No plate. Seconds after he was gone, a sputtering of light flicked across the screen.

"Whoa, who's *that*?" Lassner asked.

I held my breath. I knew what it was, but I reversed the tape just to see it again. A dodgy headlight. At 1:28 AM. Outside Ronald Shaw's garage. On the day I'd found him dead.

Lassner turned to me. "Those guys definitely didn't want their faces out there."

I leaned back in the chair, my mind clicking a mile a minute. "No, they didn't."

Nine hours. That was the time between the 1:00 AM visit and the time I barreled into Shaw's garage. The camera didn't show the backyard, the door from the house, all of that was out of range. Lenny Vine could have slipped in at any time, and at any point without the cameras picking him up. He could have climbed over a neighbor's fence or pushed his way through Shaw's front door. And the two of them could have easily incapacitated Shaw, carried him from the house, put him in that car, and then left it running. The snow that night would have covered their tracks. What went on for those twenty minutes?

Had Martini considered Shaw a liability, a threat? When I had walked through Shaw's place, it looked like he was preparing to leave. Was he also preparing to talk? I stood, stepped away from the laptop to glance out of Lassner's window at the street. I needed a moment to think.

"Get what you needed?" he asked.

"Do you think you could make me a copy of that footage?"

"Yeah, sure. What went on over there?"

He was young, looking for a little excitement, but the implication of what I'd just seen unsettled me. "A copy, please," I said solemnly. "And thanks for your time."

Chapter 32

I sat in my kitchen in the dark listening to the metronomic clicking of the clock's second hand. It was well past midnight, quiet. It felt like the entire world was asleep, except for me, but, of course, that was just a feeling. Nothing stopped the world from turning, not death, not tragedy, not trauma, not pain so deep it stole your breath, not grief so strong it threatened to turn you inside out, nothing at all stopped the world.

What did I know, or think I knew? I knew that Frank Martini, Ronald Shaw, and Deloris Poole had something going that involved Shaw placing girls, and only girls, in Poole's care. I suspected the worst. I knew that Deloris Poole was one thing on the surface and something darker underneath.

I knew Shaw had perverted his responsibilities to Bettle House and the children it served for what? A fancy car? The hell of it? I got up to pour myself a glass of cold milk.

I knew that Ronald Shaw had been extremely affected by my showing him Ramona's photos. He had been frightened, backed against a wall, and he'd run to Martini. Shaw would have broken if I'd stayed on him, I was sure of that. Maybe the others had been sure of it too?

My first thought, my fear, the one eating its way through my gut and lying on my chest like a concrete slab was that these girls were either being sold or given away, even the thought made me sick. I'd hoped the ledger and drive would have confirmed something, but they hadn't. I had hoped my visit downstate to Pittston would have provided more answers than questions, but that hadn't happened, either, except to confirm the link between Poole and the tiny place. Martini was that link.

Martini knew Pittston. He'd spent vacation time down there with his family; so confident that no one would trace him that far, he even posed for a photo at Sally Sweet's. Is that why Poole took the girls there? At Martini's recommendation? Had she and Martini rented out the Whittier place to show off the girls under the pretense of a summer outing? That's what I thought, but had no proof of—that's the scenario that wouldn't let me sleep. That's why I was sitting in my kitchen in the dark at midnight, jaws clenched, wanting to do something ungodly to the both of them, and to Lenny Vine.

Lenny. A few years back, there had been a girl, not much older than Ramona. She was a witness to a gang killing. I had a client, and Lenny had one, too. My job was to protect the girl. Lenny's was to protect the gang. I did my best, but lost because there were some things you didn't do for money; Lenny won because he doesn't operate by the same principle. Lenny Vine is wired wrong, broken. Tamika Jenkins. That was the girl I lost.

I would take the footage from the security camera to Hogan, after I paid Deloris Poole a call. Hogan wanted me to turn over Ramona, but I didn't think that was such a good idea. Martini's reach was long. He likely still had pals on the force who wouldn't hesitate to let him know the second I brought her in. Hogan might even make good on his threat to arrest me. If so, tomorrow was going to be a long day.

*   *   *

Showered, dressed, and ready to start the day, I checked in with Ramona on her new burner. She was fine. I then called her mother to tell her what was going on. It took some doing to convince her that leaving Ramona where she was for now was the best thing, but she finally got on board with it. That done, I drove to Poole's, not at all sure what kind of play I could make.

Her car was in the drive. I parked out of sight of her windows and settled in. If I knocked on her door, she would only lie again. She was obviously good at it, going so far as to employ props, leaning that cane against her sofa like it was Tiny Tim's crutch. I was done with lies—lies had run me all over this town like a headless chicken. I was going to sit back and watch for a while, see how Poole spent her time. Maybe that would lead me where I needed to be.

The farm in Pittston. No photographs at Sally's. Martini on the wall. Tonya not at her grandmother's, because she didn't have one. The butterfly necklace that might help ID her. Tonya had been a thorn in Poole's side, and hadn't given her a moment's peace. Had Shaw come in and solved the problem? If Tonya couldn't be managed, couldn't be molded, and couldn't be used for their purposes, had they simply cut their losses? Is that why she ended up under that on ramp? Was that Martini's and Lenny Vine's doing?

I'd dressed warmly and brought along a couple of blankets, too, to help the car's heat along. Even still, I was nearly frozen solid when Poole's door finally opened after two hours of waiting. I slid down in the driver's seat, watching as she stepped out onto the porch and looked around before rushing to her car and driving away. No cane, I noticed. No obvious difficulty walking down the front steps, walking to her car, or getting in it. Deloris Poole appeared hale and hearty.

She passed me going east, not in a hurry, not like she was making a run for it, just going. I gave her a good lead, then followed, hoping she was going somewhere more interesting than the grocery store or Starbucks.

Three cars behind Poole, my eyes on her back window, she turned onto the southbound Kennedy, and I dropped back another car length, confident I couldn't lose her. I stayed in the same lane. If she got off, I'd get off. I cranked the radio up, settled in, giving my gas gauge a quick look to make sure I had enough to hang in. I would be okay, unless she planned on driving to Pittston.

Ten minutes later, we were off the expressway and Poole was turning into an empty lot near the UIC campus. I eased to a stop at the corner when Poole drove in. I did not want to venture farther without cover, but even from where I was, I could hear Poole's tires roll over the hardpacked snow, draw to a stop, and then idle there.

She was waiting for someone. This was a meet. I flicked off the radio, checked my watch. A few minutes after 1:00 PM. Odd time to meet clandestinely. Perfect spot, though. Away from main streets, an empty lot, easy access in and out from all four directions, the ability to see someone coming.

I pulled off, but didn't go far. I slid into a parking spot across the street, then hunkered down in the seat, my eyes on Poole. It wasn't a very dignified position, and if anyone asked, I'd be loath to tell them this was part of how I made my living, but if a thing worked, you used it. Unless Poole was meeting with somebody from the Mob, nobody was likely going to go down the row of parked cars, checking in every window.

A dark SUV began to circle the lot, the driver making a slow circuit, like a shark closing in on dinner. This was it. This was Poole's contact. I slid down lower and watched as the SUV entered the lot, pulled around, and met Poole's driver's-side window to driver's-side window. That's when the window on the SUV slid down a crack, just enough so the drivers could talk to one another, not enough to be able to see the driver's face.

The windows stayed cracked for a time, both cars idling, slow whiffs of exhaust wafting out of their tailpipes. What were they talking about? Why were they talking about it here? If I stayed put and didn't make a move, they'd have their conversation and drive off without my getting a single bit of information. I needed to force things. I worked it through from every angle, anticipating all the ways things might go. For me, the probability of success was low. There were just too many exit points, and even if I sped in at top speed, I'd never be fast enough to get a look at the other driver before both cars raced off.

"Oh, the hell with it."

I slipped my gloves off, took a couple of deep breaths, then made a quick reverse, jerked the wheel, and tore out of the spot, flying toward the lot, spinning to a halt in front of the SUV. Immediately, its tinted window went up. I knew the SUV would reverse and speed away. I knew I couldn't cover both cars in the open lot and hold them both, but I had hoped on ID'ing the driver. I needed to know if it was Martini or, God forbid, Lenny, but the dark windows foiled that. I quickly studied the SUV as it screeched away from me, no plates, no distinctive markers or tags. Whoever the driver was, he or she had taken every precaution.

The SUV tires spit up slush, rocks, and snow, backing away from me, and within seconds, it was out of range, out of the lot, and disappearing around the corner. Poole was slower off the mark. I jumped out of my car and yanked open her driver's door, which she had failed to lock, before she could even get her foot on the gas.

"Turn it off!" I barked. "Get out."

She stared up at me, eyes wide, fear and confusion plastered all over her face. "What are you doing?"

"We need to talk."

Poole's eyes darted around the lot, looking for a way out. She had plenty of options, but I don't think she was thinking that far ahead. I'd startled her, found her out, though I didn't know what it all meant yet. The meeting she'd just had hadn't been innocent—she knew it, I knew it. I was hoping that she was now scared enough to say something that would explain it all.

She straightened, jutted a trembling chin out. "I want a lawyer."

If I had a nickel for every time somebody said that to me, I'd have a mountain of nickels to wallow in; I'd be nickel rich, a nickel-aire. But that was another life.

"I want to lie on a beach in Bimini," I said, "but that's going to have to wait. Get out. Let's talk."

She glared at me defiantly. The shock had worn off. I had no legal basis to keep her. She knew that. "Or?"

I took a step back. "Sally Sweet's. Doreen says hello."

Poole looked like I'd shot her. Her lips moved for a few moments before she could get any sounds to come out of her mouth. "Who?"

"Nice try. Want to try again? Who were you meeting with just now?"

"I don't have to tell you anything. Move your car."

I wasn't keeping her, not really. All she had to do was back up and go. But until she figured that out . . . "Was it Martini? Did Lenny Vine finally trade up?"

"You're supposed to be looking for Ramona, aren't you? Why are you following me around?"

"I've done my job, Miss Poole, I found Ramona. As to why I'm following you? Well, with Shaw gone, I have a feeling you're now the weakest link. What are you doing with those girls? Selling them? Trading them?" Poole drew in a sharp breath. I went for broke. "The old Whittier place? The outings? The thumb drive? The ledger? I'm giving you a chance to help yourself, here."

Her car flew into reverse and she three-point turned it, a look of sheer panic on her face. "Suit yourself," I yelled after her. "Ramona says hello. And a lot of other things."

Poole tore out of the lot in the same direction the SUV had

taken, her tires spitting up ice and slush and bits of gravel. I stood there, my car door open, the car dinging, then trudged back and got in it. Not a total loss. She hadn't given me any new information, but she now knew I knew more than she thought I did. She was probably on her phone right now, screeching at Martini or Vine to come save her. Good. Let them come. I drove out of the lot, cranking up the radio.

Chapter 33

I stared across the table at Barb and Marian. They stared back. We'd been doing it for about two minutes, ever since they sat down in my booth at Deek's, interrupting my lunch. I'd ordered the short ribs and mashed potatoes, my last meal before I went to see Hogan. I broke first, but only because having two nuns staring at me across the table made me feel oddly exposed, even if one of those nuns was Barb.

"The pope sent you?" I asked, leaning back. "He finally got around to excommunicating me, didn't he? I knew it was only a matter of time. Oh, well, guess I can go back to eating meat on Fridays."

Barb said, "You always ate meat on Fridays."

"Because I hate people telling me I can't. You know that. Stop playing."

Marian leaned in. "The Love Bus is a judgment-free zone. Open to all, no questions asked."

"I'm aware. I got the memo." Her eyes really were penetrating, you couldn't get away from them. She'd have made a good cop. I could just imagine the number of sweat-soaked confessions she could have gotten.

"Scoot and the others haven't been around," Barb said.

Marian pointed a nun finger at me. "You chased them away, and now I want you to fix it."

"*I* chased them away?"

"Literally," Barb said.

It was a double team. A setup. But they were right. I had told Scoot and the others to keep a low profile for a day or two, for Ramona's sake.

"You ruined it. You fix it." Sister Marian got up, stared down at me. "God loves you."

She turned on her heel and headed for the door, her boots clomping along the floor, me watching her back, my mouth agape. Barb slid out of the booth. "If you need any help finding them, call me." She smiled. "Marian can be a bit—"

I interrupted her. "Gangsta?"

Barb laughed. "She really is sweet."

I frowned. "I've *zero* evidence of that."

Barb buttoned her coat. "You'll find the kids?"

"Yes."

"Then it's done. Anything on Whip?"

"Nothing."

Barb sighed but said nothing else. She met Sister Marian, the Mafia nun, at the door and they left together, but before they went, Marian turned and gave me one of those *I'm watching you* looks that sent a slight shiver through me.

"You thinking about signing up?" Muna asked as she set my plate on the table.

"Huh?"

"The nuns."

I looked up at her. "Are you serious? *No.*"

"Good. You'd be terrible at it."

She walked away. I glared at her back.

"So!"

I kept getting messages, calls, and texts from Martini, still looking for that update. He'd pay me a visit next, which was why I was staying out of my office. Besides, he likely already knew about my cornering Poole, especially if that had been him in that SUV. So, all this update nonsense was him playing a part, just as Poole had been playing one. He was wasting his time, though. The sight of him creeping into that park with his gun drawn, with Vine, thinking I was in that gazebo with a child, told me all I needed to know about him, and nothing I didn't already know about Lenny.

Monday morning, Hogan stared at me from across his desk. I'd just shown him Lassner's security footage. He saw what I saw: two men, the blinky headlight. He also had the thumb drive and the ledger, Tonya Pierce's link to Poole, her possible ID, and copies of the photos showing Martini, Poole, and Shaw as close as pickets in a fence. I'd told him about Vine tailing me, and my trip down to Pittston, and the photo of Martini and his family on the wall at Sally's, and then Poole's secret meet with the SUV. It looked like he was waiting for more, but I was all talked out.

Still, I knew what he knew. None of it was a slam dunk, not even a half dunk. Truthfully, my ball was still halfway down the court, but I knew I was moving in the right direction. Too many people were getting nervous and desperate over all this "nothing" I had.

"So there, you now know everything I know. Deal's a deal."

He appeared unmoved. "You were supposed to come in with Titus."

"I didn't."

"I can see that. Where is she?"

"Safe. She's been in contact with her mother, my client. You can mark her off your books."

"I'm supposed to take your word for it?"

"I'd appreciate it."

Hogan's brows furrowed. "Adrienne Babcock said you were a pain in the ass."

That got me. "*Adrienne Babcock?*"

I worked a year in uniform with Babcock. She was as dull as a rusty butter knife, and as slow as molasses in January; she was also a flincher. She flinched at everything—a sudden movement, a leaf falling from a tree, a cat walking past her in the street. God forbid you had to go through a door with her. Hogan must have read my face.

He leaned back in his chair. "She's in records now."

"Oh, thank God." I said it before I had time to filter the thought.

"I looked through that drive and the ledger," Hogan said. "I didn't see a smoking gun. I've got nothing on Poole. There was nothing at Shaw's, either."

"I don't think he killed himself. He wasn't wearing shoes. Did you see that suitcase in his closet? Who packs to die?"

"He wasn't acting rationally. He'd downed half a bottle of sleeping pills."

"It's difficult dressing a dead man," I said. "They could have managed the suit. Shoes and socks are harder to get on."

"They?"

"Martini. Shaw."

"Again, I should take your word for all those conclusions you've jumped to?"

"Logical conclusions."

"Maybe *you* killed Shaw."

I stood. "Okay, I'm out. You sit here and be obstinate if you want to. Ramona's found, but she ran for a reason that's buried somewhere in all that crap I just gave you. Use it, or don't. But just so you know, this is why PIs don't much care for cops." I waved my hand around his office. "This. Right here."

"Didn't I promise to arrest you?"

"Go on then. Lock me up. Let them keep pimping girls out of an old house in Boondocksville. Go on."

Hogan watched me, no expression on his face. "Bring me something I can use next time."

I turned, disgusted. "Like there's going to be a next time."

"Babcock was right."

I turned back. "Oh, 'Babcock was right'? *Babcock?* The woman who once showed up for work without her duty belt? What she thought she was going to do all day without it, I don't know. Or, wait, why don't you ask her about the time she came to work without bullets in her service weapon? Might explain why she's in records right now."

"Get out of here," Hogan said.

But before he finished the sentence, I was already halfway out the door.

There was no answer at Poole's. I rang the bell several times, then knocked. If she was inside, she was avoiding me. If she wasn't, where was she?

"You back again?"

I turned from the bell, irritated at being interrupted. A woman stood gawking at me from the sidewalk.

"Excuse me?"

"I've seen you parked across the street, going in and out of her place. You missed her. She left about an hour ago, said she'd be gone for a couple days, and asked me to collect her mail and her paper."

I stepped off the porch, met the woman at the walk. She was maybe in her seventies, spry, it appeared, fully capable of dialing 911 or taking my license plate down, which she'd likely already done.

"Was she by herself?"

"Yes."

"Luggage?"

The woman looked me over. "You a friend of hers?"

"Yes." The lie took no time to fly out of my mouth. "We were supposed to go Christmas shopping today. She must have forgotten."

The woman appeared to relax some, smiled. "Must have. She

didn't mention anything about shopping. Looked in a hurry, though."

"You're her neighbor?"

"Viola Harris. Me and my husband live two doors down."

I pulled the photo of Ramona out of my bag. "Mrs. Harris, do you remember this girl?"

She squinted at the photo and her face lit up. "That's Ramona."

"Ms. Poole didn't tell you Ramona had run away?"

That shocked her. "Run away? That can't be. I just saw her not too long ago. She stopped by to bring me an early Christmas present."

"You know her well, then?"

"I suppose I do. She comes over to my house all the time for talks and cookies. I think she's just looking for a break from all those chores and homework and such. She told me once that I reminded her of her grandmother, which warmed my heart so, I can't tell you. Run away? Oh, where could she be?"

"She's been found. She's safe."

The woman clutched her hands to her chest. "Thank you, Jesus."

I stared at Poole's house, wondering where she might run. Or . . . "Poole doesn't have a garage, does she?"

"No. Why?"

"Nothing. I guess I'll try back, then." I got my car keys out. "The early Christmas present. Mind if I ask what it was?"

"It was a photo of me and her, and she put it in the nicest frame. I have it on my mantel so I can always see it. She's such a special child."

Something else Ramona had left behind? A photo in a frame, or a hiding place for something else she'd taken from Poole? Although Ramona swore she'd told me everything, I had a feeling that wasn't true. What if?

"Could I see the photo?" I pulled out my ID and my business card, letting her study both. "You can call to verify those first, if you want."

She looked up at me, a worried look on her face. "Ramona's not in any trouble, is she?"

"No, ma'am, she's fine, but she might have come across something that isn't quite right, and I'm trying to find out what that is."

She stared at me, long and hard. It was cold out here, but there was no way to rush the appraisal. It would take as long as it took, but my toes and fingers would suffer.

"Come on, then," she said. "I'll show it to you."

Her redbrick bungalow was neat and well kept, with white shutters, low bushes in front reduced now to a tangle of brittle twigs in for a long period of stasis before spring came around again. The small herd of wire reindeer on the snowy lawn was a cute touch. She slipped my card into her pocket and led me inside. I stood on a throw rug and slipped my boots off, then stood and waited to be invited farther in. You didn't go traipsing into people's homes, unless you were invited to, my grandmother had taught me. It was a sign of respect. I watched as Mrs. Harris took off her boots and coat, all the while crowing about Ramona. She was halfway to the living room and the mantel with the photo on it, when she remembered I was with her and turned.

"Don't just stand there, come in. Sit."

She handed the framed photo to me as I took a seat on an end chair. The frame was nice. Heavy. Ramona and the woman were posed side by side, their arms around each other, both with wide, happy smiles on their faces. Ramona looked younger somehow, the woman too. I declined the offer of tea and hesitated before making what I knew would seem like an odd request to Mrs. Harris.

"It's a beautiful photo," I said, "but I'd like your permission to remove the frame. I need to see if there's anything hidden inside."

"Hidden? Like what?"

I explained briefly about Ramona leaving things behind, leaving out a lot of detail. "She did it to protect herself."

"From what? What's going on over at Poole's?"

I held Harris's treasure in my hands. "May I?"

She looked at the framed photo, looking a little worried. "Go ahead. Do what you need to, just don't break it."

I was careful, taking my time unscrewing the frame, lifting the back away, and placing it gently on the table in front of me. There was an SD card taped to the back of the photo by a thin strip of clear tape. I carefully peeled the tape away to hold the card in my palm.

"What is that?" Harris asked.

I held it up for her to see. I doubt she'd ever seen an SD card, but I briefly explained what it was.

"Why would Ramona hide a thing like that behind our picture?"

I knew, but didn't say. Instead, I put the frame back together and handed it back to Mrs. Harris. "I'll need to take this. It'll help Ramona."

"Go on, then."

I stood, carefully slipping the card into my pocket. "Thanks for your help. I'll tell Ramona you're thinking about her."

"You do that," Harris said as she walked me to the door. "I still don't know about SD cards, but you make sure Ramona gets that."

I slipped back into my shoes, buttoned my jacket, and stepped outside. "I will. Thanks, Mrs. Harris."

She waved me on. She was still standing there at her door waving when I pulled away from the curb and drove off. Just like a grandmother would.

A hidden SD card, another puzzle piece. Another lie. I needed a computer quick.

Chapter 34

The SD card was the missing piece, the piece that made the thumb drive and the ledger make sense. It held evidence of money exchanges between clients—I suppose you could call them that—and Poole, with regular payouts, cuts, to Martini and Shaw that stretched into the six figures. That's how Shaw had afforded that Tesla. I wondered what else he owned and had hidden? I wondered what Martini and Poole had spent their shares on? Or was Shaw's Tesla the reason they got rid of him? Maybe they told him to lay low, play it cool, and he hadn't, drawing attention? He had the good sense not to drive it to work, but his neighbor sure noticed he had it. Where was that Tesla now?

Adoptions? I didn't think so. There were no corresponding paperwork, applications, or anything noted, just the money. It was possible all that other stuff was somewhere else in Poole's files; perhaps Ramona had only taken a part of what was there. But if that was the case, I didn't think Shaw would be dead, and Lenny Vine wouldn't be in this up to his neck.

I scrolled through the numbers. The initials on the drive matched actual names on the SD card. The numbers on the ledger were a code; though I hadn't realized it before now, each number was assigned to a girl. Sarita Douglas, sixteen, had been "adopted" by Simeon and Georgina Hawkins of La Porte, Indiana. Their address was there, the electronic receipt for their "purchase." Carmen Pugh, seventeen, to X. Stephenson, Denver. None of the matches appeared to have gone through Bettle House, though all of them had Shaw's prints all over them. He had been funneling girls to Poole, the ones who'd languished for years in the system, Poole would groom them, teach them, and they moved them out, got them placed, making money off the transactions. That was it. That was the ugly truth.

But what did the crossed-out zeroes mean? I looked up Ramona's code, matched it, then followed the column. For her, there was a one in the column. I tried the same with Tonya Pierce's name. She had the crossed-out zero.

I sat back in the chair, trying to figure it out. Shaw moved Tonya. Had he been moving her to someone on Poole's list? If so, what happened? How had she ended up dead, instead? There were a lot of zeroes in the column, only a few with ones. Ramona. Darla Leland. Ones. What did Ramona and Darla have that Tonya and the others didn't? Ramona didn't have much. Her grandmother was gone; her grandmother's house, where she'd once been happy, also gone. The aunt who wanted her, but couldn't get her, moved to another state, gone, and her uncle Lester was a big, fat no-go. She only had her mother, a woman struggling to right herself after years of addiction. I sat up. Ramona had *one* mother. Someone who wanted her. Someone who would raise holy hell if she came up missing, as she did when she found out Ramona had run away. Is that why Shaw never came for Ramona? I mean, maybe they'd planned to cycle her through, like they'd done the others. That's why Shaw placed her there in the first place, maybe believing that Leesa Evans was out of the picture. But she came back around, didn't she? Out of jail, clean and newly sober. She'd made it known she wanted Ramona back. Leesa Evans was the *1,* the one that saved Ramona.

I hurriedly gathered the ledger, the drive, and locked them in my safe. I didn't have time to walk them down to the basement. The SD card I slipped into my front jeans pocket, then grabbed my bag and my jacket. I needed to get to Hogan, and then I had to bring Ramona in. I had it. There was enough information in Poole's files to find and bring back every girl, hopefully before it was too late to save them. I just hoped Hogan and the rest of the cops moved fast enough to catch Poole before she made a run for it or Martini stuffed *her* into a can.

My door opened. It was Pouch dressed in olive green. He looked like a walking hand grenade. The morose look on his face made him appear as though he'd lost his best friend, which, I suppose, he had—at least temporarily. His lost expression told me all I needed to know. Whip was still out there, some-where, unaccounted for.

"I'm in a hurry," I said. "I can't talk about it right now."

Pouch's eyes scanned the office. I snapped my fingers to bring his eyes back around to me and off my stuff. "Pouch!"

"Charlie missed group. He never misses. He's in trouble."

We stood there for a moment, neither of us speaking, but both of us likely imagining the same worst-case scenario. My mind ran through it all again and I felt anxious and sick. I'd checked every place I could check: hospitals, drunk tanks, his apartment, his job, even the morgue. I shimmied into my jacket, pushing the image of Whip lying in a shallow grave out of my head. "Not now, Pouch, I have to go."

I waved him toward the door and shooed him out into the hall, locking the door behind us. I froze when I caught sight of Martini standing by the fire exit, blocking the stairs to the base-ment. It was an odd spot to pick, I thought, but then it became clear. Still, I had to check. I grabbed Pouch by the arm and walked him toward the front stairs that led down to the street, bracing myself. When we got to them, as I suspected, there was Lenny Vine, leaning against the wall, that sleazy grin on his face. My grip still on Pouch's arm, we moved back away from the stairs. We were caught in a pinch. Martini started walking toward us, Vine too, closing the vise with Pouch and me in it.

Martini asked, "Who's the little guy?"

"Doesn't matter," I said. "He's just leaving." I pushed Pouch toward the stairs, hoping Vine would let him go, only he wouldn't; he stopped Pouch with a slow head shake. I pulled him back again and stood in front of him.

"I've been trying to call you," Martini said. "You don't answer. You're avoiding me? I thought we were working this together?"

"Nobody's avoiding you, Martini. I've been busy, and I'm sure I turned that partnership down. I'm in a hurry, too, so if you don't mind beating it?"

He laughed. Vine laughed. "What about the meet with the girl. That never happened?"

"She never showed," I said. "Kids, huh?"

"But you never showed, either."

Our eyes locked. The game was over, both of us knew it. "No, I was there. I saw you and Vine." Creeping into the park up to that gazebo with guns drawn. "Looked like you two were expecting trouble."

Vine looked over at Martini. Martini's brows lifted. You could almost see the nice-guy façade melt away, revealing someone horrible underneath, someone lost enough to hire on Lenny Vine to do whatever, because maybe he didn't have the stomach for it.

"Okay, then, done with tap dancing. Where is it?" Martini asked. "Don't say *what.* You know what. And don't say you *don't have it.* You've been running to Hogan, poking into Shaw, running all over town."

I said nothing. I didn't move. Copies of the ledger and the drive were locked away in my safe, but they meant nothing without the SD card, which I stupidly now had on me. If I lost that now, I'd be back to almost square one.

Martini held out a hand. "Give me the bag."

I smiled, but it wasn't a happy smile, not the kind you gave when you saw a cute puppy or baby, it was a buy-some-time smile, an I'm-thinking-as-fast-as-I-can-but-coming-up-goose-eggs smile. "Mind if I take my gun out first?"

Martini and Vine laughed; Pouch and I didn't think anything was all that funny. Martini snapped his fingers impatiently. "Toss it."

Vine snickered. I looked over at him, not bothering to hide my contempt.

"Don't get cute," Martini said, glancing over at Pouch, his eyes traveling from his head to his toes, a bemused expression on his face. "I'd hate for anyone to get hurt here."

I handed over the bag, knowing Martini wouldn't find what he was looking for, hoping I would think of something brilliant before he realized it. I could feel the SD card in my pocket resting against my right hip. When they found the bag didn't have what they wanted, they'd search me, and then maybe they'd trash my office just for kicks. I was sick of people trashing my office. I sneered at Martini as he rifled through my stuff, his beefy man hands pawing all over my wallet, my keys, my life in microcosm. In hindsight, it might have been better to put the SD card in the safe and have Hogan come to me. But hindsight was no help to me now.

"Wrong side again," Lenny said. He was taunting me, of course. That's the kind of person Lenny Vine was. Childish, half-baked. He was referring to the last time we'd come up against each other, the time he sold a kid out to a street gang, and they killed her.

I kept my mouth shut, but watched Vine closely. I didn't

know Martini. He could just be greedy and saw an opportunity to make some money to augment his police pension. The morality of his actions he would have to answer for to his maker. Vine, I knew, would slit my throat and then stand there and watch me bleed to death.

"Not here," Martini announced, slinging my bag to the floor. "Where is it?"

I could hear Pouch breathing hard behind me. "Where's what?"

It didn't look like Martini was in a playing mood. "I know you found her. I know she talked. I know she gave you what I'm here to take back." He flicked his head at Vine. "Search her."

I fisted my hands, ready to punch Vine's lights out, or at least get a good shot in, but that's when I heard the click, and turned to see Martini with a gun aimed at the back of Pouch's head. I would have thought he couldn't do it, shoot an innocent person in the back of the head, having once worn a badge and sworn an oath to serve and protect, but his eyes told me something different. This was a different Frank Martini than the one I'd met at Clancy's.

I unfisted my hands and slowly raised my arms and waited for Vine, who eased up leering at me, to run his weaselly little kid-killing hands up my legs, around my behind and inner thighs.

"Enjoying yourself?" I hissed.

He winked at me. "Oh yes I am."

I kneed him, but it only made him laugh. He eventually found the right pocket and plucked out the card. He held it up so Martini could see it, then tossed it to him like it was nothing, instead of everything I needed.

"See?" Martini said as he slipped the card into his jacket pocket. "I knew you were holding out."

I looked at Vine. He was still standing there. Too close, smelling of old cigarette smoke and degradation. I shoved him back, both arms, as hard as I could, not wanting him anywhere near me. He took the shove, and even seemed to enjoy it.

Martini put his gun away. Mine was in the bag on the floor, out of reach. "So now you got nothing," he said. "So now you can spin your wheels all you want."

Martini and Lenny exchanged a look; then Vine headed down the stairs, whistling a happy tune, his work done. I was shaking with fury at having had the little troll's degenerate hands all over me. Pouch moved to stand beside me, watching Martini as he stopped for one final parting shot.

Martini leaned in, lowered his voice, alcohol on his breath. "And in case you're wondering, it was for the money."

My eyes burned into his. "You didn't have to tell me. I knew."

Pouch bumped into Martini, who pushed him back. "Watch it, you little freak."

Pouch backed up. "Sorry. So sorry."

I watched as Martini and the SD card waltzed down the hall and then away down the stairs. I stood there dejected, listening as the front door opened and closed, knowing that all that digging, all that pushing was wasted effort. The growl I let out was one of pure frustration.

"We need to get out of here," Pouch said.

I bent down to pick up my bag, scooping up the odds and ends that had fallen out when Martini searched through it. "You go on, Pouch. Sorry you had to get in the middle of this."

"No, seriously," he said. "We need to get the fuck out of here before they come back."

I sighed. "They're not coming back. They got what they came for." I stood, slung my bag over my shoulder, then turned to face him. Pouch stood there holding the SD card. I blinked, not believing what I was seeing. "What? How did you? *What?*"

"I can't turn it off," he said apologetically. "He was there. It was in his pocket. You needed it, so . . ."

I looked at the card, at Pouch, my mouth hanging open.

"Now we need to get the hell out of here before he realizes he ain't got it and comes back looking for it."

I grabbed the card, then gave Pouch an overly enthusiastic buss on the cheek. "*Gah!* You wonderful little pickpocket, you."

"That's not what you said the other day when you frisked me in the street."

"Shut up, Pouch, don't ruin it. Run. Let's get out of here."

We raced for the back stairs, knocked for Turk, then ran right through his basement lair to the back alley, and sweet, sweet escape. I was back in the game, baby.

Chapter 35

Detective Hogan stared at the computer screen, at the numbers that coordinated with the vague jottings in the ledger and on the thumb drive—meaningless apart, everything when all three were viewed together.

We were in the same coffee shop where we met before at a back booth away from the rest of the diners. Hogan looked across the table at me, not happy, his laptop in front of him with the SD card in it. "You're trying to tell me Frank Martini, a decorated detective with the Chicago Police Department, is pimping girls out of an old farm downstate?"

"*Ex*-detective, and don't give me that wide-eyed disbelief, we're not in Neverland. Look at this. Multiple payments going back years. Girls handed out like grand prizes at a county fair. All of it taking place in Pittston. One or two girls a year, off the Bettle books, nobody around to miss them or wonder where they went."

"That still doesn't explain how a cop gets in this."

"I don't know. Poole said Martini came with Shaw. I don't know that I believe a word she says at this point, but Martini worked missing persons for years, he had to have dealt with DCFS more than once. Shaw worked there before he went to Bettle. It's possible they came in contact."

Hogan pushed his laptop away. He looked like he wanted to vomit. "And you say he came after this with that PI Vine?"

"Vine's a PI in name only. I don't even think he still has his license. He's filth, but, yeah, him. They both came for it. They got it. I got it back."

"How?"

I took a sip of hot cocoa. "I had a hand grenade on my side."

Hogan blinked, confused, and let a moment go. *"What?!"*

"Doesn't matter how. I got it, and I made copies, and locked them away. This is yours. They killed Tonya Pierce and Shaw, and maybe Poole, too. I haven't been able to set eyes on her since our encounter in the lot. It's Martini and Vine driving this thing now."

Hogan leaned back. "They killed Pierce because she wasn't getting with the program? And Shaw because he was flashing the money?"

"You aren't exactly laying low driving around town in a Tesla worth a quarter of a million."

"How'd they get away with this for so long?"

"It's a big system. There are lot of kids and a lot of cracks."

We both sat silently for a moment.

"Martini told me he did it for the money," I said.

"He *what*?"

"He whispered it to me when he thought he had the SD card and was home free. He said, point-blank, he did it for the money."

Hogan slid the card out of the laptop and pocketed it. He shook his head. "You go looking for a runaway and you come up with this bullshit. Son of a bitch." He grabbed his coat, stopped. "Where's Ramona?"

My phone buzzed in my pocket. "As far away from the

three of them as I could get her, but I think it's safe to bring her in now." It was a text from Ramona's burner. It read simply: **Sall sw.** "Hogan, wait."

I called her number back, a sinking feeling growing, but got no answer. I sent a text replying to the one I'd gotten, but got no response to that, either.

"What is it?" Hogan asked, standing over me, the laptop under his arm.

I dialed the number again. "I don't know." There was no pickup. Then a call came in.

"Cassandra Raines?" It was Scoot.

"Scoot, what's wrong?"

"They took her. Grabbed her off the street, right in front of us. Two white guys. Maybe cops?"

I was already moving, grabbing my jacket, tossing money on the table. Scoot didn't have to say who she was or who they were. Martini and Vine had Ramona, and they were going to kill her.

"When?"

"Like just now. Like I can still smell the smoke from their van. Look, I don't do 911 or the cops, so I'm calling you. You gotta do something."

"Thanks. I'll take care of it."

"What the hell's going on?" Hogan asked when I ended the call.

"They grabbed Ramona."

"What good's that going to do them? We've got their books. And where are they going with her? Every cop in the city's still looking for her."

The text: **Sall sw.**

"Pittston. They're taking her to Pittston."

"Wait a minute. You don't know that, just like I don't know any of this is even verifiable. I've got to study this. Check stuff out. You're jumping all over the place with theories."

"Sally Sweet's. That's what she was trying to type in that text." Hogan looked skeptical. "You still don't trust me. Fine. Get out of my way, then."

"Wait. Why Pittston? If they want her dead why not do it here, like they did Pierce?"

"I'll ask them when I see them," I said, brushing past him.

"I'll call Pittston PD and see if they can assist," Hogan said.

"Don't. I've been there. The local cops practically picked my car up and threw it at the interstate. I have a feeling the cops down there know exactly what's going, and it wouldn't surprise me if they're getting a cut too." I checked my watch. It was just almost 7:00 PM. They didn't have that big a lead. I rushed for the door. "I'll keep you posted."

"Wait. You're going down there solo at this hour?"

"Yes." I pushed through the door and raced to my car, but when I unlocked it, Hogan slid into the passenger seat.

"What are you doing?"

He tapped the dashboard impatiently. "Let's go."

"Your badge won't mean diddly-squat down there," I said, starting up.

"We'll see about that."

I peeled away from the curb, headed for Pittston.

Chapter 36

We managed to avoid Pittston PD as we skirted the small town and got to the gate with the stone lions. I eyed the security camera, knowing we didn't have long, then turned to Hogan. "The place is about a quarter mile past that barrier, but we're about to have some company. Someone's monitoring those cameras."

"Whose place is this?"

"Apparently, the town owns it now." I looked out the window and saw car tracks and footprints in the snow at the gate. "Someone's been here." I pushed the door open, hearing the faint *whoop-whoop* of a police siren. I turned to Hogan. "See? They're on someone's payroll."

"So, how do you want to play it?"

"You stand a better chance of talking your way out of it than I would. Me? They find me here again and I'm going straight to Pittston jail."

Hogan flicked a look in the rearview mirror, the flashing lights of the SUV just visible from down the road. It was coming fast. "Go on, then. I'll hold off the yahoos."

"He's a real hard-ass. If he's also dirty—"

Hogan looked as though I'd insulted him. "I'm CPD."

I hesitated. "Watch your back. It's a father-daughter team. If he's desperate enough to do what he's doing, he won't hesitate to take you out to cover it up. I don't think she'll be much help to you."

Hogan again checked the rearview. "You got about thirty seconds, if that."

I got out, gave the approaching lights one last look, then bolted for the gate, climbing over it and racing up the road, my boots slipping in the snow, arms pumping. Behind me, I could hear the police SUV skidding to an urgent stop, its flashing lights bouncing blue off the snow and trees. The sound of gruff voices was the last thing I heard as I sprinted for the house, sweat already freezing to my face and body. I worried about Hogan. He was off his beat without backup. I hoped he'd be okay. I'd sent Ben a text from the car telling him where I was, Hogan had sent a similar message to Spinelli, just in case things went sideways and neither of us came back. It was added protection I hoped we wouldn't need.

When the house came into view, I stopped to catch my breath and looked around. The lights were on inside, but there was no van out front. Maybe they'd parked it out of sight in the barn? Maybe Ramona's text had been a ruse, and they'd taken her someplace else? What if I had gambled on Pittston and lost? If so, Ramona was as good as dead.

Whoever was inside the house knew by now there was activity at the gate. They might even have tracked me all the way up the road, though I hadn't seen any outward signs of cameras along the path. Yet, everything around the house was eerily quiet. I kept to the tree line, pushing closer, burrowing into my jacket.

I fell back, startled, into the shadows when the front door opened suddenly and Poole rushed out, holding Ramona tightly by the arm. Ramona was pulling against the hold, trying to free herself, but Poole had her in a tight grip. They headed for the barn in a hurry, fleeing.

Martini came out next in a rush, peering into the dark, as though something might jump out at him. He'd seemed so cocky when he thought he had the SD card. Now he just looked desperate, cornered. Where were they taking Ramona? Why were they keeping her, instead of doing away with her as they had done with Tonya? What did she still have that they needed? If they got past me, would Hogan at the gate be enough to stop them from getting away? And where was Lenny? He was not someone I wanted sneaking up behind me in the dark.

Martini stood for a time staring at the stand of trees where I was hiding, as though he could sense I was there. Did he know Ramona sent me that text? Had he seen me jump out of the car at the gate? Keeping my breathing steady, my chest pressed to a cold tree, I watched Martini look for me.

If they got to the van, my odds of stopping them diminished. Plus, I would be easy to mow down. I needed to stop them here before they got to the gate. Only, I couldn't get my frozen feet to move, or my body off the tree. And, again, where the hell was Lenny Vine?

I squinted my eyes shut and blew out a quick breath to steady myself. *"Screw your courage to the sticking-place."* The words popped into my head. Shakespeare *now*? And Lady Macbeth at that? It was funny what the brain dredged up in moments of crisis. Useful? Hell no. But I suppose you can't take the English major out of the PI, even at a time like this.

Martini gave up and headed toward the barn. One final peek around the tree. One more deep breath—hopefully, not my last—and then I shot out, giving up my cover, counting on the element of surprise. I ran up the slight rise toward the barn, eyes sharp, focused on Martini, who, at the last moment, saw me coming and reached behind his back for his gun. Racing toward him, I drew mine out, too.

"Martini! Don't!"

He fired off a round. I hit the snow and flattened out, taking a quick assessment of all my body parts. He'd missed. Thank God for darkness, surprise, and the fact that Martini was likely a rusty shooter. But there was no reverb on the round. He was using a silencer. A *silencer.* Who did he think he was, Paulie Walnuts?

I got mad and pounded a fist into the snow, wishing I could do the same to Martini's face. Keeping my head low, I watched him just a few feet away, his eyes scanning, looking for me, his arm straight, his gun aimed where he'd seen me last. He was waiting to take his next shot, like he was picking off jackrabbits in a field. Whatever happened next, Martini had already wrecked himself.

If I lifted my head, I was dead. If I moved, I was dead. But I had to get to the woods to stop Poole from doing whatever she had it in her mind to do. Ramona was just as great a threat to her as she was to Martini. I lay there shivering, my chin in the snow, my eyes on the debauched demon who had come to this.

"Too late, Raines," he shouted, his booming voice bouncing off the trees. "I'll be the last one standing." He turned, ran for the woods.

I lifted my head up when he disappeared around the side of the house, the sound of his heavy feet echoing in the still night. I scrambled up and took off after him, with quite a distance to make up. I had to get between him and Ramona.

Chapter 37

God, it was cold. What was it? Five degrees? My body was stiff and slow to respond, my clothes wet and heavy, thanks to my snow dive. Still, legs moving, racing to catch up, like there was Olympic gold at the end of it, like the hounds of hell were nipping at my heels.

I stumbled into the thick maze of dormant trees into almost total darkness, and plastered myself, heaving, winded, behind yet another one. The moon was high in the sky, but its glow didn't penetrate the tangle of canopy trees towering above my head, their web of brittle branches encased in layers of ice, twigs snapping and cracking in the wind, their movement casting eerie shadows on the virgin snow, thanks to a sliver of murky moonlight that had made it past the branches. I was a good distance from the house—no barn, no van, no gate, no Hogan. Trying to orient myself, I calculated the main road was at least a mile north, the back road maybe that far south. This was the perfect spot, out of the way, for Martini and Poole to run their operation. Who would know? Who would see or care what went on?

A gust of wind blew through, flicking snow in my face, blurring my vision. It felt as though I'd wandered into some forsaken dreamscape, some dead place at the edge of the world. Where was Ramona? Where were Poole and Martini? I moved forward, using the trees as shields, running to one, hiding behind it, listening, then moving forward to the next. I kept the gun up and ready. I didn't dare put it away, no matter how much I wished I could.

I caught movement up ahead and kept my eyes on it, all the while moving forward, next tree up. A flash of dull color. Blue? Was it Ramona? I moved out from behind the tree, into the open, and ran like hell toward the blue. I couldn't yell out her name or make more noise than my feet and heavy breathing were already making. But just as suddenly as I'd picked the flash of blue out of the dark, it was gone again, making me wonder if maybe I had imagined it in the first place.

The legs of my jeans were frozen stiff, my boots the same, as I pushed forward, eyes sweeping the dark, craning to hear even the faintest of sounds that would tell me I was going the right way, that I hadn't lost Ramona. The sound of a twig snapping froze me, and I whirled around, near panicked, only to find nothing there. Suddenly something yanked me by the jacket and pulled me behind a tree. I turned to fight, to shoot, but a hand covered my mouth to quiet me. It was Ramona.

She brought a finger to her lips, a signal for me to keep quiet. She'd gotten away from Poole, but she and Martini had to be close. I heard the crunching of feet on snow behind us, and turned around to face it, moving Ramona behind me. There was no way I wanted to confront Poole or Martini in the dark like this. We had to get out of here. I wondered if the path was clear the way I'd come, or if one or both of them had doubled back and closed off that exit? What was up ahead if we couldn't retreat? More trees? Worse?

There it was again. The crunch. It was definitely the sound of someone advancing from the south, or at least I thought it was south. Retreat was not an option. Ramona and I were going to have to move deeper into the woods, forward not back.

I turned to her, signaled the direction. She nodded that she understood me, and we began moving back. She went first, I behind her, my grip on the back of her jacket as the two of us slowly made our way. The footfalls behind us quickened. We'd been seen. Suddenly the bark on the tree ahead of us splintered. Martini had fired and missed.

"Run!" I yelled to Ramona. We ran full out, not bothering about the snow, or the racket we were making. "Don't stop. *Go!*"

There were another two pops and I felt a whiff of air shoot past my left ear. We were going to die. I checked to make sure Ramona was completely ahead of me, that my body covered hers. Maybe that would buy her a few more seconds. Then I veered us off to the side, behind another tree, waiting to see what Martini would do next. Ramona pressed behind me, I could feel her body shaking, and I doubted it was from the cold. There was someone shooting at us, someone who wanted both of us dead. It was a lot for a kid to get her head around. It was a lot for me, too. She began to whimper. I shushed her quiet.

Wordlessly I moved us forward again, quiet steps, slow progress. Where was Poole? Was she ahead of us or behind us with Martini? Was Hogan still at the gate, headed this way, or on his way to Pittston jail? There was a fourth option, but I didn't want to think about it. And Lenny. I hadn't forgotten about him.

Ramona stopped suddenly and I ran into the back of her. I whispered, "Keep going."

"No. Look."

I checked for Martini, then flicked a look where Ramona was pointing. We'd gotten to the end of the woods to a frozen creek bed. The lake she'd mentioned. We stood at the top of a steep, short hill, the icy creek at the bottom, another hill, just as steep, on the other side. Not insurmountable, especially with a gun coming behind you.

"Down the hill, up the other side," I ordered. "Go!" Another round whiffed past me, ripping the sleeve of my jacket. "Now! Don't stop for anything."

Ramona slid down the hill on her butt and disappeared in the dark. I turned, shot in the direction I thought Martini was, then pedaled back and ducked behind a tree guarding the hill, making sure no one got close to it. I checked my sleeve, flicking off goose down to send it floating off like fairy wings. No blood.

"You don't get it, Raines." It was Martini. The sound of his voice, after so much quiet, startling, chilling.

I glanced over at the hill, wondering how far Ramona had gotten, hoping it was far enough by now. "I get it," I yelled back. "You're a dirty pimp, you son of a bitch!" That's right, Cass, antagonize him.

"We're helping these girls." It was Poole this time. "Can't you see that? They were never going to be chosen. Many of them had spent their entire lives shuttling around like garbage. And the red tape. The bureaucracy. We cut through all that. We made everyone happy."

I peeked out from behind the tree, seeing them standing just feet away, in a small clearing, walking toward the hill, the frozen creek, Ramona. I needed to hold them here. I slipped left. Another tree, another vantage point.

Poole kept babbling, like she could explain and justify things. "Some families want a child, any child, after years of trying, maybe some want a kid to help around the house, maybe someone to teach a trade, pass along a vocation to. Honest work. It wasn't what you think. Fast adoptions. We created families! Happy families! Until—"

Martini kept coming. "Shut up, Deloris!"

I peered out, half a face, not much. Didn't want to get my

nose blown off. "No, keep talking, Deloris." I moved again. "I'm listening. Tell me how you sold those kids."

Martini stopped. It's what I hoped he'd do. He fired again, but I was gone, behind him now.

He turned, circling, firing wildly, frustration getting the better of him. Bark exploded off the trees, raining down on the snow. "Damn you, Raines! Don't you get it? These kids would have been on the streets, if not for us! This way, everybody gets something. Years of running these kids down for chump change. Did the department appreciate it? They swept me out. What'd I owe them? All these girls, they can fend for themselves. Who loses? Climb off your high horse. This is the real world we're in."

"She doesn't understand," Poole whined. "It wasn't even about the money. It was about making families. And I did. *We* did." I stayed quiet, hidden. When I didn't respond, as Martini likely hoped I would, Poole gave up trying to explain herself. "We have to get out of here, Frank. She probably has the police coming."

"Doesn't matter. I'll take care of this," Martini snapped. "Get the girl, bring her back here. And don't forget we wouldn't be in this mess if you'd kept your door locked."

Poole swept forward, toward the creek, and my heart seized up. I steadied and fired, my round hitting her in the left thigh. I didn't want to kill her, just stop her. Poole screamed, gripped her leg, then fell to the ground, rocking in agony. By the time Martini shot again, I was two trees away.

"Frank! Help me!" Poole begged. "I'm shot."

Martini just stood there, peering into the trees. It didn't look like he cared much for Poole's pain. It was apparently now every kid peddler for himself. "Shut up. I can't hear."

"Do something!" Poole screeched. "I could bleed to death."

"Shut up, I said!"

I crept along behind the trees, looking for an opening.

Poole rocked back and forth, blood coloring her fingers. "I swear I'll tell them everything. How you and that monster Vine killed Shaw and Tonya. Burned her like she was garbage. I'll tell all of it! I never signed on for any killing. I wanted them adopted, not handed over like—" That's as far as she got. Martini calmly walked over to her and put a round in her head. I muffled the gasp as best I could, but Martini didn't look interested in pursuing me anymore. He stood at the top of the hill. He saw the creek bed below. He knew which way Ramona had gone. I slid out from behind the tree, hoping to stop him, when a shot came from behind me, splintering the wood three inches from my cheek. I stumbled back.

"You do not give up, do you, Raines?"

It was Lenny Vine.

I watched helplessly as Martini scampered down the hill. I had no idea where Vine was, I couldn't see him, but he sounded too close. "Come out, come out, wherever you are."

I hated Lenny Vine. I eyed the hill. I had to get there. I lifted off the tree and another round exploded above me. I ran for the hill, anyway, wayward rounds pinging the snow at my feet, whizzing past my ears. I could hear Vine chasing me, but the hill was all I saw, all I thought about.

I hit the hill and jumped over the side, sliding down on my butt, Vine coming fast. I would never make it all the way down and across before he shot me in the back, like the wretched dog he was.

I hit the bottom and scrambled away over broken branches strewn along the snowy ice. My hand landed on a fallen branch about the size of a baseball bat, I grabbed hold of it, eyed the gun in my other hand, then slipped the gun in a pocket. Maybe it was the wrong decision. Maybe I'd regret it. It certainly went against all my cop training, but I didn't want to kill anyone today, not even Vine. I didn't want to kill anyone ever again. I pressed my body to the ground and waited for him to slide down after me. I could hear his labored breathing as he made his way down the snowy slope. I gripped the branch. I'd only get one shot. If I missed, he'd kill me. When Vine got to the bottom and to his feet, his back to me, I sprang forward and beaned him in the back of the head, knocking off his porkpie hat and sending him to the ground, out cold, his gun falling out of his hand, disappearing in the snow. I kicked his foot to make sure he was good and out, then I threw down the branch, picked up his hat, and flung it as far as I could, getting a perverse pleasure out of it. Then I ran up the hill on the other side, toward Ramona.

I lay flat at the top for a moment, gasping for air, my heart beating a mile a minute. Then I shot up and barreled into another stand of canopy trees. Trees! I hated the woods. At that moment, I never wanted to see another tree, *ever.*

"Stay down!"

It was Martini.

I bolted toward the sound of his voice and found him yards up, standing over Ramona, his gun aimed at her head.

I drew my gun, aimed it at him. "Move away!" Martini slid me a sly look. "I said move away!"

Martini turned, smiled, like this was some kind of joke, like he hadn't killed three people already. He looked past me, amused. "Where's Vine?"

"Taking a nap." I was aiming for Martini's heart, though I doubted he had one. I'd avoided killing Vine. I hoped to do the same here, but that was up to Martini.

Ramona pushed up from the ground and stumbled behind the nearest tree. It was just Martini and me now. Neither of us said anything for a time. We both knew what time it was, what had to happen.

"I suppose you want me to confess my part? Beg for forgiveness?"

I didn't answer. I slowed my breathing down a little more. A confession didn't much interest me. Shaw was dead, Poole was dead, Tonya Pierce was dead, and Lord knows in what state we would find the other girls . . . Right now I only had one concern here in the woods, in the dark, in the snow, in the middle of freaking nowhere, and it stood trembling behind a tree.

Martini sighed. "You're right. You don't need it, do you? Deloris, like a fool, told you most of it, and you have the rest, thanks to Ramona Titus, our little runaway. I'll just add this. It wasn't personal. There was a need, we figured out a way to fill it."

"We? How'd you get involved in the first place. Shaw and Poole I get."

"Other missing kids, other cases. I caught on to what Shaw was doing. I saw a way to profit from it."

"Did you even care who you sold the kids to?"

"At first, but money has a way of changing people, doesn't it?" He slid a tired look at Ramona. "But I can't kill my way out of this, can I?"

"You tried, though, didn't you? Put the gun down, Martini."

"Cass!"

It was Hogan across the creek, coming my way.

"Here!" I yelled back. "He's armed."

Martini laughed, shook his head. "That seals it."

"Guess it does," I said.

He cocked his head. "I lied when I said I couldn't kill my way out of this."

I stopped breathing. "Don't make me."

"I've disgraced my family, my kids." He glanced up at the trees, the sky beyond, or what he could likely see of it. "Well, I've paid off the house. I didn't blow it on a Tesla, like that idiot. I told him nothing conspicuous. At least Deloris had the good sense to bank hers offshore." His eyes met mine. "Did you kill Lenny?"

I'd wanted to. I've dreamed about killing Lenny Vine. "What happened to Shaw's Tesla?"

He laughed. "I drove it into the lake and made him watch. That car could have ruined everything. Then we find out he's planning on running and leaving us holding the bag? When it was him moving the girls, him taking them off the books at Bettle, and using Deloris to house them? No, this was Shaw with the big money dreams. Remember that when it's all said and done."

He looked around, almost wistfully, at the bare trees; then he looked at me. "Guess I made a real mess of things. Only one way out I can see."

"Don't," I pleaded. "Martini, don't—"

In one swift move, his gun came up; he pressed the muzzle to his chin and blew his head off, blood spraying the trees, blanketing the snow with gore. I jumped; Ramona screamed. Hogan rushed up the hill and stood beside me, both of us staring in horror at what was left of Frank Martini. I put my gun away, watching as Martini's blood and brain matter melted the snow.

"What the hell did he just do?" Hogan said.

I turned away, went for Ramona. "He just saved the state a lot of money."

Chapter 38

"So, what's it going to take?"

I stared at Scoot across the table, his gang flanking him, engrossed in our conversation. We were back at Deek's, in my booth.

"Why's this your business?" Scoot asked, his hat cocked rakishly on his head.

"You haven't been back to the bus, and I'm getting nun heat." I looked from one to the other. "I don't like nun heat."

"Where's Ramona?" a girl asked.

"Safe," I said. Had it really been just forty-eight hours since the woods? It felt a lifetime ago. I'd managed to get Ramona emergency placement in a good, safe home. Leesa Evans was satisfied, and determined more than ever to get Ramona back. Poole was dead, Shaw was dead, Martini was dead. It was an end, not justice. The girls they sold, thanks to the things Ramona had stolen, were on the way to being accounted for. They'd been essentially sold to clear the backlog, cut the red tape, we didn't yet know the depth of it. If they'd started out vetting the prospective parents, as Martini and Poole claimed, the money soon perverted those efforts. The police and the feds had dates, amounts, names. It would only be a matter of time before they sorted it all out. The only thing unresolved and left hanging was Lenny Vine. He was gone when I got back down the hill. His hat too. I had no idea where he was, but knew almost certainly I would encounter him again.

"As you all need to be," I added. "You won't let me help you, so the Love Bus has got to be it."

"You got a piece of it?" Scoot wanted to know.

I leaned forward, my hands folded on the tabletop. "There is no piece. They're good people aided by Jesus. Your staying away, keeping the kids away, only hurts you, doesn't it?" I reached into my pocket, drew out a short stack of my business cards, handing one to every kid, even Scoot.

"I already got one of these," he said.

"Take another." I held up a card. "This is me. You get into a jam, you need anything, *anything,* you call." I stared at the girl in the red wool hat whose stepfather had forced her to choose the streets to life at home with him. I was particularly speaking to her. "But for the love of God, go back to the freaking bus."

Scoot chuckled. "It's the old one you're scared of, isn't it?"

"Yes."

The group laughed, hard—not with me, *at* me. "I guess we'll go back, then. Help you out."

"Thank you. Now let's eat."

One of the boys spoke up. "All of us?"

"Unless you're not hungry?"

A chorus of enthusiastic yeses went up as the group scattered around, taking seats at tables and booths. Muna, smiling, dropped menus at each one, and started taking orders. Aggie was back, hovering in the background, her eyes tracking my every move. It looked like she'd be around for a while. She thought she had me all figured out. We'd see about that. "You're a strange woman," Scoot said.

I grinned. "I've heard that."

He eyed the sleeve of my jacket. I'd stuck a strip of duct tape over the hole Martini's bullet had made. It'd do until I could buy a replacement. "What's with that?"

"Tore it. No big deal. Pancakes?"

He picked up the menu. "I'm feeling more like eggs and bacon."

I thought about it. "Good choice. I'll have the same."

I took up a spot in the hallway, my back to the wall, knees up, waiting. There was no plan, no endgame. I was taking a chance. I'd been here for hours, Lila Kennison across the hall, peeking out occasionally to offer tea and snacks, bits of conversation. I'd already used her bathroom twice and ignored a call from Eli, again. We were going to have to have a talk soon. He was a good man, and we fit nicely together, but he was moving too fast, and his kid added a level of complication I wasn't sure about. I was used to traveling light and mostly alone, and he was asking for more than that. I needed to think things through.

My eyes closed, my head back, I ran through everything that had happened since that Saturday morning at White Castle, not elated but all right with the outcome. Ramona was safe. Leesa Evans had her second chance. I hoped the two of them would get together again. I'd given Evans half her money back, telling her I hadn't needed it, ginning up a heavily modified time/mileage report to show her. I don't think she completely bought it, but the money would get her one step closer to that apartment. I thought of Shaw's Tesla sitting at the bottom of Lake Michigan and how he must have felt seeing it go down, knowing Martini wouldn't hesitate to do the same to him. Did I feel sorry for any of them? I did not. There was a special place in Hell for people who abused children, and I hoped Shaw, Poole, and Martini were there right now turning on a spit. I heard heavy footsteps on the stairs and opened my eyes, watching as he appeared on the landing. He stopped, looked at me, not surprised at all to see me there. I stood up, faced him. After a moment, he wouldn't look at me, but I kept staring. He had a black eye, a fat lip, and his knuckles were bruised. He looked like he hadn't slept.

Without a word, Whip unlocked his apartment door, then pushed it open wide so I could follow him in. For a quick second, I saw something in him I didn't recognize, and it pulled me up short. I stood at the threshold, suddenly unsure of what I wanted to do.

He turned, slid me a look, then dropped his keys in his pocket. I stepped inside, closed the door behind me, and stood with my back pressed to it. Part of it was me standing between him and it, so he couldn't get past me; the other part was not wanting to get too close to whatever bad news he was holding on to. Magical thinking on both counts. Whip was twice my size and hardened by prison years, so if he had a mind to run, me holding up the door wasn't going to stop him. He wouldn't hurt me, I knew that, but he wouldn't let me stop him, either. And as for bad news, it shot off the tongue at the speed of light; distance—long or short—couldn't do a damn thing to soften it.

"Are you okay?" I asked. My hands were behind my back, my eyes on his bruised face. Worry, trepidation, crept up my throat like a repulsive, evil thing.

"I know how this looks," he said, "but I'm okay. I can't talk about it right now. I'm only stopping off to take a shower, change, and then I'm out again."

"Where? What's going on?"

Whip let a moment go. "I don't want you in the middle of this."

I lifted off the door. "*This?* Meaning?"

He shook his head. "No. The less you know . . ." He checked his watch. "I can't take long. Look, I'll call you, how's that? When it's done, when I'm out, I'll call."

He headed for his bedroom as if that was all that needed to

be said, as if I were someone else, and not me, and I could back away from anything and leave things like that. I caught up to him and grabbed his arm, turning him around to face me, up close.

"Yeah, I didn't think that'd go over," he said.

"What have you gotten yourself into?"

He gently pulled his arm free. "Not me. I told you I was out of the life, playing things straight. That's no lie."

"You quit your job. You disappeared. You ignored my calls. Barb's too."

We walked into his bedroom. I'd been there before, but he didn't know that. He grabbed a small duffel from the corner, opened drawers, and started tossing clothes in it. I watched to see how many days he was packing for, but he didn't put in much, maybe a couple days' worth.

"So not a long trip, then?" I said.

"I'm not leaving town, just getting a change of clothes."

"What the hell are you doing?"

Whip stopped, a pair of socks in his hand. "Do you trust me?"

"More than you trust me, obviously," I shot back.

He dropped the socks in the duffel. "I trust you, but I'm not getting you tied up in my shit. It's messy and it's—"

"Is it illegal?"

"I'm trying hard not to let it go that way, which is why you need to step back."

I swept the duffel off the bed, tumbling its contents on the carpet. It was an act borne of fear and desperation more than anger. "You let me worry about where I step. *Talk* to me."

He didn't say anything for a long time. I didn't, either. He flicked a look at the tossed duffel, toed it.

"Who am I talking to?"

I didn't understand the question. "What?"

"*Who* am I talking to?"

I got it. "I'm not CPD, Whip, you know that. You know who I am. *That's* who you're talking to."

He shook his head. "Why can't you just leave it?"

"Because I'm tired of losing people I care about, that's why. I'm done with it, you hear me? *Done.*"

He walked over to the window, peered out, as though checking for something, someone. He turned back to me, squared his shoulders. "I owe somebody. Not money. Money's easy. You owe it, you pay it, the deal's done. I owe an action, some skin, and I can't move forward until I offer it up. That means I'm going to have to call up somebody I haven't been for a long time. I'm not that guy anymore, but I'm going to have to be that guy."

I slowly eased down to sit on the bed. "Tell me."

He turned to face me. "I ran with a crew back in the day. Thieves. Some worse. I told you all that before. Things went down I'm not proud of. I owed a guy. He called in his marker." He exhaled as though a weight had been lifted. "That's where I'm going to have to leave it."

"What's he want you to do?"

Whip picked up the duffel, punched everything back inside. "Nothing I haven't done a million times. I'll figure it out." He stood. "Go home."

"Who's asking you to do this thing, whatever it is?"

Whip shook his head.

"Where are you going?"

Whip shook his head again. "I'm going to hit the shower, and then go. You're going to let me, and then you're going to leave it sit until you hear from me. I appreciate you wanting to help, but you can't, and even if you could, I won't let you. You're more than a friend, Cass, you're family."

I watched silently as he padded to the shower, closing the door behind him. I listened as the shower started, then left the room to wait for him in the living room. I was standing at the door when he emerged twenty minutes later, showered, shaved, and freshly dressed in a sweater and jeans, the strap of the duffel slung over his shoulder.

Out on the street, at the curb, he gave my shoulder a squeeze. "I'll call you. Promise."

I watched as he got in his truck, started it. He lowered the passenger window, gave me a wan smile. "We good?"

There was so much going on in my head, all of it a jumble. "Whip?"

"Yeah?"

"I can't lose anyone else."

"I know. You won't. I promise."

He drove away, into the night, with Christmas just days away, without my knowing where or why.

Yet.